THE BLANK SLATE

Other CV-2 Books by Raymund Eich

Stone Chalmers
The Progress of Mankind
The Greater Glory of God
To All High Emprise Consecrated

The Confederated Worlds
Take the Shilling
Operation Iago
A Bodyguard of Lies

Novels
New California

Short Novels
The ALECS Quartet

Collections
The First Voyages: The Complete Science Fiction Stories
1998-2012
Stage Separations: The Complete Science Fiction Stories
2013-2018

THE BLANK SLATE

Raymund Eich

CV-2 Books • Houston

Cover art: © Eraxion | Dreamstime.com
Cover design, book design, and aircraft carrier logo are copyrights, trademarks, or trade dress of CV-2 Books.

Third CV-2 Books trade paperback edition: June 2019

1

Of course the customer pickup counter stood at the back of the my-fab.com store, thought Clay. If asked, the manager would rationalize the location as being close to the store's complex metabolism of minia-turized laser sinterers, desktop extruders, and biopolymer fermenta-tion vats, but in his imagination, Clay could hear Nil snort: the counter at the back forced the customer to pass in-store displays, which were memes' coat proteins, designed to infect the minds of passersby.

The aisles meandered past the displays. Ceiling-mounted bullet lights glossed the surfaces of mock living rooms, where black leather couches rested on spindly carbon nanotube frames across from gi-gapixel video displays painted on false walls. A string quartet played from the interior speakers of a Lorelei sedan; the autocar's wide-open doors revealed a wraparound cabin of hidden electronics and vat-grown leather and tropical hardwood. Citrus and musk scents drowned out pheromones and neurotransmitter receptor agonists by the perfume counter. A head-and-torso robot mounted on the counter turned its blank mannequin face and lifted its arms as Clay approached. "Sir, could I interest you in a cologne?" came a synthetic voice from a speaker hidden between the mannequin's chin and nose. "We can combine masculine pheromones and oxytocin derivatives to rekindle that romantic spark."

Clay hesitated a step, then turned away, his cheeks warming and his heart rate speeding. How could the thing know? Brain activity scanners were getting smaller, but they weren't yet cheap enough for myfab to fill its stores with them, were they? He exhaled and kept walking. The store's computers saw a man with a child nearby and a glinting band on his left ring finger, rapidly cooling in the air conditioning. The store's software had guessed he and Jenny could use a romantic spark, nothing more.

His heart rate slowing to normal, Clay looked around and wondered why the displayed plenitude bothered him. Since he and Nil had sold their company a few years earlier, money had been no real concern—he could splurge on impulse purchases, like a double-neck electric bass or an indoor wood-smoker compatible with the SueChef 8800 in his kitchen, without blinking at the cost. Yet Clay had never been impulsive; his D4 receptor activity was low enough that deferring gratification came naturally to him.

Martin, on the other hand... "Kitty!" cried Clay's son, and he stomped to a robot pet display. A robot cat tensed its legs and its ears twitched, but then it relaxed under Martin's awkward petting and rubbed the corner of its mouth against his hand. A lifelike piece of work: a calico, white belly and orange eyepatch, like Jenny's old cat that had finally died a couple of years earlier. *How many times had he told her not to empty the litterbox when she was pregnant? Hadn't she heard of toxoplasmosis?*

Martin looked up at him and the vapidity of his expression soured Clay's stomach. "Wan," Martin said.

"Not today," Clay said.

"Iwan."

"No, Martin." Clay stepped closer to the boy.

The boy cringed, his expression half angry and half ready to cry. Clay's hand clenched and he stepped closer. Martin's eyes grew wide and fearful and the robot cat scampered a few steps away. Clay relaxed his shoulders and inhaled. "We have another toy for you at the back of the store. Let's go."

Martin looked at the robot cat and sniffled. He limply put his hand in Clay's and stumbled after his father.

This trip was another of Jenny's brilliant ideas. The toy waiting for them was a plush robot monkey with the ability to sing and emit scents. Somehow the combination of music and aromatherapy would cajole Martin's neurons to form more robust synapses; so said the theory she'd read on some powder-blue website full of emoticons and schmaltzy photos. *You should be happy,* she'd said, *the on-board volatile molecule fabricator is one of your MuSynths. And Martin needs to be more integrated into our daily lives, so take him with you to pick it up.* She was grasping at straws with her hopes of healing Martin. Didn't she know that?

"Da." Martin's voice sounded timid. He wrapped his free arm around Clay's leg.

Clay shook his head and sighed. "It's okay. Just a picture."

They'd reached an America United licensed products display. An animation as large as a home theater monitor, painted in viscous oil and hydrophobic fluorophores, dominating the display. It cycled from an eagle, its wings as broad as the Mall's length, rising like a phoenix to the Washington, D.C. Firestorm and back. Words resolved and dissolved above the flames, *Never forget* and *June 19, 2019.*

"Do' lie."

Clay didn't like it either. Almost four years gone, and though the country had recovered it still felt brittle. "You don't have to look." He let go Martin's hand and cradled the boy's head between his palm and his thigh. He led Martin forward, past the painting, past a case where America Freedom Force action figures battled terrorists (ecowarriors, right-wing Bible thumpers, and Uighurstani nuclear scientists), past wearable computers (mostly wristwatches and necklace pendants) branded with the America United logo, past a life-size bust of President Everton, brown hair edged with gray, eyes firm but caring, face cast in an expression of implacable strength. $1995—that had been a good chunk of money when he was a kid, four months of payments on his dad's diesel pickup; now closer to one.

Did he smell something? Clay's breathing grew deeper, slower. He glanced around the statuette for volatile molecule fabricators and blinked in surprise when he saw it. A MuSynth, a black disc the size of a man's thumbtip, had been pinned to the bust's lapel like a microphone. A cylinder the size of a pencil's crimp band jutted out, the optional MuFan attachment. The fan motor was too quiet to be heard over the background noises of distant conversations and treading feet. A serotonin emitter, designed to instill calm.

But clunky compared to the NuGlands the Defense Department had just ordered.

He glanced away with a guilty start. He had a professional interest in volatile molecule fabricators, that was all, but it would be easier if he didn't have to explain himself to passersby. "We're almost to your toy," he said to Martin, and walked on.

Two more displays. The next one they came to had another robot mannequin behind a dark wooden bar bearing wine bottles and glasses. A banner across the front of the bar read *myfab.com Oenologix—your perfect wine at your perfect price*. Jenny drank too much wine, not him. He strode on—

The mannequin spoke. "You could use a glass of wine, Clay Schieffer."

Clay swung his head around, the calming effect of the serotonin emitters now banished. "How do you know my name? And who are you to call me by it?"

Like the one at the perfume counter, the mannequin's face was the color of nickel and smooth as a doorknob, a bulge for its nose, indentations for its eyes. It spread its arms, palms out. "Don't blame myfab. They don't know I've borrowed their machine."

Clay squinted. A marketing ploy by myfab? Or a cracker's phishing expedition? "You haven't answered my questions."

"True. Pardon me if I don't answer your second one, but I can answer your first. I know quite a bit about you, Clay. I know in late 2019 you and Anil Thomas sold TS Microcatalytix to Titan Industries for $123.6 million. Have you ever wondered why?"

His mouth hung open. How many people knew that number? Other than him, Nil, their attorney, their CPAs… not even Jenny knew with that much precision—

Clay squeezed shut his eyes, shook his head once to clear it. The person waldoing this mannequin had hacked his CPA's server or played golf with a Titan Industries exec to get that information. What was he trying to do with it? "No, tell me why," he said as a challenge.

"Do you know what they did with the MuSynths?" the robot asked. It cocked its head, and spoke next with its voice changed. "Sir, do you prefer red or white?"

Clay stole a glance. A couple walked his way. They appeared to be in their 50s, but with all the antiagathic treatments on the market these days it was hard to tell. The woman had dark roots, puffy blonde hair, and makeup that artfully disguised sagging jowls and wrinkles at her mouth. She ignored Clay and talked loudly about fabric swatches to her husband. At the lapel of his denim blazer, the man wore an America United pin—a platinum eagle with splayed wings and a diamond for its eye against an outline of the continental U.S, with individual states in ruby, jade, emerald, and gold. Platinum members were the highest rank, Nil had said. With blue eyes set deep in his combover head the AU man scowled up at Clay. Clay tugged at Martin's arm and stepped closer to the bar.

"Sir, perhaps a pinot grigio?" the mannequin asked again, as the AU couple strode past. Clay nodded, distracted, and he started when he heard wine pour into stemware. The glass' base tapped the bar and he returned his attention to the mannequin and its distant master. The wine was yellow-white and condensation dewed on the goblet. He swallowed a dry, fruity mouthful and pictured Jenny shaking her head at his boorish unwillingness to savor the wine's bouquet.

He set down the glass and stared at the mannequin. "What about the MuSynths? Tell me."

"You wouldn't believe me if I did. It's better if you find out yourself."

"How the hell am I supposed to do that?"

"You still work there. You're smart enough to get into Titan's server farm in St. Louis," the company's headquarters.

Clay's face grew clammy. This was a trap. The National Counterterrorism Service was testing him before finalizing the new DoD order, 600,000 NuGlands. "I should call the feds on you."

The robot shrugged. The play of the overhead lights on its face tinged its appearance with sadness. "I can't stop you if you do. It won't harm me, though. I've been careful, they won't find me." It lifted its chin. "But Clay, I don't think you're going to do that."

Who was this stranger to claim to know him so well? Clay swirled his glass on the bar and light danced in the wine. "You don't?"

"A hunch. Feel free to send me an email. 1001001@samizdat.zj." Clay's eyebrows rose. The Republic of Zhejiang was a haven for Filipino smugglers, Russian hackers, Bahraini offshore bankers, and native Chinese IP pirates: the Cuba of the Far East. "Got it?"

One million one thousand one. Clay nodded and looked up from his wine. The person running the mannequin had dropped the connection. It stared stupidly at him and the half-empty glass.

"Da, toy," said Martin.

Ding sounded in his earbud. "You're scheduled to meet Nil at your house in five minutes," said the concierge software running on his wearable computer in its bland alto voice.

Clay glanced at the watchface of his wearable on his right wrist. *Dammit.* They met every Monday night to take stock of things happening around the business, a tradition going back to TS Microcatalytix' early days in a cramped, rented warehouse. Normally not so early, though. He'd be at least fifteen minutes late. How could he forget?

"Da!" Martin clutched awkwardly at his pants leg and pulled.

One million one thousand one.

Nil stood on Clay's guest parking spot while his Lorelei sedan thudded its door shut. The evening air clinged to him, heralding the coming sauna of Gulf Coast summer. Below the setting sun's orange light shining on Clay's red tile roof and through the upper branches of the live oaks, the house and the front yard lay in the last shadow of daytime, colors still vibrant and outlines still clear but without glare or glint. Knee-high robots, metallic pygmy centaurs, trotted across the st. augustine lawn with toys in their arms and laid them in neat piles near a swing set and jungle gym done in thick plastic and primary colors. Nil took a breath. Despite Martin's problems, Clay had a haven to return to after business hours.

Nil shook his head and frowned at the thought. He'd seen enough of other people's marriages to know it was no picnic. With antioxidant cocktail therapy, he would be vigorous and erect at age eighty; with his favored position at the head of the line for Agerix, he would be so at eight hundred. Time enough to settle down later. Still, before going to the front entrance, he touched his overear microphone to activate it and told his concierge to revise his supplement regimen to boost his mood.

The holographic doorman appeared in its wall niche to the right of the doors. "Mr. Thomas, I'm afraid Mr. Schieffer is not home at the moment. Mrs. Schieffer asked me to show you in."

Nil frowned. Whatever Clay's faults, he was usually punctual. And though he got along with Jenny—she was a fine looking woman, not a trace of baby weight, and whip-smart—a perpetual awkwardness hovered over them. She didn't approve his girlfriend-of-the-month lifestyle and his implicit rebuke of Clay for marrying, he guessed. No matter. He could charm anyone, couldn't he? He nodded to the doorman and the double doors swung open.

Clay's house was smaller than Nil's, but not by much. From the foyer one could look straight through enfiladed rooms to the granite-countered kitchen and the breakfast room beyond. Nil walked to the left, where the living room lay behind a walled off stairwell.

Casement windows and a French door ran along the right-hand wall and gave a view of the back deck, a lawn strewn with more toys, and a fenced-off swimming pool. The living room extended forty feet back to twin doorways, one to the media room and the other to the billiards room. A low bookcase separated the living room into near and far sitting areas. The near sitting area had a couch, a loveseat, and two chairs arranged in a C-shape around a coffee table, the whole ensemble in burgundy leather and polished walnut.

Jenny sat in one of the chairs, her knees tucked under her chin and a half-empty glass of red wine in her hand. She wore linen shorts and the pale curves of her thigh and calf caught Nil's eye for a moment. A ponytail gathered her black hair. She turned from the view out the casement windows to look at him. "Clay's out with Martin picking up a new edu-toy. He didn't tell me you were meeting here tonight." She extended her left arm. The sleeve of her silk, floral-print blouse fell away from the thin silver wearable at her wrist. She peered at the watchface. "He should've been home by now." Her tone of voice carried a hint of exasperation. *At Clay or at him?* Nil thought.

She remembered her manners. "Care for a seat? Glass of wine?"

"Thanks." He sat in the middle of the couch, just outside her personal space, while she touched her earring microphone and told the house to bring out the bottle and a second glass. The couch faced a fireplace, the bricks now cold until November. Above the mantel a slideshow played a photo of Jenny and a man of Chinese descent—her brother, he guessed from the resemblance—in an ROTC uniform holding a rolled parchment.

Time to say something, he said. "How's—"

"How's—" she said at the same time.

Nil bowed his head slightly. "Ladies first."

Jenny wrinkled her nose and waved away his offer. "You're the guest."

A household robot rolled up on rubber treads carrying a bottle and glass on a tray. It set down a tray on the coffee table and poured malbec.

"How is Martin?" Nil asked, a concerned expression on his face. He sniffed his wine but kept his gaze on Jenny.

"He's making progress, but it's slow. Two steps forward, one back, you know?" Nil did not, but he nodded anyway. "He wants to learn, he wants to behave properly, I can tell. But it's tough on him."

Nil sounded hopeful. "The NuGlands might help." He sipped his wine. Tart, lingering.

"The what?"

"NuGlands? Clay hasn't talked about them?"

"Not that I recall."

Nil cleared his throat to cover his surprise. "You know how the MuSynths work, right? A series of microreactors can be programmed to convert chemical feedstocks to any desired—"

"I took chemistry in college," she said with a sharp edge. "Sorry, that sounded rude."

It did, but Nil waved it off. "I forget what people know. The NuGlands are a huge step beyond the previous model. They're much smaller than the MuSynths, and as you might guess from the name, they're implantable. We can tag them to have affinity for particular body regions and lodge them on arterial walls. They get power from combusting serum glucose and can make practically any biologically active molecule. They'll put big pharma out of business." He'd given that pitch so many times it rolled off his tongue with a practiced air of casual excitement.

She frowned at a spot on the floor a few yards away, her mind apparently gnawing at the new information. "Neurotransmitters and axonal and dendritic growth promoters might help him," she said. The words came so easily and so calmly they hinted at long hours reading about brain architecture and crying for her child. "Though they wouldn't help with problems in the developmental gene expression cascade." She shut her eyes and swirled her wine, a scab over emotions rubbed raw. "Enough of my problems. How's—sorry." She winced. "I don't mean to sound catty, but I've forgotten her name."

"Minerva," Nil said, and he acted out the tactic of an apparently heartfelt confession, so ingrained by habit he barely noticed. "I wish I could forget it too."

The slideshow over the fireplace changed to a photo from the time of their buyout, Jenny, Clay, and Nil at a restaurant, all smiling— even Clay beamed with lively eyes—goblets and steak knives in view. "Sorry."

"She was flighty and troubled and too young. She pawned off my jewelry drawer and dropped out of college." He shook his head. A steeper price than he usually paid for a girlfriend-of-the-month. "My own damn fault. You don't want to hear—"

From the back of the house, behind the kitchen and breakfast room, a garage door rattling open. Jenny's eyes drooped and her mouth pressed closed and turned down at the corners. Nil had spent twenty-five years since puberty studying women for signs of lacks and clues to how to fill them. Jenny had a huge lack.

She was also his business partner's wife. He gulped wine.

"Mama!" Martin cried as he ran into the living room. A toy monkey in brown fur held the boy by the shoulders and rode his left upper arm. Clay followed, his steps slow and his expression distant.

"Sorry I'm late," he said to Nil. He nodded toward the billiard room. "Let's shoot some eight-ball and have a drink."

"I'm who moved the schedule forward tonight. There's an America United meeting I want to attend."

Clay stopped and glanced at Nil's chest, where his platinum membership pendant hung on its chain. Clay stiffened and turned his head from Nil's gaze. "Let's go," he said, and pointed to the billiard room.

"Will you have time later to play with Martin?" Jenny asked. "He'll better integrate the toy into his family schema if you do."

"It's Monday," Clay said sharply. "I meet with Nil every Monday—"

"Clay, I said, later. Can you do that for your son?" *And your wife,* Nil thought.

Clay blew out a breath and his shoulders slumped. "Yeah, sure, whatever." He strode toward the billiard room. As soon as Nil crossed the roller track threshold to the billiard room Clay told the doors to roll shut.

Clay leaned back against the bar, arms crossed, neat scotch close at hand. Nil leaned over the table, his brown eyes intent on the cue ball while he drew back the stick. "You didn't read the sales report, did you?" he asked, and shot.

"Smoke and mirrors, isn't it?" Clay said. "At least you can call engineers on their bullshit." The cue snicked the six-ball and the six-ball rattled into the side pocket.

Nil met his gaze and Clay crossed his arms tighter, expecting another lecture on how to be a senior manager. "Not this one. DoD is only the tip of the iceberg. Half a dozen federal agencies—NCS, NMHA, some even I've never heard of—plus, the biggie. America United ordered six million NuGlands."

"Six million."

"No, Clay. Six million! From AU alone! Between our royalties and appreciation in Titan's share price, that's twelve, fifteen million dollars for each of us!" Nil eyed and struck his next shot. The five-ball drove home the three.

"Like we need more money." Clay lifted his glass. Scotch smoldered in his mouth. More money wouldn't keep Jenny from sniping at him. More money wouldn't make Martin above-normal, the way the genes they'd added should have made him.

Nil leaned against the table and twirled his cue with his free hand. The platinum eagle fell away from his stout chest and glinted in the green light. "What's on your mind?"

Clay dropped his gaze from the platinum eagle to his whiskey. "Nothing important."

Nil chalked up the knuckles of his left hand, the white in high contrast to his South Indian skin tone. He bent over the table, then glanced up. "Jenny?"

Clay shook his head.

"There are other fish in the sea," Nil said. His teeth nibbled his lower lip as he struck. The five-ball rattled around the pocket mouth, kicked out. "Damn."

Nil had made that hint a few times. As if divorcing Jenny would make a difference—golddiggers would cling to Clay like leeches. He reached for his cue and walked to the table. "It's no worse than usual." Under the green light lay a clean Newtonian universe of balanced spheres and laser-planed slate: a realm within his sole control. No stranger would move the balls or shake the rails like the bumpers of a pinball table. "Fourteen the corner," to be followed by the eleven at the far end. The fourteen clinked on Nil's balls already in the pocket.

"Then what? Martin? Something coming out of R&D?"

Clay bent over his next shot but a sudden notion made him left his head. Had *Nil* sent him the message? He studied the other's fleshy cheeks and guileless eyes, looking for evidence and not finding any. It made no sense; if Nil had something to tell him he'd say it straight up. Nil peered back and raised an eyebrow. The platinum eagle shifted and caught the light.

What had Titan done? What could AU members not overhear? "I'm feeling pressed, that's all," Clay said while trying to keep his voice level. He lined up his shot. The cue ball caught the eleven off-target and pushed it off the rail and away from the pocket.

Nil seemed to accept the answer. "Let's go to Havana some weekend." A post-Castro paradise of casinos, topless dancers, new divorcées and college girls on spring break... Clay couldn't care less, but those things caught Nil's attention and he shrugged and nodded to push the conversation away from his thoughts. Nil sank his next shot, his next, his next, and the eight stood behind a constellation of striped balls. "Bank the cue, bank the eight," he said, and pointed the cue stick at the target corner.

"You're not that good."

"I'm on a new supplement for fine motor control," Nil said. The final words sounded half-forgotten when they left his mouth. He eyed the balls and struck. Thud snick thud, and the eight-ball fell into the corner pocket.

"I'll be damned in writing."

"Leave something out there and I'll take it from you," Nil said, and then cleared his throat and looked away. "I do need to run. Thanks for the drink—" he lifted his vodka tonic, mostly ice cubes, from the side table and drained it.

Couldn't Clay trust his best friend to hold any revealed secrets? How firmly was Nil tied to AU? "What's so special about tonight's meeting?"

"One of the founders is speaking tonight, and there's a platinum reception for him and some other bigwigs afterward. Good chance for networking."

"How much of it do you believe?" Clay asked, then wondered if now were the time to start wasting words. Hurriedly, he said, "I hear from AU a lot of things about President Reynolds that don't fit with what I remember of those days. And if Reynolds was a bad president, he paid for it on 6:19, right?"

Nil glanced to the side, then leaned toward Clay and lowered his voice. "A lot of AU rhetoric is nonsense," he said. "Don't fake that surprised look."

Caught, Clay shrugged. "If it's nonsense, why pay it lip service?"

"Joe citizen wants to believe there's a strong hand on the tiller after 6:19, and the bronze and silver members want to belong to something bigger than themselves." Nil shrugged. "And like I said, it's a good chance for networking. Do you want to come? I can't get you into the reception but you could hear the speech and get some face time—"

"No. Thanks. Martin."

Nil accepted the excuse as they walked to the front doors. Jenny and the boy were upstairs out of his sight. Good.

The words fit with what he knew of Nil: Clay was glad to see his business partner hadn't drunk the AU coolade and only participated for pragmatic reasons. But would that make him more likely to help Clay, or less?

2

Thank God Jenny had been out of the living room when he left Clay's house, Nil thought as his sedan descended the exit ramp nearest the Excelsior Hotel. *Leave something out there and I'll take it from you.* Christ. No kidding there were other fish in the sea, almost all of them not Clay's wife. Nil pushed thoughts of Jenny far out of mind and put on his game face. He'd soon be surrounded by executive members of AU, senior bureaucrats at federal agencies, and a wide range of local business and professional figures. He undid several buttons of his shirt and spritzed a cologne, equal parts oxytocin derivatives and odorants custom-fit to his genotype, onto his neck. He had to make TS Microcatalytix look good. He had to make himself look good.

Had Clay's mood tonight been more distracted than usual? His friend had never been an extrovert around the office, but tonight, Clay had been even deeper in his own head than usual.

Nil bolted upright. Had Clay picked up on his thoughts of seducing Jenny? He relaxed and in amusement sniffed out a breath. If he had to wager on Clay's ability to intuit others' thoughts he'd take the other side every time. Clay hadn't guessed a thing. To assume otherwise was to fall into the common trap, on hearing nothing but the echo chamber of one's own thoughts, of assuming the rest of the world thought those same thoughts too. Nil had long ago decided not to be common. Clay would never realize Nil had noticed Jenny's slender limbs and smooth skin—

Game face. His Lorelei stopped under the Excelsior's smooth stucco porte-cochere and he climbed out amid large black sedans and cars with state and federal government plates. Fifty yards away, an orchestra of traffic hummed, roared, and grumbled on the freeway. Nearby office midrises thrust banks of lighted windows into the washed-out night. Under the porte-cochere, revolving doors gave access to the hotel lobby.

The ballroom looked like any hotel conference space: taupe carpet, beige walls, the divider panels pushed back into their recesses. Umbellous chandeliers tinkled in the breeze from the vents. Murmured conversations filled the room, occasionally punctuated by guffaws and loud greetings. The crowd was a mix of AU members of all levels. Trophy wives hung on the arms of powerful men in handmade suits with gold and platinum membership pins and pendants. They recognized Nil with the barest of nods. Weaker, poorer men wore suits customized by machines and silver and bronze membership pins in need of polish. The latter stared at Nil's platinum eagle and hesitated before speaking to him in high voices. If they brought their wives the women smiled blankly, if at all, and peered enviously at the diamond- and silk-adorned platinum wives. The looks struck him as catty and rude. Jenny would never—

Other fish in the sea. Some women attended alone, or in pairs. Many wore guest passes clipped to their lapels and flicked their gazes over the cut of men's suits and the polish of men's shoes. He'd had enough of that attitude from Minerva and didn't care for more. The other solitary women were AU employees in crisp navy suits, skirts swishing as they walked, former sorority girls and black debutantes who crewed the swag and membership tables. He idly fingered the top copy on a stack of President Everton's manifesto, *No Higher Virtue*, and chatted with a tall *kali* with straightened hair and wide green eyes until the lights dimmed for a moment and he took a seat.

The chairs had been arrayed close together in three sections, the two on the wings slanted toward the podium. What at first glance appeared to be microphones hung from the ceiling, but Nil recognized them as MuSynth clusters. Some people carried short glasses of water from the tables in the corners and sweat dampened Nil's back when he relaxed in his chair: warm temperatures enhanced the contagiousness of moods. He swallowed dryly. On either side, silver members brushed against him, muttered apologies, and leaned away.

The podium stood on a dais, the latter trimmed in red-white-and-blue bunting. Behind hung a massive American-flag-themed backdrop with huge glossy portraits posted on it. President Everton's likeness held the top position directly behind the podium, and in a row below were pictures of Alexander Fisher, AU's executive director and, as CEO of Titan Industries, Nil's ultimate boss; Kiper Carter, retired Marine Corps general and AU's security policy director; AU's domestic policy director, Christopher Bishop; and tonight's speaker, AU's economic policy director, David Grunwald. Grunwald sat toward the back of the dais, next to the head of AU's Houston organization.

The lights dimmed, a spotlight lit the podium, and video displays on the front and side walls showed a closeup. The local director gave an introduction. Grunwald was an emeritus professor at SIU Carbondale "who responded to the extreme challenge of June 19, 2019 by turning thought into action" and helped form AU with other figures from the St. Louis region. Nil doubted Grunwald's role in forming AU had been pivotal, but in practice he'd given AU enough credibility on economic policy issues to win the great mass of voters who wanted both tortured terrorists (which every faction had promised) and fat subsidies for the middle-class way of life. Add a telegenic Midwestern governor and victory came easily. The local director yielded the podium to Grunwald and Nil clapped with the rest of the crowd as the retired professor stepped into the spotlight.

Emeritus usually was a fancy word for "old," but Grunwald looked vigorous, perhaps in his late 50s, though with antiagathic treatments (and Nil had no doubt Grunwald was ahead of him in line for Agerix treatments) one couldn't be certain. His hair was white but thick, no combover, and the lines of his face made him look distinguished, not elderly. He thanked the local chapter and gave an introductory joke everyone laughed at; his words came rapidly in a tenor voice and a Brooklyn accent.

Grunwald's speech delivered the usual mix of buzz phrases ("an end to selfishness," "the purpose that comes with unity"), contradictory policy prescriptions (preservation of jobs in the petroleum industry and expansion of ecofriendly solar power plants; free vat-grown meat for the poor and senior citizens, and further regulatory oversight of biochemical minifabrication tools), and veiled threats against "foolish believers in decentralized decision," "sowers of disunity," and "petty people resentful of the health care safety net that will soon extend everyone's lifespan." For his Houston audience, he added a few words about the manned Mars mission supposedly to launch late in Everton's second term. The words wouldn't stir soup, let alone men's souls, but the bronzes and silvers around Nil leaned forward and stared with rapt eyes. Nil glanced at the MuSynths suspended in the gloom and smirked. With skillful crowd-psychological engineering and aerosolized neurotransmitter agonists, a speaker could read the telephone directory and be lauded by this crowd.

After the speech, Nil slipped through the chattering mass to the elevators. The platinum reception occupied a penthouse suite. A string quartet played near the French doors to the balcony. Waiters in white jackets, security cleared by NCS, circulated with trays bearing crab cakes and beef sashimi. Blue-suited debutantes circulated the room and catalyzed conversations. About half the guests had platinum membership pins; the other half were local, state, and federal politicians and civil servants.

A stout white fellow in a machine-cut navy suit was an obvious bureaucrat. He had a fleshy, florid face, combed-over hair, and a mustache. Mustaches made a man look either French or gay, and the bureaucrat's was too wide and bushy to be French; but Nil couldn't imagine anyone, male or female, looking at his beady blue eyes with any affection. Nil munched a crab cake and eavesdropped on the bureaucrat's conversation with one of his peers.

"Goddamn Boucher got another one transferred to Dent County. Yamamoto the brain scientist. Bastard's an e.c. And Boucher gets him?"

"Boucher's got POTUS' ear," the other said blandly.

"Wish I knew why." Mustache Man's tone was sarcastic and he snorted out a breath.

One of the blue suit ladies, a blonde with a round, madeup face and an effortlessly plastic smile, took Nil's attention away from the conversation. "How are you this evening, Mr. Thomas? Wonderful. I'm Melissa, if there's anything I can do, ask." She met his gaze and he read the frank assessment, *I know you're a multimillionaire but are you the best one I can find in the room?* Perhaps some of the blue suits weren't golddiggers, but he couldn't think of any off hand. Could he find a woman who wasn't interested in his money— He smiled coldly in response. "Have you met—?" she said, and pointed to Mustache Man.

"No."

She seemed relieved to hand him off without rancor on his part. "Sir, if I may?"

Mustache Man glanced at her, past her, and took in Nil's platinum eagle. Nil extended his hand. "Hi, I'm Nil Thomas."

The other shook. "Bill Haycock." He paused. "Go ahead, everyone sniggers the first time."

Juvenile, yes, but his last name *was* humorous… Nil sniffed out a breath in amusement but cut it off when Haycock's eyes narrowed. He'd set a trap and Nil had walked into it open-eyed. Gnaw off your leg, quick. "I know what it's like. I switched schools for third grade and when I said, 'My name is Anil,'" affecting a South Asian accent he'd never had growing up in Kansas City, "everyone called me 'Anal.'"

"How'd your people get a name like Thomas? Englishman in the woodpile?"

Nil kept himself from showing offense. "There's been a Christian community in southern India for centuries," he said nonchalantly. If the other were obviously a member of the City on the Hill Society, he would have played up the apostle Thomas directly founding the Indian church, but Haycock seemed the kind to be skeptical of myths. "You work for—?"

"National Counterterrorism Service. I'm an Assistant Director stationed at the main office."

"How's life in New Washington? We appreciate the hardships it must entail for our public servants."

"It's just the ass-end of Kansas. I've been worse places. What's your line of work?"

"I'm the Chief Operating Officer of TS Microcatalytix, a Titan Industries company. You may be aware of our products, the MuSynth and NuGland—" and from that Nil was off to the races. Crowd control? Interrogation assistance? If a high-ranking official of NCS might want to hear about it, he played up how TS Microcatalytix could help. Haycock asked smart questions and he responded with smart answers. Whatever tactical error he'd made on first meeting Haycock had been overcome. Nil was in his element.

TS Microcatalytix had a two-story building in the Nolan Ryan Industrial Park near the Houston suburb of Pearland, about fifteen miles south of Clay's house. When his suv pulled into his reserved spot near the front door, he put aside the catalog of vintage 35mm SLR Leicas he'd flipped through on the ride down. Meticulously ground lenses and the mathematical certainty of optics lingered in his mind's eye. Not that he needed another camera; he hadn't picked up his gigapixel digitals in weeks. But he didn't want to think about how some stranger knew more of the company's affairs than he knew himself.

Inside the front doors, the reception mannequin smiled at him from behind its counter. "Good morning, Mr. Schieffer." Its androgynous voice echoed through the double-height space. Clay glanced at it and pressed his lips together. It had the same abstract faceless shape as the wine-tasting robot at myfab, but at least its programming still bound this one. His soles crackled on the terrazzo floor.

In front of the windows at the foot of the west stair hung a hologram showing a cartoon animation of the NuGland. A blue raindrop shape clung to the inside of a red half-cylinder bisected lengthwise. Yellow cubes flowed down the length of the half-cylinder, hit the blue raindrop, and disappeared. Green circles appeared on the surface of the blue raindrop's base and slid through the red wall. They bubbled up and popped like carbonation in soda water.

Clay hated the animation. Too simplified. Though the raindrop shape was right, the cartoon didn't show the scale: the NuGland was less than three microns long and three wide at its thickest point. The cartoon didn't hint at the person-years and computer-months required to attach the microfabricator to the arteriole endothelium's lipid raft transmembrane proteins at target points in the recipient's vasculature. (Why synthesize a neurotransmitter in the liver)? It didn't show the receptors that grabbed substrate molecules from the bloodstream, the combustion chamber that burned one such substrate, glucose, to power the unit, or the maze of microfluidic pumps and catalysis chambers which generated product. It didn't reveal the complex programming language that gave the microfabricator its flexibility or the transceiver that linked it to a doctor's orders.

It didn't tell the world the NuGland microfabricator was Clay's finest achievement.

It told Clay he had no comparable challenge left.

He trudged the stairs to the second floor landing. Paintings of central Texas landscapes, mesquite-covered hills and half-dry streambeds, hung on the far wall under security cameras, microphones, and sniffers. At the security door, the tiny red light of a retina scanner flashed in his eyes and the door unsealed with a demagnetizing thud. Two lefts, his standard morning greeting to Cynde, his secretary, and then into his corner office. The leather chair squealed under his weight and the video display flicked on and craned its neck to him.

How much email could he get by 8:45? Reports from QA, marketing, HR, compliance, and more compliance soured his mood. Finally something he cared about, an R&D report, but when he skimmed the summary ("Redesigning the geometry of the combustion chamber of the NuGland would increase power generation efficiency by 0.5-0.8%") he remembered again he had no challenge before him.

At least, no technical challenge. Last night's words of the robot operator came to mind. Clay dithered for a moment, then pushed his left index finger into a nearby pointing thimble and tapped the thimble to his wearable to establish the link. On the display, his point of view flew past the emails. Between a blue sky and a green ground, gray shapes like mesas sat at the horizon. The one on the far right would be the sales and marketing server.

*   *   *

Nil glanced up from the AU/Houston/Platinum wiki to take in Clay's suv on his left and the overgrown jersey barriers in front, between his car and the building. 8:50, Clay probably hadn't beaten him to the office by much.

Inside, Nil asked the receptionist if Ms. Colbert had arrived. Yes, now in her office. He went through the security doors on the first floor. Mostly labs down here doing wet chemistry and molecular dynamics simulations. Cooling fans on server racks hummed; racked MuSynths chugged; and compressed air pulsed to drive a fluid dynamics experiment. Down the side corridor to the freight entrance, a high grinding sound came from the machine shop and male voices laughed about something. In the main corridor the scientists, half of them refugees from Chinese warlords or Hindu national-socialists, showed deferent surprise: they greeted Nil and half-stepped aside for him. They didn't seem to notice themselves acting on innate human software programmed over a million years of evolution. Nil smiled and chatted and deftly pretended not to notice, either.

At one time, he'd known a lot about endogenous human biomolecules and MD sims to test small molecule bioactivity. Long ago, though, he'd realized thousands of people knew much more and could be hired for decent salaries and benefits packages. True success came from networking, brown-nosing, courtiership, and back-stabbing, and while all but the most Aspergerish of the people around him knew that too—more innate human software—most shied away from those skills, subconsciously using them to acquire petty things like more sex from their spouse or a five-thousand-dollar raise. Nil knew himself to be a wolf in sheep's clothing, but one smart enough to leave the sheep placid and their meat tender and well-marbled with fat.

He followed the corridor around the corner near the auditorium. Scientist offices stood on the right—Nil passed a conversation about synthesis pathways for steroid hormones and a screensaver running an MD sim—and a side corridor led to more offices. Monica Colbert's stood at the end, in the northeast corner of the building, directly under his.

Nil shook his head to dismiss the symbolism. Technically, yes, Monica was number three on the TS Microcatalytix org chart, behind Nil and Clay, but in addition to her official title, chief financial officer, Titan Industries had assigned her to TS when it bought the company and she had the ear of headquarters in St. Louis. More than the ear; every rumor pointed to Monica having an affair with Alexander Fisher, Titan's CEO. Her door was closed but light leaked underneath it. Nil knocked.

The door swung open. Monica sat behind a wide desk, cherry-stained and glass-topped, bare except for a few artfully arranged manila folders and framed photos of her with other coiffed, made-up young women with clear skin and fine bones. She wore a gray pin-stripe suit, its shoulders padded, and a maroon ascot. A loose pony-tail bound her blonde hair, save for a few fugitive strands artfully dangling past her ears. She attempted to look crisply professional, but her wide eyes and large mouth undercut the effect. "Good to see you, but can we make it quick? I'm flying to St. Louis for meetings and need to clear the decks before I go."

Nil nodded and entered the office. The door remained open as an offering to the sexual harassment furies. "I didn't see you at the AU meeting last night."

"I try to make them, you know that."

"Grunwald said the org will ask Congress and President Everton to raise the licensing and reporting requirements for chem nano."

"I'd heard," she said with a faint smile, and then she crinkled her nose. "You know that won't be a burden on us."

"Not for the foreseeable future, but I want us running a tight ship before the wind might ever change. If the executive committee underwent a change in personnel...." He let the prospect of life without Fisher's influence on Everton hang unspoken. Nil had seen multiple examples of a ranking bureaucrat getting purged and his fiefdoms suffering the same fate.

"I see what you're saying." Bland and noncommittal; he'd have to monitor the issue for a while to make sure she followed through.

Now that he'd laid a smokescreen, he raised his real topic. "One other thing. Clay's been acting strangely lately, don't you think?"

"Doesn't he always?"

Nil chuckled. "More than usual, I should say."

"I hadn't noticed. What details?"

"I met him last night for drinks and he seemed distracted. Something big on his mind."

Monica shrugged. "Maybe the next build of the NuGland? I'm worried the schedule will slip."

"No," Nil enunciated. "If it were technical, he'd be upbeat and talking at the edge of my comprehension."

"Maybe his wife's finally going to leave him."

Surprised by her comment, Nil cleared his throat. "He didn't act like it's worse than usual. Has he talked to human resources? Maybe there's a health issue…." He gabbed; he sought to gain information, not to give it away.

Monica kept her poker face. "I haven't heard a thing, but I'll keep my eyes open."

"I appreciate it. I'll let you go. Good luck in St. Louis."

She smiled, but weakly, turning up the corners of her mouth but leaving her eyes expressionless. Trouble with headquarters he didn't know about? Or had he showed too much of his curiosity about Clay's mood? Nil looked over her face but couldn't tell which, and as he scrutinized her she resumed her poker face and he realized he would get nothing more.

Clay touched the thimble to the glass-topped surface of his desk and rows of a spreadsheet shuffled up the screen. He had burrowed deep into the data structures of sales and unearthed a master shipping fulfillment database for the MuSynth. Dates scrolled by and he remembered happier months, September and October 2019, when Martin was genesculpted *ex utero* and he and Jenny made love surrounded by moving boxes on a mattress thrown down on the floor of their new master bedroom.

Wait a second. November 3, 2019, their biggest single order yet shipped: 600 units to Midwest Home Products, Erlanger, Kentucky. A quick flick to a zipcode map showed the town to be a suburb of Cincinnati a few miles from the airport. He'd seen that name elsewhere in the spreadsheet, hadn't he? Clay frowned and scrolled up to earlier dates. MHP had been sent one order previously, eight units in late July, a few weeks before the negotiations with Titan heated up. Quite a jump in orders shipped by TS' fabrication contractor in west Houston.

But he hadn't seen MHP in the sales database, right? He flicked over to an earlier spreadsheet his searching had generated, sales in the same timeframe, and muttered, "Find Midwest Home Products." No hits. Had MHP's name been entered differently in the sales data structures? He tried variants, acronyms. No luck. Had the order been shipped to them care of another company? But no single sale of 600 units had taken place in late October or early November. He told his computer to compare the two spreadsheets and highlight discrepancies.

The fulfillment spreadsheet pulled out a few rows, glowing green with data added relative to the sales spreadsheet. Shipments to MHP included 1400 units in mid-December, 1100 in late January 2020, 1600 on February 9, and then a lull. The lull broke in the summer, with orders ten-fold larger, twelve to eighteen thousand on eight occasions from early June until the third week of September. MHP's 119,300 units were the most shipped to any company in TS' first eighteen months of operations. And the sales database had no record.

Someone in fab had made up the order and shipped it to a non-purchaser? But their fab contractor would have been as automated as the facilities at a myfab store. No person could slip in an order and automated audits would have caught him if he had. More likely someone had removed MHP from the sales database.

Sons of bitches. In Titan's agreement to purchase TS, Titan had contracted to pay royalties on sales of the MuSynth, $12.40 per unit. The bastards in St. Louis had shortchanged him by $2.5MM. He seethed at the monitor for a moment, then realized he could check the sales spreadsheet against his royalties report. After a few minutes of deciphering he found Titan had paid him royalties for the 119,300 units that didn't show up on the sales spreadsheet.

What did MHP make? Another flick of his hand opened a browser to MHP's website. *Midwest Home Products, a Titan Industries company*—

A knock on the door jolted Clay. Monica Colbert stood with her hand poised over the door and her mouth open. "Have a minute?" She sounded short of breath.

Clay pulled his left hand into a fist, twice, to close all the documents on his monitor, then leaned back. He didn't have much use for her, but she generally did her job and left him alone. "Sure."

She nodded at the monitor—it was edge-on to the door, she couldn't have seen anything—and said, "Working on the next NuGland build?"

"Yeah."

"I'm leaving for St. Louis in a few hours and I wondered if you could give me an informal progress report?"

"Uh, sure, we're increasing the efficiency of the combustion chamber. And solving some of the binding issues involving caveolin phenotypes in black, uh, African-American populations." That last was a wish, not a statement of fact, but she would never know.

"Good. Everyone in St. Louis is looking forward to rollout of the next build. Sounds like we're on schedule. Talk to you later."

Clay breathed shallowly until she walked past his secretary's station and out of his line of sight. He slumped back in his chair and sucked in a deep breath. Sweat drenched the back of his shirt. He couldn't have fooled her, could he, by spitting out half-remembered details and wishful thinking?

He slid upright in his chair. Maybe he had. Colbert wasn't technical and wouldn't know any details on the next NuGland build and work being done in the labs. He never spoke smoothly, so his stumbling words wouldn't have tipped her off. She wouldn't guess what he'd been looking at. Nothing to worry about.

Except for server access logs. Clay didn't move, but his heart thudded. She could easily find out what he'd been looking at. But so what? She wouldn't know what those sales meant any more than he did. The only person with any claim as to what it meant was some anonymous hacker operating out of the Far East, but Clay had no way to weigh the other's veracity. He might be wasting company time chasing shadows.

Besides, he could sniff up information on Midwest Home Products as easily on the ride home.

3

The Titan Industries Tower dominated a cluster of mid- and high-rise office buildings in northwest St. Louis. Its curved, art deco lines of foamed concrete outwardly reflected the city's revitalization after the New Madrid earthquake of 2017, and its location, formerly site of the worst slums in the city, quietly hinted at the power of eminent domain and disaster-relief subsidies. From Alexander Fisher's office on the 49th floor, one could look past the high-rises and sports stadiums downtown, past the half-rebuilt Gateway Arch, and so far into Illinois that, through the haze, one couldn't tell where subdivisions ended and cornfields began.

Fisher stared through his reflection in the window and ignored the view. After months of hints, his wife had spoken bluntly last night, about ground rules and discretion and the best family-law attorneys in the metro area. She'd offered him the choice of discretion around the office and in St. Louis society, or the loss of half his fortune plus legal fees. Bitch. He gave her all she could reasonably expect: money for her charities and his presence at galas attended by the gossip columnists of stltoday.com. But she'd gambled she could extort more from him without driving him to pay hundreds of millions in a divorce settlement; and she'd been right.

A gentle chime sounded in his earbud. "Ms. Colbert to see you," his concierge said.

He tightened the knot of his handmade silk tie and stepped to his desktop cologne mister. He stretched his neck to receive a spray, pheromones and trust compounds. *Discretion around the office.* He smirked and told his concierge to let her in. Monica strode in briskly, smiling professionally, and he knew she wasn't worth a tiny fraction of $620 million; and from the worry lines around her eyes he could tell she knew, subconsciously, she wasn't either. The door swung shut behind her.

"What's status at TS Microcatalytix?" he asked.

A good subordinate, she didn't hesitate before giving her report. Operations ran smoothly; sales growth matched projections. He knew she assumed he'd read all that in previous reports, and she soon moved to more subjective statements. Thomas had recently upgraded to platinum membership in AU and his eagle pendant had given him entry into new networks; Schieffer made progress toward the NuG-land upgrade.

"Our garage duo's handling the pressures of stardom?" Fisher had picked up the metaphor from one of his MBA professors. Most entrepreneurs were like talentless teenagers jamming in the garage; only a few could put together music worth hearing. But of that few, fewer still had the business savvy and financials to cope with success.

She frowned. "Schieffer's been acting strangely lately. Yesterday I monitored him poking around on our sales server, and when I 'happened' to stop by his office he lied pretty poorly about what he was doing."

"Sales?" Schieffer planned to jump to a competitor or a startup and poach TS customers? Not credible. The dossier on Schieffer pegged him as a tinkerer, not a leader, and Titan's patent lawyers had his baby, the NuGland core technology, locked up.

Monica shrugged, nodded. "He was interested in shipments to Midwest Home Products in '19 and '20."

Fisher's gut tightened. He hadn't thought about the Free Samples Project in months; it was water on the bridge and should have long since flowed out to sea. The cosmos had joined forces with his wife to ruin his week. Christ, possibly his life. The problem wasn't Schieffer himself finding out what happened at MHP in those years—from the dossier, he knew Schieffer couldn't persuade a soul—but if he somehow infected others with that knowledge. Goddam—

Fisher snorted in a breath and straightened his spine. *When in doubt, lead.* "What exactly did he look at? All the data."

Monica raised her thin, curved eyebrows, but calmly said, "Let me check." She drew her display out of an inner pocket of her suit jacket and snapped her wrist to whip the display into rigidity. In the past he'd appreciated her ease under pressure compared to most of his underlings, but now he pressed his lips together and narrowed his eyes. Did she think her status in his bed exempted her from the standards he insisted on?

"Spreadsheets of total sales and shipping fulfillments from July 1, 2019 to December 31, 2020," she said. "He also browsed up a map of metro Cincinnati and MHP's home page."

"I said all the data."

"He also checked his royalties reports for '19 and '20."

Schieffer could have found the units shipped, but nothing more. Fisher eased his shoulders and lifted his head. "If he looks at that sales and shipping data again, call me immediately."

Monica nodded. "Something big?" she asked lightly.

She had gotten above herself. "Need to know."

"If I knew what he was looking for—"

"Christ, when I say 'need to know' I damn well mean it. Are we clear?"

Her face grew blank for a moment but then she recovered her professional expression. "I'm happy to do whatever's in Titan's best interests."

"Good. Anything else?"

She opened her mouth to speak and Fisher mentally cursed for making the offer. "Do you have a moment? Out of the office?"

"I have a stableful of shit on my desk today."

She didn't look happy. He rolled his eyes slightly and moved his hands in broad arcs away from his head. "We're out of the office. Five minutes."

Monica smiled wanly, a crinkle around her eyes. "We haven't gotten away any time recently. Wouldn't it be good to reconnect? We could take a weekend at the corporate villa on Maui—"

"I'm booked."

"We don't have to go this weekend—"

"I am booked solid for a long time to come."

Her chest heaved but her voice stayed level. "It wouldn't have to be a weekend, or Maui. But sometime." She swallowed heavily. "I remember you once told me how good you felt with me, how much better than with your wife—"

"Shit! You know I'm married."

"And I know you're unhappy—"

"You don't know shit about my marriage," he said, and his gaze drilled into her until she averted hers. "There's your guilty conscience. Why didn't I see it? You want half my goddam fortune—"

"Alex! No!" Her eyes were damp and her mouth pursed childishly.

"You've got promotions you only earned on your back. That's all you're going to get. Take that or take nothing."

She gasped breaths but didn't cry. "If you want it to be over, tell me."

He leaned forward with a cold look on his face. "Okay, it's over."

She sobbed then and squeezed her eyes shut. Tears glistened on her eyelashes and trickled down her cheeks.

"And don't think you've got a harassment suit, either. I've recorded every voicemail and email and saved all those salacious, inappropriate cards you sent. Be glad with what you got." He moved his hands through the air, reversing the prior arcs. "Back to work."

She ducked her head and scampered out and her sobs became choked-off cries until the door swung shut and returned the office to silence.

The toy monkey danced across the st. augustine singing nonsense syllables and Martin staggered after it. Clay sipped his scotch and put it on the glass-topped patio table, intersecting a condensation ring. He happened to glance at Jenny on the other side of the table. She sat on the edge of her seat, her hands clasped under her chin and her eyes tracking Martin. The boy plodded along the front of the flowerbed along the side fence. He would never catch that damn monkey. Clay returned to the display on his knee.

According to its website, Midwest Home Products made health, beauty, and household aesthetic products. The website splashed an ad for Auromatique, its new product line developed in a joint venture with a musicology company. The device released scents (generated by a MuSynth) in conjunction with music to perform mood engineering. Imagine if Jenny heard about that—

She gasped and then Martin cried. What now? The boy lay face-down in the grass near the edge of the flowerbed. His fists flailed and his crying grew louder. Jenny rose from her chair and Clay shook his head. "He stumbled over his own feet. Let him figure out how to stand up."

She pressed her lips together and set her fist on her hip. "If you'd been watching you'd have seen him trip over a sprinkler head." She stalked across the deck, the soles of her mules loud on the cementitious panel, and jumped down to the lawn. The monkey sat on the iron fence between the lawn and the pool, a timid look on its cartoon features.

Even if the boy had tripped he wouldn't have done worse than stub his toe, but try telling her that. Clay sighed and pressed a button on the display edge. While he stood the display rolled itself up and grew soft as cloth. As he shoved it into the pocket of his khakis, it shook and a chime softly sounded in his ear. He pulled the display out and read the name shown on the outside of the roll. M Colbert. Why the heck was she calling? Did she need to reach Nil but couldn't find him?

"You're answering that?" Jenny asked. She crouched next to Martin. The boy stood now, her hands holding his torso, his face red and petulant.

"Work calls me after hours only in emergencies." He turned his back and unrolled the display. "Answer."

Colbert sat in a car, based on the headliner and the glimpse of sky visible through the back window behind her. Thick makeup surrounded her puffy, bloodshot eyes. She sniffled. "I hope I'm not bothering you, Clay."

"I'm at home."

"I know what you were looking at yesterday. Sales and shipments to Midwest Home Products. You weren't hiding."

He slowly exhaled. Underestimating her had been foolish, but yesterday he had inflated his worry into groundless fear. "No, I wasn't. Should I have been?"

"Yes. I don't mean to sound harsh, I really don't. It's easy to think you're on solid ground when you're really on thin ice."

"I have to hide my interest in my own company's operations?"

She shook her head and the gesture triggered Clay's resentment; he wasn't naive "It's not your company anymore. You were looking at something St. Louis doesn't want you to see." She forestalled his next question. "I don't know why."

Over the previous two days Clay had jumped from conclusion to conclusion about the stranger at myfab, that he was an AU employee, a scammer, or a madman. Even after finding the MHP discrepancy in the database, Clay considered dismissing it as an innocent error. But now, while wind rustled the sun-dappled leaves of live oaks and Jenny scowled at him against her backdrop of blossoming yellow bells, intuitions crystallized in his mind. The stranger had been neither scammer nor madman; the discrepancy had been intentional.

Drop it. He could return to his corner office, comfortable lifestyle, and cavernous house and pretend he'd seen nothing amiss on the sales-and-shipping server. Mornings swimming laps in the pool like a pacing, caged predator, days shuffling virtual paper, and evenings drinking scotch, all the time shrinking inside, osteoporosis of the soul. He couldn't drop it. He would have to be circumspect—he could hire Zhejiang hackers to track the deliveries after MHP received them or private investigators to dig through that company's trash—but he knew now what he had to do. "I was double-checking my royalty statements, Monica," he said. From the corner of his eye he saw Jenny jerk her gaze away from their son and peer at Clay. "I don't want Titan to rip me off."

On the display, Monica shook her head. "You're a mediocre liar. Clay, I don't know what you were looking for. I don't care. But if you haven't found it yet I'm willing to help."

Obviously a trap. "I don't know what you mean."

"You didn't get into MHP's servers. I have high enough clearance to get you in there. All I ask is that you cover your tracks. Do you know how to use a proxy server?"

"I can." Could he trust her? Clay frowned. "What's in it for you?"

She lifted her head. "I've decided the time has come for me to leave the company. I won't regret burning my bridges."

He'd always assumed she'd been a happy employee of Titan. Granted he rarely talked to her, but did anyone ever know what someone else thought? Yet she offered him a key to the vault. What was the catch? "That's it?"

"That's it," she said. Clay checked her face for a hint to what else she wanted. Him? His money? She had worked with him for years, though, and never dropped a hint of such a thing, unless he hadn't noticed. But her expression lacked seductiveness: furrows slashed from between her eyebrows to the bridge of her nose and her jaw clenched. Her anger at Titan was real; what she offered she freely gave.

Jenny slouched in a thick leather chair in the home theater room. On screen, in a '90s coffee bar, the outwardly aloof romantic lead bantered with the heroine he'd ultimately fall for: *Restless in Redmond*, a dot-com era costume drama, comfort viewing to keep her from crying. She'd bathed Martin, dressed him in his pajamas, tucked him into bed. Clay had grudgingly walked in and kissed the boy's forehead and lied and replied to him "love you too," then slinked back down the hall to pick at his dusty guitars or filter his photos. Or make a phone call.

His distraction and resentment made sense now. He was having an affair. The realization pressed down on her. She'd seen the evidence for months, years, but had let herself be fooled by pleasant memories of the past and the man she'd married. She didn't deserve this. He'd brought on all their problems, tempting fate and subjecting Martin to genesculpting—barely approved in the fall of '19—and yet he blamed her for their son's ailment and sought comfort somewhere else. Maybe his slut would let him genesculpt his second child.

Jenny imagined running upstairs, scooping Martin from his bed, and driving off, somewhere, anywhere. Her brother lived fourteen hours away in central Kansas, and his duplex on post had a guest bedroom and a fold-out bed. She caught her breath and pushed the thought away. Before she did anything she needed proof.

Nil would know, especially if Monica really did work with them. She told her concierge to pause the movie and call him. While the call went through she realized he would lie to protect Clay, but she could read his tells. She told her concierge to run his voice and video feeds through an expression reading program to put a second perspective on the matter.

He sat in his living room, she could tell from the bronze statuettes and paintings behind him, and looked surprised to see her.

"Who's Monica?" she asked bluntly.

Nil crinkled his face. "Monica Colbert. She works with us...." He trailed off and then looked at Jenny, his eyes wide.

"Are they having an affair?"

He blanched. "Good lord. An affair?" He leaned back and rubbed his forehead. "I haven't seen it around the office. Not openly." To her eye he told the truth, and the expression reader found no sign of evasiveness on his face. "But it wouldn't surprise me." His expression grew apologetic. "I have suspected it."

"Suspected? How long?"

"Weeks? Months?"

Her face tightened. "You suspected my husband was having an affair and you walked into my house and talked to me as if you gave a damn about me and my son?"

Clay would have either wilted from or mirrored her anger, but Nil instead gave a firm look free of rancor. "I didn't want to drive a wedge between you if I had no proof."

She ended the call soon after. The room felt as large and soulless as the office she visited a couple of times a month. Nil was a better friend than Clay deserved. He'd told her the truth when asked but hadn't volunteered it in the hopes Clay would mend his own fences. Hell, he was a better friend to her than she had expected; he hadn't evaded her question; he didn't treat her as a leper for Martin's developmental disability.

He'd also spoken wisely about proof. They had two suppositions but no evidence. She couldn't flee to her brother Roger's house or retain a divorce lawyer yet, but if she so easily believed Clay was having an affair, she would need a divorce lawyer soon regardless of the proof. Their marriage was like a splintering raft. It would take both of them to lash it together; if Clay refused to help, the currents would separate them. She cried then but held a pillow to her face to muffle her sobs and catch her tears. Though across the house and asleep, she didn't want Martin to hear.

After a time, her tears subsided, leaving her eyes puffy and a mucus taste at the back of her throat. She knew she wouldn't be able to think more that night. She told the movie to unpause. The next scene soon started, Seattle summer, a sunny blue morning, and from the tracking shot she recognized the scene: the romantic lead would accidentally reveal his sensitive and loving side while dog-walking along Lake Washington. Someone somewhere lived happily ever after.

The sun climbed the cloudless eastern sky above Fort Riley and drove off the dew laid down by the spring night in Kansas. After the winter's dormancy, green tinged the lawns between the post buildings. A robo-mower worked in the distance, its motor's hum echoing off brick facades and aluminum-framed windows. The hay smell of the season's first mow reminded Roger Sung of guiding the lawnmower across his family's suburban yard as a young teen.

Roger and his first sergeant, Hardin, strode the sidewalk toward battalion HQ and Lt. Col. Mueller's 0830 meeting. Roger's thoughts churned. Would they finally be deployed? He'd hinted it to Emma over breakfast. A chance to demonstrate the Light RTD paradigm in the field, but a field 11,000 miles away. She had been happy for him but her smile had still been forced.

He rounded the last corner of battalion HQ and saw Capt. Olafson, commander of Victor Company, approaching from the other side of the building. Olafson had been too tall for helicopter pilot school, a broad-shouldered blond with close-set brown eyes and a pixie chin. His eyes brooded under his black garrison beret. "What do you think this is about?" he asked.

"What else? Uighurstan."

Olafson shook his head. "Two years of occupation and they haven't deployed us yet. You know we're the red-headed stepchildren."

Of course he knew. Heavy RTD jocks ruled the roost at DoD, thanks to the sexiness of autonomous battle tanks and self-propelled howitzers and the cozy relationship of the procurement office with the kickbacks-and-overruns crowd at the defense contractors and the kingmakers on the Congressional committees. The Light RTD paradigm used swarms of robots and teleoperated devices you could buy at myfab and its old advocate, Lt. Gen. Wickenham, now retired, had been a prickly bastard who'd made too many enemies. "Maybe Mueller and Maj. Gen. Johnson have bent the right ears. Maybe Heavy RTD is screwing the pooch in Ooo-stan."

"Those thumbdicks couldn't screw their way out of a wet paper bag. But winning or losing in Ooo-stan doesn't matter, Heavy RTD's only there to make it look like Everton is tracking down the 6:19 perps anywhere on Earth. They won't send us."

"Then what's the meeting about?" Roger asked.

Olafson glanced to either side and lowered his voice. "You read the r-mail."

Scuttlebutt, the rumor mill, backchannels; and men always said women gossiped too much. "Loyalty drugs?"

"Damn right."

Roger rolled his eyes. "They won't. We're officers and gentlemen. They don't want to fog our performance."

"Rog, get your head out. You know the technology's there. You've got a brother-in-law working in the field, right?"

He nodded. He'd never mentioned Clay had co-founded one of the big players in chem molecular fab; he didn't want to bother explaining why he hadn't resigned his commission for a soft job in industry. "Doesn't mean they'll dope us up with loyalty drugs even if they can."

Olafson shook his head and said nothing. Behind Roger, Hardin cleared his throat. "Sir, time to find out. 0826."

Headquarters occupied a low building in beige brick. Hedges

bunched under the windows and a sign along the walkway to the front door announced 1 Light Robotics and Teleoperated Devices Battalion and showed the battalion's "Army Ants" logo. Inside, vinyl tiled the floor and Roger and the others passed the cubicle-divided offices of headquarters company personnel and civilian employees.

The main conference room stood in the middle of the building. The fluorescent lights gave everyone in the windowless room a washed-out look, like corpses on morgue slabs. Roger, Hardin, and Olafson were the last to arrive. The other company commanders, Smith of Uniform, Ng the artilleryman, and Maldonado and Bauermann from maintenance and supply, wore smartcamo fatigues and stood with their first sergeants and some headquarters personnel among an array of hard plastic chairs. The graphics in their uniforms shifted with their movements and Roger focused on their faces to avoid a headache. Behind the front table sat tall, brown-eyed Lt. Col. Mueller, his narrow, triangular face pensive as usual. He talked to Maj. Gen. Johnson, broad-nosed and shrewd-eyed, the division commander, sitting to his left. To Mueller's right was a sharp-faced male civilian wearing a gray suit, probably Latino from his black hair and copper-toned skin. Sympathy seemed a stranger to his face.

Roger glanced at Olafson. The other nodded sideways at the civilian and mouthed *told you so*. Roger raised his eyebrow and shook his head slightly. The civilian didn't look like a doctor or scientist or some paunchy member of the bureaucracy's middle ranks. But what was he? And would Johnson attend a briefing prior to the battalion's deployment to Uighurstan?

Mueller called his captains to order and they took seats. "I know you're wondering what this is about," he said. "It's frustrating to shuffle paper and play red team/blue team on the back forty while the hog jockeys are getting the glory in Ooo-stan. We're better soldiers and can outperform them in any kind of war we are asked to fight."

Uighurstan, then; but Mueller glanced at the civilian next to him. "Not what we think," 1Sgt. Hardin murmured to Roger while Mueller turned back to face his subordinates.

"I now introduce Mr. Ramirez from the National Counterterrorism Service."

Ramirez spoke curtly. "Gentlemen, it's been almost four years since the June 19 attack. The fact no similar attack has been attempted since shows President Everton's original strategy, vigorous military action abroad and vigilant police work at home, is fundamentally sound. But you know as well as I do no plan survives contact with the enemy."

Roger had waded through Clausewitz in his military science courses at A&M. The preferred paradigm since the Reynolds years invoked evolutionary metaphors, war was a red queen race where each combatant had to run faster and faster on the innovation treadmill to maintain parity with the other. What strategies had the 6:19 perps evolved?

"The global coalition of forces that's been at war with the United States since June 19 has responded to President Everton's original strategy. Bound as he has been by the precedents set by his forerunner's failed policies, our enemies within the borders of the United States until now have only been faced with law-enforcement agencies coordinated by the NCS. The scourge of uncontrollable, unmonitorable minifabrication technologies—perversions of the pocket sinterers and photosynthetic MRE generators you carry with you on maneuvers—" and better known as *brownie dust* and *solar-powered shitboxes* "—has freed our enemies from supply lines, money laundering, and state sponsorship. Our enemies have enlarged their numbers, increased their armament, and improved their organizations and their training. They have carried war to our shores.

"We need you to stop them.

"For that reason, I am here to tell you that President Everton has invoked the Insurrection Act to allow the use of the United States military against armed enemy combatant formations. Major General Johnson has received orders from the Secretary of Defense to assign 1LTRD Battalion for this purpose. Questions?"

Tension filled the room. Yes, the unit had trained in counterinsurgency operations—the tactical flexibility of a light-robotic swarm made it ideal—but everyone had envisioned that training for use in shantytown streets and overgrown jungles in the Third World. Roger had never thought of operations on American soil and doubted anyone else had. He glanced around the room and most of the company commanders had hunched shoulders and narrowed eyes.

Olafson raised his hand. "Who will have command?"

"I'll work with Lt. Col. Mueller to define objectives. Orders will officially come from him. We will attach task groups of NCS agents to you as needed for particular operations," Ramirez added. Mueller's long face stayed impassive.

"What ROEs do we have to work under?" Smith asked.

"Rules of engagement paperwork is being formalized," Ramirez said. "Generally, we authorize the use of non-lethal munitions only unless your equipment takes man-lethal fire. Then you can retaliate in kind."

Domestic politics still offered some constraint. The tension in Roger's shoulders eased until another question came to him. "This is the first briefing we've received on insurgency by domestic terrorists. I've never even heard rumors from military or law enforcement personnel about this." The men nearby shifted in their chairs away from him and the ones in the rows in front of him turned around and peered his way. He knew they hadn't heard rumors either, but none wanted to question the NCS agent and the vast, secretive bureaucracy he represented. "How extensive are domestic terrorist insurgency operations?"

Ramirez smiled. "I'm glad to hear NCS' rumor abatement procedures work. You shouldn't have heard about this. We estimate twenty-five to thirty thousand people are members of domestic insurgency groups. Few such groups have become fully operational, but know-how is diffusing through these groups. Slideshow." The lights dimmed and the wall behind Ramirez, Mueller, and Johnson glowed. A photo showed a shack of weather-worn gray planks and rotting shingles, set at the edge of a brown stubbled field. The next showed an interior view of the same shack with its floorboards peeled back to reveal a stash of rifles, rocket propelled grenades, and mortar rounds; plastic-and-metal cubes, partially disfigured by solder, glue, and bare wires, but recognizable as chemical molecular fabrication reactors, arrays of miniature machine tools, corpsman kits, shitboxes, and sinterers. Stuff you could order from a wood- or metalworking tools catalog, pick up at Bass Pro near the K-State campus in Manhattan, or steal from a National Guard armory with inside help.

"Goddam," Maldonado said. "You could keep a rifle platoon in combat indefinitely with all that."

The image changed again, the same field from a different angle a few yards into a wood, the shack in the distance. In the center of the photo, a camo net stretched between pine trees and hung over a pickup truck. The Bubba's Customs logo stood plainly visible on the tailgate. A camper shell yawned open over the pickup bed and a 120 mm mortar tube thrust up from a metal frame bolted onto the bed. The frame mounted a pair of robotic arms for loading. It became Ng's turn to swear.

"We recently found this in a raid on one cell of a white supremacist group in North Carolina," Ramirez said. "They aren't alone. Not only do they have other cells we haven't penetrated, but other groups with similar armament and organization are active: the American Bantu Self Defense League, Fuerza Aztlan, GaiaFist, and others."

Roger rested his mouth against the knuckles of his fist. In a country as large and populous as the United States, thirty thousand men could join insurgent militias and not be noticed. Dropouts could live off photosynthetic MRE generators; greenies from Portland and *vatos* from south Phoenix could drive into the wilderness and play soldier at night or on weekends. But if NCS had noticed them, they must have poked their heads out of their foxholes and fired on some government official. Between r-mail and bloggers rumor would have spread, even to central Kansas.

Was Ramirez' brief a fraud or had the administration silenced journalists both big and small?

The lights came up and washed out the display. "More questions? No?" the NCS agent asked. "Then let me hand you over to Maj. Gen. Johnson and Lt. Col. Mueller. Before I go, let me say again that I thank you, Pres. Everton thanks you, and your country thanks you for your service." He rose imperiously and strode out. As he passed, Ramirez' gaze flicked over Roger's face and nametag SUNG.

A few seconds after Ramirez left, the company commanders started talking and the volume quickly built until Johnson said "Gentlemen!" Silence fell save for the last echoes ringing off the drywall. "I'm sure this came as a surprise to you. You're not alone. If you have questions, spit them out."

No one else wanted to be the first, so Roger spoke. "Have we corroborated NCS' intelligence on domestic insurgents?"

Johnson nodded gravely. "Yes. There are groups out there caching weapons and preparing for combat. You're wondering why it hasn't made the blogs? NCS has asked them to keep quiet to minimize copycatting and they've complied."

"And the ones who publish anyway get arrested," Bauermann said.

"We all know an enemy combatant when we see one." Johnson shrugged. "Also, gentlemen, this is our chance to prove the LRTD paradigm in the field. That means more respect for our arm and the formation of more battalions." New battalions would need new commanders and where better to find them than from experienced LRTD officers? Roger briefly imagined himself two ranks up the pay scale with a command entrusted to him.

Mueller looked over the company commanders. He knew them far better than the two-star general did. Mueller had lobbied his superiors to establish a light robotics unit in the Reynolds years and had commanded 1 LRTD since its formation. He had recruited his captains personally, and though he was knowledgeable about the machines they guided he was a shrewder judge of people. "Some of you are uneasy about the invocation of the Insurrection Act. I understand. This is a new step for the country and for our unit, but when people can build this—" he pointed with his thumb at the washed out display of the robotic mortar behind him "—with the example of 6:19 in their minds, it's necessary. There are enemy combatants in our country only we can fight." Mueller's gaze landed on Roger and the latter straightened his back. He had been given delicate and dangerous orders because only he could carry them out. He and his first sergeant; he and his brother officers. The mood in the room lifted.

Johnson spoke. "While we have you together I want to address another matter. I know rumors are floating around about loyalty engineering. R-mail has, as usual, turned a molehill into a mountain. I'm here to set the record straight."

Across the room, Olafson folded his arms. Roger returned his attention to Johnson.

"The Army is dedicated to maximizing its personnel's combat performance and minimizing their susceptibility to psychiatric casualties. You're familiar with both semipermanent and acute combat supplementation for those ends, and the defects in both are obvious: customizing dosages for the soldier, delivering tablets to the soldier, ensuring the soldier takes each dose as instructed, and for acute comsup, educating the soldier as to which supplement to take at which time. Those defects are solvable when we're wargaming on the back forty, but we're finding from Uighurstan they're a severe problem. Soldiers are suppressing their fear too far or not far enough. Soldiers are suffering from insomnia or narcolepsy. And worse." Johnson grimaced. *How much worse?*

"We can implant devices to reduce those problems. They'll produce small doses of supplements in precise locations in the brain at the proper time. No need for a quartermaster to deliver pills, no risk of sending Peter's genome-tailored pills to Paul, no temptation to increase or decrease the dose. You may have heard rumors to that effect and they're true. It's a much better solution.

"Now there's another set of rumors out there. That the Army or the civilian leadership wants to turn you into Pavlov dogs who'll salivate every time the President rings a bell. I have two words for you. Not true," he enunciated. "If you're worried about it, put it to rest. It won't happen."

Roger wondered what backed up Johnson's words. From the seat to his right Mueller stared ahead and bobbed his head.

Johnson went on. "You and all the men in your units will each be assigned a meeting with medical staff for implanting devices prior to embarking on the Insurrection Act missions Mr. Ramirez indicated. Questions?"

Olafson stirred but kept silent. So did everyone else. *Are you going to be the first to call bullshit on a two-star general?*

Mueller breathed in and sat straighter and the movements brought attention to him. "You won't be the only ones given these implants," and tapped his temple with his finger. "Don't worry, it doesn't hurt at all." After the meaning sank in, a couple of men laughed nervously but quickly stopped when the light colonel fixed them a look. "Where's the humor, gentlemen?"

"No humor, sir," Olafson said. "It's inspiring to see an officer lead by example."

Mueller surveyed the room, and Roger's doubts faded in the imperturbable certainty of the lieutenant colonel's gaze.

4

Monica waited for Clay outside his office. A night's sleep and skill with a makeup brush covered any remaining sign of her emotions from the previous day. After the standard greeting to his secretary, he said to Monica, as casually as he could manage, "What brings you by?"

For a moment her expression showed gladness for his caution but a displeased look soon returned. "We need to discuss some schedule changes on the NuGland upgrade rollout. I suggest your office."

Clay nodded and led her in. The door started swinging shut but she caught it and eyed its thickness before letting it go. "How sound-proof is it?"

"I've played loud music in here without my secretary hearing."

"Unless she heard but didn't ask her boss to keep it down." Monica pressed her fingers against her wearable, a necklace pendant tucked under her blouse. "If our conversation was important enough for me to wait for you first thing in the morning, it will have to last fifteen or twenty minutes."

Clay raised his eyebrow and nodded toward the door. "She's been with me for years."

"Before or after the purchase by Titan?" Monica reached into her jacket and withdrew her portable display. "I have messages to send if you want to get started. Here." She fished the pendant out of her blouse and pointed her chin toward his wearable. He lifted his wrist and heard a chime in his earbud. Data received. "That will get you into the servers at MHP and Titan HQ," she said. "Have a proxy?"

"Zhejiang," he said.

"Trustworthy?"

From Samizdat.zj—she had no need to know. "Trustworthy as any stranger."

Monica nodded and settled into one of the visitor chairs facing his desk. She bowed her head over her display and her stray lock fell down her face. Clay faced his monitor and went to work.

Fifteen minutes later MHP's receiving dock logs hung hazily on the display. The haze stirred and entries assembled themselves into a spreadsheet. Shipments from TS Microcatalytix received, cataloged, QA'd, and warehoused. A gesture revealed logs of disbursements from the warehouse to fabrication. Another gesture—

Fabricator code was only easily readable by minirobots and IIT graduates. Clay plodded through it line-by-line until it made sense. MHP's fab facility soldered the MuSynth to a board, wired it to a battery lead, and connected it to a controller chip; added a microphone and a camera to the board; then housed it in color-programmable chameleonic plastic. The home and car model differed only in size. The product was an air freshener.

An air freshener St. Louis didn't want him to know about? He had a lot of hunt left to run this thing to ground.

Monica rolled up her display and stood. "That's enough time. I'll let you go."

"Don't you want to know what I've found? Maybe your next employer could use it." It briefly surprised him that he talked about such subterfuge. The past days had left their mark.

"It wouldn't do me any good," Monica said. "My noncompetes are tighter than pantyhose." The door opened for her and she strode out.

Clay returned his attention to the display. A graphic of the air freshener hung there, innocuous and cheery, swooping pastel yellow plastic with a stylized flower on the side and a tiny MHP logo along the base. His gaze landed on the inlet and outlet ports to the MuSynth. What was the controller telling the minireactor to make?

After more minutes hunting he found a copy of the source code loaded into each controller's memory. TS minireactor code was only easily readable by MuSynths and original members of the company's R&D department. Various small molecules—he copied the profiles to his wearable and had it run them against a Czech university's small-molecule database to verify, but from the esterification steps he guessed many were fruit flavorants. Common odorants made up most of the rest. Then Clay saw the final class of molecules and he felt no surprise; his subconscious had primed him for the discovery. Neuroactives. Oxytocin derivatives, serotonin analogs, and others. He could ask Nil the precise pharmacology but he knew it in broad outline: the drugs would act on the brain to promote trust, comfort, and happiness.

Although the air freshener continually produced both the odorants and the neuroactives, it channeled them in two different pathways. It continuously released the odorants in pulses about five seconds apart, but the neuroactives were normally stockpiled and only sent to the release port on receipt of a command from the controller.

The trail faded. MHP's fab facility downloaded the command code for each unit directly from a server in St. Louis. The inefficiency of having the fab facility call St. Louis for every unit would have been slight, but Titan hadn't reached its market share by tolerating inefficiencies. What secret did Titan HQ not want MHP to have even a slim chance of knowing?

The only other thing he found on MHP's server was shipment data, tens of thousands of names scattered across the country. ...Sa, Salazar, Sampson, Saint-Denis.... All the shipments had been labeled "Free Sample." He copied over the list and browsed to a remote program to check it for statistical anomalies. While it did, he dove into the St. Louis server farm.

No password prompt or other authorization challenge; it was like walking into the house of the old woman who lived across the farm road when he was growing up, the screen door wide open and the inner door unlocked. How much had St. Louis done to Monica, if she had such high clearance but had decided to bolt? Or was the private key in his possession even Monica's?

His wearable chimed in his earbud and he looked at the display of statistical anomalies. Red and blue dots lit up a map. The red dots, shipments in winter '19-'20, clustered around Iowa, New Hampshire, and a few other states. The shipments later in '20 formed blue archipelagos in populated states along the east coast, the Great Lakes, Texas, Colorado, Arizona, Nevada, and the west coast; Missouri was mostly clear of both colors.

He turned to his office computer and dove deeper into the St. Louis server.

The search engine and document compiler found reams of code he couldn't parse, but the comment lines stood in plain English. His thimbled hand hung in midair while he read the words. *This block finds word 'Everton' in voice or audio. This sub-block limits to utterances of 'Everton' when speaker's tone is respectful. This block detects Everton's voice. This block detects lead-in music for campaign commercials V1-4, A1-8. Rev. 12-4-19: commercials V5-6, A-9-11. Rev. 2-17-19: commercials V7+, A12+. Rev. 7-29-20: bugfix commercial V34. This block scans the subject's field of vision for text 'Everton' and checks context. 5-11-20: this block compiles target address information to add parallel signaling for AU-backed House/Senate candidates.*

Pump trust molecules into the air whenever Everton spoke on streaming video or audio. Whenever someone said his name pleasantly. Whenever his campaign commercials aired. Whenever his name was written on screen or on smartpaper. A 'pedia search confirmed the red dot states were all sites of early primaries and caucuses to get Everton his party nomination. The blue dots gave him pluralities in the states with the most electoral votes.

No, it couldn't have made a difference. Only a hundred thousand people out of a hundred million voters had received free samples of the air freshener. A random sample—

Clay's face grew clammy. No, not a random sample. Those names had been picked for a reason. He wracked his memory for marketing buzzwords tossed around by Nil and feed them into the search engine working on the data on the St. Louis servers. After several false starts he found the right buzzword: "NQ." Influence quotient.

His computer assembled a workbook of spreadsheets, each for a state, and sorted each sheet by an NQ column. He'd once heard from Nil how NQ scores were calculated. The process couldn't be called data mining unless the mining engineer were Rube Goldberg: Complex sifting, sorting, fuzzy logic, Bayesian filtering. Clay searched for particular names. Sa ranked highly in Nevada; Salazar, in North Carolina.

It still couldn't have made a difference. One person in a thousand, no matter his influence, couldn't have tipped the election to Everton. Impossible.

Except for the summary documents, signed by America United and Titan personnel, which turned up in his search. *Memetic epidemiology simulations indicate persons with NQs in the 98th* percentile or higher should swing the votes of 200-250 individuals directly or at one remove.**

Inflection-point analysis indicates 400-600 high NQs in Arizona could boost Everton's polling 6-7 percentage points.

Follow up interviews about the "Free Samples" indicated high customer satisfaction with the air freshener among the targets. After the formal interview, "unscripted" discussions between the interviewer and the target to gauge the target's political views elicited vigorous pro-Everton comments and essentially no anti-Everton comments (see full and raw data sets, attached).

Analysis of polling results and vote tallies in Iowa and New Hampshire indicate our intervention made Everton the early frontrunner for party nomination.

Given the four major candidates resulting from the fractured political arena after June 19, it is clear our actions before the general election prevented throwing the election to the House of Representatives.

He'd been a damn fool during the negotiations in '19. No wonder those bastards had offered such a good deal for the company. They'd wanted to monopolize the political uses of the MuSynth. Titan had made Everton the president, thanks to Clay and Nil. If Titan and America United could do that, how much more potent would their plots be with the NuGland plugged into millions of people's brains?

Clay copied everything he could find to his wearable and then readied another copy to send to an anonymous private account. Where to open one? Zhejiang? *Eggs and baskets*. He opened one from a Cuban ISP and sent it and then realized how tight he felt in his gut. Deep breaths to think.

He had to expose America United's plot. How, though? He could rant in the blogosphere, only to be dismissed as a loon until NCS agents rammed down his door. He shook his head. He needed advice from someone he could trust.

He backed out of the servers and went across the second floor to Nil's office. Nil knew marketing and public communications, he'd know how to get this information public.

Halfway down the hall Clay hesitated, picturing the gaudy platinum eagle dangling at Nil's neck. Where did his friend's loyalties lie? Nil didn't believe in AU's ideology, he'd made that clear the other night. He belonged to America United out of convenience, not belief. His commitment to the organization couldn't survive this news, certainly not from his business partner. His confidence renewed, Clay strode on.

In his office, Nil sat, his gaze on a rubber-footed display standing on the glass-topped desk, his expression showing he was in conversation with someone. He waved Clay into the office. The door swung shut and Clay pulsed his fists while Nil nodded at the camera mounted on the display. "Follow up and get back to me. Later." He turned his attention to Clay, freeway traffic visible outside the window behind him. "What's new?"

"Do you know what they used us for?"

Nil frowned. "Who? What? Start at the beginning."

Clay inhaled and hoped his voice would sound more calm. "Titan and America United. The election campaign in '20. They bought MuSynths and wired them to other devices to instill trust in socially influential people whenever Everton came on television or radio. It gave Everton the presidency."

Nil looked stunned. When had he ever been at a loss for words? The silence daunted Clay and he filled it with details of the database discrepancy and the Titan internal documents, and Nil's face showed recovery from his initial surprise.

"How did you find all this?"

"Servers in St. Louis. I can't say more." Clay added, "I'm not making this up—"

"I'm sure you aren't." Nil looked into the distance, out the window to the north where the industrial park gave way to horse farms. "I'd suspected something like that had happened."

The words took a moment to sink in. "You did?"

"Why was Titan so interested in buying us? Yes, we've been a profitable acquisition, but I wondered if there was more. Buying us let them decide what customers could buy MuSynths. It makes sense."

"You suspected? For years? Why didn't you tell me?"

Nil's eyes widened briefly. Slowly, he said, "I had no proof."

"We have proof now. We have to do something."

"Do something?" Nil's face grew haggard. "Do you know what Everton can do? If we say something like that about the President we'd be locked up as enemy combatants faster than you can say six-nineteen."

"If he can do it it's because we gave him the authority. All the more reason we have to do something." Nil's haggard expression deepened and Clay raised a hand to placate him. "We can spread the news anonymously."

"Who would believe it? It would sound like the 6:19 conspiracy theories you hear from the Christian socialists and the green libertarians."

"No, it...." Clay remembered another voice. *You wouldn't believe me if I told you. You need to find out for yourself.* "Even if we don't publicize it we have to do something. Our dog went mad, it's up to us to shoot it."

Nil's slowly shook his head. "Why rock the boat? Someone had to be President. Why is it bad we made a tidy profit off the person who did?"

Clay blinked and his mouth hung open before he spoke. "They treated people like puppets."

"That's how the world works. Brain activity scanners and surreptitious drugs are how men land one-night stands and women land husbands. It drives sales and marketing of every product you can buy. A politician is just the star of another content stream."

"Goddamn, that's cynical."

Nil laughed, a high pinched mirthless thing. "You want cynical?

A lot of people are better off by what Everton did. They can believe the country has a common purpose. They can sleep at night without worrying about another 6:19 because they trust him to stop it before it happens. That's why no one would believe us if we went public about Everton stealing the election with MuSynths; no one would want to hear it."

Clay shook his head. "There's want to hear and need to hear."

Nil's eyes showed world-weariness. "I've seen a lot of people, men and women, in all sorts of situations. Almost everyone would rather hear a lie that meshes with their beliefs than a truth that makes them question them."

Like Jenny pretending their retarded son would somehow become normal. "You think we should let this go."

"Our lives are too good to throw away in a foolish gesture."

Clay thought of mornings in the lap pool and Nil's world-weary look. "Are they?"

Nil blinked in surprise. "They're better than a detention camp. Haven't you heard what I've said?" He peered across the desk. "I really think we need that weekend in Havana."

Sure, clinking $10,000 chips and visiting the finest bordello on the Malecón would somehow imbue their lives with meaning. Maybe osteoporosis of the soul was contagious. Clay wanted to round the desk and shake Nil by the shoulders to jar him from his passivity, but he squeezed his fist behind his back till the urge faded. His friend would not be able to help him. Disappointment flooded him but he tried to cover it. "Let me check my schedule and get back to you about it. Maybe next month?"

He trudged back to his office. Nil would not help him, but surely the stranger would. One million one thousand one. Had he known what Clay would find or merely guessed? Either way, if he wanted Clay to find the secret of Everton's election he must have a plan of what to do with that secret. Unless the stranger worked for the government, AU, or Titan and intended to entrap Clay. The thought made him sweat; dots swam in his vision. He slunked into the men's room and leaned his forearms on the marble vanity, then splashed water on his face until his thoughts calmed.

No one had a reason to entrap an apolitical entrepreneur with no enemies. Even if he'd ended up on a blacklist through some misfortune, the victim of a database error or the target of a grudge grounded in an event he'd long forgotten, why would the stranger use such dangerous bait? They couldn't be certain he'd keep knowledge about the Free Samples Project and its role in electing Everton to himself before they could arrest him. He held his face in front of the dryer and nodded to himself. The stranger was no enemy. Time to find if he was a friend.

Nil stared out the window at the parking lots of other buildings in the industrial park. *Clay, who were you trying to fool?* Nil could read his business partner well enough to know he hadn't been convinced to bury his discovery; his acceptance of the Havana trip had embodied one of Clay's standard tactics, feigned agreement to get another person off his back long enough for him to do what he intended to do in the first place. He would spread the secret of Everton's election campaign; worse, he would do it cackhandedly and NCS would track him down. Clay was a dead man walking. Nil imagined a cordon of armored vehicles surrounding the building and an interrogation under an fMRI brain scanner. Even if they released him, AU would marginalize him and Fisher would force him out of Titan Industries. Better not to come to that—

Sweat soaked the back and armpits of his broadcloth shirt. Clay was his closest friend. Betray him, even to save himself? Perhaps he'd misread him. No, that was wishful thinking and only a fool would cling to it. Clay had walked out of his office ready to reveal Everton's secret to the world. He could hope Clay would realize the danger before he acted. Was that unreasonable? If anyone would think twice before doing something rash, it would be Clay. He would heed the threat of arrest and prison. Yielding to it would carry no shame.

Even if he didn't heed the threat.... Nil swallowed thickly. He couldn't betray his friend. He had enough money to last a lifetime, even an antiagathic-extended lifetime. He knew his power much better now than he had fresh out of college; he could easily rebuild his fiefdom. With enough preparation time, even brain scanners could be fooled. With hypnosis, biofeedback, and the right cocktail of neuroactives he could practice a lie until habit left its tracks in his brain like truth. *Sales in 2020? What about them?* Clay's fall might be inevitable but who wanted to carry on his conscience the knowledge he'd pushed him?

Clay's fall was inevitable. In the distant parking lot a woman waited for her car. The sun glossed her black hair and a breeze rippled the hem of her minidress.* *The car rolled to a stop in front of her and she climbed in, supple motions and pale slender legs. Clay believed he could think his way out of any jam but didn't realize people were more complicated than microscale chemical engineering. He would cackhandedly reveal Everton's secret. The raid would come soon after. Agents hopped up on testosterone supplements wielding brain scanners.* Cut the ignorance act, Mr. Thomas.* Building a fiefdom in a detention camp? Enemy combatants were denied antiagathic treatments. Clay's stubborn selfishness would drag others down with him and he would not care; worse, he would think it his due and wonder why anyone around him would complain.

"Call Bill Haycock, NCS."

The display refreshed. Haycock looked better than he had a few nights previously. His grooming hadn't changed: same ill-fitting suit, sagging jowls, bags under his eyes. Bright, diffuse light illuminated him as if he stood outdoors. But on a wall behind him a screensaver chased its tail across a smartpaper whiteboard and small frames showed live video feeds, golf holes on a rainy hillside and an irrigated patch of desert. His office, Nil realized; though maps and floor plans of New Washington were classified, rumor had it government offices hunkered windowless behind blast walls and under masses of soil. Haycock frowned. "Mr. Thomas."

"Assistant Director Haycock, thank you for taking my call. I wasn't sure whom to talk to."

"What about?"

Nil felt light-headed and forced himself to breathe deeply. "I know how concerned President Everton is with the potential for misuse of molecular fabrication. And mental illness, the six—the June 19 perps were crazy to plan it and crazy to stay in Washington when they knew it was going to happen. My business partner, Clay Schieffer: he's mentally ill."

Haycock squinted. "Not my department. I'll forward you to technology permitting before they review his license."

"There's no time for that. He's a threat to himself and others. He's lost touch with reality. He said the most unbelievable nonsense about Everton's campaign in 2020."

Haycock's eyes widened. He took control and reverted to his bland expression, but Nil had seen enough. He looked away from the bureaucrat and shook his head as if sad about Clay.

"What sort of nonsense?"

"That Everton's campaign used our products to trick people to vote for him. Completely unbelievable. I've met the President and he would never dream of it. He's a strong leader and everyone can see it. Everyone except Clay. I don't know what's wrong with him but he needs help. Someone with his skills and his degree of insanity is a threat to society."

"Where did he get this idea?" A frantic edge tinted Haycock's tone.

Nil pretended to ignore it. Clay had struck something deep and hidden. "No clue. Have enemy combatants gotten to him with propaganda? My God, is that possible? Right under my nose?"

"Our enemies are capable of a lot. Thank you for bringing this to our attention."

"I'm glad I can help keep America safe. I'm glad we have men like you to do that job." Nil smiled weakly. Too much butter? No, Haycock was the type who craved even brazen flattery.

Haycock stared into the space behind his camera; the sound muted and his hand covered his mouth. Abruptly the audio feed returned and Haycock met Nil's gaze. "It helps we have loyal citizens like you. Don't worry, he won't hurt anyone."

"He'll get psychological help?"

Haycock squinted, a gaze honed over years to make anyone, friend or foe, uneasy. "Like I said, Mr. Thomas, he won't hurt anyone."

* * *

Night had stolen over Houston, driving the last tint of blue low to the western horizon. The headlights of Clay's suv swept over the empty parking lots and boarded windows of old lowrise office buildings, vacated by telecommuters and virtual companies. Green-eyed possums stared back and then darted away.

The stranger had given him an address between the TS Microcatalytix building and his house. A half mile away on the other side of the freeway, Learning Machines Stadium glowed in spotlights like a beached white tanker. The navigation display showed a few more twists and turns through the office park to get to his destination and Clay fidgeted in his seat.

The trip had been uneventful. Sending the copied data to the stranger's email address took only seconds; stopping at a U-Ship-It to send a flash drive with the copied data overnight to a mail drop in Chile took longer. His arms had shaken when he handed the package to the robot at the counter, but the robot was too simple to notice and whoever might have observed him via the security cameras sounded no alarm. Probably thought he was a solo practitioner sweating to meet a deadline. He told the suv to make it colder, then shivered in the blast from the vents.

The suv slowed for a stop sign. The navigation display showed a right turn coming up. Clay shut his eyes and let his head loll to the headrest.

The suv stopped for a long moment. It started forward and Clay leaned to the right, into the expected turn, and lurched and opened his eyes. Had he misread the nav display? No, the green pathline ran to the right and the red travel line overwrote it.

"Shouldn't you have turned right?" he asked the suv.

"I'm following the path you indicated," it replied.

Clay frowned, unused to such an error and lacking a ready reply. "Run a diagnostic on yourself."

"As you request." The suv had passed through the intersection but now slowed. A parking lot entrance lay to the left, small puddles dropped by an afternoon thunderstorm lay along the curb. The suv turned into the lot and three cars and a van, all painted shades of blue or silver with metallic sheens in the illumination from the streetlights, waited in a concave semicircle around it. Jackers who could hack an autocar?

Men in bulky black windbreakers and mid-forearm gauntlets lurked around the cars and whipped their heads up to watch him. Not robbers. Yellow block letters emerged on their chests: NCS.

Adrenaline flooded Clay. "Abort destination. Wipe it."

The nav display blinked out.

"Reverse!"

The suv rolled to a stop in the center of the semicircle. NCS agents duckwalked toward him.

"Reverse, dammit!"

The suv cut its engine.

The NCS agents peered in the windows. "Open the door, Mr. Schiffer," said one in a gruff baritone voice.

He seized on the mispronunciation. "Shiffer? That's not me."

"Looks like you on the warrant," said another male voice, higher-pitched but more resonant. The second agent shoved a smartpaper against the window, text facing Clay: his picture, his name spelled correctly.

"I've never seen a warrant before. How do I know that's real?"

The first agent's arm jerked forward and the suv window's safety glass starred around the impact point of a pistol butt. He punched again and the entire window crazed, looking like the surface of a barely frozen pond. The other agent shoved the sheet of broken safety glass into the cabin.

The first agent reached in for the manual door lock and Clay extended his leg and kicked at his arm. The gauntlet stiffened against his sole. He frogkicked again and again and finally aimed at his hand, but too late. The lock clunked open and the agent pulled the door wide, then grabbed Clay's ankle on his next kick and dragged him off the seat and out of the suv.

He writhed, kicking aimlessly with his other foot and reaching for the second agent's legs to pull him off balance. His butt landed hard on the base of the door, then again on the pavement. Grit ground up his leg; pain bloomed in his vision when the back of his head hit the asphalt.

The second agent shoved a plastic cup, mounted on the muzzle of a black plastic object sized and shaped like a pistol, toward Clay's mouth.

He slapped at it but a third agent pulled his arms away. He twisted his neck but the second agent held the cup in place. Though soft plastic, the agent drove it over his mouth and nose and jammed his head against the parking lot. Gas hissed inside the cup. Clay held his breath a few seconds but soon had to gasp for air. He inhaled a mouthful of the gas and felt lightheaded. In the distance, a car hissed down a street.

"Resisting arrest," the first agent said. "That's *prima facie* evidence of enemy combatant status." Clay had trouble hearing over the cottony buzz in his ears.

"You doing law school part time? Speak English," the second agent said.

Clay's eyelids fluttered. "On its face," he said, but the soft plastic muffled his voice and none of the agents heard.

Another inhalation and his pains faded and the agents seemed to be at the lip of a well with him at the bottom. One million one thousand one, you bastard, I'll get you…

The feds lifted him. His world was upside down and grayed out; his vision jumped with each step they took. They laid him on a firm surface in a dark box and a pair of doors shut. The gray he saw went black.

5

Nil's Lorelei pulled up in front of Clay's house. It turned off its engine and headlights and the street's lighting returned to a midnight constellation of streetlamps and biomethane lanterns. He sat for a moment and composed himself. Clay's discovery and willingness to reveal it had posed Jenny a danger but she didn't need to know what had happened. She would not believe the news and would blame the messenger. He climbed out of the car and slipped his eagle pendant into his shirt where it rested coolly on his skin. The twin lanterns on either side of the front doors hissed and the holobutler appeared in its niche. "Good morning, Mr. Thomas. I don't believe you're expected. Mr. Schieffer is not home but I'll inform—"

The front doors swung open and the butler stopped speaking. Jenny stood in the foyer and clutched one of the doors with her left arm. Shadows covered her face but her voice came frantically. "Nil, you've seen him?"

He winced. "I wish, but no. I was in the neighborhood and after your call I wanted to stop by. I'd hoped he'd made it home by now."

Cool air spilled around him into the humid night. Jenny shook her head and the door rocked in her grip. "Oh god, I'm sorry, come in," she said. The wing of the house leading back to the garage was dark, but in the front sitting room, first on the right, a table lamp glowed next to a green cloth-covered couch with a magazine face-down on the wrinkled cushion. The room had a window the shape of a pixelated triangle made of translucent glass blocks that showed their reflections like cubes of distorted memories. "I've been sitting here trying to read and looking up every time a car drives by."

She wore jeans and a baggy Rice sweatshirt that hung on her to mid-thigh and didn't flatter her figure. "I trust I didn't give you false hope when I pulled up," he said.

"No, I'm glad you came by. Have a seat. I'll get the kitchen to fix you a drink?"

"Vodka tonic, thanks." He sat on the edge of a matching green loveseat perpendicular to the couch. He couldn't bring himself to sit back.

After she told the house his request, she said, "This isn't like him. I know things are bad between us—" She fixed her gaze on Nil, then nodded. "I didn't think you'd be surprised."

"I've heard his side of the story." He felt he'd teeter off the loveseat if he said the wrong thing. What put him off his game?

"I'm sure it's all my fault the genes he put into Martin clashed in my uterus." She closed her eyes, took a breath. "Nevermind. He said he'd be home around nine but his concierge would have messaged me if he got delayed. Three hours? Something's wrong."

"I left the office around six-thirty," Nil said, "and his suv was still in its spot." Both statements were true.

"He's not at the office. I never have trouble reaching him there and I called the security desk and they said he wasn't in his office and his suv is gone from the parking lot." She looked into the distance and sniffled. "He's at his mistress' place."

"That's possible."

She looked warily at Nil. "Are you covering for him?"

Nil showed his palms. "We both know he's a bad liar, but even then he's good enough of one to say 'midnight' if he'd be out till midnight."

"Unless he lost track of time," Jenny said. She gazed at the wall and Nil imagined her mind's eye picturing Clay in an adulterous bed.

"I doubt it. If he's not tinkering with his microreactors he's got one eye on the clock."

Jenny slouched on the sofa. A household robot rolled up with Nil's drink. The time had come to lay the groundwork. He took a deep drink.

"I wonder if there's something else entirely."

She wrinkled her brow, though betrayal and jealousy remained in her expression.

"Lately Clay's been distant and secretive," Nil said. "From you, me, and everyone else. Has he talked about politics?"

"He doesn't care about politics."

"I thought that too, but he recently surprised me by asking what I thought of President Everton." Monday night in the billiard room he'd been trying to gauge Nil's involvement in America United, and now it was clear why: to see if he could trust Nil with this dangerous falsehood he'd been searching for.

"I've never heard him talk about Everton. What do you think he's gotten into?"

"There are people out there who could use his skills to do something dangerous...." He let the words hang, then looked at Jenny.

"Enemy combatants? Recruiting him? He wouldn't fall for that."

Nil shrugged. "He's been looking for something we aren't able to provide him. They could promise him a challenge and give him a purpose and he might take them up on it."

Jenny frowned. "I don't know."

"I don't either, but it's crossed my mind."

She pulled her knees to her chest and wrapped her arms across her shins. Nil sipped his drink and let her imagine her husband as an enemy combatant.

Jenny lifted her head and the swift motion caught Nil's attention. She stared at the glass block window without seeing it. "Is that him?"

"Where?" Nil asked, and then a low whine sounded from the back of the house, followed by the higher whisper of suv tires and motor.

Jenny scampered out of the sitting room and toward the garage. Nil took a breath and followed slowly. If Clay hadn't yet been arrested, how would he explain his presence there to him? The truth: Jenny had been worried when he hadn't come home and she deserved better than to sit there alone. He strode down the enfiladed spaces, the dining room in farm-grown hardwood, the kitchen with the SueChef, its arms retracted and its idle light glowing green, in the ceiling.

He reached the doorway from the kitchen to the utility room and looked ahead to the garage. Jenny stood in the doorway, silhouetted by an overhead light, her limbs trembling. She gasped and ran into the garage.

The suv sat immobile, its front and left side gleaming of carnauba wax and glass cleaner. Jenny stood on the far side and was visible as a shadowed figure through the tinted windows. She leaned in the right rear window. "Oh my god oh my god."

Nil joined her. The window had been smashed and a few shards lurked in the frame. "Careful," he said.

She pulled her head back out of the window. "He's not here."

"What? Open, both doors," he told the vehicle. The doors clamshelled open; the cabin was as empty as the day of the car's fabrication. No Clay, no sign of struggle, no disposable i/o devices or hobbyist catalogs in the door-mounted map pockets or strewn on the floor.

"Where did he go?" Jenny asked, and then she clambered onto a front seat and yanked the nav display around on its neck to face her. "Where did he go?"

"Ma'am?" the suv said.

"Last trip. Show me."

Nil climbed in next to her and took the rear seat facing her. Their knees brushed and he leaned closer to see the display. A green line drew a direct path up 288 into the city from the industrial park.

Departed TS Microcatalytix 11.51p.

Arrived Home 12.09a.

Passenger: Clay.

"Eleven-fifty? Clay in the car? That's not right."

"My data indicates it is correct."

Jenny tightened her grip on the display and shook it back and forth. "I said it's not right! It's not—" Her hands fell to her sides and she breathed raggedly, panic showing on her face until she closed her eyes and deepened her breathing. Nil sat impassive, but started when she opened her eyes and dropped her jaw.

"Oh god, Nil, were you right?"

A medium-pitched whine woke Clay. He jerked his head around to check his surroundings. Bad idea. His vision swirled under bright lights and he felt sick to his stomach. He lowered his head to his knees and breathed deeply until the urge to vomit faded. Cautiously he sat up and opened his eyes.

The light was far dimmer than he'd first thought. He sat on a thinly-padded ledge. NCS had dressed him in a short-sleeved powder blue jumpsuit, no belt, no pockets, and a pair of white shoes tied by white hook-and-loop fabric. The inside of his left forearm itched, about a third of the way from his elbow to his wrist. At the site of the itch were bands drawn on his skin with a permanent marker. He wanted to scratch but resisted the urge.

Clay glanced at his wrist to check the time, but his wearable was missing. He touched his ear, searching for his earbud, but then let his hand drop. Of course the feds had taken it, though after taking his wearable they could have left it; without his wearable to send output , the bud was as useless as an earring and less attractive. Speaking of jewelry, an indentation ringed his left fourth finger, but the gold band was gone.

He had more important things to worry about. His missing wearable meant the feds knew what he'd found.... Clay shook his head, disappointed in himself for thinking that. They'd known he'd found out about the Free Samples Project before they picked him up. Nothing they pulled off his wearable would worsen his fate.

He sat near one end of a long, narrow room painted the same shade of pale blue as his jumpsuit. The walls were made of a rigid foam that yielded slightly when he pressed his fingers into it. The walls had no windows. A ledge ran along each of the room's long sides. The room could probably seat thirty people comfortably—forty or fifty if comfort weren't a concern—but only fifteen other men sat here, most of them unconscious, heads leaned back against the wall or lolled on their neighbor's shoulders.

The dim light came from bare bulbs mounted every dozen feet on a power strip running down the center of the ceiling. Between the bulbs hung black shapes like small wasp's nests. Each shape was an array of tiny cylinders fixed to an array of small boxes. Clay's eyes widened and his skin tingled. MuSynths.

The room rocked slightly, shifting Clay in his seat and nodding the heads of the unconscious men around him. The whine hadn't stopped since he'd woken up and he matched it to the shaky feeling. Airplane engines. He glanced around. This was the cabin of a plane?

A bullet camera in the nearest corner aimed itself at him and his chest tightened. He would be under surveillance every second and the monitors would be hidden, like the security guards who may have seen him twitching at the U-Ship-It last night. Last night? They could have knocked him out for days. The thought set him shivering and he plunged his hands under his arms.

He took a deep breath. The lost hours or days would never return. He needed to put them aside and focus on his situation. He was probably on a plane—traveling where? He stared at the camera and then felt pressure in his ears. They were descending. Clay looked around again, some base part of his brain looking for fresh clues that he knew weren't there, when a mist hissed out from the arrays of MuSynths. Spots swam in his vision and he felt light-headed. Let me stay awake and think, damn you....

Clay woke with pain in his ears and the ledge jolting underneath him. The bulbs shone brighter and cast harsh light on the groggy, unshaven faces around him. He worked his jaw to help his ears pop and rubbed his chin. Morning stubble chafed his fingers; NCS had nabbed him only the night before. The whining airplane engines had been replaced with a deeper, softer rumble from the far end of the room, to Clay's left, and the rumble tone rose and fell and Clay realized he and the other prisoners were inside a shipping container on a tractor-trailer's flatbed. They could be riding down a freeway in the middle of a big city's rush hour and no one would give them a second glance.

He shook his head. No one would put a detention camp near a big city, where average citizens could inadvertently ride by and see something that would start them wondering. Clay pictured a compound ringed with coiled razor wire and armed guards, miles from a US highway in some sparsely populated place where the big-shot locals wore bronze AU pins—a dying farm county or a tribal reservation. Nil would have a guess. Clay shook his head again. Clever Nil would never end up in this place.

As the truck drove on, the other prisoners woke. With sidelong glances Clay watched them go through the same steps he'd already taken: looking around, looking at themselves, looking at each other like new boys in school searching for a clique to join. Clay felt glad he didn't have the compulsion to find a slot in a hierarchy. Halting conversations sprung up, men in low voices asking *Why am I here?* Not all of them said that, though, and Clay guessed the ones who did not voice that question, like him, knew why.

"Where are we?" whispered the man to Clay's left. He reminded Clay of rice-rocket racers he'd seen on Chinatown streets: pudgy, spiky black hair, acne scars on his cheeks and neck. He didn't look like a 6:19 perp, assuming anyone knew what a 6:19 perp looked like.

"In a shipping container being towed to a detention camp."

"Detention camp? I didn't do anything!"

Clay shrugged. "I'll take your word for it, but it won't help you much."

The other looked around more and Clay expected to be left alone for a while, but no such luck. "I did some genomics work in my basement, but a lot of people do, that can't be why."

"You should assume they can hear every word."

"But I didn't do anything wrong. Okay, I didn't have a license, but the only coat proteins I fabbed came from viruses that don't infect people." He stopped, scratched his arm. "What did you do?"

Clay's first thought was to not answer, but then he realized he had a chance to spread the truth. "I found out that Everton stole the election, and how."

The other looked perplexed. "You mean the Indian AI."

Clay's eyebrows rose.

"Don't you know the story? The Indians secretly programmed an AI. It hacked all the voting machines. It gives Everton instructions through an implant."

A Paki crater sat in the middle of Bangalore and the Hindu

national-socialist government had gutted the computer science department at IIT. Even in the U.S. full AI was a decade away. Clay laughed. "No."

"Uh huh, then what was it really?"

"America United used neuroactive drugs to make people support Everton."

The other peered at him, then shook his head. "They didn't line up fifty million people and give them drugs."

"No, they—"

"Got any proof?"

"I had it. They didn't let me keep it."

"Convenient for you," the other said, and turned away.

Clay remembered his final conversation with Nil and his cheeks warmed. No one would believe the truth, especially not with an absurd red herring floating around. He'd thrown away his freedom for nothing.

The engine's rumble lowered in pitch and the truck slowed. The other prisoners looked around the vessel and the bullet camera pivoted its aim from face to face. Clay held his breath and stiffened his back against the foam wall, but the MuSynths in the ceiling remained silent. The truck downshifted through more gears, then stopped. Men looked around in alarm in the second before the truck made a wide right turn.

A time later—ten minutes, maybe fifteen—the truck stopped again for about a minute, and then trudged along in low gear for a while. After the next stop the truck reversed, its warning chime beeping, until it tapped into some thick, yielding surface and jolted the men in the shipping container. Their voices became a chorus of fear and confusion. Over the din Clay heard bolts snap back and hinges squeak on the far side of the foam end wall, and then drills unset screws and the end wall gapped away from the vessel's sides and let in slivers of light and cold air. The end wall rose up and revealed a loading dock.

Clay remembered tedious days handling cattle on his father's ranch. A concrete floor lay twenty feet below a sheet-metal awning. Two sheet-metal walls defined a space further divided by tubular-steel fence panels, which narrowed from the open end of the shipping container to form a chute about three feet wide. The chute went straight until it reached the back wall of the dock and then turned right, where it led to a doorway in the wall barred by a six-foot turnstile. Outside the chute, guards in dark blue uniforms rested their forearms on the panel bars and peered at the prisoners. Overcast daylight and bare bulbs lit the dock.

"Get out of there," boomed a voice over hidden speakers. "Single file down the chute."

The men around Clay nervously made eye contact with one another. Sitting here wasn't going to spare anyone; if the feds wanted them dead they could have gassed the inside of the shipping container. Clay stood and jumped down to the concrete floor, bending his knees before he landed. He strode, head down, toward the chute and rubbed his forearms against the cold. Behind came the shuffles and thuds of others following him and then a wave of coughing. A sulfurous smell wafted from inside the shipping container.

Clay strode down the chute. The guards stepped back from the fence panels, but watched him with hooded eyes while muttering to each other. Someone burst out in cruel laughter. Clay shivered— colder than he'd thought—and turned toward the turnstile. Maybe he was doing what they wanted, but he did it on his terms. He still had choices, even here and now. The turnstile buzzed and he pushed it forward.

More sheet-metal walls loomed in front and to his right. The path turned to his left, where a second turnstile showed the path doubled back the way it had come, but with the back wall of the loading dock between the two portions of the path. The second turnstile buzzed and he went forward.

Clay walked into a small room with metal-clad walls and a door, not a turnstile, in the far wall. Behind him another prisoner scraped his shoes in the vestibule between the turnstiles and rattled the second turnstile against its lock.

Four men—three uniformed guards and a brown-haired civilian wearing a four-inch-long gray plastic strip across his knuckles— watched Clay. Filters clipped across their septums lodged in each of their nostrils. One of the guards glowered. "Your barcode," he said nasally.

"My what?"

The guard jabbed at Clay's chest and an electric shock made him fling wide his arms. The civilian waved the plastic strip at the itchy markings on his forearm. The plastic strip beeped in satisfaction and the door swung open. Two more guards walked in. "Start moving."

Clay blinked and shook his head after the shock, but didn't move. One of the guards grabbed his upper arm and pushed him out the door. He stumbled but kept his balance.

The space outside the processing room looked like a warehouse stacked high with crates and catwalks. The guards grunted, ordering him to a steel-mesh stairwell in a corner of the warehouse. Clay climbed and glanced through the meshwork at each landing. The stacked crates were cells laid four levels high, and most held men in powder-blue jumpsuits. Clusters of spotlights and cameras, microphones and MuSynths, hung from the ceiling on long poles. A faint sweet aroma hung in the air and Clay felt suddenly tired.

"Third level," one guard said, and Clay trudged out of the stairwell and along a catwalk. "Turn."

The catwalk was six feet wide and Clay forced himself to walk down the middle of it, refusing to be cowed by either the height to his right or the inmates to his left. On the edge of his vision he glimpsed the cell interiors, pale blue concrete walls behind a front gridiron of bars. A few prisoners spoke as he passed—

"Mm, mm, what a white boy doing here?"

"Fear not, brother, there is nothing finer than to be persecuted for His name's sake."

—but most looked lethargic or asleep.

The guards stopped him about two-thirds of the way down the catwalk. The cell was six feet wide by eight deep, with a cot in the back left, a hole in the floor in the back right, and a sink in the middle of the rear wall. A display panel had been painted on the right hand wall in thick uneven strokes. Fluorescent lights shone overhead, embedded in a glass block that jolted him with a reminder of the front sitting room of his house. He hesitated at the entrance and the guards shoved him in. He caught the edge of the sink and stood up. The cell door slammed shut before he turned around.

Clay crossed and gripped the bars. Across the gap rose the next block of cells and he studied them. Most men slept or slumped across their cots gazing at video displays. Despite the comment he'd heard, most of the prisoners were white, but not all; welcome to Everton's color-blind America. Distant noises echoed. The air still smelled faintly sweet. Everything felt unreal and he remembered confused, freshly-steered male calves scampering away from the corral, their scrotums bleeding and their testicles thrown into the dust.

For Roger, the time after his meeting with Johnson, Mueller, and Ramirez passed quickly. On the back forty at Fort Riley, under the first spring rains, the companies rotated through training with Ramirez and detachments of NCS agents. Roger left the command humvee to join his soldiers in the operations trailer, where they watched camera feeds from their machines and shouted to them instructions punctuated by pointed thimbled fingers. Roger looked at the bird's-eye from the company's drone aircraft. Crawlers lurched from cover to cover, their treads flinging mud, and interdicted the supply base of and surrounded the NCS agents playing red team. These games were not new, but imminent deployment gave them a purpose. Riding back in the command humvee to company headquarters, jawing about the training with 1Sgt. Hardin, Roger realized he and his men were ready to perform.

His confidence faded one night, after tucking in his son and daughter and sitting down for a movie with Emma in the media room. The neighbors behind the wall were either quiet or away from home, probably the latter. Before he told the display to play, she wanted to talk. She was glad his deployment wasn't going to Ooo-stan, but instead involved month-long shifts in the U.S. With two weeks' relief, but her tone of voice, ignoring anything outside their family, made him uneasy at her pettiness. Yes, he loved her and the kids, but he loved his country, too, and he knew it was more important than his family's convenience.

The day before Tango Company's first mission, Lt. Col. Mueller ordered him to the base hospital. Roger sweated as Dr. Iammarelli poked and prodded him. He sat on the exam table, the paper crinkling underneath him and fears of the implant filling him, and told himself to relax. His brother-in-law had invented this; the light colonel had done this; it was safe. A nurse came in and gave him an injection while the doctor chatted, and after she left Roger asked when the drug fabricator would be implanted.

"When?" Iammarelli grinned. "It just was."

That afternoon it became clear there was no loyalty drug in the implant. Roger, along with the other company commanders, met with Ramirez. The NCS agent pushed thick folders titled *Rules of Engagement* across the table, and then began talking. Roger scanned through his folder while Ramirez discussed the use of civilian attire in certain circumstances.

Uniforms are to be worn at all times when offbase on mission, he read, and glanced up. Ramirez stared at someone else and didn't notice. Roger kept scanning, his gaze searching for more discrepancies.

Use of man-lethal munitions is expressly forbidden, he found several pages later. Roger marked the page with his finger and his expression grew cold. He listened until Ramirez repeated his comments from the first meeting, that they could switch from non-lethals to bullets if fired upon.

"That disagrees with p. 82," Roger said.

"What's that?"

Roger opened and read, then stared at the NCS agent.

In response, Ramirez covered his mouth and yawned. "What I say takes precedence."

"It should be written down," Roger said. Down the table, Olafson cleared his throat and shifted in his seat.

"Lt. Col. Mueller approved my verbal amendments. Take it up with him."

After the meeting, the other company commanders walked away, careful to ignore Roger. He went to Mueller's office and knocked. The lieutenant colonel was in and listened to Roger's description of the meeting with a growing frown. "Mr. Ramirez is an honorable man with our nation's security at heart. Capt. Sung, I approved his verbal amendments."

Roger blinked. "Permission to speak?"

"Go ahead."

"With all respect to Mr. Ramirez' honor, if we were caught off the reservation we could end up twisting in the wind."

Mueller shook his head. "Don't worry about that. If anyone in the battalion is off the reservation they're going to come for the Indian chief. I wouldn't put any of us on the line if I didn't trust Ramirez and this whole operation. Anything more, captain?"

"No, sir." Go upstairs to Johnson? The two-star general would tell him the same thing and word would get back to Mueller. Roger saluted and walked out.

Otherwise, the last few days before their first mission left Roger the warm tired glow of useful effort. The enlisteds soaped clean their crawlers' carapaces and swept dirt out of the treads with small brushes. The platoon sergeants hounded their men through PT. Tango Company was ready.

Their families gathered to see them off. Roger swept his daughter up in his arms and gave Emma a companionable kiss. His son sniffled but acted strong when Roger climbed into the humvee. He did this for them; Emma knew that and would tell the children. Roger swallowed around a lump in his throat and gave them a final wave as the humvee drove away.

Their first mission came the next day, off a winding state road in the Missouri Ozarks. Roger split his platoons to barricade the road six hundred yards on either side of the target's house. Crawlers slipped under barbed wire fences, zipped across the weedy fields and, acting on simple programming, helped each other over fallen, rotting trees in the woods behind the house. The crawlers crashed the doors and raced in. One man was at home, unarmed and easily paralyzed by the non-lethals. Within minutes the agents bundled the unconscious enemy combatant into a windowless van and drove him away.

He hadn't looked like an enemy combatant, but while the NCS agents sifted for clues through the full ashtrays and the empty tequila bottles in the house, the crawlers in the backyard pried up a weedgrown convex shell, an overturned C-band satellite dish, big as a child's wading pool. Underneath lay a plastic-lined pit racked with bullpup assault rifles and ammunition magazines. Roger's eyes bugged. He'd sworn an oath to defend the Constitution from all enemies, both foreign and domestic; and he had to thank Ramirez for alerting him to the domestic ones.

6

Clay woke groggily. A single light glared on the catwalk. He shut his eyes and pulled the thin cotton blanket closer to his neck. The light grew brighter and a harsh voice whispered, "Shay-fur."

Couldn't any of these people pronounce his name correctly? Or did they mangle it on purpose to drive home his inferiority? A flashlight shone in his eyes. Spillover illuminated the flabby white guard holding it. Another guard, white, with a moustache and sharper cheeks stood there and three men—in civilian suits? Clay squinted against the glare—were behind them. "What do you want?"

"Get dressed," said the sharp-faced guard.

Clay had been sleeping in his jumpsuit for warmth. He put his feet in his shoes and remembered to close the hook-and-loop fasteners manually. No chips and sensors to do it for him. He sat and blinked and wondered why they'd woken him.

"Don't give me that shit. Get up." The cell door rattled open.

"Where are you taking me?"

"You insubordinating?" the guard asked. He thumped his right fist against his left palm.

"No, boss." Clay stood and the guards and the other three men stepped back. Yes, civilian suits. The catwalk was mostly dark, the spotlights on the poles dimmed for nighttime. The flashlight beam bobbed up and down the catwalk. The other prisoners either kept their distance or were deep in drugged sleep. A few times a day advertising appeared on the in-cell displays for genome-optimized formulations of tranquilix, free to any prisoner who asked. Whenever the advertising appeared Clay turned his back and did hindu pushups or jump squats till sweat dewed on his skin and the advertising went away.

Interrogation? No one had interrogated him yet, but when he'd seen other prisoners get pulled from their cells it always happened during daytime, and no one in a civilian suit was anywhere nearby. But then, he wouldn't be interrogated in the usual fashion, Clay guessed; he knew something the prison guards wouldn't be cleared to know. But perhaps the three suits were cleared. Perhaps they would steal him away to someplace more secret—

Perhaps they would kill him. He hesitated and one of the guards pushed him in his back. "Keep moving."

His knowledge was dangerous to Everton, even if very few people would believe it. They could have tracked his email and sent agents to strongarm his Cuban ISP; if they moved quickly, they could have intercepted his overnight shipment of the flashdrive to 1001001's South American maildrop. The only fugitive data on the Free Samples Project he knew they had not yet mopped up lay between his ears. Rather than kill him in the prison, where inmates and guards could chance to hear or see, he could die on some lonely stretch of road. He grew anxious at the thought. *No, they weren't going to kill him*, but he realized he had no evidence to support the thought.

In the processing room, the lights flickered on. Clay hadn't noticed the desk and the locked cabinets before or the path worn between the door and the turnstile to the dock. Clay headed toward the turnstile and the flashlight guard said "Stop."

He stopped, turned. The three suits formed an arc around the two guards. The suit in the middle looked to be in charge. "We'll take him from here."

"We have to outscan him," the sharp-faced guard said, but didn't move.

"I'm not stopping you."

"I can't. Union rules."

The suit on the left laughed until his boss glanced in his direction, then grew silent. "Then get your scanner operator here."

"I'm not authorized to call him in after hours."

Boss suit shook his head. "We're taking him. You solve your own problem."

"We have to outscan him. Standard procedures."

"Listen," the boss suit said as he raised a finger.

"There's no need for that," the sharp-faced guard said.

Boss suit pointed at the guard's chest. "We're NMHA. We're under the authority of Health Secretary McLaren on a mission of importance to the President."

"I don't care who you are, we have procedures we have to follow."

Boss suit turned to his subordinates. "Take down their names, badge numbers—"

"Both of us?" flashlight guard asked. "You want to take him, go right ahead, I'm not stopping you."

The sharp-faced guard glared at the other.

"We don't have to scan him! The operator can enter the data manually! It's in the handbook."

The sharp-faced guard nodded at the boss suit. "I'd forgotten, we can do it that way. It'll take me a minute to find the form."

Boss suit checked his watch and minimally nodded.

Clay counted his breaths while the guard rummaged through the cabinets. His breathing slowed as he studied the suits from the edges of his vision. NMHA? The mental health agency didn't need a hit squad. Maybe they had a new interrogation technique, advanced brain imaging or the like. Inhale, deep. He'd find out soon enough. If he stayed on his toes he could figure out how to handle it.

The form was easy, but it took closer to three minutes for the guard to find a pen with enough ink left to write on the dumbpaper. He cleared his throat and put on a gruff face for Clay. "Barcode."

Clay exposed his forearm. The guard squinted and wrote numbers, at one point overwriting a four with a nine. "I need a receipt," he said and handed the form to the boss suit. Boss suit scrawled his signature and handed the form back and the guard ripped out a canary-yellow copy and rattled it until the suit who'd laughed at union rules picked it up.

Through the turnstiles, the dock stood bare, the fence panels stacked against the far wall. A van had backed up and stood with its rear doors open about two yards from the edge of the loading dock. Two bland government-issue sedans idled on either side. A fourth suit stood near the back of the van. "Get in."

He could jump to the ground and run for it. Clay shivered and his breath steamed in the sodium-vapor glare lighting the dock. Over the van he glimpsed bright stars, Orion's shoulders and the members of other constellations he couldn't identify. One of the stars in the Big Dipper was the north star, right? But which one was the Big Dipper?

"Move," said the third NMHA man in a high, rabbity voice, and he shoved Clay for emphasis. He lowered his head to watch his footing, and as he did he saw rows of sheet metal warehouses stretching across a plain. He climbed into the van without urging. No place to run. The doors shut and Clay shivered more.

He rode for a while, until the van slowed and a buzzing sound grew. The van stopped and the doors opened to show a large patch of concrete. The NMHA agents stood in a semicircle around the back of the van, and behind them a small passenger jet stood, engine whining, logo of a bankrupt airline on its side. Portable stairs stood in place. A searchlight snapped on, its beam locked on Clay, and he squinted and climbed down. The NMHA agents shifted around him as he trudged to the portable stairs.

Run, a thought urged, but he put it aside. Even if he could elude these four, how many others lurked? And beyond them, how far could he go on a cold night in strange territory wearing a prison uniform?

They weren't going to kill him. Why send a jet to pick him up if his destination was a shallow grave? He lifted his chin and climbed the portable stairs.

Inside the door, a guard stood behind a sheet of bulletproof transparent plastic. "Down the aisle." Clay passed more bulletproof plastic, tinted dark, on both sides of the aisle. From behind the plastic came murmured voices and the tap of input devices. Halfway between the emergency exit row over the wing and the back of the cabin, the guard said over the intercom, "Here." Within five minutes they were airborne.

He tried to sleep but couldn't, and so returned to a question that had been on his mind for a while. Who had betrayed him to the feds? Monica was the only one to know he'd accessed the St. Louis servers; the stranger with the email address was the only one with a hint of what he'd found. Clay still couldn't figure why the stranger would entrap him, but why would anyone else? The engine noise dropped in and out of his hearing and then he fell asleep.

He woke on the descent. After landing the plane taxied for a while before the agents put him in another van. He glimpsed distant hangars and sodium-vapor lights before the door shut. He dozed off-and-on while the van followed a curving road over rolling hills. It slowed and turned and nearby a gate rattled open along a track set in the pavement. A slow journey for another minute, down and up more hills, ended in an enclosed place where the sound of the van's engine reverberated and then cut off. The back doors swung open.

A parking garage. A blonde, casually dressed in capri pants, a pastel yellow blouse, and a corduroy blazer, stood in front of three burly men in blue jeans and black bomber jackets. The blonde cocked her head. "Mr. Schieffer? I'm Dr. McKing."

Clay swung his legs over the edge. "Where am I?"

"Dr. Boucher will tell you in the morning." She pronounced it *Booshay*. "I'm sure you're tired and would like to refresh before then. If you'll come with us we'll show you to your room." She started walking and the soles of her flat shoes echoed off concrete walls. Clay fell in with the guards, one in front of him and two behind. A stairwell ended one flight up. They led Clay into and across a hallway that curved away in both directions and had windows running along the top of the far wall. A door with a biometric scanner stood under the windows. Two of the musclemen turned on flashlights. McKing pressed her hand to the biometric scanner and a thin red line crossed her eye. The door swung open. They stepped out and Clay paused. The night was much warmer than his previous location and the sky held a quarter moon and a bright spread of stars.

"Keep moving, Mr. Schieffer," said one of the guards behind him. "You can enjoy the view later."

The flashlight beams bobbed along a paved path, but between

them and the moonlight Clay could see their destination. A low building in a bland modernist style stood before him and its walls curved away from his vantage point. The path led around the curve and it appeared the building had a round floor plan. From the path a lawn lapped at the building's base. A knee wall, two feet high, gave way to picture windows stretching six more feet to the building's eaves. Inside lay rooms dimly visible through the moonlight and security lamps that reminded him of a cramped modernist hotel. Maybe a third of the rooms had the lumps of sleeping figures under blankets. One person, a lanky man visible by a small cone of light cast by a wall lamp, sat reading in an armchair next to the window and looked up in surprise.

McKing halted at another biometric door. While it scanned her Clay looked around. Another building curved around their destination and he realized it was the one he'd come out of. At the other building's eave a camera hung, aimed at the door in front of him. Even if they were kind enough to let him see natural light and sleep in a real bed, they would still observe everything.

The door hummed open and one of the guards behind him nodded at Clay to enter. To his left was an orderly station topped in white melamine. Behind the counter, robots snoozed in their charging cradles and a bored, quiet-looking young white man with an acne problem, quickly minimized a window on his display. "This is him, doctor?"

McKing nodded, turned to Clay. "We'll show you to your room in a minute, but first we'll need you to sign in." The orderly slid a clipboard across the counter. *I, Clay Schieffer, do understand that I am remanded to the custody of Dr. Francis Boucher—*

"What if I don't sign?" Clay asked, and made sure his voice sounded surly.

McKing yawned and covered her mouth till it ended. "Willy, stamp his form." The smartpaper generated, in bright red, *Patient refused to sign* and the doctor scribbled her signature next to it.

"One more thing," McKing said. Willy set out tweezers on the countertop. "Stay still, it hurts less than waxing." Clay didn't react until after she pulled a hair from his left eyebrow and dropped it into a small plastic bag. "For our genomics file." The pinprick of pain from her tweezers soon faded.

"Your room's along here," she said, and turned left after the orderly station and led him down another curved hallway. He visualized a floor plan of concentric rings. "Number Three." A smartpaper display on the door had been programmed to show his name. "We've exempted you from the normal schedule tomorrow morning. When you're awake the duty personnel will take you to meet Dr. Boucher. If you have any special requests please let us know and we'll see what we can do." He almost believed her, but the guards eyed him impassively and he told himself not to raise his hopes.

Clay stepped into the room and the wall lamps came on. A quick glance confirmed his earlier assessment of the rooms, but compared to a concrete cell a cramped hotel room was a dream. Carpeted floor, a bathroom with a shower, sink, and stocked toiletries cabinet, a digital clock displaying 4:03, table and round chair, a comfortable-looking bed—

Three pairs of trousers, three polo shirts, underwear, and socks lay neatly folded on the bed. At its foot stood two pairs of moccasins, one red, one brown, and a pair of blue canvas low-rise sneakers. He checked the labels inside the pants and saw the myfab clothier logo and his name. His name lay printed under the myfab cobbler logo on the insole of the shoes.

He was still in a cage, but at least a gilded one.

Next to the piled clothes sat a manila envelope. Its only label was a barcode sticker and something inside rattled when he picked it up. He dumped out his wallet, stripped of cash and cards but otherwise intact, and his wedding ring. He flung the wallet to the table. His finger was the easiest place to store the ring.

He took a quick hot shower, not caring about splashing water on the floor, pulled on underwear, and fell asleep on top of the bed covers.

Clay woke slowly, then jerked his arms and legs, startled and forgetting where he was. Strips of sunlight lit the picture window's sill and the carpet near the window. Outside, across the ring-shaped courtyard, the wall of the outer building showed featureless concrete and a visual slice through the short, high windows. A pair of cameras mounted under the eave aimed past each other, watching the court-yard's outer perimeter, and a third aimed at his room.

He pulled a shirt and a pair of pants off the clothes piles. Comfort-able, though did myfab.com routinely turn customer data over to the feds? Clay pushed his feet into the brown mocs but stopped halfway, the heel grips flopping underfoot. He didn't know where he was, or what they planned to do to him, but they weren't going to set him free anytime soon. As for what they intended, he could sit here and wonder or he could see what Dr. Boucher had to say.

In the hall he walked toward the orderly station. On the way he passed glass panes with drawn curtains and a closed door on his left, the smartpaper reading *Morning Group Session* and muffled voices talk-ing within. Two orderlies and a guard stood behind the station, and one of the orderlies, a chubby blonde with permed hair, came around to Clay. "Mr. Schieffer, are you ready to meet Dr. Boucher?"

"Can I get breakfast first?"

"Oh, sure. The cafeteria's over here." She led him further around the curve, past the outside door he'd come in from and toward the room where the man had been awake the night before, and into a quarter-circle room in the center of the building. The cafeteria had no outer wall, but instead a long, narrow planter filled with vegeta-tion whose names he didn't know and whose cousins he'd parched to death in his office. An array of skylights filled the ceiling. Chairs and tables looked like they'd been picked up from a coffee-bar sur-plus store, and an array of Snackerias, SueChefs, and other equipment filled the south wall.

"You get a base number of cafeteria points every day," the blonde orderly said. "The doctors and therapists can give you more, I can't, so don't try to butter me up. Use them wisely because otherwise you'll be stuck eating the nasty stuff squeezed out of those military gadgets. It's free but it looks like turds and probably tastes like them too."

She walked away and Clay ignored her advice. The order kiosk read his handprint and showed 40.00 points in his account. He spent 16.85: pancakes, bacon, scrambled eggs, orange juice, cappuccino. The juice was sweet and tart and the bacon snapped between his jaws without crumbling. Sunlight crawled onto his table and he felt almost normal. Just what they wanted, he guessed. He slowed his eating while the thought sank in.

Afterward, he tested them by walking the other way out of the cafeteria. To the outside of the building the rooms were closed, but on the inside the curtains were open on a window revealing a fitness room stacked with cardio machines, free weights, and physioballs. Just past it, another door led to the outside; sunlight glowed on the vinyl tile and a sprinkler flowed on the grass outside.

Rubber soles squeaked toward him. "Dr. Boucher would really like to see you," the blonde orderly said. Behind Clay came the sound of throat clearing. A glance over his shoulder showed the guard, clad in black and expressionless.

They herded him back around the building, where the orderly returned to her station and the guard walked with Clay out the north door. He steered him to the right, past the naked windows of the inner building and the bland, camera-watched wall of the outer, to an entrance to the outer building. Biometrics machines scanned the guard and the door swung open.

The hallway Clay had seen the night before ran the perimeter of the ring-shaped outer building, he guessed. It looked the same in the glimpse he caught walking a few steps to the left to an open door. The guard pointed with his head. "The doctor's office."

The office had picture windows, but unlike the cells, these faced outward and no cameras peered in. Outside, the ground fell away from the building down and up a shallow valley, yellow-brown with early spring, crowned by woods on the far ridge. A black asphalt line descended the valley's far slope and came up to the building. Beyond the ridge, a yellow-green hill rose in the distance; a line of trees slanted up it along a tan-colored gash of dirt road.

The office had a cantilevered glass desk at the far end in front of a wall of bookshelves. Near the door, thick-lined brown leather couches faced each other and a matching armchair sat perpendicular to both. In the armchair sat a man of medium build, with a long face, green eyes, and dirty-blond hair trimmed close over a widow's peak and a beard. He wore dark gray slacks and a gray pinstriped shirt, open at the collar, under a blue denim blazer. "Mr. Schieffer, hello, I'm Dr. Boucher." He remained seated, hands in his lap. "You admire the view?"

Clay said nothing, but his cheeks felt hot from having revealed too much. *Too much?* Boucher could guess he wanted to be free.

"Have a seat, either one." Clay took the one facing the picture windows while Boucher looked past him to the guard. "LeRoi, come in, please." The door shut behind the guard and Clay sensed his presence behind him like a human wall.

The doctor opened a manila folder on his lap and his eyes darted over it. Clay looked from the windows to Boucher and back several times waiting for him to speak, but he ignored Clay for a time. Finally he looked up. "You're lucky I have President Everton's ear," he said.

"Lucky?"

"Without me you'd be sitting in a cell in South Dakota until you died of old age. Never mind the better food, the softer bed, the grounds privileges, and so forth. You have the chance to leave here within a few months."

Like hell. Could it be possible for him to be freed even with the dangerous knowledge he carried? Clearly Boucher had enough authority for NMHA agents to pull him from his prison cell in the middle of the night. But even the authority to free him didn't mean Boucher would do so. "What's the catch?"

Boucher met his gaze with effortless aplomb. "There's no catch, Mr. Schieffer. We don't subscribe to the incarceration paradigm. The idea that warehousing a man for a length of time is rehabilitory is categorically false. It doesn't even work on people who are criminal, let alone people like you."

"People like me."

"I understand the President's object in arresting enemy combatants, though I don't agree with what he does with them. After the June 19 attack the masses sought those whom they could define as morally culpable for the attack and then exile from the community. Criminals, in other words, to be punished. It's an urge instilled in us since our ancestors wielded antelope femurs against each other on the African savanna a million years ago and the President is stuck leading a nation afflicted with that urge.

"As I said, I don't agree, because the concepts of 'crime' and 'punishment' are antiquated," Boucher added. "You're not a criminal, Mr. Schieffer. However, the fact that you engaged in behaviors that led NCS to arrest you demonstrates that you are mentally ill."

The purpose of this place came clear. Clay narrowed his eyes. "I'm not crazy."

The doctor raised his eyebrows and then turned his attention to the manila folder. "Your file shows erratic behavior and public nervousness. Your current demeanor shows distrust for duly constituted authority, inappropriate belligerence, and difficulty concentrating in social situations. In other words, psychosis."

"You say *I'm* crazy?"

"We prefer the term *mentally unwell*. But you're fortunate you've been diagnosed in the present age. Unlike the crude treatments and scattershot drugs of the past, today we can sculpt a therapy regimen to your personality and your brain chemistry. Within a few months you could be restored to well-adjusted, socially appropriate behavior."

Clay inhaled and wondered how many molecules of oxytocin entered his lungs with each breath. He refused to trust Boucher or his lackeys, airborne drugs or not.

Boucher flexed his hands on the manila folder and it rattled. Erratic behavior? Public nervousness? What was written there about Clay's arrest? What was written there about the person who'd informed on him?

"My staff will work with you on an everyday basis. Large and small group sessions, medication regimens, and the like. You are at the cutting edge of therapeutic modalities, Mr. Schieffer. Although making use of our therapy is your choice, and one you can reject, as I said, you're lucky."

"Cutting edge? Why me?"

"If we can help you return to mental wellness, it will move us closer to the day when those cell blocks in South Dakota can be torn down and their inmates returned to productive life. Also, you are one of the strongest engineers yet swallowed by NCS." The words struck a chord of flattery in Clay's emotions, and realizing that made him more angry. "I'm certain part of you would rather spend the effort you now fritter away on psychosis on actions that can improve our society instead. Now, if you'll excuse me—"

Clay bolted from the couch and leaped at the folder in Boucher's hands. Clay pulled and it slid through the doctor's hands, but not fully out. They wrestled and Clay pushed hard off the floor and shifted his weight. The armchair tilted on its side legs and tipped over and the two of them crashed onto the floor. Clay yanked the folder from the doctor's grip, opened it, scanned for names—

The guard landed heavily on Clay's back and pressed him against the floor. Surprised, Clay lost his grip on the folder. LeRoi flung it a couple of yards toward the desk and then pulled Clay's arms back and twisted them. Clay grunted in pain and bunched the muscles in his legs.

"Tendency, to violence," Boucher said, breathing hard. He picked up the folder. "Possibly, excess testosterone."

"Go to hell," Clay said. The guard twisted his arms further and he gasped.

"Want me to apply some, what do you say, negative reinforcement?" LeRoi asked.

Boucher sucked in a couple of breaths. "You learned how to do that in the penitentiary?"

"Wouldn't even leave a mark."

Boucher let that hang for a moment. "Let's hold it in abeyance. Not now."

"Doctor, he attacked you. You can't let that go."

For a moment there was no response. From outside Clay's sight came a thwack, the manila folder hitting Boucher's desk broadside, and a few seconds later, the dull thud of the chair's feet swung down to the carpet. "He'll almost certainly come to repent of it. And if he doesn't, he can die of old age here, too."

The guard frogmarched Clay to his room and shut him in. Clay spent the next hour rubbing his upper arms and taking a closer look at the room. Thick bolts held the round, swiveling chair to the floor, and the window was made of thick plastic. Even if he could break the window he'd have to bypass the cameras and either scale the outer building's wall or penetrate the biometric security on its doors. He wasn't getting out that way.

At eleven-thirty came footsteps in the hall. Someone knocked. "Open," Clay said, but the door didn't. All manual. He opened it by hand and saw the man he'd glimpsed in the middle of the night: pale and long-faced, with a narrow nose and dolorous eyes.

"Kenneth Delacroix," he said and extended his hand. Clay shook it and gave him his name. Others loitered down the hall, watching sidelong.

"We have a couple hours for lunch and unstructured time," Delacroix said. "Please join us. We can tell you more about this place."

If Clay was going to survive without being broken, let alone escape, the more information he could get the better. He nodded and followed the others to the cafeteria.

In the line at the order kiosk Clay stood in front of a broad-chested man who had a few day's stubble and east Asian eyes. Clay held his hand to the machine and when the display refreshed the man behind said, "Holy smokes," in a flip California accent. "Sorry, wasn't trying to look over your shoulder, but negative 226? Your first day? What did you do?"

They'd docked him points, apparently. "I took a swing at Boucher."

The other looked both shocked and pleased. "Sweet. Wish I'd done that." He cleared his throat. "Phil Yamamoto."

Clay replied with his name and shook Yamamoto's hand. The kiosk display said *Minimal nutritional requirement will be dispensed.* "Hopefully I won't regret it."

Yamamoto made a sour face. "I've tried that crap. Nasty."

The SueChef extended its arms and placed a plate on Clay's tray. A gray-brown disc the size of a hockey puck, a soft white pile the same size, and rows of green and orange cylinders as large as pills forced down livestock's throats. The SueChef added a small paper cup of water.

Yamamoto pointed to a table where Delacroix sat with another man. The other introduced himself as Uri Kerensky.

"Can you tell us about yourself?" Delacroix asked Clay. "Why did they nab you?"

They might not believe him either, but Clay saw no harm in saying it. "I found out how Everton stole the election." The gray-brown puck tasted like bland, desiccated meatloaf.

Delacroix's eyebrows crinkled in sympathy and he handed over a pat of margarine. "For the mashed potatoes," he said, then, "Well?"

"Neuroactive drugs," Clay said, and sniffed and glanced quizzically at the ceiling. "Tied in with a detector for Everton's voice and image. Promoting trust in influential people."

Delacroix pressed his lips together. "I'm not surprised," he said, then glanced up. "I'm sure they're doing it here."

"It doesn't mean they'll get you, though," Yamamoto said. "Ken's the old man and he's not giving in."

Delacroix's expression hinted at sadness for a moment but held firm. "Almost two years. I was the first 'patient.' The sod hadn't taken root in the courtyard and the old farm fences were still on the site."

"Where are we?"

"Missouri. License plates in the staff parking lot."

The margarine did help the mashed potatoes. "Farm fences, you said? Parking lot?"

Yamamoto sliced an herb-crusted chicken breast. "You didn't see the robotic foot bridge last night? It's near the exit over the freight dock. A robot arm will extend a ramp to let you climb up and down over the office building."

"It costs points," Kerensky said. He stared evenly at Clay. "And it's just a bigger cage."

"Why'd Boucher have you brought here, Clay?" asked Yamamoto.

Shame suddenly flooded him. These men, and the thousands of others in South Dakota, had been locked up because of what he'd done and allowed to happen. "Because I did the basic engineering work behind Everton's theft of the election."

Yamamoto blanched. "Boucher wants you to keep at it. Dammit." He shook his head, his expression sick and frightened.

"Phil's a professor at Carnegie Mellon," Delacroix said. "He does basic research on neuron/circuit interfaces."

The big picture clicked. Dread ran down Clay's back. "Boucher wants to 'cure' brain scientists and engineers so we'll work for Everton." Clay looked at his plate and the remaining food seemed even less appetizing than it had.

"I thought it was just me," Yamamoto said. "That I was influential for being a professor and that's why he wanted to turn me."

Clay felt the need to say something. "He wants to turn us all," he managed, feeble-sounding. "What about you, Kenneth?"

"I'm no engineer," Delacroix said. "Are you familiar with Treasures in Heaven?"

Clay cocked his head. "AU's Christian affiliate, right?"

Delacroix pressed his lips together and Clay realized it was not. "After the attack on D.C., many of us felt the need for a spiritual renewal in our country. We took our name from Matthew 6:19: earthly treasures—welfare programs, protected jobs, military might—can rot or be stolen, but treasures in heaven can't. AU ginned up the City on the Hill Society to compete for the hearts of believers. As for how I got here, after the election, you can connect the dots."

"I don't recall your organization," Clay said. "There were a lot of meetups and affinity mobs after June 19."

"I'm resigned to our present obscurity," Delacroix said, slightly wistful. "I've heard Everton had his impact on it; the new leadership is timid and membership and donations are far down."

"Boucher's hoping you—"

"Say *hail Everton full of grace* so I can be let go to merge what's left of TiH into City on the Hill. No thanks."

"Even if you said it they wouldn't believe you," Yamamoto said to Delacroix.

"Brain scans?" Clay asked, knowing the answer.

"Brain scans."

Clay stabbed his fork at an orange cylinder. It squirmed under the tines before a second stab speared it. Before eating it he turned to Kerensky. "Uri?"

"My story's similar to Kenneth's. I was president of Greensmith. The environmental NGO."

"You guys do emissions trading?"

"Did. It folded after my arrest." Kerensky looked wistful. "More than that. We had a vision for market-based solutions for all environmental problems. Give people property rights in environmental goods, and low-transaction-cost markets to trade them, and you'll do better for the world than ten thousand bureaucrats in Washington, Old or New. They framed us on charges of supporting ecoterrorists."

Delacroix stood and lifted his empty tray. "Clay, I wish we could have met under better circumstances. I'll see you at the afternoon brainwash, one-thirty." Yamamoto and Kerensky left soon after and Clay grimly chewed the rest of his lunch.

On his way out of the cafeteria a rotund man, bearded, with small ears and a wide flat nose, hustled up to him. "Hello, I'm Quentin Van Wijk." Clay shook his damp hand. "We've got an hour, let me show you around."

Van Wijk led him out the south door. Spring sunlight warmed Clay's arms. "Don't we need biometrics to get back in?" he asked.

"The doors are unlocked during the day. Here's the footbridge." Van Wijk stepped on a paver set alone in the lawn around the inner building. Electric motors whined and hardware clanked on the roof of the outer building and a set of metal mesh stairs descended to them. Clay felt suddenly clammy despite the sun, remembering the cell block he'd left twelve hours earlier.

"This costs points, doesn't it?"

"I already paid." Van Wijk huffed up the stairs and Clay slowly followed. More metal mesh, in cross-section like an inverted U with long uprights, formed a tunnel around them. Another tunnel in the same style crossed the roof of the outer building. Cameras hummed to focus on them and they waited at the outer edge of the roof for the footbridge to lift off the courtyard and land in place for them to descend to the outer grounds.

The cleared ground fell away, down a slope jutted with limestone, to a high barbed-wire double fence about three hundred yards away. If he didn't stumble Clay could sprint it in forty-five seconds, and if he could find a way through the two fences, beyond lay a patch of woods with forested hills visible in the distance.

"I can guess what you're thinking," Van Wijk said. "It won't work.

They have cameras everywhere, plus military robots with visual and IR cameras and other sensors, armed with sedative darts, plus perimeter fencing. A half-dozen men have tried it and they've all failed. One guy tried a second time and they shipped him back to New Mexico." The footbridge clattered into place and Van Wijk descended. Down the slope a small flat shape, like a steel pizza box with tank treads and a toy gun coming out of the top, turned toward them. Barely visible in the distance, a second robot zipped along the base of the fence. It stopped at the point along it Clay had already picked out as the destination for his downhill sprint. The robot aimed its dartgun at them.

Spring green tinged the dormant grass and soft cumulus clouds ambled overhead. Instead of an eighty square foot cell, he had a four-hundred acre one.

"So escape's going to be tough," Clay said. "Thanks."

"Not tough. Impossible." Van Wijk walked southward around the perimeter of the office building. The building's windows saw them coming and grew opaque, preserving the staff's privacy from the inmates.

"I saw you talking to Delacroix," Van Wijk said, breathing heavily. "He's a stubborn idiot. Don't follow his lead. Give Boucher what he wants."

"That's what you're doing?"

Van Wijk looked agitated. "Do what you like, but fighting them won't do you any good. Don't you want to be free? Get out of this place, go home, get back to your life?" He stopped and took a couple of breaths. "They're keeping up my blog. They must have someone drafting entries and running them through software to mimic my style. When they let me out I can go back to it and my readers won't know I was away from it for months when I became an Everton loyalist."

"You could tell them what happened."

"And get sent back to New Mexico?" Van Wijk snorted. "No way."

Clay followed him around the building toward Boucher's office on the east side. In the parking lot stood a dozen cars, ranging from a new Ambassador luxury sedan to an old manual-drive Buick retrofitted with an autopilot. A low sprawling sign read *NMHA Dent County Research Facility*. Van Wijk asked the same questions as the others, but

Clay let the breeze carry them away unheeded, down the valley to a creek crossed by a one-lane low-water bridge. The blogger fell silent and Clay trudged back to the footbridge. It swung down for him. No charge for the return trip.

At one-twenty-five gongs chimed and footsteps sounded in the hall. Clay peeked out of his room and saw the sign across the hall read *Afternoon Group Session*. The display across from his bed lit up with the message *Unexcused absence from a Group Session incurs a 20 point fine.* He sighed and stepped into his sneakers.

On his way to the door he stopped in the bathroom and a thought came to him. Could he resist the neuroactive chemicals Boucher's staff pumped into the air? Like every other bald ape, he'd like to think he mastered his thoughts, but that's what Everton had counted on '20. Force of will could help, but why not take insurance? He tore off a sheet of toilet paper, rolled it up as finely as his long fingers could manage, and pinched off two small pieces. In the toiletry cabinet he found an atomizer of cologne. He sprayed each pinch of toilet paper with the cologne and wedged one up each nostril. The citrus scent deep in his nose made him wince. Perhaps a fool's errand—he didn't know the mesh size of the paper fibers but they were certainly wider than aerosolized oxytocin analogs—but worth the attempt.

The meeting room had white walls hung with abstract paintings, smears of color glowing in lozenges of sunshine coming through skylights. A guard stood just inside the room, arms folded. A dozen green plastic chairs stood in two concentric arcs and faced the corner of the room. An Asian male—of Korean descent, Clay guessed, from his tight upper eyelids and chubby cheeks—sat in a plush chair with thick arms. He wore a lab coat over a chalkstripe oxford shirt, and his black hair parted down the middle and pomaded flat. He watched them enter with a breezy smile.

Clay was late. He entered the back row but found a man in every chair, probably claimed by their occupants by accident months ago and now taken out of habit in a form of unconscious, emergent property rights. Delacroix, settled on the back row, nodded to Clay but didn't give up his seat. The only open seat was on the front row, between Yamamoto and a dapper fellow, lightly tanned, with a narrow moustache and a businessman's hairstyle, both salted with gray. He gave his name as Javier Zuniga.

"We have a new patient," the facilitator said. He leaned toward Clay. "I'm Dr. Kim. You don't want to introduce yourself?"

"No."

Kim shrugged, pulled a stylus and a smartpaper from inside his lab coat, and scratched a note before speaking to the entire room.

"Yesterday Dr. McKing facilitated your discussion about people for whom you have affection who in turn respect the broader principles of our society and our government. We're going to switch gears a little bit today, though I'll be asking you to think about the people in your lives.

"Each of you has people who are concerned about you. That's a good thing, isn't it?"

"Absolutely," said Van Wijk.

"Does that mean they approve everything you do?" Kim peered into the back row. "Kenneth, didn't Paul rebuke Peter for going astray?"

"That's true."

Kim nodded as if Delacroix had said something profound. He glanced at Clay, then the others. "I know some of you wonder why you were arrested by the NCS. How did that agency find out your misdeeds? Isn't it possible that someone who cared for you told them what you'd done?"

Someone on the back row murmured "bullshit," but hoarsely, a reflexive denial. Everyone else tensed. Clay noticed his hands had clenched.

Kim's breezy smile returned and he spent a long moment reading his smartpaper. "For example, Clay. What person who cared for you might have informed NCS of your misdeeds? Do you have any guesses?"

Clay glared at him. "No."

"No guess at all? There aren't many candidates. One of your coworkers or subordinates, such as Mr. Thomas or Ms. Colbert? Your secretary, perhaps? Or a family member?" Kim frowned at the page. "I can't tell from this how strong your marriage is—"

"Jenny didn't inform on me." Clay pressed his fists into his thighs. They wanted him to lose his cool, so be damned if he would. Jenny might be mad at him, maybe even for good reason, but she wouldn't have turned on him.

Kim smirked. "I know it's a therapy cliché, but denial is not only a river in Egypt."

Clay gritted his teeth. The cologne stung his nose. "It wasn't Jenny."

"Then who?" Kim stared at him.

The stare rocked him. Part of Clay wanted to blurt *one million one thousand one* but instead he swallowed hard. The stranger might not be a friend but he wasn't going to hand him over to those he knew were his enemies. Clay drew a breath and stared back.

"Why don't you tell me?"

7

Clay soon learned the Hospital's routine. In the group sessions, the facilitator pressed multiple buttons in his victims' psyches, dressing like an authority, pretending to like them, calling them out on statements inconsistent with past admissions. "Didn't you say Everton had accomplished a good thing by reinstating central authority after the mistakes of the Reynolds administration?" McKing asked Kerensky one morning, and the quiet man turned red-faced and tried to swallow back the word *yes* as he muttered it.

The trust molecules in the air helped, but the hospital staff elicited most of those admissions through simple bribery. For a half-pound of beef fajitas or a caramel mocha with real whipped cream, men would say Everton's crackdown on suspected enemy combatants was necessary after 6:19. Delacroix declined these bribes, and Clay imagined the other's stare poised to chide him whenever he was tempted to agree with the facilitator. Bored of the military surplus food, he finally did, in an afternoon session with the sunlight fading in and out through passing clouds. He avoided Delacroix's gaze the rest of the afternoon but shame still warmed his cheeks.

From overheard conversations and the brutal cheerful questions asked by the facilitators, Clay found most of the others had been here only a few months. Delacroix had been in far longer than any of them and apparently had seen many other prisoners released before

him, "cured" of their "psychoses" by Boucher's program. How had
Delacroix resisted the trust molecules? However he had, it was plain
Yamamoto, Kerensky, and others did so as best they could by orbit-
ing Delacroix, transferring the urges both to trust, instilled in them
by aerosolized small molecules, and to belong to a social order, tran-
scribed by brain ribosomes after an epoch of primate evolution.

One tactic the facilitators also wielded was to bring up the names
of those released—Guillaume, Marqus, Eric, others—and show photos of these men on the decks of fishing boats, with their arms around
wives beaming amid diamonds and black velvet, or in AU meetings
glowing with the torches of faux brotherhood. Van Wijk spoke of the
released with frank envy; Delacroix, with stubborn nonchalance.

The orderlies administered four drug calls daily. They had per-
sonalized DNA information and, Clay surmised, a stack of MuSynths
feeding into a tablet press or liquid formulator. Every patient had a
single tablet or plastic cup, a cheerful color that suggested a candy
flavor—orange, banana, chocolate. Antioxidants and Agerix, muscle
builders, fat burners: everything needed for health, fitness, and extended life. And, unspoken, the neuroactives of Boucher's choice. Zuniga and Van Wijk took their doses, but Delacroix walked by shaking
his head. Clay, embarrassed, declined his as well.

He wondered when the facilitator would mention Clay's company
had designed the drug fabricators. Probably when it would do the
most to isolate him from the other prisoners and leave him no choice
but to embrace Boucher's cure. He coughed and felt an itch inside his
nose from his toilet paper filters. Alone in his room, he would throw
them away, the sharp contrast of blood against the bleached paper
drawing his gaze as they arced to the trashcan.

After dinner, nights were unstructured until lights-out at ten. On
the display in his room, Van Wijk played a trivia game based on Everton's book *No Higher Virtue*, with correct answers returning random numbers of cafeteria points. "It's open book and when you
win points, you can win big." Dumbpaper books bowed the library
shelves, mostly mystery novels and pro-government soldiers' mem-
oirs from Uighurstan. Clay used the elliptical trainer and the free
weights in the fitness room. Nine-thirty he stalked on heavy legs back

to his room. He'd lost himself amid his exertions but the plain white walls and the cream-colored vinyl floor brought him back to his confinement. Someone had shut him into this cage and turned the key. Someone would pay. He approached the cafeteria, sweat trickling off his jaw and his sneakers squeaking on the vinyl.

Delacroix looked up through the leaves of a ficus tree. He sat alone at a table near the cafeteria's north entrance. "Clay, have a minute?"

He wanted to avoid the other's gaze that evening, but Delacroix would keep asking and tomorrow would be no better. Let the other say his piece and be done with it. Clay entered the cafeteria but hesitated when he saw the table in front of Delacroix. Thin crinkly pages and tiny print marked a bible open closer to front than back. "What do you want?"

"There's something I'd like to talk about."

Clay glanced from the bible to the other's face. He hadn't encountered the false chumminess of evangelizers since college and felt angry at himself for not seeing it when he'd met Delacroix the day before. "No thanks."

"Sorry? Oh, I'm not asking about your beliefs. Please, sit."

Clay inhaled, then pulled a chair away from the table. Its feet barked over the vinyl.

Delacroix laid a ribbon between the open pages, shut the bible, and slid it to the side. "I'm not going to give you grief for playing along with them this afternoon, either. You know they'll try to hang you on that hook—"

"I know."

"Okay, I'm sure you do. That puts you ahead of Marqus and Eric." Delacroix interlaced his fingers and rested his hands on the tabletop. "I want everyone who comes into this place to resist it. There's a lot of ways it can defeat you. Taking their cure is just the most obvious."

"What's so subtle I don't see it?"

"What happens when the day comes Everton sets us loose?"

"Without taking Boucher's candy?"

"If Everton locks up people's minds, what harm can we do without a key? Those locks are out there—your technology AU used three years ago is just the beginning. Yamamoto's not the only one wiring into people's brains. You're not the only one putting drugs in them."

"Okay, let's say in ten years they let us out without being doped up. Looks like a victory to me."

"Not if you lose your—" Delacroix gave a lopsided grin. "If *soul* bothers you, call it *humanity* or *ethical center*. Survival alone is not enough, not if you pay too high a price." He rested his fingertips on the bible's white leatherette cover. "I was reading about King David."

"Trust in God and we can kill Goliath?" Did he sound bitter? Why shouldn't he?

Delacroix ignored Clay's mockery. "After that. When he was king he had everything, so what did he want? More. He saw Bathsheba bathing and seduced her. But then he wanted even more. Her husband Uriah was in the army, so David ordered his generals to let Uriah get killed."

Footsteps in the hall made Delacroix look up. The foliage obscured Zuniga's face. "Gentlemen."

"Evening," Delacroix said. Clay nodded.

After Zuniga walked away, Clay unfolded his arms. "So David was a scumbag. What of it?"

"It got me thinking. There are things we shouldn't want because it's immoral for us to have them. But there are also things we shouldn't want because getting them costs too much. I saw how Kim baited you with who informed on you and how you bit on it. I understand. In your shoes I'd be furious and looking for revenge. But who informed on you doesn't matter. Let it go."

"Yeah? And if I don't?"

Delacroix narrowed his dolorous eyes. "I don't know you well enough to say. Boucher might be able to make the judo throw on you, use your anger to get you to submit to his treatment. The sooner you get out the sooner you can take your revenge, right? And whether or not you'll still want to take revenge once you're out is irrelevant because Boucher will own your...ethical center.

"Then again," Delacroix went on, "maybe staying angry will help you preserve your independence until they let us out. Call it ten years. Then what? By then everyone outside will be as brainwashed as they're trying to make us in here. The person who betrayed you will no longer be morally responsible. What good would taking revenge do? Plus you'd end up dead, or in prison, or in a place like this but with strong arms holding you down while they inject you with the same drugs we can refuse to take."

Clay leaned back and rubbed his chin. "That's a lot to think about."

"I'm sure it is." Delacroix looked up to the clock high on the wall over the cappuccino maker. "It's almost lights out. I'll let you go. Take care."

Clay nodded. After Delacroix left he sat and massaged the burning muscles in his arms while he thought.

The low sun lit Clay's Spanish tile roof and the littered toys lying in the shade of the front lawn. Nil could take in the days since that Monday evening with a glance at his calendar, but it felt like months since he'd waited alone with Jenny for Clay to return from myfab. He walked slowly from his parked car to the front door, treading as softly as he could on the steps leading up from the driveway.

The cage of tightly woven voxel wires lit up. "Mr. Thomas, let me show you in." The door swung open.

"She's not expecting me."

"You're welcome anytime, I've been told. She's in the living room with Martin."

Jenny sat cross-legged on the floor with her son and a mob of brightly colored toys whose diverse textures were visible in the soft glow of table lamps. Her ponytail hung limply at her nape and her face was in shadow. "The duck goes quack quack quack," she said, her voice thin. She passed a toy duck in front of her son's face. Its feathers brushed his nose and his closed eyelids.

She greeted Nil and Martin opened his eyes wide and staggered to his mother's far shoulder. The boy's mouth quivered and his hands bunched around the strap of her blue tank top.

"He takes a while to warm up to visitors these days." Her face looked haggard.

Nil had nieces and nephews; he didn't enjoy dealing with small children but could pretend for brief stretches. He squatted a few feet from Jenny but lost his balance and fell to his knees with one hand outstretched to prop him. He craned his neck to look at Martin, but after a glimpse of the boy's eyes he turned to Jenny. "How are you?"

"Staying as strong as I can, for him. Have you heard anything?"

Nil slowly shook his head.

Absently, Jenny put her arm around Martin and pulled him closer. "Me neither." Her chest fell and rose. "Clay's really an enemy combatant."

"Looks like. He wouldn't have disappeared without telling one of us. Kidnappers would have called about a ransom. And I can't believe he would have harmed himself."

She tightened her lips and stared at Nil. *How can you be sure he was arrested?* He imagined her asking. His palms grew clammy while he thought for a preemptive lie. "What galls me is I didn't see it," she said. "He was withdrawn and belligerent for months. We shared this house with someone dangerous and I didn't see it."

Nil felt relieved. "I worked with him and I didn't see it either."

"And then I can't believe that he was dangerous. He had been good to me for years. He displaced his guilt at tempting fate," she said, and winced and pulled her son closer until he squirmed in her arm, "onto me but we could have worked through that. Well, I would have been willing." She dropped her arm from Martin's shoulders.

The boy looked carefully past her and Nil smiled a toothy grin at him without meeting his gaze. Martin smiled bashfully and hid his face against his mother's shoulder.

"It's his bedtime."

Her words gave him an opening to pursue his true purpose in visiting. "He's a good-looking boy. He must get it from you."

Jenny looked quizzically at him, then stood and lifted Martin to her hip. "I'll bathe him and put him in bed. You're welcome to stay, get a drink."

"Thanks. One for you?"

She waved the question away and walked past Nil. She wore khaki shorts and he watched the muscles bunch and release in her narrow calves. Behind the fireplace on the far wall, her feet sounded quick and heavy on the stairs.

Water surged in the pipes and Nil got a vodka tonic from the bar in the billiard room. Balls littered the green felt and his fingers drummed the bar while he waited. He snatched his drink from the BarQeep's silicone hand and stalked back to the living room. He sank into the tan cotton couch, the mob of toys in front of him and a video display to his left. The quinine rolled bitter over his tongue. Shadows deepened over the back lawn and biomethane lanterns around the pool flickered on.

Seducing a woman was an art. The female psyche wanted both to be dominated, held firmly by strong arms and a piercing gaze, and to dominate, to believe she had chosen both her bull and when to intice him with her red flag. He savored the bitter quinine until the night sky purpled over the yard.

Her footsteps came slowly, heavily down the stairs and he wondered how so slender a woman had a thudding walk. "I think he's asleep. He's been having trouble. Clay never helped him to bed but Martin can tell he's gone." She sat on the same couch as Nil. Her eyes were baggy.

"There's a lot on your mind. More than Martin."

She blinked and started, then shut her eyes and breathed deeply before turning to him. "Why am I surprised it's obvious? I've been tossing and turning and waking up in a sweat. Not about Clay. About me."

She wasn't going to ask him to use his AU membership to do something for Clay. Nil had gauged the situation correctly. He touched his fingertips to the slight bulge of muscle on the outside of her shoulder. "You have nothing to worry about."

She didn't move.

"They can question Clay with a brain scanner. Even if he lied and implicated you they'd tell it was a lie."

Jenny leaned away from him and he let his hand return to his lap. "They'd question me anyway."

"The technology's getting better all the time. NCS could have scanned you without your knowledge."

"What? That's…. Maybe."

"You have nothing to worry about. Anyone can see you're innocent. Pure."

She pulled her legs up and turned toward him. Her knees formed a barricade and her hands covered her lap. "Why are you here?" Jenny asked sharply.

"I hadn't seen you for a few days," Nil replied. "I wanted to make sure you were well."

"That's all?"

"What's on your mind? Please."

"You come in here and say things—"

"Say? Things?"

"I'm good looking? I'm pure?"

Nil leaned back and folded his arms. "What are you saying? Sure, I'm flattered, but whatever Clay's crime, I still owe him some loyalty—"

She braced her hands on her knees and peered forward. "Excuse me?"

"The house can open the door for me anytime. You come and sit next to me. What should I think?"

She sat back and pulled her hands back to her lap. "It means you're welcome here. That's all."

"Sorry. It's been stressful for both of us." He drained the last mouthful of his vodka tonic and stood. "I won't take more of your time. My best to Martin. Take care." He looked around for a table to rest the empty glass and one of the household robots rolled up, arm extending and tray leveling

"I—okay."

Outside, the sky was gray-black with city night as he stepped into the Lorelei. The engine hummed to life and reversed. He knew the game as well as a golfer having hit a long straight drive or a poker player reading a tell with pocket kings in hand. Jenny would wonder if she subconsciously was trying to seduce him and would fret he might not come back. He had her where he wanted and he felt shamed at the crassness of the thought. All love involved seduction, didn't it? Clay had chosen a path that threatened all three of them, hadn't he? But as the sedan reached the street he didn't look back at the house despite knowing Clay was not there.

* * *

Clay lay on his back, the sheet loose over his body and the blanket kicked to the foot of the bed, trying to fall asleep. He felt warm, with beads of sweat crawling down his body and his head. Along the wall to his left, a sliver of moonlight faded in and out as clouds passed. His right ear itched and he rubbed it with the flats of his fingers. He closed his eyes and his thoughts faded—

"Clay," a bland synthetic voice whispered in his right ear.

His limbs jerked and he lifted his head from the pillow. He stared to the right of the bed with wide eyes but saw no one. Sweat beaded on his forehead and cold gripped him.

"Sorry to startle you," the voice whispered again. "Don't worry, you're not hallucinating. Don't speak yet. I haven't found any bugs in the room but they can read lips through the cameras outside. Plus they have sensors in the window frames The panes are like the tympanum of a microphone. They can record your voice."

The stranger. How? A moment's thought showed him. Clay remembered a happier time a few years ago, listening to Jenny talk about the formix robots she worked on, tiny and simple with their hive-and-drones control architecture. The stranger had sent a formix robot through the cracks in the walls and lodged it in his ear to speak to him. Clay searched his memory for the hive's control range. Only a few dozen yards, back then, and though he couldn't recall her talking about it since the range had undoubtedly gone up. Call it a few hundred yards. The stranger could give orders to the hive from anywhere with internet access, but the hive had to be on or near the Hospital grounds, and to site it and start it scavenging bits of metal and plastic to build more ant-like robots, he'd been close and still could be.

"Roll onto your side, with your back to the window," the stranger said. Clay complied. "This might feel a little uncomfortable, but some more formix are going to climb over your neck and jaw. They can pick up muscle movements around your larynx and mouth. Subvocalize what you want to say and I'll pick it up."

Clay nodded, assuming the robot in his ear could sense the motion. The formix soon started climbing over his neck. Itching, he clenched his hands to keep from scratching. The itch turned to pricks like a weed's tiny burrs.

Test, test, he subvocalized, his lower jaw dropping for each vowel.

"You're coming in fine."

Good, Clay replied, and then the product of confused thoughts bubbled to the surface. *Before anything else you have to convince me why I should trust you.*

The other drew a breath. "I didn't put you in here."

Clay stared at the gray wall and it turned black as a cloud occluded the moon. *Talk is cheap.* The darkness held for a longer time than it had before.

"You took a game theory class in college, correct?"

Given what the stranger had said in their earlier conversation, in Houston such a long-seeming time before, Clay wasn't surprised the other knew that. All he remembered from the class, though, were the two-by-two grids of Prisoner's Dilemma and a young professor with curly brown hair and a Bronx accent.

"I'm either a friend or an enemy to you, though you don't know which. You can either trust me or not. If I'm an enemy and you don't trust me, you're no worse off. If I'm an enemy and you do trust me, the worst that can happen is they catch you trying to escape. That's not so bad. Boucher has never sent anyone back to the camps for trying to escape once.

"But if I'm a friend, not trusting me makes you no worse off, but trusting me could make you much better off. Freedom, Clay."

He remembered an earlier afternoon, the spring sun warm on his face and the greening valley sloping down to the fences. The stranger's words made him crave escape. He took a breath to keep himself from overestimating the odds of success as a result of wanting it badly. The world wouldn't conform itself to the strength of his wishes. But it would comply with reason, and the stranger's logic was tight. Even though it meant running the risk of betrayal, his wiser move was still to trust the other. He could die of old age here, too.

Plus, with freedom, he could find out who betrayed him and exact his revenge.

What's your plan?

"As you've noticed, I have a hive of formix on site. Your wife's employer does good work. At h-hour, the formix will knock out electrical power, both the main feed and the auxiliary generator. The cameras, the doors, all will lose power."

In his mind's eye Clay pictured the layout of the Hospital. *So will the footbridge.*

"Can you climb the courtyard wall of the outer building?"

The sky had been dark for a while and Clay shivered and pulled the sheet closer to his neck. His attention focused on the cotton gripped in his hand. Could the camera mounts on the wall of the outer building hold his weight? Long enough. *Yes. What about the security robots?*

"There's a front coming in. The cloud deck will be solid. Visibility will be very poor—"

Infrared.

"—and I'll trigger their recall-to-base command after they lose radio contact with Boucher's security people. They're good machines but Boucher's security men aren't as wired together as the military. The crawlers on this side of the creek will beeline to the back of the building. The ones on the other side will have to cross the bridge and will then come up the driveway. When they're the only ones out, head north toward the fence. Without the crawlers around you should be able to climb through. Standard barbed wire, you crossed fences like that on the ranch growing up, correct?"

How can I tell when to make the move?

"You'll have trouble seeing them, but listen for the first wave. I'll try to say something but I'll be busy and may not have a chance."

Onto the roof, wait for a break, run to the fence, climb through—
Once I'm out, then what?

"You'll be on someone's farm. Hang a right, avoid the farmhouse—do you need to avoid cows?"

Only the dangerous ones.

Silence from the other was followed by uncertain laughter. "I'd rather assume that's a joke at my expense than that there are flesh-eating cows in backwoods Missouri."

Good assumption.

The other's voice sounded more lighthearted. "You'll come to a two-lane asphalt road. Look for a gray midsize sedan."

Clay realized he had only one more question. *When.*

"It should be solid clouds by midnight. I'll give you a five-minute warning before I blow the electrical system."

The tiny robot in his ear fell silent. Clay rolled onto his back and stared at the dark ceiling. Transient breaks of moonlight came rarely through the picture window and their frequency lessened as the night wore on. He scratched at the formix on his neck and the stranger directed them away.

What would he do with freedom? He would be on the run, hiding with the stranger from NCS and the rest of Everton's agencies. He would have little opportunity to find his betrayer and even less to avenge himself.

Perhaps Delacroix was right. Perhaps the question didn't matter. But he would have time to find out whether the question mattered or not and where to focus his energies in either case. For the next few hours, only escape mattered. He rehearsed his steps over and over. Outside the front had blown in and clouds fully covered the night sky.

"Five minutes," the stranger said in his ear. Clay jerked, surprised despite himself. He laid still and tried to recall how he'd prepared for cross-country races in his adolescence. His memory unearthed forgotten rock songs that came back to mind like ancient desert roads swept clear of sand. *Round the hanging tree—*

"Now."

The building fell silent, as if it held its breath. No air tumbled through the vents, no nightlights glowed under the door to his room. Clay scrambled out of bed. He sat on the floor next to the bed, on the side away from the window, and pulled on jeans, a polo, and a thin jacket. Across the courtyard the high thin windows of the office building showed no light. He stepped into his sneakers, then stepped out of them and stuffed one in each outer pocket of the jacket. The sheet hesitated, tucked tightly under the foot of the bed, but he pulled it free and zipped it into his jacket. He piled clothes and pillows in his place and tugged the blanket over them as high as he could. With luck they wouldn't notice he was gone even after the lights came back on.

He cracked open his door. Darkness cloaked the hallway but sound carried from the orderly station. Cabinet doors barking open and Willy's voice. "Germano, where's the damn flashlight?"

Clay crouched low, his knees stiff, and padded on his bare feet down the hall away from them. "I tell you it was under there."

The voices faded as Clay put more distance between himself and the orderly station. Clay breathed a little more easily as he crept by Van Wijk's room. Behind the next closed door, Yamamoto snored loudly.

Clay came to the building's south door. The night outside was barely tinged with gray, some moonlight diffusing through the cloud deck. He squatted at the door and pressed his face to the glass. No one moved outside. Clay reached for the doorknob. Willy and Germano would find the flashlight soon. He opened the door and wind rustled outside. He slipped through and gently pulled the door closed.

The night had cooled and he felt glad for his jacket. Still no motion. Clay crouched and scampered across the courtyard to the base of the office building's wall. Low, dense shrubs, tight as coiled springs, scratched his bare feet. From inside his jacket he pulled the sheet, a faint white blur in the dark night, and looked up. The camera was a black, angular shape against the dark gray clouds.

He bunched each end of the sheet in his hands and held it behind his head as he jumped. Clay whipped the sheet forward and caught the camera. His feet scrambled at the wall but then found it and he started climbing up. In the camera mount a masonry screw groaned. *Hang on.* Metal whined under his weight and his arms ached as his feet climbed. His right foot reached the outer sill of the window along the top of the wall and he pushed with his leg until his center of gravity stood over the roof. He landed, belly-first, certain someone in the building below must have heard his landing.

He took a breath. The grit of the flat composition roof nipped at him through his clothes and his feet were cold. He had the sheet with him but he noticed a change in the weight in his jacket. One of his sneakers had fallen. He peered over the edge and saw the thin line of its pale trim. It hung half-submerged in the foliage of the shrubs, the navy canvas about as dark as the kelly-green leaves. With luck no one would see it till morning.

No time to waste. He crouched and duck-walked down the center of the ring, as far from the roof's edges as he could manage to keep from being seen from the ground. Against the lighter roofing material stood the darker rectangles of solar panels. Clay detoured and crouched lower. His quads burned and the grit pressed into the balls of his feet. He traveled as lightly as he could and hoped no one worked late in the building below. Plumbing stacks and a kitchenette vent lurked to stub his toe, but he saw them contrasted against the roof and made it safely to the north side of the building. He glanced back. The inner building looked small and low from his angle. A flashlight beam bounced around the interior near the north door and the orderly station.

He crept away to the outer edge of the roof. The wind rustled and the ground was almost as dark as the sky. Clay lay flat and saw spotty, jerky motions but couldn't tell if they were the security crawlers returning to base or tricks being played by his eyes.

A dull but fast clacking sound—Clay imagined a zipper made out of Martin's chunky snap-fit building blocks—came to him then from the northwest, further along the ridge where the Hospital buildings stood. He peered in that direction and saw a flat, square shape approach the building and turn along its western side, toward the loading dock.

A few seconds later came another sound, this from the north. Two sounds, actually, two machines treading on parallel tracks at an angle upslope. They followed their peer around the building. Clay breathed as quietly as he could. The sound repeated, this time from the northeast, and he didn't see the crawler until it crested the slope. It clacked away and left Clay in silence.

He felt suddenly timid. Where was the stranger's voice?

He had said he might be busy. Clay rubbed his hands, feeling cold, and remembered the lay of the land as seen in daylight, the valley falling away to the creek on his right. The last robot had come in the direction of the furthest point on this side of the creek. He counted out breaths and listened to be certain. ...three, four, five. No robots approached. Time to go to work. He jumped off the roof and landed, knees bent, on thin turf.

Go! He had three-eighths of a mile to cover, downslope on uncertain terrain, barefooted in the dark. He jogged, twisting his path around every darker shadow that could be a hidden rock or an overgrown hole. The only sounds were his breath and the wind. He was alone with the thickly veiled moon. In three minutes he would make it to the fence.

Pale whiteness suddenly lit the grass around him and threw his shadow downslope. From the distance came Van Wijk's voice, smug and out of breath and fighting hoarseness. "I told you he was trying to escape!"

Clay looked over his shoulder. The blogger stood in the parking lot outside the office building, next to a guard holding a bright blue-white flashlight. A second guard sat in a golf cart and the standing guard climbed next to him. The flashlight beam bobbed and returned Clay to darkness.

He sprinted toward the fence, angling down the slope and heedless of hidden obstacles. His breath came fast and harsh and his heartbeat filled his ears. He glanced back and the cart had closed to about two hundred yards. The fence stood another three hundred yards in front. He wouldn't reach it in time.

The stream bisecting the property burbled to his right. They couldn't take a golf cart across it. Clay turned and sprinted for it. The water was low but rocks lay jumbled over the stream bed and jutted above the water's surface. He slowed, the water chilling his feet and the rocks slimy on his bare soles. The cart clacked and its electric motor hummed. The guards' feet pounded after him.

Clay reached the far side and turned to the fence. The guards splashed across the stream, grunting and cursing. Clay ran, his lungs fiery and his legs aching. He could make out the fence posts—

Hands closed around his ankle. He slipped the tackle but stumbled, and then the other guard wrapped him in his arms and drove him into the ground. Clay squirmed and wriggled his arm free. He swung his elbow and struck the guard's face hard enough to make him loosen his grip. He felt an itch in his right ear, was the stranger coming or leaving him?

Clay writhed further, but a large bulky shape loomed over him. Pain bloomed in his cheek and his head snapped back. He grunted despite himself.

"That's right," LeRoi said. "I think you need some negative reinforcement." His fist caught Clay over the left eye. His head sagged and spots filled his vision like gray static until he saw nothing more.

8

Clay woke with a headache and squinted against cloudy morning light. His left eye was half-shut and he lifted his hand to touch it. A cuff around his wrist stopped him. He tried his other arm and both legs, first gently, then thrashing. Cuffs restrained all his limbs.

"Nice try," Boucher said. His face was impassive but anger lurked under his tone. "No one's gotten that far. How did you blow the electrical system so thoroughly?"

To stall the doctor, Clay looked around the room. He lay on an examination table: a paper sheet rippled between him and padded black vinyl when he shifted his body. The cuffs were blue plastic and more blue, a glistening gel, covered his feet. Liquid bandage and anesthetic. He'd seen the like once, holding Martin while Jenny smeared the goop over the boy's scraped knee. Boucher's staff had stripped him and redressed him in a too-short hospital gown. He shifted his weight again and insulated wires touched his torso, suggesting sensors attached to his chest and belly.

The examination room smelled of disinfectant and seemed crowded, with Boucher, the blonde orderly, and one of the guards nearby. The orderly worried her lip with her teeth, but the guard stood as impassively as ever, arms folded, a tattoo half-hidden on his forearm. The picture window didn't help the room feel larger; it gave a view down into the valley to the site of Clay's recapture. *God damn*

Van Wijk. I'll pound that bastard's head into the floor.

"Glass, opaque," Boucher said, and the view turned dark gray. "You haven't answered me."

"The question again?"

"Playing dumb will only make it worse. How did you blow the electrical system?"

He felt a stupid urge to gloat, *wasn't me, it was the vast hidden conspiracy out to rescue me.* He resisted; if they hadn't found the formix nest he wouldn't lead them to it. "I didn't."

"You happened to wake up, guess the electricity had failed, and then run for the fence? Do I look stupid?"

"Only a little. I hadn't been able to sleep. Being awake it was obvious when the electricity failed, you can normally hear the air in the vents. I planned what I'd do in a power outage shortly after I got here, so I did it."

Boucher bent closer until his face loomed in Clay's sight. "You planned to hop the fence, walk a thousand miles, and swim to Cuba?"

"No. Mexico."

Boucher narrowed his eyes. "Don't get cocky. You could be of great value to society, were you cured, but if your psychoses are intractable we'll cut our losses. You're a hair's breadth from being returned to South Dakota."

"My psychosis is more intractable than Delacroix's?"

"Delacroix has a large amount of social capital among a sizable demographic that potentially could be tipped to full loyalty to our nation. For practical purposes he's irreplaceable. All you have are good tinkering skills. Dozens of scientists and engineers would work well enough in your place."

Good tinkering skills? Clay fumed at the insult, but doubts stirred in his subconscious mind. He had little social capital; not enough to guide his wife back to loving him, not enough to avoid betrayal at another's hand. He wanted to sink deeper into the examination table as Boucher stared at him. When the doctor turned away Clay felt relief, like walking into air conditioning on a summer day.

Boucher nodded to the orderly and the guard. She stepped to the left of Clay's face and the guard went to a table along the interior wall of the room. He pulled on a pair of stiff black gloves and his forearm tattoo became fully visible, the words *Caucasian Forces America* surrounding a Maltese cross ringed by a double helix. He came closer, held his hands up, flexed his fingers. The gloves creaked and light from the ceiling fluorescents reflected in their facets.

"You have forced us to try stronger medicine," Boucher said from near Clay's feet. The blonde orderly lifted her hand. Between her thumb and forefinger she held a tablet, flag blue and as long as the last two bones of her little finger. Clay swallowed and pressed his jaws together.

The guard reached for Clay's mouth. The facets of the gloves pressed solidly against his skin and the guard levered his lower jaw open. Clay tried to bite but the guard's hands were too strong and the gloves felt hard as a spoon against his teeth. He thrashed his head but the guard pushed his head back into the table cushion. Clay grunted and pressed his tongue against his palate. The guard reached a finger to his tongue and pried it away. Clay fought the urge to gag.

The orderly shoved the blue tablet between his tongue and his palate and jumped back. The guard held his hand over Clay's mouth.

"You can swallow it or you can choke," Boucher said. "Your choice."

Clay swallowed it, grimacing. The tablet felt dry and thick. Something scratched him on his calf, just above the ankle cuff. The tablet bulked in his esophagus and he grimaced more.

"Give him some water," Boucher told the orderly. Clay opened his mouth for a jet from a squeeze bottle. The tablet descended further. "Give him more if he wants. Leave him here until the electrogastroenterogram shows he's moved his stomach contents to his intestine. If he vomits, do it again."

"Yes, doctor." The orderly sounded as wrung out as a dishrag. The guard simply nodded.

"You'll return you to your normal schedule after that," Boucher said to Clay. "But remember, you're a hair's breadth from being returned to South Dakota."

* * *

From his plush linen couch, Nil frowned at the home theater display. R-tex' smashed chassis lay grayed-out behind the words *Reloading*. He knew how to solve the level: send E-mac through the narrow passage to the control room to open all the gates while C-orb stacked crates to block the main path of the guardbots, buying time for R-tex to find and kill the boss. But some ill-glimpsed part of himself between his conscious mind and his hands on the controller kept steering his machines into suppressor beams and roving crushers. Return to the start of the level and try again—

"Sir," Latour, his household software, said, "there's a Jennifer Sung Schieffer to see you."

He tossed the controller onto the leather-topped coffee table, next to an empty plate streaked with ketchup and a half-drunk glass of beer. Contingencies swirled in his mind. "Is anyone with her?"

"She's alone."

The seeds he'd sown in her mind had germinated. Nil told the game to pause and the coffee table to open its drawer. He pulled out a breath spray, spritzed his mouth, then stood. "When I get to the foyer, show her in."

The front doors opened as he took his first step onto the foyer's chessboard marble floor. Jenny wore a yellow, floral print sundress. She hesitated in the doorway, and the flickering lantern light on the front porch glossed her black hair and danced on her bare shoulders. "Come on in."

She entered just far enough for the door to close behind her, then glanced around. Through the transom window, the lanterns gleamed high on the double-height walls. To left and right, the study and the dining room looked like a photo shoot from a design blog, clean and precise from disuse. She slipped out of her mules and nudged them into the corner with her bare toes.

"Where's Martin?"

"In bed. I hired a sitting service. I needed to get out of the house." She then looked away as if she'd said too much.

"Thanks for coming by. Care for a drink?" Nil returned to the great room without asking her to follow. He stopped in front of the couch, the room filled with the glow of recessed lighting and the grayed-out display, and turned to her, intensifying his gaze. She stood between two pillars at the cusp of the room and her eyes widened for a moment.

"A drink?" she said, and her face showed caution battling impulsiveness and winning. "Ice water."

"Right away, ma'am," Latour said.

Nil had heard fly fishermen talk about letting the trout run with the hook for a time before reeling it in. He waved at the living room. "Have a seat."

Jenny joined him on the couch and a robot rolled in from the kitchen. It handed her a tumbler of water. Ice cubes buoyed a lemon wedge. She sipped and studied the display. "You're a gamer."

He shrugged. "It's a harmless vice, why not indulge it from time to time?"

She sipped again, then held the glass for a time before she took a long swallow and firmly set it down. "Nil, no more games."

"Sure." He looked up and kept his face as guileless as he could. "Display off—"

Jenny laughed, cutting but not cruel. "I'm not a nineteen-year-old girl. I know the kind of man you are."

He admired her frankness; so much better than college girls whose brave façades masked childish fears and longings. "Yes, you do."

"Then why me? Even with antiagathics I'm not as young as I once was—"

Nil rested his fingertips on her shoulder. "Youth is overrated."

"They don't know what they're doing and just lie there?"

"They're flighty and foolish." His fingertips stayed in contact with her skin. "You're neither."

"I'm a bad mother."

He didn't want to think about Martin. "You do an incredible amount for him."

"I keep worrying I did something wrong. Other than tempt fate by going to the genetic engineering clinic. Did I have a drink I shouldn't have, or...?"

"No. It's normal to wonder, but you didn't do anything wrong."

She peered sidelong at him. "But Clay did?"

The house hung dark and silent around the bubble of light cast by the lamp on the end table. "Clay had every good thing a man could want. He threw it all away."

She reached for his hand. Her skin ran smoothly over his knuckles but then she pulled her hand away. "What would we tell him?"

Nil took a deep breath to keep his heartbeat calm. He gazed into her eyes. "We can figure it out in the morning."

Silence filled the room for a moment, but then she took his hand in both of hers and stood, pulling him up. He rose from the couch and she led him out of the great room only to hesitate on entering the hallway crossing the house. To remove the need for words, he squeezed her hands and moved his to the right.

In his bedroom, the gray light of downtown seeped in through the windows in the sitting area and spilled over the comforter and pillows. Colored lights burned on the roof-edges of skyscrapers. Jenny turned and he closed his hands around her upper arms and kissed her deeply. Then he guided her to the bed.

After, their legs brushing amid tangled sheets, Nil stretched on his back, half-awake and content, while Jenny lay curled up next to him, his arm around her and her cheek resting against his ribs, over his heart. His pituitary gland secreted more oxytocin than the MuSynths sold to Everton's campaign ever had. It had been good. Not simply the sex, though she had known what she was doing and hadn't just lain there; but also she had scratched emotional itches so deep and so ancient in the depths of his mind he had forgotten he had them.

Pheromone perfume? Probably, but every other woman who'd reached his bed in the past decade had worn it. That hadn't made the difference. He couldn't recall the last time he'd had such a moving first encounter with one of his lovers. He wondered why, idly with the lassitude of afterglow, while her fingers spun his sweat-damp chest hair. From time to time a smooth firm metallic object slid over his skin.

Her fingers stopped and he felt the muscles of her face firing into a pensive expression. She needed to leave, Nil guessed, and he set his subconscious to find how best to convince her he truly wanted to see her again.

"Tell me something," she said.

He ran his fingertips over her left forearm. "Of course."

Jenny stirred then, rolling onto her stomach and rising onto her elbows. Her hair had come loose and hung lightly past her now-serious eyes.

"Did you call the feds on Clay?"

After a few blinks Nil turned to face her and propped his head on his forearm. He had a choice of tactics, the truth or a lie, and his intuitions prompted him with one. "Yes."

She gasped, but of course she would, regardless of her deep self. "Why?"

"He came to me mired in paranoia and conspiracies and threatening to do something rash with our technology. NCS would have caught him before he did, but they would have packed the rest of us off to South Dakota along with him." Nil spoke with as much nonchalance as he could muster and left off with an unfinished tone.

She inhaled, thinly but long in duration. "And."

He met her gaze. "I think you know."

"For me."

Nil's cheeks lifted. "For you."

Her eyes widened. She drew up onto her knees, thighs together, and her hands covered her lap. "You informed on him to get to me?"

Nil raised his arm toward her. "To free you. Aren't you worth it?"

She scampered off the far side of the bed and hunted for her clothes with quick glances to the floor. She needn't be so wary of him; he would let her leave; she would be back. Jenny found her panties, stepped into them, raised them with quick shivers of elastic. "How could you do that?"

"To see how lovely you are, and how little you received of the love you deserved...." *Don't panic. She'll work through this. And pretend you had no choice.* "...what else could I do?"

"Something other than stab your best friend—my husband—in the back!" She lifted her dress and he caught a last glimpse of her small pert breasts before the yellow cotton fell over them.

Nil returned his gaze to her face and shook his head as cynically as he could. "You no longer loved him."

She stiffened, and her voice came thinly. "You think that means I love you?"

9

Saturday afternoon a cool, dry wind swept over the concrete plaza outside the Titan Industries tower. Haycock climbed out of the cab and trudged to the lobby doors. With luck Fisher had called him and Ramirez here out of an excess of caution, and not because something critical had popped up; but if Haycock could describe his luck in one word it would be *bad*.

Shoes slapped the concrete and a dark motion caught Haycock's gaze. Ramirez in his blue suit and tie stepped away from a shadowed concrete bench into the full sunlight. They shook hands and Haycock studied the other's face for some sign of gratitude.

"How's the new assignment?" Haycock asked.

"It was about time we got the Army on our side. Tactically they add a lot."

"I'm glad it's working. A lot of us pulled strings to make it happen." And Ramirez, his subordinate on the org chart, had made it work to his advantage.

"We sure did. Let's go in."

Boxy concrete planters held soil for saplings slouching on stakes and formed a gapped barricade between the plaza and the skyscraper's lobby. Magnets sealed the glass doors and Ramirez rapped his knuckles until someone moved at the guard station deep within. The guard was a paunchy, gray-haired white man whose face was blotched by gin blossoms. A few paces from the door recognition lit his face.

The guard pressed a button on a stand jutting out of the floor. "Mr. Ramirez, what brings you back here?"

"Good to see you, Stevie. We're here to see the boss."

The guard peered at Haycock. "You are?"

"Bill Haycock, NCS."

"You work for Mr. Ramirez?"

"With him."

The guard returned his attention to Ramirez. "Mr. Warren's not in today."

"The boss boss. Mr. Fisher."

Stevie waved them in. The soles of dress shoes clacked and the guard's rubber soles squeaked. In the weekend emptiness, the sounds echoed off gypsumboard walls. "He's in his office. You know the way?"

Ramirez nodded. They approached the guard station and Stevie reached for a clipboard with a sign-in sheet. "Let's skip that," Ramirez said. "You know who we are."

"Mr. Ramirez, you know the procedure—"

"I certainly do." He smiled and strode to the elevator bank. Haycock followed and didn't look back at the guard. He'd know his place.

Unlike.... He gazed from under his eyebrows at the back of Ramirez' head. The other would be in that security guard's plastic shoes right now if Haycock, head of NCS' St. Louis bureau on 6:19, hadn't told Fisher about a disgraced former agent looking for work. The elevator climbed and the pressure change jabbed Haycock's ears.

The doors dinged. The real estate up here was too prime for cubicles; gray light trickled through the blinds and slumped out of the doorways of spacious, windowed offices. Ramirez led the way to Fisher's corner office. The door was ajar and something inside ticked rapidly.

Fisher stood at the window, looking at suburban Illinois. He drummed at the sill with a pen. Ramirez coughed and knocked on the door while Haycock looked at the carpet.

The ticking stopped. Fisher turned, then lifted his left wrist and studied the watch face of his wearable. "I thought you'd be here by one."

"I was in the field," Ramirez said.

Fisher wanted to vent, Haycock sensed, and he saw little harm in being slightly servile in response. "Flights out of New Washington are tough to find at the last minute. But now that we're here we're glad to do whatever you need."

"Come in. Door, close. Security, full on." The NCS agents went in and the door swung shut. From the chairs facing Fisher's desk Haycock saw purple bags under the CEO's eyes and a muscle twitching in his cheek. Behind the desk, Fisher waved at the chairs and dropped into his own. He leaned forward and rested his forearms on the desktop.

"The Free Samples Project has lost containment."

The words sank in. Ramirez spoke. "We expected rumors to eventually spread. The preemptive counter-rumor strategy—"

"Not rumors, Ivar. Evidence. Spec sheets, controller code, and lists of target consumers have been copied out of Titan's servers. We can't have that posted on a server out of the Far East."

Haycock let out a heavy breath. "Goddam crackers. They'll need a while to figure out what they've got which gives us some time—"

"It's not crackers. And he's had a while. This happened several days ago."

Ramirez pulled a smartpaper and stylus from inside his suit jacket. "One man? What's his name?"

"Clay Schieffer."

Ramirez started writing but Haycock raised his hand to stop him and smiled. "It's okay. We already got him."

"You've arrested him," Fisher said.

"Yeah. Over a week now."

Fisher pressed his lips together. "Well?"

Haycock's eyes briefly narrowed. "I received a tip that indicated Schieffer was presumptively disloyal. With his skills in molecular-scale chemical fabrication, I decided he merited immediate protective confinement."

"It's been over a week and you didn't tell me?" Fisher's face reddened. "Christ damn it. Presumptively disloyal? He told someone about the Free Samples Project?"

Haycock's eyes narrowed again. However rich Fisher was, however deeply he'd wormed into Everton's ear, he had no place to second-guess a government employee doing his duty, regardless of how much cash he slipped the two NCS men under the table. "A tip indicated he was presumptively disloyal."

Fisher took deep breaths and put on a look of exoneration. "You can still fix this. Where is Schieffer? Gitmo North?"

"Let me check." Haycock unrolled his smartpaper display and scratched at it with a cheap plastic pen. Schieffer's file showed him logged on admission to the South Dakota facility. "Good guess."

"He needs to die."

Haycock nodded. "I'll call the warden—"

"No. I don't want anyone outside the Project's need-to-know perimeter asking questions when Schieffer breaks his neck falling from the top of a cell block. You go, you pull as many strings as you need to, and you take care of it yourself. Are we on the same page?"

The urge to argue nudged Haycock, but Fisher had too much power to fight impulsively. He could survive another day of travel. Maybe he'd have time to hit a hotel bar near the airport and buy cosmos for facelifted blondes. "We are."

Fisher turned to Ramirez without a further glance at Haycock. *I'm not a lapdog or a mercenary.* Fisher said, "There's someone else who was involved in Schieffer's plan. Monica Colbert. She acquired my, a private key that allowed Schieffer to spoof authentication to access the servers."

"She knows about the Project?" Ramirez asked.

"I have no idea but I don't fucking care to take that risk. Do you?"

"We can scan her," Haycock said, "with the new portable device."

Fisher stared at him and his voice came low and slow. "I already know she betrayed me."

Ramirez mirrored the CEO's tone. "I'll take care of it. Who else?"

"Schieffer's wife?" Haycock called up a photo of her through his wearable. No matter how beautiful, no woman received a free pass from the machinery of justice; and despite antiagathics and free radical scavengers Schieffer's wife was a decade beyond the question of having enough beauty being on the table.

"I don't know what she knows. Too much extreme action can backfire." Fisher nodded at Haycock. "Here's a use for the new portable scanner."

"I'm heading to Houston already," Ramirez said. "I'll interview her."

Fisher's eyes widened and pointed his index finger like a conductor making a stroke with his baton. "Great idea, Ivar."

Haycock shifted in his seat and sat taller. Fisher had wealth and influence and could shift people around NCS headquarters like a prepubescent girl playing *Virtual Dollhouse*.

To Ramirez, Fisher added, "Anyone else who we are certain knows?"

The other agent shook his head and Haycock filled the gap, his voice thin and higher than usual. "I've got one." It meant burning a tip, but there would come others. He snorted out a breath. "Anal Thomas."

The CEO frowned and checked a display on his desktop. "He's been a pleasant surprise since I bought TS Microcatalytix. He could almost make the jump to Titan. And he's a platinum. How do you know? He was your tip?"

"I am certain he knows Schieffer dug out the data. No telling if he has a copy."

Fisher's gaze flicked over the display while he stroked his chin. A smirk crossed his face. "I see his membership's paid up through the end of next year. Ivar?"

"I'll add him to my list of Houston action items."

The CEO nodded and tapped the display. "Do either of you have anything for me? Good." He fiddled a key in a drawer's keyhole in his desk and slid it open. The hardware made a smooth steel hiss. Fisher pulled out two thickly-packed white envelopes and tossed one to each of them. "Till next time." He shut and locked the drawer without a second look.

At the first few payments, Haycock had thought of Judas and his thirty pieces of silver. He thought of it again for the first time in a long while.

*   *   *

A team of miniscule hominid robots split into platoons and marched over the breakfast table, veering stiffly around a blue-rimmed plate sticky with leftover pancakes and syrup. Not remotely formix, Jenny thought, and sipped her coffee. Too specialized. To her right, Martin turned his head from one platoon to another as they formed lines, one of three and one of five; meanwhile the operation symbol, a toy car with sandwich boards front and back, rolled into place between the two platoons and flashed a plus sign. The robots started counting off in bright, tinny voices. "One!" "Two!"

"Ms. Schieffer," the house's computer said in her earbud, "you have a guest."

Why the hell couldn't he leave her alone? "Mr. Thomas isn't welcome. You know that and he does too." Multiple times she'd told him. Did he think she had bluffed about cracking the combination on Clay's pistol safe?

"It's not Mr. Thomas. Rather, it's a Mr. Ramirez."

She set down her coffee. "I don't know a Ramirez."

"Three!" said the tiny robots. "Five!" "Three plus five!"

"He tells me it's urgent."

A video display hung above the wainscoting on the wall to her left between two still-life paintings. She pointed at the display. "Show him."

Ramirez wore a gray suit and matching tie against a white shirt. Two men in similar attire stood just off the front landing and more men waited at the street, in and around two generic American cars the color of cheap sparkling wine.

"Who are they?" *Who wore ties in this day and age?*

"Law enforcement personnel."

Jenny slumped and felt sick to her stomach. They'd come for Clay, where they now coming for her? Had he said something to make them think she was an enemy combatant?

Did he think she had denounced him, and was this his revenge?

"Eight!" said the robots, and they extended their arms to Martin like a chorus line at the end of a song-and-dance routine.

She could have the house tell them she wasn't here, and then sneak out the back with Martin... where one of their agents would be posted in the alley.

What did she have to fear? Clay had been arrested on false pretenses. She would tell Ramirez what happened and once the truth sunk in he'd be released.

"Stay here," she said to Martin. "I'll be back soon."

The boy frowned but then the robots started moving again and he returned his attention to them while Jenny went to the foyer and raised her shoulders. "Open."

The cast of characters hadn't changed, but she could see a wider angle, from the side fence of her yard to a workman's truck parked several houses down the street. Ramirez glanced, in a smooth, economical motion, to one of the men behind him. The other pulled a pair of sunglasses from an inner pocket of his bulky jacket and put them on. Ramirez turned back to her and she realized the sharpness of his features: eyebrows like narrow brushstrokes, cheekbones like a gemstone's facets. He looked both more handsome and more cruel than he had in the video display. "Ms. Schieffer? I am Ivar Ramirez, NCS."

"Is this about my husband?"

"We have a warrant from the security court to search the premises." He slipped a trifolded sheaf of blue-backed smartpaper from within his jacket and handed it to her.

She yanked it from Ramirez but didn't look at it. "I don't object. You'll find nothing. He's innocent. You can let him go."

Ramirez stepped across the threshold and without thinking she backed away. Agents hustled up the sidewalk and into the house. The one in sunglasses followed Ramirez in and waited behind the lead agent's shoulder.

"What makes you think we are holding Mr. Schieffer?"

"Because I know why he's missing. His business partner, Nil Thomas, called you to arrest Clay, to get him out of the way."

Ramirez raised an eyebrow. "Why would Mr. Thomas do such a thing?"

Her cheeks felt warm. She glanced away and her voice fell. "Professional jealousy."

"Professional jealousy."

His tone made her flinch. "It's all true! Take me to your headquarters and run me through an fMRI. You'll see I'm telling the truth!"

From far behind her, one of the agents swore and Martin bawled. "Maaa-meee!"

Jenny stalked away from Ramirez. "What have you done to my son?"

Martin kept crying even after she crouched next to him and wrapped her arms around him. On the tabletop, six robots clawed at the air like upended beetles. The agent, a white man with a fleshy, pink face, rubbed the back of his head and scowled. "I was checking under the table when one of those little robots jumped into my collar." His hand descended to scratch at the back of his neck.

"Jumped?" Jenny said. "It fell."

Ramirez stood at the passageway to the kitchen and drummed his fingers on the counter. "What's that, Lundquist? You were attacked by an autonomous mechanical device?"

Agent Lundquist took a moment, but then he smiled like a schoolyard bully at Jenny. "Yeah. An autonomous mechanical device."

"It's a toy robot. It fell!"

Ramirez glanced over his shoulder at the agent in sunglasses. "Are those toy robots?"

"None I've ever seen, sir." He stared at Jenny as he spoke.

From the table, Ramirez took one of the robots and waved it at the wearable on his wrist. He cocked his head and listened to some audio through his earbuds, then threw the robot back on the table.

Jenny felt a nodule of fear in her gut. She held Martin more tightly and his crying subsided.

Ramirez glanced at the plate on the table. "The pancakes smell good. You made more than you needed?" A noise crashed on the floor above. Ramirez glanced up. "I think we'll be a while. I haven't had breakfast. Mind if I sit?"

He went ahead before she could speak, picked up a spare fork, and speared a pancake. "Lundquist, get the kitchen to warm up some syrup."

Lundquist grunted and went into the next room. Jenny stroked Martin's hair. The agent in sunglasses kept staring at her.

Nil slouched across the bench seat of the old pickup truck when the cars rolled past slowly enough for him to read their federal license plates. He pulled the ballcap, blazoned with the logo of the Mexican soccer club América, lower over his eyes.

It hadn't been the pheromones in Jenny's perfume. It had been her. Unlike a college girl intimidated by his status, unlike a golddigger casting a gimlet eye on his wealth, unlike a *desi* woman whose parents echoed the ticking of her biological clock, she was assured and confident and comfortable in her skin. He shook his head. The words crossing his mind didn't capture what stirred deep within him.

Small wonder his previous attempts to speak to her since their night together had failed. If he couldn't articulate what he felt to himself, how much poorer his chances of telling her. She had slammed her door and told her concierge to ignore his calls. He refused to let that be the final word. Even though he had felt foolish, walking onto a used car lot on Harrisburg near the Ship Channel amid the rustle of plastic pennants and Latin American flags, frowned at by the Hispanic proprietor for apparently being a Honduran in need of a cheap truck who spoke no Spanish, dressed too well, and paid cash without haggling, it was necessary. Even though he'd been sitting near her house for an hour, hoping she would run an errand or take Martin to the small city park a few blocks away, he would continue to wait for another chance to explain himself.

Even though the feds parked in front of her house and walked to her front door.

Leaning against the pickup's right-hand door pillar, he pushed himself a little higher. From under the brim of his hat he could see the ground floor of her house under the canopies of the front-yard oaks. Three feds lingered near the door. Would she think he had pulled strings to do this? That he sought revenge against her, or he displayed the agents like a peacock's tail to show his prowess?

Why were they here?

They would interrogate people close to an 'enemy combatant.' Find out what they knew—

He jolted further upright. She knew nothing. Would they believe that?

The door opened and Jenny stood in the doorway, strong and proud. She pulled the warrant from the lead agent's hand and, unbowed, let them in.

What had he brought upon her?

What had he brought upon himself? If they were interrogating Clay's family and colleagues, they would come to him. Despite Nil's indirection in the phone call with Haycock, the assistant director already knew he knew the secret of Everton's election.

He relaxed, aided by the humid air of the pickup cabin. He was a platinum member. He'd proven his loyalty to AU with his checkbook. That would keep him safe.

Wouldn't it?

After a time, the feds emerged and went to their cars. Jenny was not with them. They hadn't arrested her. Had they done something worse? She appeared at the doorway and relief filled him, but it soon gave way to worry; Jenny watched the feds with a guarded, sullen look, and Martin clung to her leg and hid his face against her thigh. She was safe, for now, but the look given her by the lead agent made him wonder how long she, or anyone, would stay safe.

The lead agent climbed into the middle car in the line and running lights bloomed on all three. "Engine start," Nil said. "Follow those cars."

The engine hummed, but the autopilot, an aftermarket unit mounted where the steering wheel had been, said through its front-panel speaker, "Instructions not understood."

Too imprecise. "Follow the second car currently parked across the street and two houses ahead."

"Instructions not understood."

Nil squinted and quoted the license plate of the rearmost fed car. The line of cars slipped away from the curb.

"Instructions not understood."

Dammit. Hopefully the autopilot would let him navigate on the fly. "Head west." The truck lurched into gear and the draped bundle of kinked wires festooned with orange wirenuts connecting the autopilot to the engine swung with the motion. "Turn right." Ahead, the freeway sliced over the street. The feds turned northeast, toward downtown, and he followed.

It would be a convoluted path to Nil's house, in a gentrified neighborhood west of downtown, but a poorly-trained autocar might take it. The feds turned south onto 288, and he nodded. "To the office," he said, and the autopilot was smart enough to get the location from his concierge without asking him. He rode past warehouses and horse farms, retro-urbanist planned communities and a Buddhist megatemple. What would the feds find at the office? Had Clay stashed a copy of the data he'd stolen?

Nil followed his thoughts so closely that he almost missed the feds exiting for Pearland, four miles before the office. Why here? Unless construction or a multicar accident blocked the freeway ahead, no autocar would take this route to TS Microcatalytix.

The feds traveled deeper into the suburb, past golf courses and a myfab and a Youniverse store facing each other across a busy street. They weren't going to the office. Nil frowned and scratched instructions to his wearable on his display. *Who has an address near here?*

The answer came quickly. *Monica Colbert, Broadway and Main Condominiums, Pearland, Texas.*

Monica? She'd been acting erratically lately, but what involvement could she have? Regardless, Fisher's cloak would shield her from investigation. Unless her erratic behavior came because she knew Fisher's protection had been withdrawn.

How had Clay gotten into Titan's secure servers, anyway?

The feds turned right behind Monica's condominium complex. Nil went straight and glanced down the side street. Between the complex' back fence and brick-and-cinderblock warehouses on the other side, brakelights bloomed on the feds' sedans and chameleon camouflage rippled with the colors of concrete and brick over a line of trucks and humvees.

*   *   *

Roger strode through the condo complex with Hardin and one of his platoon commanders, Lieutenant Wilson. Their boots clunked on the concrete walkway and their uniforms shifted coloration to match gray siding and mottled tree trunks. Humid air made the subvocal microphones pasted onto their throats itch.

Wilson was the greenest of his lieutenants, less than two years out of ROTC, but he worked hard. His platoon had taken the lead in the operation and performed flawlessly. Months of training in the ghost town on Fort Riley's back forty had paid off. The enemy combatant's condo had been secured and the e.c. Taken prisoner.

They passed between two buildings and came to a parking lot in the middle of the complex. Morning sunlight glinted on the aluminum roofs covering the parking spaces. The feds' sedans and a matching van with tinted windows stood in the driveway, blocking parked cars. On the far side of the lot stood the e.c.'s building. The condo furthest on the right. Roger led his men between the feds' cars and under the awning over some parking spaces.

One of the NCS agents—Lundquist, if Roger remembered his name—stood at the front door of the condo second from the right, flanked by two of his subordinates. A young couple, some combination of Latin and South Asian, clad in college tees and pajama bottoms, stood bugeyed at their threshold.

"There's nothing to see," Lundquist said. His voice sounded pinched and nasal from his nostril filters. "This is a routine law enforcement activity." He nodded slightly and the agents lifted aerosol blowers. The pistol-shaped objects sneezed a mist into the couple's faces. Their eyes drooped and the woman leaned groggily against her mate. "A routine law enforcement activity," the agent repeated. The couple stumbled back into their condo and the door shut them in.

Roger halted. "I didn't see memory disrupters in the RoEs."

Lundquist stepped between the two robots and scowled at him. "Captain, what are you doing in uniform?"

Don't change the subject on me. "My job."

"You're supposed to wear civvies—"

"If Ramirez requested."

Lundquist grunted, then gestured toward the e.c.'s condo. "He's upstairs."

"I asked you about—" Roger began, but the agents turned their backs and walked away.

Hardin spat and Wilson sniffed out a breath while Roger fumed. The feds wouldn't capture dangerous prisoners without the unit's help. They would boost morale by remembering that.

The condo's front door stood cramped between a stairwell and a small, doorless closet hung with coats and jackets. A pair of small pink running shoes slouched on the closet floor. Offset in front of him was a bathroom, its door open, stray cat litter tracked across its vinyl floor.

"We nabbed ourselves a rugmuncher?" Hardin said.

"Green and animal-rights terror factions have sizable female memberships," Wilson said.

"For lesbian terrorists it's a hundred percent."

The lieutenant laughed. "They still have to raid the sperm bank."

"Wilson, I read the same report you did," Roger said. "I think you're right." A prickly thought eased in the back of his mind and he started up the stairs. Photos and video of a family in the desert Southwest and college girls bundled up on the frozen shore of Lake Michigan played in small frames along the stairwell walls. Terrorists recruited from the upper classes, didn't they? Status didn't give an e.c. immunity.

Two of Wilson's crawlers guarded the top of the stairs but swung their muzzles wide when their software identified Roger and the other men as blue team. The stairs landed at a den. More crawlers milled around like dogs circling the feet of their masters. Ramirez looked up and raised his eyebrows slightly. "Captain, I wasn't expecting other members of your team," he said, and Roger's mouth suddenly felt dry. The lead agent swept his gaze to Hardin and Wilson and smiled. "Won't hurt for them to see this."

The prisoner slouched in a swivel chair of red plastic webbing. From the smoothness of her skin she looked under thirty. She wore faded gray sweats and had turquoise polish on her toenails. Her blonde hair hung limply and her fingers brushed the chair's casters. Roger barely recognized her from the displays on the stairwell walls; the skeletal-muscle relaxer took all the tone from her face, save for faint twitches around her mouth and eyes.

Behind her a coffee mug squatted on a desk, next to a display showing a half-composed letter. Wilson leaned past the prisoner. "'I hereby resign from Titan Indus—"

"Immaterial," Ramirez said, his tone firm.

Wilson looked back at his captain and raised an eyebrow.

A Titan Industries employee was an enemy combatant? A high-ranking employee, if she resigned in writing. Roger's body rocked from his heart beating. "Keep reading."

Ramirez' tone sounded even more firm. "You are ordered to stop." Wilson's eyes showed white and he jerked his gaze between the agent and his commander.

Roger cringed inside, but Ramirez' tone was too strong. "Stop," he told Wilson. His lieutenant stepped away from the display. His hands shook until he clasped them behind his back. The prisoner's gaze moved slightly toward Roger but then sagged back and lost focus.

Ramirez turned to one of his subordinates. "Got a clean one?" The other agent nodded and pulled rubber gloves from his pocket. He snapped them on and rolled them up his arms, over his wearable and the cuffs of his shirt and jacket. He reached into his jacket for another item in a crinkling plastic bag. From the bag, the agent in rubber gloves pulled a small revolver.

Wilson's voice, picked up by his subvocals, crackled in Roger's earbuds over a private channel. "What is he doing?"

"Sir," Hardin said with the disguised world-weariness of a senior NCO who knew circumspection, "it's an old trick."

Wilson was too green. "Trick?"

Roger glanced sidelong at Ramirez. He was the kind of sick bastard who would do this stunt. *Fake execution*, Roger said through his subvokes. *Sidearm loaded with blanks.*

Wilson breathed hard. "Isn't that torture?"

"Not if your man is in the White House," Hardin said.

Ramirez spoke in the flesh. "I've seen plenty of enemy combatants who'd rather die than be captured," Ramirez said. "I'm sure you have too, Captain Sung."

The lead agent nodded, and the one in rubber gloves holding the revolver approached the prisoner. Her eyes briefly widened and her head twitched.

"What are you talking about? Ah, you're trying to sell this show."

"Sell? Show?" Ramirez sounded like this charade was being played at face value.

This man was above him on the chain of command. The weight of that thought burdened Roger's shoulders, but he forced himself to act despite it. "A pistol with blanks, a fake execution, we've seen it done."

Ramirez glowered. "My after action report will write this up as a suicide. Yours will do the same." The rubber-gloved agent wrapped the prisoner's right hand around the revolver's butt and aimed it at her trembling eye.

Suicide? He said that to frighten the prisoner, but a blank could destroy an eye at close range. This was wrong. Behind him, Hardin and Wilson stirred and shuffled closer to their captain.

Ramirez glanced at the other agents, then peered at Roger and his men. Wilson hyperventilated and Roger's toes curled in impotent anxiety. "I know what the six of us found in this room today," Ramirez said.

A gunshot rang out and the prisoner slumped, half her face a pulp of tissue. Blood smeared the display and dripped to the chairmat. The room stank of blood and propellant. Hardin stood frozen. Only Wilson's gasping breaths and the plink of blood onto the plastic chairmat sounded.

Sweet Christ it wasn't a blank.

Roger's hands trembled and his gaze lit over the dead woman, needing but not wanting to see. Enough. His hand slid up to his holstered pistol as he looked at Ramirez, visualizing target rings over his chest. But the agent's stern face caught Roger's attention and stayed his trembling hand. Ramirez' right hand pulled back his jacket and lingered over his holster. His voice was barely audible over the shot echoing in Roger's ears.

"Either you found the prisoner already dead when you entered this room," said Ramirez, "or you won't leave it."

10

The cheerful yellow light of morning slanted through the windows of battalion headquarters and made Roger feel exposed, as if the sunbeams scanned his soul. A cleaning robot licked the floor with its flat roller and Roger's boots squeaked through a film of drying solvent as he paced down the hallway. Civilian employees and HQ personnel greeted him, their faces open and pleasant, but he knew they saw something foul in him and shared cagey glances behind his back.

Mueller's batman sat at a desk outside the battalion commander's office. The door stood quarter-open and a thin slice of sunlight glowed low on its face. The batman looked up when Roger approached and waved his hand at his computer display. "Captain, may I help you?"

"I need to speak to the lieutenant colonel."

The batman frowned but took a closer look at Roger's face. "Right away, sir." He hustled out of his chair and rapped on Mueller's door. "Sir, Captain Sung wishes to speak with you. Yes, sir." He pushed the door wider and waited for the captain to enter.

Inside, door shut, Roger said, "Good morning, sir."

Mueller sat behind a desk stacked with smartpaper bundles and old dumbpaper files in manila folders. He set one folder down and looked up over the reading glasses perched near the end of his nose. "You look like hell."

Roger started and blinked his dry eyes. He hadn't slept well for several nights but at least he'd shaved that morning. "My apologies."

"I didn't it mean it like that." He nodded to a chair in front of the desk and said, "Sit." Roger did. "Whatever you came to talk about is serious, isn't it? Trouble here? Trouble at home? Don't hesitate, I need my men on an even keel."

Roger wetted his lips. "Home is good. No issues in the barracks."

He took a deep breath. "But I have to talk about our last operation."

Mueller peered down his nose at the bundles on his desk, reached for one. "Pearland, right?"

"That's correct."

"I knew something was going on. It's not like you to be late in preparing an AAR. Agent Ramirez submitted his—"

Roger stiffened and pressed his lips together. "It's a lie."

"Beg your pardon?"

The chance to talk frankly soothed the ache in his soul. "In his AAR, Agent Ramirez lied about the prisoner's death. She was alive and neutralized with skeletal muscle relaxer when we found her."

The commander's eyebrows briefly jumped. "Then how did she commit suicide?"

Roger sucked in a breath. The light colonel was going to make him say it. "At Ramirez' order, one of his men placed a pistol in the prisoner's hand, turned it around against her, and pulled the trigger."

Mueller sat up straighter and shook his head. "I can't believe it.."

"I saw it. No further from me than you are. Wilson and Hardin saw it too."

Mueller shook his head again, slow and wide. "He strikes me as a good man. Hard, yeah, but every time I work with him my respect grows. He ordered the execution of a prisoner?"

"Yes, sir."

"That doesn't make any sense," the lieutenant colonel said, and he scowled. "Why shoot a prisoner and write it up as suicide? Why do it in front of you?"

Roger blinked. In the moment when his eyelids were down he saw the dead woman in his mind's eye. "He wanted to break us. Show us he and NCS have more power than we do."

"Sounds like he did break you."

The words boggled Roger. "Sir?"

"Three of you saw this thing coming down? Against just Ramirez and his triggerman—"

"There was another agent—"

Mueller angrily shook his head. "Two or three doesn't matter. You and your men were armed as well as they were. But you didn't try to stop him."

Part of him wanted to sink into the chair and vanish from his commander's gaze, yet Roger mastered himself and forced himself to sit erect, feeling like a man leaning into a stiff wind, and bore the rebuke. "I did not."

Behind the desk, Mueller folded his hands together and his voice grew milder. "I wasn't there. I don't know if I would have done any differently in your shoes. Then again I don't know if I would have done any differently in his."

Mueller was a good officer and a good man. How could the lieutenant colonel take Ramirez' side? But he would listen, at least. "Sir, I don't follow."

"We've been at war now almost four years since June 19. You don't know what kind of enemy the prisoner was. Atrocities elicit paybacks—"

"Sir. She was in her twenties. We found no military or terrorist hardware on the premises. She worked for Titan Industries, of all places. She could not have belonged to a terrorist faction."

Mueller pushed his chair back and stared out the window. Several times, Roger wanted to interrupt his silence, but his anguish held his tongue. A wall clock ticked out seconds. "Let's suppose for a moment you're right about her. He shot a person in cold blood, in front of witnesses, and was certain he could get away with it. A man who can do that has power and a lot of it."

Roger nodded. "He threatened us."

"Christ damn it. You've kept quiet?"

"You're the only person I've told, sir."

"Hardin? Wilson?"

"They haven't spoken to anyone."

"You're certain? Make sure they keep quiet. If Ramirez did what you're saying he could break us all. I need you; all my officers, all my men, here on post or out in the field. Not in a camp in South Dakota."

What could they do, even the entire battalion, against NCS? "I'll urge them to be silent."

"I see why you haven't filed an AAR. You have to do one. You have to be silent there too."

"Sir, with all due respect, to lie on an official report…."

Mueller yanked his reading glasses from his face and rubbed his eyes. "Be selective in how you tell the truth. Anything else?" Mueller peered across the desk. "Do not blame yourself. You can't undo that prisoner's death. A good man can't imagine all a bad man is capable of doing. If he doesn't stop him before the act that doesn't make him responsible for it."

Roger wished it were that simple. He wished the image he saw when he blinked would fade from his memory. But Mueller couldn't extract it for him and an officer sucked it up. "Yes sir."

Clay shuffled into the meeting room. The scabs of healing rock scratches and insect bites itched his feet. He found a seat on the back row near the inner wall and kicked off his mocs. His nostrils itched and he squinted against the morning sunlight coming through the sky-lights.

McKing facilitated this session. She bobbed in her chair and smiled with too much energy as the inmates took their seats. "Everyone here?" she asked. She bounded to her feet. "Today I have some very good news. The medical staff has conferred and we've concluded that one of you has been cured of your antisocial thoughts and is ready for release."

Clay folded his arms and scowled at Van Wijk. The blogger sat front row center, and he craned his neck to McKing and looked as happy as a dog expecting a treat.

"Mr. Zuniga," the doctor said, "we're very happy for you."

Van Wijk slumped in his chair for a few seconds, then twisted his bulky body. On the second row, Zuniga showed no surprise. "I have learned better skills to control my antisocial urges. I thank you and others on the staff for teaching me." The other inmates glared, but he sat tall. His eyes and face showed pride.

"What are you going to do when we've released you?"

He stroked his chin with two slender fingers. "I shall return to my work and talk with my wife about all that I have learned here. And play golf."

The session wore on. The inmates reacted to the news in a number of ways. Most turned sullen, muttering sarcastically after Zuniga spoke and responding to McKing with one-word answers. Van Wijk, in contrast, lavished praise and agreement on both Zuniga and the facilitator, echoing their words and mirroring McKing's body language. Delacroix sat quietly, his gaze on nothing and his attention clearly on his thoughts. His expression soured as the morning passed; unhappy with human frailty, Clay guessed.

After the session, the inmates avoided Zuniga, speeding their paces as they walked by him and launching stiff, banal conversations with others. Clay intended the same and would have left Zuniga alone with Van Wijk; Zuniga, though, turned away from the fawning blogger. "Clay, I would speak with you after lunch."

"Why should I bother?"

"You can tell me at great length I am a terrible person, if you wish. But there are things I wish to tell you in return."

Clay's stomach growled. They might give him bonus points for talking with Zuniga and get him off his military surplus diet a day sooner. "Find me after lunch."

Low conversations filled the cafeteria. Kerensky talked in a wistful tone about winery tours in the hills above Santa Barbara; Yamamoto gave no reply but his expression showed his thoughts ran down similar paths. Clay picked up a tray of tuna disc, sweet potato wedges, green bean slivers, and limestone-filtered water and looked for a place to sit. Delacroix sat alone, but he gulped food and had an angry expression that Clay took to mean he wanted no company. He found a table and ate alone.

What did Zuniga have to say? Whatever the staff wanted him to. *Give them what they want and get out of here, we'll fly to Pebble Beach for a round of golf and then go to dinner with our wives.* Instead of this cage, we'll pace a larger one where you can't see the bars after you've had a few drinks. Clay sniffed out a breath and drank from his glass of water. Let Zuniga talk; it would give Clay the easiest points he had yet earned.

Clay carried his tray to the dishwashing robot and found Zuniga waiting for him, wearing a gray polo shirt, baggy corduroy trousers a slightly darker shade, and canvas sneakers. He glanced at Clay's black moccasins. "You should wear tennis shoes."

"I only have half a pair. Ask your buddy Van Wijk about it." Zuniga did not reply and a question came to Clay. "They trust you to take me onto the grounds?"

"They don't know I'm taking you onto the grounds. But yes, they trust me. And they fixed the bug in the security robots' hardware."

Clay handed his tray to the outer arms of the dishwashing robot. It opened its slot and its smaller arms snaked out and plucked away the plate, fork, knife, and glass. "Okay, Zuniga, I'm ready."

The other led him around the corridor toward the south entrance. "You can call me Javier, if you wish."

"I don't."

Zuniga laughed, and the sound made Clay feel mocked. "Do you enjoy playing the adolescent?" The south door opened for them. A robot mower hummed across the lawn and the courtyard smelled of freshly-cut grass. The pedestrian bridge swooped toward the landing. As he slowly climbed the stairs, Zuniga looked to both sides. His hand drifted up the rail. His expression seemed thoughtful.

"You'll miss this place?" Clay asked. *Yes, I have learned who I am supposed to be—*

"No. But I am glad to have been here."

"Glad you were a prisoner?" Clay hesitated, but Zuniga did not fill the gap. The urge to make the other squirm bloomed in the back of Clay's mind. "Glad they pumped drugs into your synapses and brainwashed you into loving President Everton?"

They descended the outer side of the footbridge. In the woods downslope, behind the fence, foliage swayed in a breeze. Security robots zipped like fleas along the fence.

"I have chosen to be cured." Zuniga continued down the stairs and onto the wild grass, but Clay stopped, unable to process the absurdity. Zuniga halted and looked back.

"Of course, you do not believe me. But consider, Delacroix has inhaled the same neuroactives and sat through the same indoctrination sessions as I. He has not been cured. He has even grown deeper into his neurosis, reading his Bible and fancying himself a martyr like the jailed apostle Paul, with Everton as distant Nero. The drugs are not sufficient" Zuniga breathed deeply. "For that matter, neither has Van Wijk been cured."

Clay shook his head and hurried down the stairs. "Van Wijk—"

"—he's sandbagging. He thinks if he parrots their words and tells them of others' infractions, they will release him. I do not need the Doctor's scanning equipment to read his mind."

Zuniga's tone of certainty made Clay pull his elbows closer to his body. "Maybe you're right about Van Wijk. But without the drugs and the brainwashing you would be as uncured as Delacroix."

"They may have helped," Zuniga said, "but they were not necessary. Why have they released me? I have learned a complex society needs a clear hierarchy and it is my place to defer to those above me and receive deferment from those below. I have not simply learned this, but I feel it in my heart. Yet this knowledge was always present, waiting for me to open my heart to it. I could have opened my heart to it in the instant before they opened the van doors in the freight dock. Or in the instant before NCS arrested me."

He collected his breath, then glanced away from the building. "Let's walk."

"Right here is fine."

Zuniga took a few steps. The wild grass bent under his feet. "For your sake, I do not want others to overhear what I will tell you."

"Tell me what?"

Zuniga walked along the ridgeline away from the building. Clay pressed his lips together and loped after. A few clouds like cotton candy drifted eastward. Beyond the woods, outside the Hospital's perimeter, something glinted along the base of the tree line on the far hill, probably a littered beer bottle on the side of the dirt road. The half-mile might as well be a million.

He caught up but Zuniga kept walking, at times glancing over his shoulder at the building. "That's far enough. I don't want to make you late for the afternoon session."

Clay raised his eyebrow. The payoff had better be worth it.

Zuniga's expression grew serious. "You gain nothing by resisting Boucher and his staff."

Laugh or punch at the other's face? After a moment both urges struck Clay as being as flat as an old soft drink. "That's all you have to say?"

"They are the only allies you have. More so than anyone outside this place."

"Like hell," Clay said, but doubts nudged at him. No, even if Jenny had no affection for him anymore, she had not put him here.

"I have listened in the group sessions, overheard conversations, and investigated via the internet. I surmise who put you here. I surmise why."

Clay's heart thudded. "That's not important—"

"Your wife is a beautiful woman." Zuniga's gaze landed on Clay's face. After a moment, he lightly drew a breath. "And your business partner—is it fair to call him your closest friend?—is a platinum member of America United and a noted womanizer. What was Delacroix saying about David, Bathsheba, and poor Uriah?"

Clay sputtered and his hands clenched and unclenched. "He wouldn't. He didn't."

"Who else? True, your wife no longer loves you—"

"Nil didn't betray me."

Zuniga leaned closer, a smirk at the corners of his mouth. "You know I am correct, Clay, even if you do not wish to admit it. You have no trustworthy friend anywhere out there. But with your skills, Boucher would welcome you to join his efforts."

Clay blinked and lowered his head. His cheeks felt warm and pressure throbbed behind his eyes.

"I'll wait for you by the pedestrian bridge," Zuniga said. The grass rustled under his feet. Clay faced away from him, away from the building. Only the security robots with their visible and infrared cameras could see his face.

*   *   *

Nil lay on his stomach in the ditch. Insects crept up his camo pants and pollen from the trees along the road clogged his sinuses. His binoculars, paid for in cash at a pawnshop in Little Rock, had been fabbed for someone with wider-set eyes, but they well enough resolved the flat round building on the ridge a mile away and people near it. Though the other's back was turned, Nil knew the lanky frame, the slouching shoulders, and the dirty-blond hair. He had found Clay.

His stomach growled and his skin crawled with dust. Sunday morning, he'd crept as close as he'd dared to Monica's condo complex and heard a gunshot from somewhere within. Shaking, he'd followed the feds and the military vehicles north on the freeway, past the tall cramped hospitals of the Texas Medical Center and around the skyscrapers downtown, exiting near his neighborhood. Past shotgun shacks and four-story townhouses, turning on his street. He'd driven by a few times on the cross street and glanced down the block. Feds and soldiers had stood on his driveway and his traitorous house opened its front doors for them.

He panicked and drove out of town, ending up at a picnic area off Interstate 10 to gobble down a candy bar and orient himself. From a prepaid cellphone store at the next exit, he bought a cheap, anonymous phone. Monica didn't answer his call and he threw the phone away and started driving north, off the interstate. That night, at a roadside picnic area buffeted by passing tractor-trailers and the stink of a nearby hog farm, he'd lain awake across the pickup's bench seat and thought.

They were silencing people whom Clay had told. Jenny had been in the dark, so they'd let her go. Monica apparently had known. But why would Clay tell her? Nil puzzled for a time. She must have helped Clay dig deeper into the server farm in St. Louis. God knew he didn't have the clearance. For that they'd taken her into custody. Or worse.

Shivers then erupted over him and he curled his knees up and turned his face to the old pickup's bench seat backrest of torn cloth and crumbling foam. Through Haycock, they knew he knew. They had come for him. Despite his platinum membership, despite his charm, they would do to him what they did Monica. He had misread them—he'd trusted the assistant director—and he would pay with his freedom or his life.

His hands trembled as he pulled the platinum eagle from his neck. Its leather strap dug into his nape before it snapped. He worked the door handle by hand and the latch clunked open. As hard as he could, he threw the platinum eagle into dense brush down a slope behind the picnic area. An animal scampered where it landed and Nil locked the pickup door. With luck he would sleep.

Sleep eluded him. Had he trusted Clay, had he respected Jenny, he would be warm in his bed and able to look at himself in the mirror. He'd wronged them both. Self-loathing washed over him and tossed him like pebbles on a stony beach; but deep in the night the emotion's tide ebbed. He would never sleep in his bed again, but he at least had a chance to meet his gaze in the mirror without cringing.

A note he'd saved on his wearable confirmed his recollection of Boucher's words at the penthouse suite at the Excelsior: *Dent County*. The only one in the country lay in southeastern Missouri. He smiled in the pale blue glow of his pocket display.

Yes, a long shot, he thought time and again in the next day, at the drive-through lane of a Taj Mahal restaurant in Arkadelphia, at a military surplus store in North Little Rock, on winding roads in the Ozark hills. Clay could be in a cage somewhere in New Mexico or South Dakota. But if Boucher took brain scientists, he might take Clay.

And so he had.

Near where he'd parked the truck around the hill out of sight from the NMHA facility, gravel popped under car wheels. Nil pulled up the hood of his camo sweatshirt and hid his hands under his chest. He inhaled dust; burrs scratched his face. His limbs tensed in fight-or-flight urge but he lay still to let the smartfabric settle on a pattern. The car's engine grew louder but the car didn't slow. It headed down to the T-intersection with State Route E and Nil glanced at it. That same blue Guangzhou Motor Works sedan he'd seen the day before. Who rode in it?

Not important. What did matter was getting Clay out. He had an old pickup and a dwindling clip of bills. Bribery? It would cost more than he carried, and he had to assume the feds had frozen his accounts and would trace an ATM request. Crash the front gate and drive to the building? The pizza boxes on tank treads would stop him. They would have to see him, though, and his smartfabric camo could fool their visual processors. Their visible light processors, he realized; doubtless they could see in the infrared too.

Would a sporting goods store in a nearby town sell survival blankets of aluminized polyethylene terephthalate? Could he cut them to fit under his clothes without letting his body heat leak out the cuts like the beam of an infrared flashlight? Or would he line his clothes so well with them that he'd afflict himself with heatstroke?

He had to try. Nil decided to wait till nightfall, then head to the nearest town for fast food, survival blankets, safety pins, and a utility knife. The sun crept down the western sky, and his thirst and hunger dazed him and led him in and out of sleep.

Where—? Nil came fully to his senses and shook his head to orient himself. Red sunset smeared the horizon and only the pizza boxes stirred inside the fence of the NMHA facility. In the parking lot, a Lorelei sedan stood closest to the building's front door.

He'd noticed it yesterday afternoon, but now it was well after five o'clock. What was the boss doing here so late?

Movement on the state route caught Nil's attention. On the patched gray asphalt, mottled blue-black with fresh tar, a convoy of three cars the color of cheap sparkling wine slowed as they approached the facility's front gate.

11

The car waited on its side of the two-lane, turn signal blinking, for the gate to open. Ramirez sat on the back seat and scowled at the watch-face of his wearable. Eight o'clock and his day not over. He glanced up. The lead car idled at the mouth of the driveway and the halves of the gate hadn't moved. Inside the facility's fence stood woods gloomy in the twilight. "What's taking that prick?"

On the front seats, Lundquist and O'Neill said nothing. At least they knew a rhetorical question when they heard one.

And at least Boucher had been willing to let him visit, the one redeeming feature of this whole fuck-up. Haycock had arrived at Gitmo North to find an empty cell where Schieffer should have been. Rather than stay until they tracked down the inmate, he'd flown back to New Washington and put Ramirez on the task. Sure, he was higher on the food chain and had deskbound duties at NCS headquarters, but if he wanted Fisher to keep slipping him envelopes of cash and saying good things about him to Everton, he ought to follow orders instead of delegating.

Pick a master, any master. Or the rest of us will pick one for you.

Still, Haycock had given him the order. Ramirez had ordered Sung back to Fort Riley (where he could goddam well stay, Smith and Olafson weren't insubordinate. And why hadn't the loyalty drugs from the implant worked on him as fully as they had on Mueller and the rest of the unit?) and went to South Dakota to find Schieffer. A mis-entered transfer log. What incompetent platinum member had gotten the information systems contract for Gitmo North? Whoever he was, though, he was untouchable; but the guards on duty when NMHA came for Schieffer were not.

Finally, a rattling sound, and the gates rolled back. The trees on either side loomed over the driveway . As they approached the drive-way's curves, their headlight beams penetrated a dozen yards below the tree canopies, swallowed by brush and mossy fallen logs, reflected by the eyes of possums and raccoons. At points along the driveway, cameras hatted with leaves and camo netting watched them from twelve-foot concrete poles splashed with brown and green paint.

The driveway left the woods and the building came into view on the far side of a treeless valley. The setting sun silhouetted it and sodium-vapor lamps dabbed the parking lot with light. Boucher's security crawlers flanked the line of cars, treads clacking. The doc-tor would call it an honor guard, but Ramirez assumed Boucher distrusted his visitors. As if he had the right. And why the hell did he deserve military hardware, when NCS had been forced to log-roll and blackmail for months to get 1 LRTD Battalion detached to it?

The driveway descended to a low-water bridge and the crawlers peeled off. About time—but more waited on the other side of the stream and escorted them into the parking lot. Old cars, panels scratched and windows dusty, slouched in the lot, along with a new black Lorelei in the spot nearest the building. Behind the aluminum-framed front doors and picture windows a few lights burned dimly in a reception area. A translucent gray picture window glowed to the right. Ramirez left four agents with the cars and led Lundquist and O'Neill to the front door.

A stout black man, built like a former linebacker softening into middle age, waited for them outside. One of Boucher's first projects from the state pen, when Everton had been governor; he couldn't be anywhere near as controlled as Mueller and the soldiers. "The doctor's been waiting for you."

Birch paneling clad the reception area's walls. Chairs clustered to-gether to the left, a C-shaped reception desk filled the back right corner, and a life-size portrait of Everton on the right-hand wall stared at the clustered chairs. The mannequin behind the reception desk stirred to life and turned a quizzical expression toward Ramirez, but the guard waved his hand at it. "Not now." The mannequin froze. The front doors closed behind Ramirez and his men and a door on the back wall close to the reception desk clicked and swung open.

Near the baseboards, nightlights glowed in a curving hallway. A low, wheeled robot whined over the carpet down the hall and kicked up the smell of deodorizer. The first door on the right stood open, though another guard, this one Caucasian, blocked the view through the doorway and raised his hand to stop Ramirez while the black guard walked in. "He's finally here," the black guard said to someone inside.

The second guard stared at Ramirez and the NCS agent scowled back. The only difference between the guard and the bastards Ramirez shipped to Gitmo North was patronage; but it was enough to make this thug believe himself Ramirez' equal.

From inside the room, an effete male voice said, "Show him in."

The guards parted and Ramirez and his agents passed between them. Boucher, all moping face and sloped shoulders, sat behind a deep, thick desk. His narrow beard made him look competent, like an actor playing a psychiatrist's role, but Ramirez briefly wondered how Boucher had gotten Everton's ear years ago and if any of the rumors of Everton's history of mental illness were true.

Boucher glanced at the other two agents. "You didn't say you'd be bringing others."

"It must have slipped my mind. Where's Schieffer?"

"In his quarters, I suspect. LeRoi or Ryan can track him down."

"You suspect?"

Boucher pushed himself straighter in his chair. "This isn't a prison camp. We rehabilitate people instead of warehousing them."

Maybe Everton had a streak of guilt about locking up criminals and Boucher knew how to play him. Funny, though, Ramirez had never seen such a weakness in the President. "Just give me Schieffer and a room to interrogate him."

In the bookshelves behind Boucher, a clock ticked. Boucher

stroked his bearded chin. "Ryan, bring Schieffer. I'm sure the agent can interrogate him here as easily as he can anywhere else."

Clay pulled the five of diamonds halfway out of his hand, then frowned. Either Yamamoto or Kerensky had a higher diamond singleton, if he remembered correctly, and would be stuck with the lead on the next trick while high hearts and the spade queen remained out. He threw the diamond five. Yamamoto tossed the diamond three and Kerensky played off. Clay hissed a breath out his nose. No escaping big points on this hand. Once he was out of here he would never play hearts again.

"Guard up," Delacroix said. Clay collated the trick by feel while looking up at the cafeteria entrance.

Ryan stalked in and wagged his index finger at Clay. "Come with me. The doctor needs to see you."

"It's after eight," Kerensky said.

"Stay out of this. Schieffer, come with me."

Anxiety filled Clay. This wasn't normal. Yet he stood, shrugged. "I was going to lose the game anyway."

"What's Boucher doing here so late?" Yamamoto asked.

"I'll let you know." His heart beat faster and his palms felt damp. He'd been on good enough behavior, hadn't he? Were they shipping him back to South Dakota? "Probably nothing," Clay added, but the others' faces showed none of them believed his words either.

Ramirez sat on one of the couches arrayed between the door and Boucher's desk. Lundquist and O'Neill stood behind him and the guard LeRoi blocked the doorway. Ramirez toyed at the seam of the couch cushion.

Boucher asked, "Why didn't you interrogate Schieffer when you had him in South Dakota?"

The agent's hand paused at the seam. "It's classified." He returned his attention to tugging at stray threads.

"You didn't know who he was, I'll bet. You thought him some poor fish caught in your net."

"We have further questions for him."

"And they're so important you didn't inform NMHA you wanted to ask them."

Insolent bastard. "NCS doesn't have to tell anyone anything. We've remanded these enemy combatants to you as a courtesy—"

Boucher laughed. "Have you told the President? He wouldn't agree."

"I'm here on Everton's orders."

"The signed document is in your pocket? The President himself cares about the interrogation of one man? Don't insult me."

When your opponent raises against your bluff, reraise. "Don't insult *me*."

Boucher smirked and reached for a telephone handset on the desktop to his right. He held it loosely to his right ear. "Get me the President's office."

Lundquist and O'Neill stirred behind him, but Ramirez kept his gaze on Boucher though his heart sped its rhythm. Relax. Everton's aides would take tens of minutes to decide what to tell the doctor. Schieffer didn't have tens of minutes, and footsteps trodding down the hall toward the office proved it.

In photos and video, Schieffer looked to have that breed of introversion that social weaklings interpreted as aloofness; but despite the guards blocking his view Ramirez saw Schieffer had been beaten. His shoulders slumped, and his eyes shifted like a fearful animal's. He should be fearful. Boucher's attempt to pull rank would come too late to save him.

"Bring him in," Ramirez told the guards. The two glanced at Boucher.

"I said bring him in."

LeRoi narrowed his eyes. "The doctor hasn't said it."

Boucher remained behind his desk, phone cradled near his ear. Ramirez rose from the couch and glared down at the doctor. "You wanted to see what we're going to do to your pet? You're goddam going to see." He drew his sidearm and stalked toward the doorway.

"No," Boucher said, slowly, calmly. The guards closed rank and concealed Schieffer's wide white eyes. Lundquist and O'Neill stood abreast in front of their superior, five feet from the guards.

"Schieffer's going to die," Ramirez said. He released the safety, powered on the laser sight, and cocked his pistol.

"Doctor said no," LeRoi said. The two guards drew their pistols. Ramirez' junior agents slowly drew theirs in response.

"NCS says yes." Ramirez leaned forward and the red spot slid down the ceiling and wall toward LeRoi's chest.

A gunshot sounded, then another, and Ramirez squeezed the trigger. LeRoi's eyes widened and his mouth twisted in agony as he slumped backward. More gunshots rang and Ramirez swept the red spot across Ryan's white supremacist prison tat to his chest. He fired and a wound bloomed in the center of the guard's chest. Ryan lost his balance and slammed backward to the floor.

Over the echo of the gunshots ringing in Ramirez' ears came the groans of wounded men. Lundquist and O'Neill were both down, eyes glassy, blood bubbling in their mouths and nostrils. The two guards were in worse shape. Their blood pooled and their pistols slid from their grips. LeRoi pressed his fingers against his chest and blood welled between them.

Behind the guards, the doorway stood empty and Schieffer was gone.

"—Infiltrators posing as Federal agents. Repeat, infiltrators posing as Federal agents. I authorize maximum force."

Ramirez turned to Boucher. The doctor's face looked ashen and guilty and he shouted into the handset, "One of them is in here. Yes with me!"

"You hung up on the President?" Ramirez asked, and in his ears his voice sounded muffled and distant.

"My security will be here any second. You don't have a chance. When Everton hears what NCS has done, if you aren't dead you'll wish you were."

Ramirez shook his head. "The winners write the after action reports." He fired two shots into Boucher's chest. Blood spattered the desk and the leatherbound books on the shelves behind. He had enough rounds in his clip to shoot each of the wounded guards in the head. His breath sounding ragged in his ears, he looked into the hallway. Where was Schieffer?

Clay ran down the hall and stole glances over his shoulder. No motion, no sound—two more gunshots, then a third, then a fourth. Far behind—

From around the curve ahead of him came voices and the squeak of robot treads. He ducked through a dark, open doorway. His chest heaved. The NCS agents wanted to kill him. A robot clacked by, its motor whirring. The shadows of two running guards flashed across the doorway.

Get out. He could try the hallway and break for the rear entrance, over the freight dock and next to security. No chance. Break a window? The room was gloomy away from the splash of light near the door, but he made out a small office, two desks next to the window each facing a side wall, under shelves bowed with textbooks and bound journals. A fire extinguisher, a paperweight—two chairs. Gunshots echoed down the hall. Clay grabbed a chair by the sides of its seat cushion and jabbed its castered legs at the window. The smartglass crunched and fractured but clung together and to the frame. More gunshots. He extended his arms and swung the chair with more force. The window crunched even louder, but one of the casters punched a hole and wedges of the smartglass split apart. He peeled them back, then shielded his face with his forearms like an outmatched boxer and climbed out. Shards lashed his skin and needled at his jeans.

The night was cool and gray-dark. The remnants of twilight backlit the woods behind the fence at the base of the ridge. He ran north, downslope, the same direction he'd tried a few nights before. His black moccasins were stiff and made his footing uneven. The cuffs chafed his heels. Time enough to worry about blisters after he walked to Mexico.

Something lit the grass around him and he glanced back. Lights glowed in the office and silhouetted the lead NCS agent, head like a bullet and shoulders narrow, in the torn window. Clay crouched and kept running. When he glanced back again the agent had left the window.

Gunshots rang in the parking lot and Clay dropped to his stomach while the percussions echoed off the sparse slopes. He glanced at the parking lot. Figures in suits crouched behind nondescript sedans. Another gunshot, the muzzle flashing over a trunk lid. Clay wasn't the target: robots clacked under a car standing at the edge of the lot and made fart sounds. Metal pellets thunked on the side of one of the sedans and sparks arced into the air and hissed and skittered across the asphalt.

Clay breathed a little easier, rose to a crouch, and started running down to the stream. Maybe Boucher had called back all the perimeter patrols and he could clear the fence. He approached the stream and glanced uphill at the parking lot. More gunshots, more sparks. No one seemed to be following him. He stepped into the stream. The water lapped over his shoes and was so cold he gasped for breath.

On the far side of the stream, a large shape the color and texture of the ground beneath it moved. "Clay!" it whispered.

He stopped moving despite the frigid water flowing over his feet. It couldn't be, yet he knew the voice, the whites of the close-set drooping eyes, the shape of mouth revealed by the teeth. "Nil?"

"Yeah, it's me."

Clay splashed across, his fists clenching and his brows lowering. The lines of Nil's face became faintly visible. "What the hell are you doing here?"

Nil showed his hands. "I don't blame you for being mad. But punch me in the face after we get out of here."

He would, all right. Yet how had Nil found this place? Why had he come? "Why the hell should I trust you?"

Nil leaned closer. "Because they want to kill me too. We'll talk later, let's go. I have a vehicle. In the woods at the top of the hill." He started up the slope and soon became invisible. Clay started after and guided himself by the other's heavy breaths. He soon caught up. "Just inside," Nil said, gasping, "treeline."

Clay crouched lower and peered into the darkness. Every odd shape could be a foe in camouflage and Nil, gasping, could be leading him into a trap. But the NCS agents wouldn't have brought Nil along for any reason Clay could see. Boucher wouldn't have invited him here either. Nil's explanation made more sense than those.

The thunking, sparking sounds from the parking lot across the valley had faded. Two last gunshots echoed before returning the night's soundstage to crickets and whippoorwills

The slope leveled off before the trees. The driveway formed a black streak across the dark gray ground and led into the gloomy woods. Behind a couple of trees, straight lines defined a hulking shape. The Lorelei was sleeker, darker, wasn't it?

"That's not your car."

"Long story," Nil said, short of breath. "Let's go."

A large spot of light crawled up the driveway toward the woods and revealed the shape as an old pickup truck. The beam locked in place, glinting off the pickup's cracked windshield. Clay dropped to his belly and looked back at the building. A searchlight glowed on one of the fed cars. Behind the searchlight, barely visible, figures moved across the roof of the outer building, from the courtyard to the perimeter, and jumped down.

Nil stared wide-eyed at the illuminated pickup. Clay yanked his forearm and pulled him off-balance. "Get down!" Nil stumbled to his hands and knees. "You tipped them?"

"No! Christ, Clay, they're going to kill me!"

Across the valley, a starter chattered and an engine revved up.

"Shit, they're coming!"

Blinders dropped around Clay's consciousness. Introspection would be a luxury for the next few minutes. Only one thing mattered. "Follow me. Run."

He crouched and ran away from the beam, into the woods. Springy branches of shrubs whipped his face. Behind him, Nil rustled through the brush. An owl hooted. Rabbits scampered away from them.

Clay paused near the fence on the north side of the grounds to let Nil catch up. No robots or feds in sight. In the woods behind them, near the parked pickup, a car door slammed and faint light glowed. Driving away wasn't an option. Nil stopped, hands on knees, sucking wind.

"Through the fence," Clay said.

"You're a magician?"

"Between strands, city mouse." He went to the inner fence and with his fingertips probed the two strands at thigh height for stretches of wire between barbs. He hooked his fingers around the strands and pulled. "Go through, then hold for me."

Nil bent and moved slowly through. "I'm caught. Shit, what do I do?"

"Tear your clothes. Go!" Fabric ripped and Nil stepped through. He reached for the wires and hissed when he caught a barb. Clay slipped between the strands. The outer fence proved easier, but when he stepped onto the soil of the neighboring farm, Clay heard a whirring sound and glanced up. A few feet away, a concrete post stood between the two fences. He couldn't see the infrared camera but he knew it saw him.

"Keep moving. Across the main road. They'll bring reinforcements to cordon off the Hospital."

Nil gasped for breath but followed. The woods faded to pasture. Cattle were dark shapes, mooing uneasily, all on their feet from the gunfire at the NMHA facility. The air smelled of fresh cowshit. Eyes white and udders swaying, the herd trotted away from Clay and Nil.

A few hundred yards ahead a single sodium-vapor lamp glowed on a pole between a two-story white, wood-sided house and a milking barn. In the house, lamps burned behind drawn curtains.

"Across the road, hurry." Clay jogged toward the two-lane.

"Can't." Nil gasped for breath.

Clay stopped, glared over his shoulder. "You don't want to die? Move." Clay resumed jogging and Nil pounded after him.

The fence was easier, wooden posts and saggier wires. They crossed the road and walked in the ditch on the far side for a minute. Beer bottles rattled underfoot. A sign labeled the farm they'd trespassed *Meramec Farms Organic Dairy*.

"Caught your breath? I don't have any erythropoietics," Clay said coldly. "More cross country."

"I'm not trying to," Nil said, "slow you down."

"We need more distance." Clay led the way through the fence and across another field. Unlike the organic dairy farmer across the road, this field's owner had failed to adapt to the wave of vat-grown food; thigh-high weeds scratched at them and a thistle pricked Clay's hand in the dark.

From the north, a siren blared. Clay crouched and Nil sank to his knees. Headlights illuminated swatches of the field and the siren dopplered closer. "Time to hustle."

Nil groaned and picked himself off the ground. Clay jogged. Behind him, Nil was a stooped blur in the darkness. The ground sloped up toward a line of trees and Nil fell further behind.

He didn't need him. He would have gotten this far if Nil hadn't appeared and he'd get even farther if he abandoned him. But the feds would get him, crossed his mind, but then Clay glanced over his shoulder and saw the laboring shape and remembered the cage in South Dakota and the NCS agent in Boucher's office who wanted to kill him.

Clay inhaled deeply and sped his pace. No, he wasn't going to avenge himself on Nil; he was the better man.

Running alongside the line of trees, the pale gash of a dirt road became visible. He stepped through a fence separating the overgrown field and the dirt road's right-of-way. To the left, the gravel ribbon ran down to a sharp-angle intersection with the blacktop road. To the right it rolled up and over the terrain.

Nil staggered up to the fence and leaned, gasping, against a post. "Where to?"

"Away from the blacktop." Clay nodded up the dirt road and held the fence for Nil, then jogged away. Gravel crunched underfoot like Martin's breakfast cereal. Jenny would be sitting with him at the table off the kitchen, Clay could see it, and anger welled in his gut. He almost turned to look at Nil, but didn't, and realized his fists had clenched. He relaxed his fingers and slowed his pace. The night was cool and he'd barely broken a sweat. They could go several miles before needing water. To the right, the line of trees deepened into a few acres of woods.

"Oh, god."

Now what. Clay turned. Nil hunched, head turned to the southwest. Between the dull yellow lights of Meramec Farms and Orion low in the western sky, an orange glow wavered above the asphalt road and woods.

"They set it on fire," Clay said. "NCS fouled up and they're burning the evidence."

"Oh, god."

Clay stared at the glow until noises jerked his attention away. A gasoline engine purred and gravel popped under tires. Headlight beams bobbed over the canopy of the woods behind the fence. "Off the road!" He pulled Nil toward the fence and shoved him to the ground. They crawled under the bottom strand of wire and into the undergrowth.

The sound of popping gravel came closer. Clay scrambled behind a bush and looked through the thin branches while Nil lay next to him, panting. Light spilling from the headlights showed a swooping fish shape and metallic blue paint.

"I've seen," Nil said, "that car."

Clay gritted his teeth. "Shh."

The car halted even with them. The headlights cut out and plunged the scene into blackness. Over the idling engine came the grinding of an opening window.

"I have an infrared camera," a male voice softly said. It sounded distantly familiar to Clay, but he knew the cadence of the words.

Nil turned his head to Clay, his breathing still ragged.

"I'm your best way out," one million one thousand one added. "And if I were the feds you'd be dead by now."

"We can trust him," Clay murmured.

"Who?"

"I don't know." He stood and walked toward the car. After a moment Nil hurried after him. Leaves rustled underfoot. Clay crossed the fence and went cautiously toward the car. It could all be a ruse, some cruel trick played by the stranger; but if it were he would at least see his face and learn who had done this, if not why. He crunched over a miniature berm of gravel piled on the road's edge. Nil bounded closer.

The window wound down further and a shadowy figure rested its forearms on the sill. "It's been a long time, Clay."

"I don't remember you." Too late, he realized that probably sounded tactless.

The stranger chuckled. "I wasn't very memorable. And you're—?"
"Nil Thomas."

"Really?" The stranger said nothing more for a time. Sirens sounded in the distance on the state road. "Climb in and we'll get out of here." The door unlatched and the stranger scooted into the back right seat. Clay and Nil sat opposite him and the door swung shut. "Lights off until my mark. Back to arvie, shortest path, window up." The window motor whirred and the car made a three point turn and started back along the dirt road. It curved and crested a rise. "Headlights on. Interior lights low."

The stranger looked gracile under the cabin's high ceiling and pinpoint lights. A pile of small electronic devices, homemade provenance shown in visible insulated wires and thick globs of solder, lay on the bench seat next to his nervous hands. His red-tinged madras plaid short sleeve shirt and tapered-leg jeans made his chest look shallow and his limbs short and slender. He had drab olive skin and a large head crowned with dark brown hair carelessly combed. He gazed at Clay with a mirthful expression crinkling his crow's feet. "Still don't remember me? I shouldn't be surprised, I wore such thick glasses."

Clay remembered his face now, but was less certain of his name. "Osvaldo?" In his dorm at college, a year or two younger, tolerated at the periphery of his social circle. He hadn't thought about him in years.

"I still went by that, didn't I? Call me Wally. Wally Guerra." He reached his hand and shook with Nil, then Clay. His grip's strength surprised Clay. The car slowed at a four-way intersection with another dirt road, turned right.

He'd majored in comp sci, or was it econ? And he'd surprised people when, as part of a prank, he'd hacked the elevators in the neighboring dorm. Nothing else, though, came to mind and then Clay remembered why he hadn't thought of Osvaldo—Wally—in years. "The alumni newsletter said you had died."

"Like Michael Jordan, reports of my demise have been greatly exaggerated."

"A drowning. On vacation in Cuba."

The mirth faded from Wally's face. "We have a lot to talk about once we're clear. Speaking of which," he said, and lifted one of the electronic devices, a handheld barcode scanner with the LED ripped out and replaced. He passed the lens over Clay's body from head to toe. "They didn't plant you with a transponder."

Clay hadn't thought of that. "I would have noticed."

"Would that you would." Wally shook his head, then looked up as the car slowed. "Here's home."

The car stopped a hundred yards from an intersection with another blacktop two-lane. Over the sedan loomed a bus, a great gray box with a handful of smartglass windows. The car popped open its door. The bus' engine rumbled, diesel timbre and bass pitch. Wally stepped out and waited for Clay and Nil to join him.

"Hitch yourself up," Wally said to the car. He swatted it on its curving front panel below its windshield and it backed up. He straightened and looked at the horizon, over rolling hills and acres of woods. The orange glow from the burning Hospital washed out the pale stars of Orion's belt. Faintly from the distance came the sound of sirens. "Guys, it's time for a road trip."

12

The prison bars pressed the edge of the cot but he turned over and doing so ended up on a boat. It rocked beneath him and Jenny told the SueChef to sauté bacon and Clay woke up.

He lay on a narrow mattress. Popcorn texture on the ceiling of the motor home stared back at him from a foot away. Light reached him from his right through a set of plastic safety bars. "Retract," he told them, then contorted himself until his feet reached the ladder and he climbed down. A video display, six feet wide and four high, filled most of the wall under his bunk. It showed what he guessed to be the feed from the front external cameras, a divided four-lane highway rolling under their wheels with straggly fields on either side. If he hadn't slept late, the shadows suggested they traveled southeast.

He turned. No boat, no Jenny, but the smell of hot bacon wafted from deeper in the motor home. The living room revealed Wally had spent a lot of money; to Clay's right, two rotating chairs, low-backed and cushioned in green and blue stripes, stood locked into a track system barely visible between loose lips of carpet, under a desk which hung, edge down, on a motorized pulley. To his left, an L-shaped sofa wrapped along the wall from the front door to the open passageway leading further back. Narrow, shadowed gaps showed that what looked like walls were cabinet doors with hidden hardware. Under the display, on the walls, under the couch, the motor home had far more storage than appeared at first glance. More tabletops hung close to the ceiling and swayed slightly on their chains when the motor home slowed or switched lanes.

Nil sat in the corner of the sofa, smartfabric camo wrinkled, his legs stretched toward the door. His eyes were baggy and his voice sounded tired. "I told the SueChef to make breakfast…."

Clay scowled and stalked over. He pulled back his fist; Nil's eyes widened and he turned his chin slightly away. Clay threw a hook punch and squashed the corner of Nil's mouth against his molars.

Blood dabbed Nil's lip and he breathed heavily. "I did ask you to wait to punch me in the face, didn't I?"

His anger had been simmering, but instead of the punch venting it, it boiled over. "You son of a bitch!" He windmilled punches at Nil's face. Nil pulled up his forearms and his knees and dropped to his side. Clay's punches mashed Nil's forearms until footsteps pounded toward them and wiry arms tugged at his elbow.

"Clay!" Wally yelled. "What's going on?"

He let Wally pull him away from Nil and caught his breath. "He betrayed me."

"To NCS?" Wally's eyebrows rose. "That's why you were arrested?"

Nil lay on his side and blinked. "Yes," he said. Blood trickled on his lower lip. He pushed up with his arms and slumped his back against the sofa cushions. "It was the biggest mistake I ever made—"

Wally knelt closer, arms twitching. "In person? Did you meet with them in person?"

"Phone call."

Wally's fingertips drummed his upper lip and his hand muffled his muttered words. "No transponder implants. Wait, you're an AU member."

"I was."

"Wearing a pendant, lapel pin?"

"I said I'm not a member anymore. I threw the pendant away somewhere in east Texas."

"Software." Wally clutched at Nil's left wrist. "Give me your wearable."

"I've been offline—"

"Has your spyware? Give it to me." Wally fumbled at the strap and slid the wearable off Nil's wrist. He sprang to his feet. "Lower the desk. Chair at center." At the other side of the room the desk dropped from the ceiling while an electric motor whined. One chair backed out of the way and the other moved into place. Its mount locked into the track with a thunk.

Wally sat and slid open a drawer.

"Wait a minute," Nil said. Wally pulled a jeweler's toolkit from the drawer and spun a screwdriver between his thumb and forefinger. He popped the battery and it rolled on edge a few inches across the desktop before toppling and clattering to a stop.

"We'll fix it later," Wally said, and spun the chair around. "Arvie, change destination. The campground south of Peoria. Take the next side road but no hurry after that." He nodded at Nil. "Now you're clean."

"He still betrayed me." Clay glared at Nil over crossed arms.

He shook his head. "It's my biggest mistake—"

"Because Jenny said no?"

"What?" Nil crinkled his eyebrows, but then they rose and the corners of his mouth fell. "Jesus, Clay, how could you think that?" He stared up at Clay's eyes. "I couldn't do that to you—"

"You couldn't? You have lines you won't cross? You locked me in a cage!"

"Because I was afraid! Afraid you would tell someone you shouldn't about Everton's election and NCS would drop the hammer on us both. I've seen them up close. They're powerful and ruthless and I was too cowardly to risk my own skin. Yes, cowardly. And for nothing."

Wally sat with crossed legs, cycling his weight across the heel of his lower foot, yawing his chair. "Nothing?"

"They came after everyone who knew. Or might know." Nil shot out his hand, palm facing Clay. "Jenny's safe."

"How do you know?"

"She called me. She thought my America United connections might help her. NCS agents barged into her house and interrogated her. From what she said I figured out they had a portable brain scanner and decided she didn't know what you'd found."

Clay's head sagged. Even if she'd stopped loving him she deserved better than a prison camp. "She didn't."

Wally stopped yawing his chair. "I'll check on her."

"Monica Colbert, too," Nil said. "They raided her place. Not just NCS, military too." He looked up at Clay with rebuke in his eyes. "Why did you tell her?"

Clay shifted his weight to his back foot. "I didn't. She helped me get into the St. Louis servers but I didn't tell her what I found. She didn't want to know."

"I—am lucky I had some notice the feds were cracking down. I left the house, the car; I paid cash for that old truck we left behind at the NMHA facility. I realized I had to make it up to you. Any way possible."

Not only was talk cheap, but Nil bought it at a volume discount. Parts of Clay's mind debated each other below verbalization. Did Nil's contrition make a difference? Why should it?

Wally spoke. "You came to break Clay out."

Nil nodded.

"How did you know he was there?"

"I'd heard of the facility. I had a hunch of what—" He looked at his naked wrist. His mouth fell open and he backhanded the air. "I don't remember the name of the facility's head."

"Boucher," Clay said.

"Thanks, was trying to do." He swallowed. "From the sound of it Clay was the kind of man Boucher wanted to brainwash."

The motor home slowed and turned its great bulk left into a crossover. Clay let the motion drop him onto the sofa between Nil and the door. The guidance signs and the forward view showed they would be taking a two-lane state road in Tennessee. Clay guessed they'd pass nothing but fields and small towns for a while.

"What were you going to do if you broke me out?" Clay asked, still looking at the display.

"Lie low while we made plans."

"That's it?" Clay turned his head. "I could have done that with-

out you. I could have escaped without you. I don't need you, Nil."
Maybe he had, once, in a world of meetings and cocktail parties; but
that world was as distant as Mars. He looked at Wally. "We could
drop him off somewhere."

"Clay, no!" Nil said. "I know you're mad at me, but please, I can't
survive long. They'd find me and kill me."

"You'd have a chance. I wouldn't hand you over to them."

Across the room, Wally shook his head and yawed his chair. "Clay,
we can use him."

"Use him? For what?"

Wally stopped fidgeting and fixed Clay with his mild brown gaze.
"Like I said, we have a lot to talk about." He sniffed deeply. "After
breakfast."

They went to the cramped kitchen. The SueChef extended its arms
from the ceiling and laid their food on a small table against the wall.
Bacon, scrambled eggs, and *pico de gallo* wrapped in warm tortillas;
orange juice flecked with pulp; espresso and tubular paper packets of
turbinado sugar. Clay ate quickly. "It's been a while since I've eaten
real food."

Wally looked over the rim of a bloody mary. "What did they feed
you?"

"Something out of a military surplus extruder. Horrible taste, horrible texture."

Wally stirred his drink with its celery stalk garnish and shook his
head. "They don't know how to cook it. Or they didn't try."

Clay frowned at his plate. Bacon bits and cilantro leaves mingled
in the juice of diced tomatoes. "You've got one?"

"Two, one in each emergency kit. I'll cook something from it for
you. You'll be surprised." He glanced at their empty plates and waved
toward the living room. "It's more comfortable out there."

Nil took his same place, on the sofa backed against the kitchen wall,
and pressed a teal-blue bruise reliever sponge the size of a racquetball
against his eye. Clay sat near the door. A tabletop descended from the
ceiling to hold his second cup of coffee and he wiggled his toes amid
the beige pile carpet. What felt like an insect bite itched on the outside
of his right ankle but he ignored it. Wally pointed at a spot on the floor

and a chair moved there to make the triangle equilateral. The motor home crossed rolling hills.

"Last night you picked up that Clay and I knew each other in college. More like I knew him then the other way around. I was just a scrawny Messican from the Rio Grande Valley with thick glasses and poor social skills. Clay, if I haven't changed much, don't burst my bubble."

"You're still scrawny, but otherwise—"

Wally's head lolled back and he laughed. "I prefer *bantamweight*. Where was I? College. I triple majored in comp sci, econ, and psych because I was interested in what they nowadays call inflectology."

Clay frowned. "I thought that was just some MBA buzzphrase."

"It's real." Nil said. He shifted the bruise reliever to his chin. "I'll grant there are suits who spout the jargon without knowing what it means, but the field is real."

"It's the social psychology of tipping points," Wally said. "Marketers use it to try cooking up fads, like back in '18 when the Puca Sambuca children's craze hit." He shook his head. "But advertising is little kids fingerpainting compared to what a Rembrandt can do. When you know what you're looking for it's everywhere large groups of people interact. You see it in the financial markets: cycles of accumulation, markup, distribution, and collapse, but it happens with anything you can quantify—not just stock prices, but business market share, military unit morale—"

"Support for presidential candidates," Clay said. His gut churned and he knew it wasn't solely from drinking too much coffee.

"A tool is a tool," Wally said. "After graduation I took a job on Wall Street. My team were observation quants, looking for cycles and figuring out how to ride them." His expression grew wistful. "Everyone should be a twenty-five-year-old millionaire in Manhattan at least once in their life."

The forward view vanished from the display and a map of the United States replaced it. A green arrow pointed north over the Tennessee-Kentucky border, between the Cumberland and the Mississippi Rivers. A red splotch bloomed in northern Idaho and an alarm bleated through hidden speakers.

Wally spun and looked up. "Zoom in. No, not on us." The image lurched and focused on the red splotch; it resolved into a stretch of land between a national forest and a reservoir east of Lewiston.

"What's going on?" Nil asked.

"The past few weeks, they've started using the military. Sounds like you saw that, Nil. Everton's obliged by the text of the Insurrection Act to announce when the U.S. Military is going to be used against domestic enemies. But they only do it on obscure channels and after the military is at its jump-off point. Closer." The display zoomed in. The red splotch covered a few hundred acres of hilly terrain off a narrow country road.

Clay asked, "Who's the target?"

"Track that address," Wally told the motor home. "Return to default image." The forward view returned to the display. A sign welcomed them to Kentucky.

"If you were young and rich," Nil began.

"—and single. I know where you're going."

"Why give it up? Why fake your death?"

Clay leaned forward, another question on his mind. "Why seek me?"

Wally nodded, his head, shoulders, and chest bobbing as a unit. "October '18. I was meeting Gangfeng and Guillaume, a couple of other quant nerds from the office, for lunch. Gangfeng said he'd seen anomalous price and volume action for stocks with operations in the mid-Atlantic region, Richmond to Philadelphia. That got Guillaume thinking about strange action he'd seen in currency futures. We took a long lunch to talk about it and then stayed late that night to brainstorm ideas and tease meaning from the data." He inhaled deeply. "About two in the morning, we predicted 6:19."

Clay's mouth dropped open.

"I call bullshit," Nil said.

"Not the date. Not a hydrogen bomb assembled from decommissioned Soviet warheads and rigged to the GPS coordinates of the Treasury Department. But something a few months in the future its perps thought would be big enough to flatten Washington DC."

Clay finally found words. "Someone destroyed Washington to

make a killing in the stock market?"

Wally frowned at the carpet and yawed his chair for a moment. "They made a lot of money—even though their expenses were in the billions—but it was opportunistic. Destroying DC was their plan."

"Who were they?" Nil asked.

He grinned. "I have no hard evidence. Just a hunch."

"What's your hunch?"

Wally shifted to the edge of his chair. He tried to sober his expression but the grin kept reemerging. After a last inhalation, he said, "The People's Republic of China." His control failed and he guffawed.

Nil shook his head. "Double bullshit. The PRC stuck its nose in the Indo-Paki War and got burned. Their police state couldn't hold—"

"They had bad regime loyalty data and their army district commanders shorted the instrument. Yes. The Mao Dynasty only held on to Beijing and the two neighboring provinces. Yes."

"Then why the PRC?" Clay asked.

"They got involved in the Indo-Pak War in hopes of crippling India and setting themselves as the only non-US superpower. After the war turned against them and riots and warlords led to disunion, the US was the only superpower. If the US were crippled they would have a chance to catch up. You see the video and read the blog entries, they're slowly reunifying China."

The motor home slowed at a four-way stop overseen by a flashing yellow light dangling over the intersection. At the corner stood a convenience store. Clay glanced out the side window behind the sofa. An old farmer leaned against a pickup truck and watched them pass.

"You predicted it but you didn't tell anyone," Clay said.

"We thought for a while what to do. Guillaume wanted to call NCS. I was sure NCS wouldn't believe us or, worse, would arrest us as co-conspirators. Gangfeng figured we were safe in New York so why not ride the perps' coattails and cash in ourselves? Like we wouldn't really have been arrested for that. So we kept mum for a while."

"A while."

"The more I thought, the more clearly I saw the situation. Whatever happened in '19 and '20, the Presidential election would go to whoever promised the most hawkish foreign and domestic antiterrorist program. To whoever promised a police state."

Nil frowned. "It would depend on which party—"

Wally burst into more laughter. "Sorry. You take slogans and soundbites more seriously than I do. Whoever could most credibly promise a war against Third World dictators and Russian physicists— and fringe subcultures at home—would get everything else on his agenda. More welfare, less welfare, more immigration, less immigration, affirmative action, illegalizing robots, it wouldn't matter."

"Why worry about a police state?" Nil asked. "You were a Wall Street millionaire."

Wally's eyebrows rose. "I grew up five miles from Mexico. Bad government can ruin a country for centuries. I didn't want that to happen here."

"You turned rebel for that?" Nil looked cynical. "No one's that noble."

His expression turned candid. "I had selfish reasons too. Wars and police states are expensive, and under universal suffrage, where better to raise taxes than on the rich? And then there's Ben Franklin's most famous quote."

Nil said, his tone questioning, " 'Those who would give up a little security to gain a little liberty—' "

"Oh. His second most famous."

" 'Early to bed—' "

"Make it his third." Wally twisted his mouth and looked at the ceiling. "His fourth?"

Nil fell silent, but the words came to Clay. His face grew clammy and he peered at Wally. " 'Three may keep a secret, if two are dead.' "

"Exactly." The other started and jerked his hands away from his body. "Whoa, not like that."

Clay believed he hadn't killed them. "Then like what?"

"I couldn't trust them. Gangfeng would get greedy and forensic accountants after the fact would find him and grab the rest of us. Guillaume would be too trusting; they wouldn't believe him before the attack but they'd scapegoat him and the rest of us after. So I went underground. I shifted money offshore. I bought the best false ID available in the Caribbean. Then Osvaldo Guerra went scuba diving near his fancy hotel on Cardenas Bay and never came to the surface."

"Three months before 6:19," Clay said.

"I came back to the country under an assumed name, paid cash for the motor home and the GMW, and have ridden around the country ever since. Collecting data. Making contacts. Drawing up plans. Until the time came to topple Everton. That time has come."

"It has?"

"Here," Wally said, and scurried to his desk. He pulled out a thick smartpaper and unrolled it. The ends drooped over the coffee table. "Everton loyalty chart."

"A what?" Nil asked.

"An Everton loyalty chart. I started putting it together during the '20 presidential campaign. Blog aggregation, search term interest, plus some other stuff I've been adding over time." His fingertip traced a hashwork of bars starting in the spring of 2020, rising higher and higher until mid '21, but since then churning back and forth, the bars longer than before, but the value almost unchanged after two years. "Here we have two years of distribution. People turning from AU loyalists to self-aggrandizers until only self-aggrandizers were left." He tapped the chart three months previously, mid-January. "It turned from distribution to collapse here."

The hashwork had edged down since then, but both the value and its volatility remained high. "Looks like noise in your signal," Clay said. "Fooling yourself there's a pattern."

Wally grinned and shook his head. "Didn't you hear that part about being a multimillionaire at 25? It's the start of the collapse phase. I put the probability at 98%."

"Meaning there's a 2% chance it won't." Clay spoke quietly. No cage in South Dakota for him if NCS caught him; rather, a bullet in his brainpan and his ashes scattered—

"How much certainty do you need?"

Clay slouched on the sofa. "If loyalty to Everton is collapsing what difference does it make who takes the lead? Why not stay safe and lie low?"

"I've charted historical loyalty to other regimes, like Soviet Russia and Mao Dynasty China. From the inflection point of the chart to the end of the regime can take decades. Do you want to live on the run that long?"

"No...." The absurdity of Wally's choice welled up in Clay. "But why me?"

Wally's expression turned quizzical. "You don't see it? Clay, you made the MuSynths and the NuGlands. You know how to use them better than anyone else."

He saw the task Wally had in mind. It loomed before him like a mountain with a marathon course ascending it. "I'm just a tinkerer."

"Not even close. Everton used your technology to seize his position. The same technology is the only way to dislodge him."

"Is that all I am? A tool for your use?" Clay glared at Wally. "You put me in harm's way and who gave you the right?"

"I didn't put you in the South Dakota camp or the NMHA facility. But because you've been there, you know what they're capable of. Give Everton a few more years and he'll do it to everyone. Do you want that?"

Clay's chest deflated as he exhaled. "No. But I'm not the kind of man you need to overthrow him."

"Why not? You're taller than he is." Wally grinned.

"Seriously, we can't do this. The three of us against NCS and the Army?" Clay blinked and saw Ramirez, cold stare and cocked pistol, in his mind's eye. "Cuba's not that far." Jenny didn't know anything. She wouldn't suffer for his sake. He could go in a clean conscience.

"I know it's a lot to think about. But Clay, eight months ago I sat right there—" Wally said, and pointed at his spot on the sofa, "—and I read your name and what TS Microcatalytix had invented and I couldn't sleep that night. Maybe you were friendlier to me than most of our classmates and I'm biased for that reason, but a hunch told me you were the key person to bring Everton down."

How could he have been friendly to someone he barely remembered? "I'm not nineteen anymore. Not that I could have done this then."

"You're selling yourself short—"

"I'm the wrong man." He barely knew what drove himself, let alone anyone else. The things that inspired him didn't matter to anyone else. He couldn't lead anyone against anything. Forget changing the world. They could find a cabin near the beach in southeast Cuba, where life was as slow as it had been before Castro's dictatorship, and drink rum and smoke cigars and hope NCS never found them and sent a black ops squad against them. He knew real cages now, whether built from steel bars or aerosolized neuroactives, and a quiet den in which to lick one's wounds and sleep in the sun was not one.

Wally bent forward, rested his elbows on his knees and his chin on his interleaved hands. "You've not been yourself."

"I said I'm not nineteen anymore."

"Lately, I mean."

"I've been in a mental hospital. How would you be?"

Wally leaned back and ducked his head. He glanced at Nil and Clay's gaze followed. Nil looked impassively between the two of them, but suddenly blinked and moved the bruise reliever away from his mouth.

"NMHA ordered NuGlands," he said.

"So?"

Nil glanced at Wally and the latter nodded vigorously. "They implanted you with at least one," Nil said. "Maybe several, depending on what they wanted to do to your brain chemistry."

Wally added, "What else would Boucher do with them?"

Clay rolled his eyes. "I know my own mind better than either of you. If there were something like that in my brain, I'd know."

"You've changed," Wally said. "Compared to when I first contacted you. More timid, more resigned."

"You know what I've been through?" Clay glared across the room.

"How many people would come out of the Hospital promising not to rest until Everton were defeated? You would have been one of them."

Clay paid attention to his mind for a moment, but dismissed what the others said. If he could tap his thoughts they would all ring crystal true. "I know my own mind."

Nil worried his lower lip with his teeth. "Not as well as you think. That's not a put down," he added as he flashed his palms. "It's true for us all. Thoughts pinball around our minds and we act on some of them without knowing why. But we make up stories that we do know why, that we are in control, and we tell those lies to one another and to ourselves."

"Not me," Clay said.

Nil inhaled. "I know at least something about human psychology."

The flat understatement caught Clay's attention. He looked from one to the other. Nil's brow was troubled and Wally had a pained expression. How could they both be so certain? "I'd know if they had implanted me."

"They could have done it in your sleep," Wally said.

"Not their style."

"Even if you made them angry? After Van Wijk foiled your escape?"

Clay clamped his jaws for a moment, recalling the examination room. "They shoved a pill down my throat. No, that can't have done it. Stomach acid would have knocked out the units." His ankle itched again and he reached to scratch it but halted his hand halfway. What if it wasn't an insect bite? What if Boucher had injected him while the orderly and guard distracted him? No, he knew his thoughts; his brain wasn't lying to him.

"Then while you were asleep," Wally said.

"No. I know my own mind."

Wally frowned at the floor for a moment. "Let's say for a second they lodged NuGlands in your brain. Would they show up on MRI?"

"If they were there."

He turned his owlish gaze on Clay. "Can you humor me for a couple of days?" He didn't wait for an answer. "Arvie, get us to Phoenix, asap."

Thirteen

They crossed back into Missouri across the "temporary" pontoon bridge at Cairo, Illinois in the early afternoon. Wally argued with the motor home while traffic squeezed from two westbound lanes to one, but it assured him this was probabilistically the quicker route even if they hadn't been hung up past the last exit. "Don't come this way again," he told it, as it crept onto the detour lanes to the pontoon. The old bridge's eastern tower stood as naked as a stripped tree trunk. Twisted steel poked at a cloudy sky.

The unfinished halves of the new bridge hung a quarter-mile up-river; slender, yellow webbings of carbon nanotube and titanium alloys straining for each other. It looked too slender to hold six lanes of highway deck even if it were finished.

"After the '17 earthquake, DOT under President Reynolds fast-tracked replacement bridges," Wally said. "After the election, the original contractor must not have given Everton enough kickbacks. Enemy combatant charges." They crept up on a sign where animated bulldozer icons apologized for the delay and morphed into smiling outlines of the joined states. At the lower right corner stood a logo, Gupta Engineering, a Titan Industries company.

A few miles west of the river, rain plunked the motor home's roof and soon built up to a steady rattle. They left the interstate for a two-lane road that curved over forested hills and cut into limestone banks. How close were they to the Hospital? Clay didn't ask, but he ducked lower in the sofa and peered out the window when they waited at traffic lights in small towns, fearful of police vehicles. No sheriff's deputies or state troopers stopped them, though, and he wondered how much of his fear came from his mind and how much from Boucher's.

Nil spent the day avoiding Clay and pressing bruise relievers to his face, but after a dinner of drive-through samosas and tikka masala naan wraps, another interstate ticking under their wheels on the way to Tulsa, he sat on the other side of the sofa and rolled a sheaf of smartpaper up in his hands. "We don't need Wally's contact to start mapping where, if, the Hospital implanted you. If you're interested."

"You never told me you had MRI vision."

Nil waved the smartpapers. "Human neuroanatomical atlas. If you can self-report accurately—"

"You think I can't?"

"It's tougher than it looks." He spoke in his tone of weary, worldly wisdom, and from experience Clay knew he was right to use it more often than not. "Tell me specific ways you've been thinking differently since you arrived at the Hospital. If it's because of an implant tweaking your neurochemistry we can map it to the proper locus in your brain."

Orange light slanted at sharp angles through the windows and Clay lay back and stared at the ceiling and sifted his thoughts, with long stretches between utterances. Everton and NCS seemed more powerful. His mood was bleaker and more fatalistic. He was quicker to anger and slower to trust the people near him. Nil searched the neuroanatomical atlas and scratched notes. "Somewhere in the orbitofrontal and prefrontal cortices. Brodmann's areas 10, 11, and 47."

"English?"

"Sorry." Nil jabbed his index fingers at his forehead, an inch above each eyebrow. He browsed further and named other parts of the brain as the windows opaqued against the deepening night. Clay tuned out the Latin terms and listened further to the chatter within his mind.

Wally derailed his train of thought by bounding from the back room with a chart in his hand. "See, Clay?" He shoved it in front of Clay's face and flicked his fingernail against the back of the sheet. The same Everton loyalty chart, but today's bar lunged downward. "That's the burning of the NMHA facility rippling through the bureaucracy. Turf wars out the wazoo. There will be a half-assed rally tomorrow but then it's downhill after that."

"Sure," Clay said to placate him.

Wally fixed him a mirthful look. "Fifty dollars?"

"I'm cash poor." His wallet had burned in the fire.

"I'll take an IOU."

Morning found them on a US highway crossing a desert of yucca, solar power stations, and striated mesas. The road signs named towns in New Mexico and Clay shivered. Somewhere out here lay another island in Everton's archipelago of prison camps. Wally and Nil were fools if they thought they could fight him. Everton would wield his army of NCS agents, soldiers, and informants and crush them. Perhaps NCS would scatter their ashes right here, on this scoured desert between Portales and Roswell, where the wind would slowly herd their remains into dry gulches and a thousand years of flash floods would wash them out to sea.

Maybe NuGlands were talking—

Bah. Even if there were NuGlands in his head, the changes in his thoughts had been laid down the old-fashioned way, by the formation and growth of synapses while in South Dakota. The Hospital. Nil's office.

Clay glared across the cabin at him but then shut his eyes and breathed deep cycles. At least his one-time friend hadn't tried to seduce Jenny. Thanks to that, the possibility existed he could forgive him someday. Though god knew when.

Early evening they pulled into an RV park on the north side of Phoenix. "We'll take the GMW," Wally said. Behind the motor home the sedan unhitched itself and waited for them. The sun hung low in the west but not low enough; the air desiccated them and the concrete baked their soles as they walked ten yards to the car.

The sedan joined traffic on the freeway eastbound and exited near Scottsdale. Clay assumed they were heading for a hospital or clinic, but the car carried them past a golf course and into a neighborhood of long low houses, gently pitched roofs tiled with solar panels, and Southwestern Zen gardens on oversized lots. "Where are we going?"

"Daniel's."

Clay looked at Wally. There had to be more.

"He dropped out of grad school when his parents died to move into their old house. He's a little eccentric…. Wait, that's what I think. He's very eccentric."

"Eccentric enough to have an MRI in the basement?" Clay asked.

Wally blinked a few times. "That's eccentric?"

The car stopped on a hillside in front of a stucco-clad house featuring a jumble of roofs and divided-light windows. Quadrupedal robots spat water at cactuses and palm trees in the front yard. "Can we trust him?" Nil asked.

"He doesn't know 6:19 happened," Wally said.

Clay glanced up and down the block. Split level modernist ranch houses peered down the slopes. "He doesn't get many visitors?"

"No."

"His neighbors know about 6:19, and I'll go double or nothing that they gossip like old women at a church social."

Wally craned his neck and checked the street. "Geemer, pull into the driveway."

The front door opened and swathed them in cool air. The motor on the door was a retrofit, gray and bulbous as a tumor and grinding as it unreeled the cable to close the door. Inside, a monitor popped on and an animated butler guided them to the basement.

A robot mopped the terrazzo floor of the living room and slid out of their way. Above the robot's reach, though, dust clung to the frames of cowboy paintings and the brown couches showed sun-faded patches and cracked leather armrests. A coffee table bore smartpaper catalogs for electronic parts and animatronic sex dolls. More monitors warmed up to guide them. A glance in the kitchen showed a bare white refrigerator and a mound of pizza cartons and soft drink bottles pushing up the lid of the trash can. The basement door opened. Something in the depths hummed and Clay recalled some serial killer movie where the perp's mummified parent sat in an unused room.

Daniel stood at the top of the basement stair. Despite his diet, he cut a reasonably trim figure, though a middle-age paunch tented his T-shirt. His pale face contrasted with his brown irises. "You're Clay? You removed your wearable already. Good. The ring, though." He pointed at Clay's left hand.

He'd forgotten he'd been wearing the wedding band. He twisted it off and looked around with it. Nil stood the closest. "Here." He dropped it in Nil's palm. Nil looked startled and clenched his fist around it.

"Nothing else? Earbuds, pocket displays? Come on down."

The air felt cooler and more damp. The whine of equipment became louder. Cheap metal racks covered two walls, laden with computer equipment and hundreds of translucent plastic storage drawers stuffed to their tops with small parts. Below a tiny window on the side wall, the MRI hulked like the head of a white plastic beast with a wide mouth.

Daniel sat at on old keyboard and monitor. "Lie down, either direction, preferably on your back. I hope you're not claustrophobic. You'll need to lie still a few minutes."

Clay contorted himself into the mouth of the MRI and lay there. It might be pointless, but if NCS didn't raid while he lay here, no harm would come. How big an if? His heart thudded a couple of times but he breathed steadily and calmed himself. Nothing he could do. The housing above the scanning mouth was too close to focus his eyes on it and he let it go, accepting the incompleteness of his vision. He could feel the absence of his wedding band from his hand. The humming of the MRI grew louder and deeper and mechanical parts clunked together in the housing overhead.

"That's it," Daniel said. "Come on out. Head upstairs if you like."

"When will we see the results?"

"When the processing's done. Soon." A printer rattled and whined. "Very soon."

Clay found Wally and Nil in the living room, seated on couches on opposite walls. The dividers in the windows cast long shadows across the terrazzo and the mopping robot's cleaning fluid glistened in the sun. Daniel came in a few minutes later with a bundle of oversized papers as thick as a bible. He dropped the bundle on the coffee table. "I set the processor to false-color anything that met the specs of a NuGland."

Wally licked his fingertips and started pushing pages. Clay looked over his right shoulder. The prints were grayscale saggital sections, white bone, gray tissue, black liquid—it felt as uncomfortable to Clay as seeing himself on video—and Wally moved through them quickly enough they looked like a flipbook animation.

He stopped. Clay swallowed. Against the gray background stood a red dot, an inch inside his skull from his eyebrows.

The GMW drove back to the RV park through the hot desert night. The only sounds in the cabin, other than cold air blown out the vents, came from Wally and Nil, as they flipped through the bundle of brain section printouts and murmured when they found more NuGlands.

Clay sagged against the headrest. How many units had lodged in the arterioles of his brain? What neuroactives, in what doses, emerged from them and diffused to his neurons?

"How do we get them out?" Wally said.

"Out? We can't." He breathed deeply. "But we can turn them off."

Clay's voice sounded distant to himself, but then he realized the NuG-lands were the source of that sensation. Turning off the units would be trivial and he perked up when he recognized that. "Let's do it."

Nil cleared his throat. "Don't shut down the NuGlands, Clay."

The car rolled on while silence ruled the cabin. Anger and bewilderment tugged at Clay. "What am I supposed to do instead?"

"Reconfigure them."

Clay blinked. "To do what?"

"Everton's the enemy, right? You say you'll do whatever it takes to turn him out of office? You can make doing that a lot easier."

Clay pushed his feet against the floor and sat taller. "You think I'm not angry enough?"

"Anger's not what you need. It's a question of innate tendencies. You need to be less idealistic about how people should behave. More adept at manipulating others. More ruthless."

"More like you."

Nil blanched. "Compared to Everton and his people, I'm a child. Look inside yourself. Could you shoot Ramirez if you had to? Could you keep him alive if it served your purposes? Either one might be necessary."

Perhaps it was a paradox, but the thought of taking either action left Clay cold. "You want me to change who I am."

"I want you to succeed. Do you want to topple Everton?"

Three men in an RV against the most powerful man in the world? "Someone must."

"Could you have done it, the man you were, that night we shot billiards at your house?"

Sullen about Martin, sullen about Jenny; sipping scotch and wishing he could be in the laboratory, talking with his staff scientists and hoping another technical challenge would present itself. Clay slumped.

Nil softened his expression. "You have to change either way. You could try without this; you could unlearn old habits and form some new ones, perhaps with a neuronal plasticizer to help form new synapses. You might reach the same point, but later and less complete, than if you reconfigured the NuGlands you already have." He jabbed his finger at the bundle of papers.

Clay avoided their gazes. His mouth felt dry and he told the refrigerator under the seat cushion to slide out its bin. He grabbed a bottle, swigged water, and groped for a way out. "Wally, this isn't necessary. You said loyalty to the regime is already collapsing. It'll be easy to push Everton off the cliff, won't it?"

Wally winced, pulling his upper lip high enough to show his teeth. "I worked in observation, not manipulation. There's a lot of people who'll be pushing back."

Clay swigged more water. He wished he could sit back while Everton's regime dried up and blew away like dusty soil. Yet even if a miracle obscured his trail to the NCS, and he could let someone else do the hard work of toppling Everton, what tipping points would fall unnoticed to moot the victory, to replace Everton's tyranny with another? He could trust no one else and Nil was right: he lacked the innate traits to succeed.

"I'm in," he said. "What do we have to do?"

"It'll take some time," Nil said, "to find all the units and decide what to have them do." He pulled the brain section printouts from Wally. "To start, you should generate a monoamine oxidase A inhibitor at the moral circle locus in the pars opercularis...."

They left Phoenix, heading north, and worked late into the night, discussing compounds to synthesize and the locations to do so in the constellation of NuGlands revealed by the brain section scan. Clay's reference materials on the NuGland were trapped on his wearable, but Wally plunged headfirst into a cabinet under the couch and handed him a sheaf of locked smartpapers. Writing the code to affect the changes was easy, even late at night with exhaustion and increasing elevation pulling down Clay's eyelids. Wally pulled a transceiver from another cabinet and told his wearable to communicate with Clay's NuGlands. Clay knew what it would do, yet it remained hard to believe a coded RF burst could change how he thought.

Wally had a handful of Midwest Home Products air fresheners and a stack of smartpaper notes on them stashed in one of the cabinets hidden around the living room. The code Clay had overnighted on a thumb drive to Chile had been copied and bounced around the world, with one set arriving in Wally's wearable.

They spent the next few days at an RV park in Durango, Colorado, tinkering with the air fresheners, the three of them cramped in the living room of the motor home. They kept the puffer triggered to release on audio or video of Everton, but instead of molecules to stimulate trust and complacency, Clay rewrote the process control code to release serotonin antagonists and anxiety inducers and Wally modified a worm to install the new code on the air fresheners already deployed. Not just Sampson and Salazar, but tens of thousands of others who had bought generic MHP air fresheners since Everton's election wouldn't know why they started hating the president that spring. The thought disquieted Clay for a moment, but Sampson and Salazar didn't know why they'd started liking Everton three years previous, and neither did their friends and neighbors influenced without knowing in chat rooms, supermarket aisles, and church fellowship halls.

"Not everyone will take," Clay said.

"Not everyone," Wally replied, "but enough."

The cramped quarters of the motor home forced Clay outside several times a day. Snow topped the deep green slopes of the southern San Juan Mountains and the RV park's pool was drained and covered. Clay took the jogging trail but soon gasped in the high altitude. The cold early spring air burned his throat, yet he pushed on to finish two miles, and went out the next morning to jog three.

A few of the people in neighboring RVs glanced at him the first couple of days: the gay couple with the Jesus fish on the back of their towed camper; the grizzled anglo, Marine Corps tat on his upper arm, owner of a motor home bigger than Wally's, accompanied by two women half his age. By the third morning they ignored him. He returned the favor.

In addition to coding the worm, Wally spent other time seeking exploits into the servers of America United and government agencies. Late the third night, while Clay and Nil mashed controller buttons and trash-talked during a game of NUL Ultimate Flying Disc '24, Wally ran in, more hyperactive than usual, a smartpaper in his hand. "Look at this! Woot!"

Singh's long forehand pass had almost reached Mpondo, alone in the back right corner of Nil's endzone, when Nil paused the game. Clay gave him a mild shove. "Loser."

"Don't blame me," Nil said, "blame Wally. What do you have?"

"Brain implanted NuGlands. Thousands of military personnel so far and they're rolling it out further everyday." He held the smart-paper for them to read. "The first wave was at the joint forces bases in the USA Capital District around New Washington—Fort Osborne, Fort Stockton, and Fort Everton. The second wave was at Fort Riley—"

"Fort Riley?" Clay asked. "That's my brother-in-law's post."

Wally drew the smartpaper back. "His name's Roger? Find Roger Sung," he told the smartpaper. After a moment, he nodded. "They implanted him weeks ago. Coding to enhance obedience to the command structure."

"Where's the cutoff?" Nil asked. "I'll wager fifty dollars the generals exempted themselves."

Wally shook his head. "How foolish do I look? Sort by rank." His eyes widened. "I should have taken your bet. Says all the way up to two-star general."

"Everton's worried about the military's loyalty," Nil said.

"Looks like it." Wally stared at the paused screen where the flying disc hung over the right sideline. "That's really good news if we can hack the implants in division commanders. I'm sure we can. Clay?"

Could he do this to Jenny's younger brother? To anyone? Great action would be required to dislodge Everton from the New White House, and if they were to turn some soldiers against the president while others remained loyal, that great action would involve combat. If not Roger, than someone else's brother, someone else's son, would be killed. "In theory."

"I'll work up a worm—"

Clay's thoughts returned to his brother-in-law. "Is this something we should be doing?"

Nil frowned. "We talked about this."

"Everton did the same thing," Wally said.

"That's an argument in favor of it?"

Nil stared at the paused display. His profile was grim. "We have to look out for ourselves."

"The worst that happened to anyone manipulated by Everton is a life of harmless ignorance. The worst that can happen to someone we manipulate is arrest or death."

Wally tapped his toe. "Farm animals live in harmless ignorance, don't they? Until you take them to the slaughterhouse?"

Clay saw the point. People could give up their freedom to the rule of angels, but would suffer greatly when devils staged a *coup*. Yet still…. "It doesn't seem right."

Nil inhaled deeply and he turned to Clay. "We're a long way," he said lightly, "from being able to do anything. No need to argue now." He picked up his controller. "Let's make it best-of-three."

He amended the terms to best-of-five after Clay won the next game. Clay took the series in four.

He dreamed that night about a NUL draft, head-to-head between him and his former boss at his last employer before he and Nil started TS Microcatalytix. The player pool held more than Singh, Mpondo, and other stars; the old Marine and the gay couple were included, and the first woman to be considered for NUL, Monica Colbert, played by Jenny in a blonde wig. He chose Jenny, Singh, and the old Marine. His former boss brought transport for his players, but Clay turned his head to see them climb a ramp into a gray steel stock trailer like the one his father had used to take their steers to the stockyard.

Two inches of snow fell overnight, and Clay woke early from a restless sleep to see empty pull-throughs and lawns hidden beneath powder as fresh as a clean canvas. "You were right," he told Wally and Nil while potato pancakes sizzled on the stovetop under the eye of the SueChef.

The armed forces were not the only organizations whose members had been implanted. Over the next few days, Wally assembled lists naming low-level NCS agents and federal bureaucrats. America United offered a new program of discounted dues to members who chose "loyalty confirmation." They deserved whatever the reprogramming would give them. Nothing personal, but all these implantees had chosen the wrong side.

But what to reprogram them to do? AU and the government's original programming gave them ideas. The original programming had

increased the activity of various cortical loci involved in the construction of social authority: the implantees were primed to attach greater
weight to symbols and abstractions of hierarchy. Org charts, job titles,
ideas of authority; some of the same loci involved in religious behavior. From true believers in an abstract Everton, Clay and the others
could turn implantees into skeptics. Other sources of hierarchy—the
male primate tendency to gauge others' and one's own ability and willingness to dominate or be dominated—had been left untouched by the
feds and AU. But Everton could maintain his hold that way on only a
handful of his underlings at any time.

They also debated how virulent to make the reprogramming
worm. Wally insisted on a slow spread and stubbornly held his
ground until Clay and Nil saw his wisdom. A fast-acting worm would
be noticed and quickly countered by antivirus software; but one that
spread slowly and imperceptibly co-opted system resources would be
ignored, just as higher animals' immune and DNA maintenance systems had ignored biological viruses that turned asymptomatic. Also,
reprogramming wasn't instantaneous in affect. It would take a few
days for a change in brain chemistry to manifest in changed behavior,
so there was no need to hurry.

After a week in Durango, they had the worm coded. Wally slid an
old-fashioned wireless keyboard across the table to Clay and let him
press enter to release it into the computer ecosystem. "Now we wait,"
Wally said.

Clay looked out the window at dirty piles of slushy, melting snow
in the parking lot. "Somewhere else."

From southwestern Colorado they drove east, into Pennsylvania, but
cold weather lingered and Clay suggested heading south. Wally over-
rode the motor home's desire to turn west at Baltimore and ordered it
south toward the ruins of Washington.

The old capital's northern suburbs had survived, but the closer to
the city, the more for sale signs mushroomed in front yards and the
more windows stood boarded up. Scorched buildings soon appeared,
then passed to burnt ones, then ones defined solely by rubble and

twisted steel beams. The freeway veered west and turned into ground-level tracks of crazed concrete detouring around the abutments of former overpasses. So few cars came the other direction that Clay forgot his intention to count them. A tall chain link fence walled off the former city. Patchy grass and a handful of trees had grown back in place of all that had burned in the firestorm. No one in the motor home spoke until they were well into Virginia and cars clustered in the parking lots of restaurants along the freeway.

They rode south into Georgia, through red-soil towns along the Chattahoochee River, and ended up at an RV park in Quitman County, on the Georgia shore of Lake Eufaula. Alabama showed as a piney fringe across the lake. The picnic tables were shabby and the other tenants stared at Wally's large, expensive motor home.

Within hours, an antsy feeling gripped Clay and the walls of the motor home's living room seemed to close in on him. "There's got to be more we can do."

"There's a saying on Wall Street," Wally said. "Some men can be right. Some men can sit tight. Few can do both."

Clay shook his head and stalked out. Between two cramped pop-up trailers, a cluster of boys, seven or eight years old, poked sticks at the belly of a trash-collecting robot they'd caught and flipped. Its legs churned the air and one of the boys looked up at Clay. His expression showed guilt at being seen, laid over the curiosity imparted by a smart drug.

Personal waterjets whined across the water and fishing boats dotted the lake. Clay walked to a gazebo near the boat slip and a short pier stumped with boat tie-ups. A couple of waterjets bobbed along the pier's thick rubber bumper.

Clay settled at a bench deep in the gazebo's shadow and opened a web browser. Twenty minutes later he stumbled across Delacroix' blog. After his surprise wore off he spent an hour reading the archives.

Delacroix had escaped the Hospital and somehow reached the Caribbean. He laid out Boucher's agenda, debunked a rumor Clay had not heard, in which enemy combatants had attacked the Hospital the night of the escape and fired incendiary rounds to start the fire, and repeated the words of "a fellow inmate, probably dead," who claimed

Everton had manipulated the electorate in 2020.

You're not the only one who escaped, Clay sent securely. *Remind me never to play hearts with you again.*

Delacroix replied to him a few hours later with astonished words. He wasn't the only escapee—Kerensky and Yamamoto had followed him to the Caribbean, and they'd seen others run for the fences the night of the fire. He didn't offer an explanation for his journey out of the country, and Clay didn't ask. Either many had risked much to serve as conductors on an underground railroad, or Delacroix had turned into an Everton loyalist and his blog was a scam. If he even blogged; Clay recalled Van Wijk's comment about ghostbloggers. To know whether he could trust the other, Clay would have to rely on his mirror neurons' ability to predict the thoughts of others.

He was suddenly glad of Nil's suggestion to reprogram his NuG-lands.

Back in the motor home, Wally recalculated his Everton loyalty index in light of Delacroix' blog, but its downward drift barely steepened. "People don't believe him."

"All he has is hearsay," Clay said. "If he had hard data on the Free Samples Project, people might believe him."

"You want to send some?" Nil frowned. "If the site is a fed hoax—"

"The feds already have data on the Free Samples Project."

"But not on our location."

Clay looked Wally over. "You couldn't scrub our tracks?"

A few minutes later, Wally sent a copy to Delacroix.

Over the next days, the Everton loyalty index turned more steeply down. Still, no collapse. "How many people can we send copies to?"

"Every current events blogger," Nil said.

Wally frowned. "That's a lot of packets. Runs the risk of someone tracing all that traffic."

"Is it worth the risk?" Clay's tone made it clear he thought so.

Wally's gaze wavered, and then the smartpaper bearing the loyalty chart caught his attention. "It is."

They sent anonymous copies slowly to scores of bloggers, from Eric Demosthenes to Locke Smith. Demosthenes asked for more information, who he was, how he found it, but Clay ignored the personal questions in his reply. A few posts and video streams took it up at first, with more following in the next few days. Pro-Everton posts followed, denouncing the anonymous emailer, contorting facts to paint the copies as fraudulent, hinting other bloggers credulous enough to believe the copies were accurate—

"How can they say that?" Clay asked. "They've seen all the details."

"People see what they want to see," Nil said.

Wally was upbeat. "They're giving it oxygen. The only bad press is an obituary."

Clay inhaled deeply and checked the loyalty chart. The decline had grown steeper, but Wally counseled more patience. The chart would break sharply, he insisted, some massive insider selloff, probably starting some Monday after a weekend of a million guarded conversations at the golf course, the church social, the strip club. Amid the hidden panic they could finally act.

Still, Clay wished it were enough to simply be right, without needing to sit tight.

One Sunday, Nil challenged Clay to more *NUL '24* on the motor home's main screen. Nil's play had improved, but not by enough; he left a soft midfield for Singh and Clay's other handlers to work the disc downfield. Yet Nil's transition offense had improved, sending his sprinters on deep corner patterns on turnovers. His handler, Gryzbowski, picked up the disc and launched a long backhand—

A United States map replaced the game on the display. A red splotch bloomed in southwestern Georgia and an alarm bleated through hidden speakers. "What now?" Nil asked.

The controller slid from Clay's hands. "Zoom in."

The display zoomed. A red splotch covered a stretch of the Lake Eufaula shore in Quitman County, Georgia.

13

Wally jumped up. "Move! Move! Arvie, wipe all the smartpaper." He scurried to one of the hidden cabinets under the display and pulled out a bulky backpack. "Tell Geemer to unhitch." He looked at Clay and Nil on the couch. "Move!"

The door swung open. Wally wavered as he stuck his arms through the backpack's straps and took the steps to the concrete pad. "I can grab that," Clay called as he stepped into his sneakers.

Wally cinched the straps. "I've practiced this, you haven't." His gaze turned away from the lake. "Dammit."

Clay and Nil hurried after him. The ground sloped up from the lake to a low ridge that bowled in the RV park. Trees covered most of the ridge and leaves littered the shingled roofs of the park office and the snackeria gazebo. The driveway curled past the park office and through a saddlepoint in the ridge carved out and lined by concrete retaining walls. A humvee, smartcamo shimmering, stood across the driveway in the saddlepoint. Two pizza boxes crouched behind the near tires and their turrets articulated, sensors and armaments like dogs' noses.

"We're not getting out of here in the car," Wally said.

More pizza boxes glinted among the trees. Two sharp cracks sounded behind the park office and the snackeria gazebo and pizza boxes wobbled like weakly-thrown flying discs and clattered on each roof.

Compressed air in their bellies? No time to wonder. "Boats," Clay said.

"I don't have one," Wally said.

"Theft will be the least of our crimes." He stared at Wally, grabbed Nil by the arm and pushed him toward the boat slip. "Let's go!"

They ran to the end of the motor home and turned left, down the driveway behind their row of RVs and hook-up pads. Motion glinted between the RVs. Nil's feet pounded the concrete and his breath came raggedly. Clay glanced back. Where was Wally? At his car? "Wally!"

Wally said something to the GMW and patted it on the front door pillar. It backed out of the spot,then put itself into gear. Its engine throbbed and it accelerated up the driveway out of the park. Wally hurried after them. "Creating a diversion," he said, gasping.

They hurried toward the boat slip and pier. Plastic and metal crunched behind them. A glance over Clay's shoulder showed the sedan buckled against the quarter panel of the humvee, steam rising from under both crumpled hoods. Robots zipped around the crashed sedan.

They ran onto the pier and stopped short. Only one craft lay tied up, an old waterjet shaped like a snowmobile, its paint faded and a flat cushion peeking through cracks in the plastic upholstery of the single seat.

"That can't carry three," Wally said.

"We'll make it carry three." Clay ran toward the waterjet. The pier's weathered gray boards flexed and groaned underfoot. He pulled the tie-rope over the mooring post and flung it at the nose of the craft. Feet-first he jumped into the water. The shallows were warm from the sun and the muddy bottom squished under his canvas sneakers. He climbed on the waterjet and the sun-baked plastic warmed his crotch. Dials and buttons covered the dashboard. How did you start this thing? Had the owner taken the key?

A splash behind him, and Wally climbed on. He huddled on the seat, pressed his chest against Clay's back. Clay slid forward as far as he could, until his knees scraped the underside of the dash.

"There's no room," Nil said from the pier. The plastic treads of the military robots clacked loudly on the concrete driveways. The diversion was over, and part of Clay noted how much louder the treads sounded on concrete than over grass.

"Try!"

Nil jumped into the water and clambered for the seat. The waterjet wobbled under his weight and reared back, forcing Clay to lean far forward to keep from tipping. Nil let go suddenly and the nose slapped the water. The pier and the water's surface gave his voice an odd echo. "It won't work."

The clack of treads grew louder. A glance showed shapes gray as concrete thirty yards from the base of the pier.

How far was the Alabama shore? A mile, give or take; twenty minutes if he pushed hard. "You get on! I can swim!"

Nil shook his water-slick head. "Not fast enough! They'll be on the lake if they aren't already! The two of you have to go!"

"Not without you!"

"You don't need me. The two of you can topple Everton."

"Nil—"

Anger flashed in his eyes. "Goddammit, Clay, I betrayed you once. I won't again." A small splash hit the surface near them. Paralyzer darts from the military robots. "Get out of here!" Nil pushed the waterjet away from the pier. More darts splashed nearby. He gave Clay one last look and turned to face the oncoming robots.

Wally reached past Clay and pressed the starter button. The engine throbbed and water burbled behind them. "We need to go," Wally shouted.

Clay faced the far shore and twisted the throttle on the handlebar. The waterjet surged forward and wind whipped his face. Wally reached his arms around Clay's torso and pressed his chest against Clay's back. A memory, Martin teetering against Clay's leg and clumsily wrapping his arms around it, distracted him for a moment.

The moment passed and his thoughts returned. Part of Clay wanted to turn around and do something, anything, for Nil, but a glance over his shoulder, past Wally's wind-whipped hair, showed Nil slumped face down in the water near the boat slip and pizza boxes dragging him up the concrete ramp.

Clay turned away and peered across the choppy water, searching the Alabama shore for a hidden, forested cove to hide the waterjet and start their way on foot.

"Head south," Wally shouted over the engine noise and slap of the craft's hull against the water. "We're too close to a bridge here. If we head south they'll have further to go around the lake to follow us."

"What if they're on the lake?"

"If we see their boats we head straight for the shore."

Clay oversteered to the left. The watercraft slewed and the cold taste of fear filled the back of his mouth. He eased his grip on the handlebars and adjusted course, southbound at thirty miles an hour.

The RV park soon fell out of sight behind them. They glanced fearfully at passing boats but the military and NCS weren't on the lake. A pair of old black men in a flat-bottomed aluminum boat, fishing rods slack in one hand, brown bottles sleeved by foamed rubber in the other, glared at them for going fast, but no one else showed any hostility. A white, scrubbed family on a northbound motorboat veered too close, but dad waved apologetically while the kids' upturned faces watched something in the sky. Clay lifted the fingers of his left hand from the handlebar in reply, then reopened the throttle. A few high clouds hung overhead like cotton candy on invisible ropes, but Clay saw nothing else. Tension seeped out of his shoulders as they sped on.

Why had Nil stayed behind? Yes, someone had to, and he'd been right he was the most expendable of the three. Yet even though Nil had betrayed him before, Clay's arms shook and he strangled the handles of the waterjet to keep himself from turning around.

Roger forced himself to match the pace of Lt. Col. Mueller down the driveway of the RV park. Hardin and the battalion sergeant followed behind them while crawlers clacked by.

The entire mission had been chaotic, from their abrupt deployment out of a limbo of barracks duty to Mueller's decision to join the company in the field. The battalion's other companies were tied up in extended operations in the Sierra Nevadas and the Adirondacks, the execution of NCS warrants leading them into running firefights against prepared insurgents; Roger assumed only extreme necessity could have pushed Ramirez to activate his company again. But the unit's morale had broken during its punishment for Roger's moment of conscience; though he couldn't prove it to himself his intuition told him it had happened. Roger sweated in the Georgia sunshine and hoped a cloud would shade them for a while.

Ramirez had commandeered the largest RV in the park, a motor home the size of a bus, as his command center. Mueller trotted up the steps and Roger trudged after. A massive display across the front of the room showed a highlight reel from a flying-disc video game left running by the enemy combatants. Forces of evil, out to topple our civilization. Right.

Though a large RV, the living room was still crowded by Ramirez, some unfamiliar NCS agents, and Roger's lieutenants—Wilson, Treviño, and Marsden—and their platoon sergeants. The windows had partially opaqued but the yellow-orange glow of sunlight suffused the room. An air conditioner labored but the room felt hot and itchy to the nose. Mueller nudged forward and Roger followed. A glance showed Lt. Wilson in the corner with his eyes white and his Adam's apple bobbing with nervous swallows.

Roger tracked Wilson's gaze to a chair near Ramirez. A man sat there, awkwardly, coughing. Roger shifted his head to see around Mueller. The man in the chair slumped forward, his hair waterlogged and strands of tangle tape swaddling his arms from shoulder to elbow, each hand, and both his upper and lower legs. He coughed again, a wet sound that would trigger sympathy if Roger heard it come from one of his kids. The man in the chair lifted his head. His hair was wet-black and plastered down his forehead, and his eyes, narrowly set and hooded, surprised Roger with their stubborn pride.

Roger knew the prisoner, and the realization stunned him for a moment until he thought of how. A party at Jenny's house during his last extended leave: Clay's business partner, Nil. What was he doing here? And who were the two people who'd fled on the stolen waterjet?

"Captain Sung," Ramirez said. The agent looked worse than he had a few weeks earlier, deeper bags under his eyes and whiteheads splotching his cheeks. Sweat glistened on his forehead. "Glad you could find the time to join us. Why wasn't this individual subjected to skeletal muscle relaxer?"

Roger stepped forward. Nil looked up at him, but his eyes showed only hostility, not recognition. *Why would he remember my name or face? Just as well he didn't.* Roger turned to Ramirez and met the NCS agent's gaze evenly. "Lt. Wilson didn't explain? His robots dosed him with the relaxer when he was in the water. They are programmed to retrieve people in that state, tie them up, and inject antidote. The assumed purpose of the relaxer is to retrieve persons for interrogation."

"Are you getting cute with me?" His bullying seemed hollow in the hot, cramped space. Most of the men glanced quizzically at each other, but Hardin sucked his teeth.

"I'm stating a fact, Agent Ramirez." Roger glanced at Nil long enough to see he didn't recognize his voice either.

Nil lifted his head and leaned back in the chair. "So you're going to interrogate me?" he said to Ramirez. "Why don't I speed the process? Yes, I have knowledge of the Free Samples Project. Candidate Everton used airborne drugs to manipulate the brain chemistry of the electorate in order to win the 2020 election. The commander-in-chief stole his position by fraud."

For a moment, the military men caught their breaths. *Could it be true? Would Nil know that?* But he did work for Titan Industries and Roger knew him well enough to know he was the kind of man who could find things hidden to others.

Ramirez glowered, but his demeanor showed no surprise at Nil's allegation. "You're talking bullshit."

Nil smiled. "You're in on the secret, I see." He lifted his head and made eye contact with the officers and sergeants. "How many of the rest of you are?"

Ramirez slapped him, backhanded. "Speak when spoken to."

"Or what?" Pain twisted Nil's face. "You'll shoot me the way you shot Monica Colbert? At least I know something about the Free Samples Project, unlike her. She didn't know a damn thing and you shot her anyway, and for what? She angered someone at Titan Industries? Whose payroll are you on?"

"You're goddam brave for a man about to die."

"You would have shot me in my house on a Sunday morning if I had been home. I've been about to die for weeks. Not that my death would help you. The truth is out. Not just among the honorable soldiers you're using. How many bloggers have posted links to the Free Samples Project files? How many mirror sites around the world that you can't shut down? Killing me won't do you any good. Why bother?"

Ramirez' gaze turned cold. "Because it will feel good to shut you up." He drew his pistol from inside his jacket and Nil had enough time for a look of alarm and desperation to form on his face before Ramirez fired two bullets into his chest. Blood bubbled from his mouth and his eyes turned glassy and he slumped to the floor. Lt. Treviño, standing the nearest, stepped back, face paling.

"What's your problem?" Ramirez asked. "Afraid of a little blood on your boots?" He turned to the rest of them. The room reeked of blood and propellant and fearful sweat. "We've got two more enemy combatants on the loose, so why don't you get the hell out of here and hunt them down? Or do we have enemy combatants in here too?"

The men were still. Roger's gaze clung to Nil's face despite his urge to look away. Ramirez' purpose was nothing but murder to conceal a crime from the eyes of justice. He couldn't claim to be on the same side, upholding the same oath, as Roger.

"You heard the man," Mueller said. "Out of here. The captain and I will discuss operations and the rest of you better be saddled up in ten minutes."

The lieutenants and platoon sergeants hurried out, then Mueller led Roger to the stairs. Roger glanced behind him and Ramirez glared back, his look venomous. Nil's words had been true; Everton's authority was illegitimate and his use of this sadist with a government ID compounded his crime. Roger didn't flinch, despite the agent's expression, despite Nil's corpse slumped on the carpet. Yet outside of the motor home, the hot, sunny day, freshened by a breeze, that should have felt clean and bright instead struck him like a spotlight, wielded by a divine inquisitor brooding behind the clouds, peering through the matter of Roger's field beret and skull as if they were made of glass and seeing all the stains on his soul. The sunlight made Roger sneeze.

Mueller led the way to the snackeria gazebo. His boots clunked against the concrete and Roger watched his face for some sign of his thoughts. The lieutenant colonel was as patriotic as any man Roger knew, but he was also a man for whom the code of military justice was not a set of words on paper but a principle to live by and to deviate from at one's peril. Carrying out immoral orders, and ones issued by an illegitimate authority at that, ran contrary to everything Roger knew about his commander.

What molecules were being produced by the implants in Mueller's brain? Ones promoting subservience and smothering moral doubt.... Roger's footsteps faltered and sweat dampened his collar.

What about the molecules produced by Roger's own?

The gazebo's shade made it easier to breathe. Mueller nodded at one of the picnic tables around the snackeria. "Give me a report."

Roger unrolled a smartpaper across the green meshed steel and a map appeared of the lake, its shores, and the two nearest bridges, upstream at Eufaula and downstream at Fort Gaines. "We're here," he said, and a spot appeared on the map on the Georgia shore a couple of miles south of the Eufaula bridge. "Our drone aircraft," over the lake near the dam, "is following the enemy combatants into an arm of the lake here."

"Do you know who they are?" Mueller said.

A zoom photo from the drone overlaid the map. The waterjet and its riders stood against the blue blur of water, their hair whipped by the wind and the view of their faces highly angled. The driver was tall and had dirty blond hair and though his face could not be read Roger knew. "I can't make visual out of that."

"That's fine. Ramirez gave me a photo." This one overlaid the other and the map and showed a disheveled face, unshaven, and the collar of a prison camp jumpsuit. Mueller parted his lips. "You know this man?"

He'd be a fool to lie. "My sister's husband. Clay Schieffer."

"How do you feel about your brother-in-law being an enemy combatant?"

Roger inhaled, he hoped with a sound of determination. "Ties of blood and marriage notwithstanding, a threat to our civilization is a threat to our civilization." The same caveat applied to ties of order and duty.

Mueller nodded, slowly, gaze piercing. Clay's mug shot disappeared. "Any make on the other?"

Slender build, dark hair. An adolescent? None of his relatives, Roger could account for all the teenagers on his side of the family. A short adult male? Jenny? But if her, where was Martin? "None."

"He's slippery. No traction in any database."

"The vehicle registrations?"

"To a limited liability company out of New Mexico. Ramirez will have to send agents to Santa Fe to dig further." The breeze gusted and the rumble of a motorboat echoed over the lake. "Time's wasting. What's your plan?"

Roger wiped the zoom photo from the display. The map showed Clay and the other moving further into the arm of the lake. "I'll send two platoons by land, one over the north bridge at Eufaula, the other over the south bridge at Fort Gaines, to envelop the probable landing area."

"The other platoon?"

"We need both a reserve and a force to block any possible escape by water. The remaining platoon would require boats—"

"I'll tell Ramirez to override civilian vessels in the area and bring them in for your use. Who goes where?"

"Wilson goes on the lake. His platoon's seen the most action so far today and could use some time off the line; their robots have learned a little more about riverine actions from," he said, and paused over the right euphemism, "detaining the prisoner; and their platoon is short transport after the eecees crashed their car. Marsden has the most field experience, even if it was heavy RTDs in Ooo-stan, so he can take his unit by himself over the north bridge. I'll travel with Treviño to the south bridge and cross there."

Mueller stared at the map for a moment. "Sound plan. Go brief your lieutenants."

Roger, with Hardin at his side, as always, climbed the low ridge and glanced back to see NCS agents spraying memory disrupters into parked campers. They passed under pecan trees and topped the low ridge. Columns of humvees and ops tractor-trailers stood along both sides of the driveway. "Tell the platoon commanders to fall in for a briefing," he told Hardin.

"Yes, sir." Hardin paused and his voice lost its crispness when he spoke again. "Permission to speak?"

"Speak."

Hardin cast sidelong glances from under lowered eyebrows. Softly, he asked, "Do you think it's true?"

"What's true?"

"What the prisoner said. The president cheated when he won the election?"

For minutes now, it had been as if through a fog of thought Roger had seen a road-fork, either path of which he could have stumbled down; but if he was going to reach either destination he had to man up. He could not stumble at the behest of molecules forced into his brain. He had to read the sign at the road-fork, know what toll he would have to pay whichever path he took, and pay it.

"Would Ramirez be performing extrajudicial executions if it weren't true?"

Hardin made no reply.

The lieutenants waited for them outside the company headquarters humvee and straightened their backs. Wilson and Treviño looked uneasy and Marsden, half a foot taller than the others, seemed lost in thought. Roger briefed them on the plan. Marsden perked up at being given the most independent role, and Wilson's expression softened when he heard his platoon would be held in reserve. "I'd be surprised if the enemy combatants return to the lake to break out of the encirclement," Roger said, and Wilson relaxed further, blinking and letting out a long breath. Roger glanced at Marsden and said, "Regardless of who captures them, the company will reform before returning here. Questions? Time to move."

The enlisted men wrangled their robots into the trailers. Hardin took aside Treviño's platoon sergeant. They guarded their expressions and kept their voices low. After Marsden and Wilson left, Treviño approached. "Sir, I have a question. I've been hearing r-mail and you know that can't be trusted, but... the things the prisoner said before the NCS agent shot him...."

"He was telling the truth," Roger said. "Think about it. Why else would NCS kill him?"

Treviño looked at the ground and spoke quietly. "We're bringing in innocent men so Ramirez can shoot them? What am I missing?"

Roger turned his head but realized his next words were too important. He had to stand before man and god and tell them both which path he took. He looked Treviño in the eye and said, "Ramirez can only shoot them if we bring them in."

Clay pulled the waterjet into a cove on the Alabama side of the lake. A halo of mud a few feet wide ringed the shore of the cove. Tree roots and a weathered face of limestone flanked a narrow dirt path, peppered with shoe prints and animal tracks, leading away from the lake and into woods behind. "Looks as good a place as any," Clay said. He steered the waterjet closer to the shore until the underside slid over mud, then cut the engine. Birds and a distant motorboat chattered in the silence.

Wally jumped off and sloshed through thigh-deep water to the mud. The pack was better balanced than it first had looked; tight and snug, with most of the weight borne over the hip. Clay realized again how much planning Wally had done. He had to listen to him.

Clay stepped off and strode through the water until Wally, face turned to the sky, raised his palm. Clay stopped and Wally's gaze roved the sky for a few seconds. "There's a small plane up there."

Clay checked the sky, but saw and heard nothing. "You sure?"

"Its underside is covered in smartcamo but you can catch the motion. Watch the edges of a cloud."

Water logged Clay's shoes and of course the military would have robot planes. "I believe you. That means they know we're here."

"Let's hustle," Wally said. "We need to stick to woods."

"Any ideas where to go?" Clay asked.

"Just out of the way before the military gets here. Now's not the time to plan further."

Or to look back in remembrance. They could do nothing else for

Nil, despite the pull in the back of Clay's mind. "How fast can you move with that pack?"

"Fast enough."

Clay had his doubts, but Wally had surprised him before. They climbed the track away from the cove and Clay started a jog. Wally matched the pace. The woods were damp and cool, scented by rotting leaves and pollen. The terrain rolled but climbed slightly away from the lake. They had spent half an hour getting here and it would take the military at least as long to get around the lake. Could they be here already? Clay sped up and peered into the undergrowth, looking for pizza boxes.

Half a mile from the lake, a dirt road cut through the forest. On the far side, two barbed wire fences met, one with taut wire between green metal posts palisading a treeless field grown with weeds, the other made of rusty wire and weathered wooden posts as leaning as the dense trees behind them. A *No Trespassing* sign, freshly painted, dangled from a rusted strand, but Clay saw no cameras or microphones. "Sky clear?"

Wally looked up and nodded.

They sprinted across the dirt road and then climbed over the fence. The woods soon concealed them from any overhead eyes.

Brush forced their path to meander and logs kept them watching their feet. Their jog slowed to a walk. Clay offered to carry the pack but Wally shook his head. Crows cawed and the two men skirted a clearing where a gray shack leaned under its tarpaper roof. A satellite mini dish climbed from the chimney cap and pointed south. The shack's broken windows made Clay hope no one lived there.

"Hold it," said a gruff voice ahead of them. Fear curdled Clay's stomach but he and Wally paused. Figures in old dumb camo moved among the trees. Footsteps crunched twigs behind. One of the figures, a grim-faced white man, his face tanned and wrinkled like leather and a rifle in his hands pointed at the ground, stepped forward. Visible on his woodland-pattern shirt was a poorly stitched logo, a maltese cross ringed by a double helix.

"I didn't realize this property belonged to Caucasian Forces America," Clay said.

Some of the men amid the trees murmured. The leader said, "Now how you know us?" His tone was guarded.

"I met a member, a former member, a late member, now. He had a tat of the logo. Ryan, I think was his name. He'd done time in the Missouri state pen."

"We don't keep membership logs of other chapters," the leader said. "We're not America United or a Taj Mahal franchise."

"A former member?" asked someone behind Clay. His voice sounded a little more intelligent than the leader's.

Clay twisted at the waist but couldn't get a close look. "I assume he was an apostate. That he quit. While in prison."

"We can check the lists on the webforum to back up the story," the man behind him said to the leader. "Former members to be denied fellowship."

The leader ignored the man and instead peered at Wally. "Who's this?"

"He works for me," Clay said.

"Jobs Americans won't do?"

"That pack is heavy." Clay rolled his hands palm-up. "I apologize for crossing your property. If you could show us the way out, we'd appreciate it."

The leader pursed his lips. "It's posted, no trespassing."

Clay didn't feel reckless, but rather confident; yet despite remembering the touch of the enter key under his pinky part of him marveled that he felt either. "You don't want to turn us over to the sheriff."

The leader shifted the rifle in his hands. "Why not?"

"NCS agents and U.S. Army soldiers are hunting for us."

"And I'm the mastermind of 6:19."

"Haven't you seen the robot plane?" Clay pointed one long finger at the canopy of the woods. CFAers looked up. "If you turn us over to the sheriff, NCS will come by to ask questions. Now I don't know nor do I care what half a dozen ol' boys are doing in the woods with rifles and camouflage, but the federales might."

Behind the leader, CFAers cast nervous glances at each other, but the leader narrowed his eyes. "Maybe we don't turn you in."

"They'll send robots over every square inch of the countryside looking for us, live or dead. Now what was I saying about ol' boys in the woods?"

The leader scowled and sniffed out a breath. He extended a camo-clad arm and a pudgy finger. "Nearest fence is a half mile. You got fifteen minutes."

Downslope, with less undergrowth than before, they made it in eight.

Treviño's platoon rode up the bridge into Alabama. From the corner of his eye Roger caught a glimpse of the faces of Treviño and his platoon sergeant, and over the radio crackle he caught the tone of voice of the rest. The mood was ominous. Roger wished he could tell them they were only going through the motions of capturing the fugitives, but even r-mail could be traced if handled incautiously.

The only fly in the ointment was Lt. Marsden. Roger hadn't had the chance to talk to him privately, but if Marsden did indeed capture Clay and the other fugitive, he had his orders to reform the company before returning to the RV park on the Georgia shore. Roger would talk to him then. He had built rapport with his lieutenants in the years of training on the back forty at Ft. Riley. Marsden would listen. Especially with the implant in his head. The more Roger thought about it the more he knew the brass had imposed loyalty engineering on the sly. But could a handful of molecules so precisely enhance loyalty to birds and stars on men's collars or NCS ID cards in men's wallets? Loyalty and obedience followed hierarchies more complex than any org chart.

Hardin, crammed next to Roger on the rear seat of the humvee, inclined his head. "Sir, a message from Wilson. He sounds agitated."

"Patch him through," Roger said. A background hum came through his earbud, followed by Wilson's voice.

"Captain. Things are not right. Not right at all—"

"Easy, lieutenant. What's not right?"

"It's the lieutenant colonel. He just contacted Marsden and me and ordered us to report to him directly."

Breathe deep. Don't let Mueller into your Boyd loop. "He did. Why?"

"I asked him, sir, and he… he said he didn't trust you. He said one of the enemy combatants we're hunting is your brother-in-law and you would let him escape."

The import of the lieutenant's words sank in. Had Mueller gleaned Roger's thoughts? Or did he project motivations given him by his own guilty conscience?

"One of the fugitives is my sister's husband. That's true." He invested his voice with more volume and authority. "But why did Mueller think I would let him escape?" Roger raised his voice and lowered its pitch to carry even further. "He knows I took the same oath he and you and everyone of us did and he knows I will follow any order that is lawful."

In his earbud, Wilson's breath deepened and slowed. Across the humvee's cabin, Treviño and his sergeant turned their faces to him. They'd overheard enough to know something strange was happening. "Did Mueller change your orders?"

"No sir, we're to remain on station in the lake. My platoon is most of the way to the target site."

"Then carry on."

"Sir?" Wilson asked, frantic again.

"Still here."

"Should I follow his order to report to him directly?"

Roger took a moment and hoped it was long enough for the right string of words to spool up. "Lieutenant, I trust you to follow your commission oath, your conscience, and all written rules of engagement. I am absolutely certain you will do that."

Wilson's breaths grew calm again. "Thank you, sir. Wilson out."

Patches of woods extended from the CFAers' overgrown farm northwestward along both sides of another dirt road. Clay broke a sweat and Wally finally passed the pack to him. They trudged through the woods and skirted clusters of old houses, sheds clucking with chickens, mobile homes supported on concrete blocks, windows treated by aluminum foil. A few piebald mongrels barked, but children scratching in the dirt or throwing basketballs at leaning backboards and net-less rims didn't look up. For the next hour, little changed, except the music thumping out of teenagers' cars turned from thrash country to neokrunk and the knots of aimless children from mostly white to mostly black.

The woods thickened. They followed a path crossed by roots and flanked by thick clumps of grasses. "Think we're clear?" Wally asked.

"Not yet. How long can you keep moving?"

"I've got energy bars in the pack when we get hungry." His tone grew serious. "More company."

A tall black man in patchy smartcamo stepped out from behind a tree and leveled a machine pistol, barely longer than his forearm, at them. "Hands up."

Clay clapped his hands to his head and sweat ran down his cheeks. This man looked better trained than the CFAers. These men—more smartcamo blurs lay rifleman-prostrate on both sides of the track, weapons raised.

The spokesman didn't move. "Are you Army? Marines? NCS? Some other agency?"

"None of those," Wally said. "Civilians."

"Uh-huh. Quanell, verify that."

One of the men from the ambuscade approached, lifted the pack off Clay's back, patted the two of them down. "No weapons. This one—" He pointed at Clay. "—has no ID. This one—" Quanell's voice became quizzical. "James Everton?"

"I get that a lot," Wally said. "I'm not him."

"What makes you think we're military?" Clay asked the spokesman.

"You're not one to ask questions."

"They're looking for us," Wally said. "The drone aircraft you can barely see, the convoy that's crossed over from Georgia—"

"Convoys," the spokesman said. He lowered his machine pistol and stepped closer. "Why they after you?"

"Have you read Fariq Buchanan's recent blog about the Free Samples Project?"

The spokesman snorted. "Buchanan's an assimilationist sellout."

"I'm sure he is, but have you read his recent blog?"

"I have," Quanell said. "Proof President Everton can't be trusted. He fed mind-control drugs into a whole bunch of American Bantus to get them to vote for him."

"Fewer than you think," Clay said. "He targeted ones who appeared influential—"

"Assimilationists and minstrel-pappies," the spokesman said. "So you read Buchanan's blog, so what?"

"We gave him the information on the Free Samples Project," Wally said. "Him and dozens of other bloggers. That's why they're after us."

The spokesman took a moment to think. "Where are you going?"

"A place where we can lie low," Wally said. "Any ideas?"

"Not here. We'll fight in order to defend this *ibutho* or this Autarkic Zone. But trouble'll find us soon enough without us looking for it."

"Understood."

"You want to stick with the woods, head south of west till you come to the four-lane. Turn left, stay in the woods, and there's a bridge over a creek about a mile down. You can cross under there. Follow the creek. The Choctawhatchee is about four miles downstream."

Clay lifted his hands away from his head and raised his eyebrows in a question. The spokesman nodded. Clay adjusted the pack and looked at Wally, but his partner wore a frown. "Autarkic Zone? You're talking about economic self-sufficiency?"

The spokesman lifted his chin. "You think an American Bantu doesn't know the meaning of a three-syllable word derived from the Greek?"

The skin crinkled around Wally's eyes. "No, should I? But you've obviously read Smith regarding the division of labor and Ricardo on comparative advantage—"

"Molecular fabrication technology has demolished those concepts—"

"Reduced them, but not to zero—"

"Wally!" To the spokesman, Clay said, "Sir, there isn't much I'd enjoy more than an arcane economic debate, but we do want to get out of your Autarkic Zone before the military and NCS hunt us down."

They jogged through the woods, passing weedy fields and putting rabbits and squirrels to flight amid the underbrush. Clay turned to speak and found Wally checking the watchface of his wearable. "Can you get a signal?"

"No, but I want to send a query when we get into wireless coverage. How many CFA camps or American Bantu Autarkic Zones are there? How many *ibuthos* and how many armed men?"

Clay needed a few seconds to come up with a response. "We're alone in the ass end of Alabama and you're thinking of recruiting an army?" He lightened his tone toward the end of the question. Wally had a good idea, even if it seemed well beyond their grasp.

Sweat ran down his face but Wally grinned. "How'd you guess?"

After fifteen minutes the highway came into view fifty yards past a tall fence coarsely meshed with steel links and down a gentle slope studded with slender bamboo stalks. The highway was no interstate; two lanes each direction, purple lines of fresh asphalt like veins across the road, but cars and pickup trucks passed infrequently, one every ten or twelve seconds. Clay and Wally stayed behind the fence and turned south.

"What's that sound?" Wally asked. From ahead of them, along the highway, wooden cracking sounds carried over the bass hum of machinery.

They followed the fence as it curved with the road. The source of the noises came into view. Two robots, three-armed, bright yellow, plastic pyramids ten feet tall, traveled in their direction on slow, squeaking treads. They gripped the mature fastgrow bamboo with their two hands and their third arms swung carbide-edged scythes, flashing in the sun during the backstrokes and thunking through the bamboo trunks on the forestrokes. It seemed instantaneous, the gripping and the scything, but Clay assumed there were ten-fold more safety mechanisms in each robot than in a family sedan, or else lawsuits would have grounded these robots during the Reynolds administration.

The pyramids handed the logs back over their heads without looking and dropped them across the open claws of headless, bipedal carriers. Once fully loaded the carriers walked stiffly downslope to flatbed trucks, while smaller quadrupedal robots scampered on prehensile feet over the logs and cinched cords around to bundle them. The flatbed trucks idled and the trailers' suspensions oscillated with each bundle laid down. The logs would be shipped to Mobile or Pensacola, Clay guessed, and then by barge out to the Gulf and then overboard to the hypoxic depths where they would rot in slow motion, their carbon sequestered for hundreds of years. Global warming abatement. It was one of Reynolds' few policies continued by Everton; Clay, newly cynical, assumed the Treasury received sequestration payments under some favorable treaty with the developing world.

"They're on to us," Wally said sharply.

Clay glanced through the link fence at the yellow pyramids and the headless carriers and the small quadrupeds, but they continued their duties, as oblivious as ants. Alarm widened his eyes and jerked his head when he realized what Wally meant.

"Military?" he asked, but in a lull between the crack of the scythes and during the downrevving of a pyramid's engine, he heard in the woods behind him the clack of pizza box treads. The fence's twisted wire made four-inch rhomboids. "Climb over! They won't be able to follow!"

"They'll be on the road, too."

"We have to try." Clay grabbed the fence, wedged the toes of his shoes into the mesh, and started climbing. The pack tugged at his shoulders and the fence rattled and rippled when Wally joined him in climbing.

Clay crested the fence and started down when he glimpsed motion in the woods. "Hurry!" he said, and jumped. His knees twinged when he landed and he remembered why he'd taken up swimming. Wally jumped too and they started running through the bamboo forest toward the yellow pyramids. Clay's shoulders ached and pain needled the tops of his shins.

Through the thin screen of the last bamboo, the robots loomed over them. The nearest yellow pyramid swung back its scythe. The sun glinted on the blade, the hydraulics in its arm whined and the twin brown plastic screens over its sensor mounts stared at them like angry eyes. It reached a hand toward Clay but stopped in mid-motion. "Across the highway!" Clay and Wally ducked between the two robots and behind the second one and in front of a waiting carrier, its open claws painted red like cuckoos' mouths on the ends of its upraised arms. They emerged from the robots' shadows with nothing but four lanes of asphalt and the median ditch between them and the half-grown bamboo forest on the far right-of-way.

A dozen pizza boxes waited for them, three on each of their flanks and six hull-down in the median ditch. Humvees and tractor-trailers stood on the opposite lanes.

Clay stopped and hunched while pizza boxes crawled close to the fence behind them. A voice boomed from speakers hidden on the central humvee. "Don't move."

Clay jerked his head up. The voice sounded familiar, or was his mind tricking him?

The humvee swung its door open and a tall white male stepped out. He'd never seen him before. A pizza box fired its dart and lodged in his arm. It fell limply to his side and a wave of paralysis crawled through his shoulder and into his torso.

14

Treviño had the most light-robotics experience of Roger's lieutenants, and he had enough leadership skill to look the other way when the men of his platoon spent time in barracks equipping their robots with non-regulation hardware and software. The platoon drove northward on a four-lane highway; trucks and humvees stopped one or two at a time, and in addition to dropping off cheap cameras and microphones, they also hacked into traffic-monitoring cameras or listened with parabolic microphones deep into the woods. Even traveling fast, Clay and the other could not have made it further than the highway by now. Though Treviño's men had found no sign of them, the odds were better for them than for Marsden.

"Sir," Hardin said. "Wilson again."

The lieutenant's agitation had returned. "Sir, Marsden captured them! He radioed Mueller and me a minute ago to report it."

Adrenaline pounded Roger's heart. "And?"

"Mueller ordered both of us to return our platoons to base. I told him I would comply but I haven't left yet. I had to talk to you first."

Roger's palms felt slick. "Don't leave your post yet. I'll raise Marsden and confirm he's captured the fugitives. I'll communicate after that. Hang tight. Sung out."

Treviño had overheard. "I'll pull in the outrunners, sir."

"Do it. Hardin, get me Marsden."

The carrier wave bore distant shouts and squeaking equipment. "Captain?"

"What's your status?"

"Status? Ah, no contacts yet."

Roger's face fell with the lie. Treviño's eyebrows crinkled and Roger mouthed *No contacts yet*. A horrified expression stole over the lieutenant's face. How could Marsden ignore the chain of command? The loyalty drugs. Damn Everton.

"Treviño hasn't seen them either," Roger said. "Anything more to report on your end?"

"No sir."

His mood sour, Roger spread a smartpaper across his knee and called up a topographic map of the area overlaid with unit positions. A couple of miles to his north, over two transverse ridgelines on the topo map, a circle surrounded a cluster of vehicles and bore the label* Marsden*. South of the southernmost ridge, a county road T-ended. Roger glanced at the contours and guessed Marsden couldn't see it from his position.

"There's a small paved road intersecting the four-lane about 1100 meters to your south. I'm drawing that as the boundary between you and Treviño."

"Understood, sir."

"Sung out." The carrier wave faded from his ears and Roger shook his head slowly in disgust.

"He lied to you, sir?" Treviño asked.

"Either him or Wilson," Roger said. Treviño and Hardin's expressions told him they agreed with him which was more likely.

"When would he tell you he'd captured them?"

"After they delivered them to Mueller and Ramirez killed them both."

The convoy rolled on for a moment.

"Pardon me, sir," Hardin said, "for listening in, but it sounded like they were readying for departure."

Roger took a deep breath. The world had gone terribly wrong and what could he, alone, do to turn it right? How much more could Clay, a man of deep and powerful thoughts, do if he were free?

"Lieutenant, pull the column onto that small road at the boundary. Pull up the trailers so the enlisted can see the same point and park us there. I have to speak to them. And quickly, we don't have much time."

The convoy slowed and turned off the highway onto a narrow road under a dense canopy of trees. The platoon's four trailers slanted half across the road and bent the branches overhead. The trailer doors swung open and the robot wranglers and other enlisted men crowded the openings while Treviño's Humvee rolled to a stop. Roger stepped to the pavement and then climbed onto the hood of the hummvee. Absorbed sunlight and the engine underneath made the hood hot underfoot. He took another step up to the roof.

Roger's heart thudded and his mouth felt dry, but then he realized Everton had made his job easier by priming their loyalty to the men above them. The buzz of conversations among the enlisteds dropped to a murmur as Roger turned his gaze to each truck in turn, picking out individual men, black, white, Asian, Latin, to make eye contact before he spoke.

"My fellow Soldiers," he said, and the last conversations on the trucks ceased. "When we were detached to assist Agent Ramirez and the rest of NCS, we looked forward both to action and to a chance to fulfill our oaths of service. At first, our actions and our service aligned. But over the past few weeks, and you've either heard the r-mail or you'll lie and say you didn't—" He smiled and many of the men smiled in response. His face grew solemn and the mens' mirrored his. "You've heard we've captured suspected enemy combatants whom Agent Ramirez has killed without trial. You've heard he did it earlier today. You've heard he'll do it again as soon as he gets custody of the remaining two fugitives." Roger checked their faces. A few men put on the withdrawn look of one wrestling with moral doubt, but most had guarded expressions, the people shot by Ramirez were enemy combatants, right? There was a war on.

"Some of you have also heard the rumor of what the prisoner said today before Ramirez killed him. Put those rumors aside. I'll tell you the truth. The prisoner said President Everton was elected by pumping drugs of trust and complacency into people's brains. I heard him with my own ears. Read a blog about the Free Samples Project," he said, and saw a few men blanch or jerk their limbs in startlement, "and you'll see the evidence the dead prisoner and the two fugitives gave the world."

He went on. "How could we tell if the prisoner's words are true and his evidence is authentic? I wrestled with that question for long minutes after hearing him speak before it hit me. Why would Ramirez kill him if he'd lied? The prisoner told the truth, no more, no less. A truth Ramirez and his superiors will use extrajudicial executions to suppress." It was a buzz phrase from their classroom sessions on law-of-war, but with luck he could charge it with meaning. Those men not yet fully convinced looked down when his gaze approached them.

In the trees behind the trucks, crows cawed.

"My fellow Soldiers, each one of us swore an oath to support and defend the Constitution of the United States against all ene-mies, foreign and domestic. That means more than just the plain text prohibiting criminal punishment without trial. It means our country where law, and not men, reign supreme, and where each individual is sovereign over his own mind and his own choices." He looked at their faces and imagined the implants in their brains. A needle of hypocrisy pricked him but he stifled it.

"You know Ramirez will kill the two fugitives if they are caught and handed over to them. Kill them for telling the truth. Kill them in clear violation of the same Constitution he swore to support and defend, as if its constraints do not bind him." Roger took off his field beret and scratched his scalp through his crewcut. "He might have that chance. Lt. Marsden's platoon has captured them. Lt. Marsden is three-quarters of a mile up the road preparing to hand them over to Ramirez." More crows, and Roger knew he had to hurry without seeming rushed.

"My fellow Soldiers, you have a choice. You can look the other way as our Constitution is violated, as the rule of law dies the death of a thousand cuts, as men violate their oaths and arrogate to themselves power their fellow citizens have not granted them, as our Army and its centuries of proud tradition are co-opted to make us into thugs in the service of tyranny; or you can reaffirm your oaths and turn against the true domestic enemies of our Constitution. The first way looks easier and safer. There's no denying that. But there's no denying that if you take that first way you will be cursed, by God and man, the judgment of history and the dictates of your own conscience." He scanned the thronged men in the trucks and Treviño and Hardin standing next to the hummvee with their faces turned up to him. He had them all. "But the choice is yours. If you take the first way, go—" he said and pointed to the northeast, to Mueller and Ramirez. "We hold no malice toward you but we must follow the path our oath compels. For the rest of us, we have two innocent men to rescue. Let's get to work."

The silence held a moment longer, but then active voices, the men most convinced, broke it, and the rest followed. The men dropped ramps from the truck beds to the road and the crawlers zipped down. Roger and Treviño with the squad sergeants and came up with a plan. The first squad, a few of whose crawlers were equipped with machetes and powered hacksaws, would split into two teams, cut through underbrush and fences, and flank the road between Marsden and Ramirez, then knock out Marsden's vehicles with shots to the tires and engines. The second squad, some of its crawlers equipped with muscle-paralyzer grenades, would head up the road and neutralize the men of Marsden's platoon. If they couldn't neutralize them before they formulated orders to their robots, the first and second squads would also fight Marsden's crawlers. The third squad would remain in reserve and also sacrifice a few of its crawlers in a diversion, heading south while equipped with transponders programmed to spoof Treviño's vehicles. The men sat with their handheld computers and issued the orders to their machines, and Roger saw their last doubts recede while their training took over.

The decoys left before the others, then first squad clacked away into the underbrush while second squad waited a few seconds before heading down the narrow road to the four-lane. They would take a couple of minutes to reach Marsden, and the ambush itself would take a few minutes more. Waiting was always the worst part of any operation, as men tried to stifle their animal urges to fight or flee. Thoughts, banished in preparation, infiltrated through the blind spots in one's defenses. Roger, Hardin, Treviño, and Treviño's platoon sergeant stood around the hood of the hummvee and the smartpaper map sprawled across it.

The die was not yet cast, but it was only a matter of minutes. They would be outlaws. Men as ruthless as Ramirez would work hard to run them to earth. A harsh thought chilled him. "Reminder, 15 minutes: get Emma and kids off base," he muttered to his wearable.

"Marsden's moving," Hardin said. The cluster of vehicles began to move north. The lead crawlers of first squad had just come even with them.

"Come on," said one of the men of first squad, legs dangling off the open back end of a trailer and his gaze locked intently on a handheld display. "Cut the goddam fence. Yes!"

First squad's robots flowed through a hole in the fence and around the pyramidal shapes of highway department robots. Treviño's wearable, driving the smartpaper display, animated muzzle flashes and fed recorded sounds of small arms fire through their wearables. Three seconds later the sounds, muffled by trees and distance but real, reached their ears.

Marsden's trucks and humvees soon stopped moving. Second squad's robots sped around bamboo stumps and onto the road. The animations showed the grenade launchers fire and drew sickly green clouds over the trucks. Robots waited around the trucks, paralyzer guns at the ready. Soon the green clouds were drawn over all the vehicles. Treviño overlaid a threat map. Cool yellow tinted the area around Marsden's platoon and faded slowly to green.

"Let's go," Roger said.

His hummvee led the way. Cars and pickups had pulled to the shoulder and their passengers peered over the dashboards. Marsden's vehicles slumped on their wheelrims and stood oblivious to the lane markings. A few wisps from the paralyzer grenades wafted out of the backs of the trucks.

Hardin was first out of the command hummvee, rifle unslung and gaze roving over the area. Glances into the trucks showed paralyzed men. No one looked hurt and Roger was grateful. Marsden's men deserved to walk away.

They dragged Clay and the other fugitive out of Marsden's command hummvee and leaned them against the vehicle's quarterpanel. Roger gently turned Clay's head to face him and his eyes widened slightly in recognition. "We're getting you the antidote asap. Medical, here, now!"

A medical crawler clacked up and extended a needle on a telescoping arm. It jabbed Clay, then his companion. Clay opened his mouth to speak but a coughing fit grabbed him and bent him over, his mouth contorted and his hands clenched over his mouth.

"Roger, what are you doing?"

He squatted next to Clay. "I'm risking a firing squad for me and twenty years in Leavenworth for every man in this platoon to save you. It better be worth the risk."

Clay nodded, then coughed more.

"Is it true? What your friend Nil said, about the free samples and Everton's election?"

"Every word. How is he?"

Roger pressed his lips together and looked his brother-in-law in the eye. "Ramirez killed him."

"God damn." Clay squeezed his eyes shut and banged his head backward against the hummvee.

The other man spoke. "He killed him? It makes no sense. The genie's out of the bottle now. The loyalty chart is obviously over the tipping point—"

"Obvious to us," Clay said. His eyes brooded.

"Oh, my manners. You're Clay's brother-in-law? I'm Wally." A twitch started in his left forearm and soon his arm shook from shoulder to hand before subsiding. "That's nasty stuff."

Clay looked up. Roger knew his habitual baseline expression and something about it had changed since he'd seen him last. It showed him more aware of other people's minds but less concerned about the contents. "What about these men?" he asked.

"We have to bug out," Roger said. "We don't have any place for prisoners."

Clay raised his voice and lifted his gaze in the direction of the hummvee cabin. "So we need to shoot them all?"

Roger sucked in a breath. Had Clay really said that, and with the intent to be overheard? He could understand Clay's anger but he wouldn't coddle it. "No. We let them be. NCS will be along to revive them."

"We'll let that happen?"

"We'll cripple their vehicles and their robots. They won't be able to pursue." Roger glanced at Hardin. His first sergeant nodded and moved off to communicate the order to Treviño and his men.

Clay's mouth grew firm and he narrowed his eyes. Roger had to nip his anger now.

"Besides," Roger said, "isn't Everton the one who shoots innocent people in cold blood?"

Clay blanched and blinked a couple of times. "Okay, let's go."

Roger extended his arm and pulled him up, then did the same for Wally. "My men need a few minutes to disable the equipment. Go introduce yourselves to Lt. Treviño." He waved in the lieutenant's direction. "I have a couple of calls to make."

Wally opened the hummvee door and pulled out a pack that looked as heavy as he was, then he and Clay left Roger alone. Roger's gaze drifted into the hummvee cabin and in primate reflex settled on Marsden's slack face. Marsden showed no expression but shame washed over Roger and he turned his face away from the lieutenant and his senior NCOs. No. He wasn't looking to gloat over these men. He turned back and looked the lieutenant in the eye. Marsden had done what he had thought was right and Roger could not fault him for that. But a way to say that without sounding condescending eluded him, and the muscles around his mouth twisted, unhappy with his lack of words, unhappy the situation had forced him to turn against his subordinate.

Speaking of subordinates… he walked away and Hardin followed at his side. "Raise Wilson."

Wilson's voice soon filled his earbud. "Sir. What are your orders?"

"Orders? I'm not in a position to give you orders any more. I've taken custody of the prisoners from Marsden and he didn't yield them voluntarily."

"Sir?"

"You have a choice to make. You can return to Mueller and

Ramirez and conform to the chain of command. You may take some lumps for refusing Mueller's order to cut me out of communications. Your other option is to join us in mutiny. You make that decision. God bless. Sung out."

His arms and legs felt heavy with post-adrenal fatigue. He and Hardin approached Treviño, Clay, and Wally while enlisteds crawled under the hoods of trucks and sprayed black paint on the solar cells and vented methanol from the fuel cell tanks of Marsden's crawlers. "Not quite done, sir," Treviño said.

"We have a minute." He reached into his shirt and pulled out his dogtags. A small photo of his wife, a single frame, printed on with fading ink, showed on the face of non-issue ceramic pendant the size of a one-dollar stack of quarters. In the photo she smiled and gave him a look of love he didn't deserve. He pinched it and held it close to his mouth. "Call Emma."

After long moments, her voice came tinnily out of the pendant. "Roger, what's wrong?"

The fear he knew he'd stirred up lay hidden behind the competent tone in her voice. "I'm perfectly fine and I love you very much. But do you remember all those times we talked about what to do if something very bad were happening?"

"I'll get the kids. I'll take them to—"

"None of your relatives or mine. That's where they'll look. Just get off base and lie low for a while. I'll be in touch as soon as I can."

It took a few moments, and when she finally did speak her voice sounded pinched. "Okay. Do what you have to. Stay safe."

"I will. I love you."

The call ended and Roger slid the pendant back inside his shirt. Enlisteds stood around Marsden's trucks while coolant pissed out of the radiators and crawlers lay in hibernation next to evaporating pools of methanol.

"We're ready," Treviño said.

Roger nodded. "Let's get out of out here."

15

Sunday night, they drove across Alabama down dark roads. They tuned the vehicles' smartcamo to forgettable colors and split their vehicles according to the Berger flocking algorithm, taking parallel routes and uneven spacings. It would reduce the chance of detection, but Clay wondered if they could retain control of men miles away. They stopped before dawn in dense woods on an abandoned farm in the Appalachians and spent the day resting and hiding. No drone aircraft would see them through the foliage and no satellite was scheduled to be overhead. Crawlers patrolled a perimeter, but radio chatter showed the military had not yet responded to Mueller's report or calls from Ramirez to his superiors at NCS.

Alone and cramped in a hummvee, Clay asked Wally, "When do you get today's—" he yawned through the next word "—bar on the loyalty chart?"

Wally checked his wearable's watchface. "A few hours." He fell silent, save for the tapping of his toes. Clay tried to sleep, but the spring day lay warm and heavy around them and he felt too antsy. He climbed out of the hummvee and walked under the forest cover. Men slept on the ground next to their trucks, packs as pillows and berets as eyeshields. A few played cards and looked at Clay with expressions ranging from diffident to awestruck. The latter made Clay feel uncomfortable, but he had to get used to it if they were to have a chance to succeed.

He found Roger sitting against a tree, frowning at the ground and flicking a stylus against a clipboard. "Working on today's company report. There's no macro to explain leading the unit in mutiny. Sit if you like."

Clay lowered himself to a cross-legged seat on the grass. His knees made him wince and he thought about shifting to a more comfortable position, but instead he put his heels together and pressed his knees toward the ground in butterfly stretches. "It can't be easy for your men."

"It's not easy for me; from the first ROTC class they drummed the idea of civilian control into us. Why would it be easy for the enlisteds?" He flicked the stylus against the clipboard a few more times, then stopped it in mid-motion. "Something happen?"

"Are the men happy about this?"

Roger shrugged. "I wasn't joking about twenty years in Leavenworth for each of them. They know they're already on the hook for it, regardless what they do. They won't turn against us. Staying with the unit is no guarantee of survival, but it's the best chance they've got."

Clay realized how little he knew about the military, but wasn't it like any organization crewed mostly by men? Though he had to grant how little he knew even about that, despite what he'd been learning in recent weeks. "How'd you get them to join you? You're their boss but there must be more than that."

Roger cocked his head. "It's okay, Clay. I know how they used your invention."

"My invention."

"That implantable whatzit, I forget your name for it. They put it in all of us. Loyalty engineering. But they couldn't tune it so it only made us loyal to high brass and politicians in New Washington. It made us loyal to the people we should be loyal to. I realized that and ran with it."

Clay felt a sudden chill and pulled his arms over his chest. "Christ."

"What?"

"We hacked it. The NuGland is reprogrammable and Wally was

able to pierce its security. We released a worm a couple of weeks ago to reprogram it. We turned off the loyalty engineering and replace it with self-centeredness and disdain for authority."

Roger's eyes widened. His gaze roved over the nearby clumps of soldiers. "But they..."

"Why did they follow you?" Clay wore confidence like a hand-tailored suit. "Because loyalty isn't just to symbols and abstractions. It can be to people as well. They didn't follow you because you're above them in the hierarchy and you've got bars on your collar. They followed you because you led them."

Clay yawned. The grass was soft and unmarred by anthills. "We'll be here a few more hours?" He stretched out and soon fell asleep.

The sun had slanted low in the western sky by the time he woke. Roger sat deep in thought over the clipboard. Wally ran toward them, a smartpaper accordion-folded in his hand. He grinned as if he'd cornered a market. "It broke. Gapped down at the open and declined all day."

"What broke?" Roger asked.

Wally squatted next to them and opened the smartpaper to show them. The recent weeks' downtrend in the loyalty index had steepened its descent.

"What is this?"

Wally blinked as if he'd only just realized how foreign the things that interested him were to most others. He described the data collection and its graphical aggregation. "A whole weekend of social events among people our NuGland hack turned bearish on Everton, and then they heard what you did and started thinking 'if he can do it, why not I?' "

"Is it time to act?" Roger asked.

Clay studied the chart but from the corner of his eye glimpsed Wally look at him before answering the question. "Everton will realize something's amiss and put on longs. Blandishments to the wavering, threats against those who've fallen away. He'll trigger a rally but it won't hold. Insiders will start liquidating and that'll drive the index even lower and make it less likely for Everton to raise an effective defense."

The day's bar hung on the chart like an icicle off a wintry eave. Millions of people, disdainful of Everton and not knowing why, just needing a push to form an avalanche and sweep him out of office. Millions of people summed up in a half-inch mark on a piece of smartpaper.

"We act now," Clay said. "We reveal who we are, how we found out about the Free Samples Project, what NCS has done to try silencing those of us who know about it, and that Everton and every other America United politician are illegitimate and have to resign. Then we go to the gates of New Washington and stay there until Everton leaves office."

Roger looked pensive. Wally, gaze on the loyalty chart, tugged at his lip with his thumb and index finger and bobbed his head. "Don't push it that far, yet. Name names, point fingers, but don't call for Everton's resignation."

Clay's confidence, like newly bulked muscles, wanted to be flexed. "Why not?"

Wally didn't bend. "The masses will call for it soon enough."

"What do we need to do?" Roger asked.

"I'll talk to my contacts about leading civil disobedience. Delacroix can help too. Everton won't compromise. At that point, we can turn a wheatfield outside New Washington into Tiananmen Square."

"Remember how well that worked out?" Roger said. "We have to be careful. If we go public they'll send the military after us."

"Can you defend us?"

"Against the entire U.S. military?"

"Clay's NuGland hack made a lot of men and units unreliable," Wally said.

"Like my superior? The lieutenant who captured you two?"

Why was Roger so timid? Clay looked at him and his frustration softened. Roger had risked a great deal already and they were asking him to risk even more. He needed persuasion, not disdain.

"We don't have to worry about the entire military, do we?" Clay asked. His tone sounded more honestly ignorant than he expected. "The forces in Uighurstan and elsewhere overseas are off the table. Everton would act quickly, wouldn't he? It would take time to bring soldiers in from the east coast or California. Can they just hop on the bus and get there the next day?"

Roger nodded. "I see what you're saying. They're most likely to use forces already stationed in Kansas. Ft. Riley and the army and air bases in the USACD."

Clay kept up his act. "They'd still outnumber us?"

"Fifty to one."

"The unreliability Wally was talking about will bring that down. Some units might even join us."

Roger shook his head. "I still don't like those odds."

What else could they do? Reveal the facts but then remain in hiding? Better to not even bring that up. "What could make them better?"

"Preemption."

"No no," Wally said. "We can't attack first. Nonviolent resistance is a moral high ground we don't want to give up."

Memories of a night in the Hospital came to Clay. "We can pour sugar in their gas tanks, like Wally did to Boucher the time I almost escaped. Formix."

Wally waved his hands. "That was easy. One hive ordered to perform a handful of tasks. What we'd need would be a lot more than I can do."

"Given how much you can do," Clay said, his tone warm—

"We know a formix roboticist," Roger said flatly.

How many times had Jenny told her marital woes to her brother? Obviously many. "Jenny knows more about it than Wally. That's true."

"You don't sound convinced," Roger said. "I assume she's your best lead—"

"For formix, yeah, but there might be another way. Wally can crack computer networks...."

Wally's eyes grew even wider. "Not New Washington. There's an internal USACD net but the only portals to the wider internet are heavily monitored."

"The internal net must have wireless legs we can sneak into."

Wally shook his head. "Only at very short range. Not from ten miles outside the walls. Clay, I'll ask people, but don't expect anything and don't expect it soon. Formix is the better choice."

Clay blew out a breath.

Roger cleared his throat. "I know things are tense between you," he said. "Suck it up. I'm not saying that just because she's my sister. She's the best lead any of us have, unless Wally's got some expert up his sleeve?"

"Sorry. I bought mine off the rack."

They were right, Clay realized, and then wondered why he resisted that conclusion. He wasn't the same man he'd been while pacing around the house, resenting her because he'd run out of challenges. Maybe they didn't love each other anymore, but he didn't need a crude, weak tool like love to get from her what he needed since he'd added so many more to his toolkit. "Let's swing by Houston on our way to New Washington."

They spent the rest of the afternoon and evening hard at work. Wally ordered nondescript civilian vans, pickup trucks, and RVs from car dealerships in Atlanta, Birmingham, and Chattanooga, one of which came with a new wearable computer for Clay. The vehicles drove themselves to the valley and arrived after sunset along with the night's first whipporwhill calls. The new vehicles could drive inconspicuously day or night. By midnight the enlisteds had off-loaded the old trucks and loaded their crawlers and supplies onto and ripped out the control circuits and self-monitoring devices from the new ones. Around one in the morning, they sent the old tractor trailers to drive at random until they ran out of biodiesel. Rumbling away, headlights bouncing down the dirt road, the unit followed them away from the hideout and scattered westward.

Clay rode in an extra-long van with Wally, Roger, Hardin, a couple of enlisted men, and a dozen crawlers. The crawlers slept stacked in the cargo area between the rear doors and the final bench seat. Clay lay across the third bench seat, scrawling the words of a draft speech across a borrowed smartpaper with glitchy pressure sensors in the lower right. He'd started in the afternoon with the opening *My fellow Americans,* but as they approached Birmingham around two a.m., he dropped it for *Fellow citizens.* The text proceeded in fits and starts, like a sailing ship in a fickle wind. Behind him the enlisteds snored. *You've heard by now of the Free Samples Project…* with links to sites around the world hosting the data he'd liberated. He refuted pro-Everton counter-propaganda that America United bloggers had posted. *I know the Free Samples Project worked because I invented the technology Everton abused to steal the election in 2020. My name is Clay Schieffer….*

Clay went on, mentioning the murders committed by the NCS to cover up his discovery of the information, as well as the use of the Army to hunt people down. The America United blogs would denounce him as an enemy combatant; they would paint him as the man who gave the hydrogen bomb to the 6:19 perpatrators, and despite it being a lie he could not prevent those words. He backed up and added a passage, *I'm not a political person, though I voted for Reynolds in '12 and '16,* and he realized after writing the words he had invoked a continuity with the world before the attack on Old Washington when in reality Reynolds hadn't known him from adam. *I speak for tens of thousands—* no, if he was to make up numbers, that was too few. *—Hundreds of thousands who don't care who is in office, so long as he leads a lawful, honest government that will stay out of their way as they live their lives as best they see fit.*

Deep in the night, he walked unsteadily toward the front seats of the van. Wally sat in the manual override seat, his legs propped on the dashboard and crossed at the ankle. A few taillights glowed ahead on the interstate.

"What do you think?" Clay asked as he synched the speech from his new wearable to Wally's and took the shotgun seat. Dark billboards blocked wispy moonlight and roadside transponders scrolled ads for clean restrooms and 24-hour buffets across the info display in the center of the dashboard.

Wally made a few scratches with his stylus. "Pretty good. Practice it aloud to help your speaking rhythm before we shoot video. You'll need a suit and tie, too. I'll get a software package to scrub your video feed on top of that. Make you look even taller, more symmetrical." The dim glow of the instrument panel caught his cheek as he turned to peer at Clay. "Something else on your mind?"

"Timing."

"Timing?"

"Do we broadcast before or after I talk to Jenny?"

Wally looked thoughtful and rubbed his chin. "I'm sure the feds are watching her."

"To find me in case I talk to her. That's a given. Let's say they find where I am. When would they be more likely to arrest me?"

"Before you press send. Arresting you afterward is an admission by Everton that what you've said is true. Plus transmitting this speech will boost your social capital. They'd have to take more care planning your arrest."

Clay stared through his dim reflection in the windshield. "Then we film and send the speech before we get to Houston."

Wally's feet fidgeted and his voice dropped even lower in volume. "The downside is they might punish Jenny to get at you, or ransom her for your good behavior."

That was all? An insight bubbled out of his subconscious, one the old Clay would have turned away from: Jenny was replaceable; he was not. "Then we go with plan B. Another formix roboticist. Or plan C, none at all."

"You would cut her off?"

"If it were her or me?"

Wally glanced over his shoulder. "What would that do to her brother?"

Behind Hardin lying across the front seat, Roger slept, head leaning against the side wall of the van. Clay had always been dispassionate in his dealings with others, but his old self had ascribed it to disinterest. Other people raised obstacles when he tackled such important challenges as fitting a chemical factory into ten cubic microns. But now he saw the source of his dispassion as the understanding that other people were items in the toolkit. Nil would be proud. "We demolished Roger's loyalty circuits and he threw away his career for us. Our hold on him is deeper than anything a few implants can change."

Wally grew still. "You do have reason to be confident." He stared out the windshield and Clay studied his profile. What was he getting at? He wanted to overthrow a president, didn't he?

"I'll review the speech in the morning," Clay said. "Let's send video before we reach Houston." He reclined the shotgun seat.

The RV rolled westward down the interstate. Every five miles, towns full of AU silvers and bronzes slept, and Clay wondered at the ways a man like Everton could have used the loyalty of so many.

The van rolled to a stop in the alley behind Clay's house. He stepped out into hot humid midafternoon and glanced both ways. Amid the jumble of garages, sweetgum trees, and utility cables, the cameras placed by NCS were obvious if one knew what to look for: gray plastic boxes the size of a man's thumb tucked near cable junctions high on the utility poles. Their crawlers had knocked out the cameras and paralyzed the agents staking out the house. They had a few dozen minutes before NCS would notice and deploy more agents to the site.

The garage door had a PIN pad next to it. Jenny hadn't changed the code. The door rumbled up and Clay walked into the garage. He sweated under the collar of his new suit, fabbed in the hours before dawn at a Youniverse in the suburbs of Jackson, but he was glad he kept it on. Jenny would be surprised and hopefully impressed.

His suv stood, dusty, a new window in place of the one smashed during his arrest. He would have to thank Jenny for that, an easy icebreaker and expression of gratitude. Her sedan sat next to the suv, Martin's child seat in the rear. He would have to be as charming as he could. It wouldn't be much. No time to dither. Clay walked quickly past the cars and the electronics closet and in through the rear door. Water jetted into the washing machine and the valet robot reached its arms into its hamper and fed the machine clothes. He approached the entrance to the kitchen and glimpsed a shadow cast from the right—

"Clay!" Jenny said. With both hands she held a pan over her right shoulder, like a batter waiting for a pitch. "I heard the garage door and didn't know what was happening." She didn't lower the pan. "How did you get past the agents outside?"

"I had help. Roger is with me, with some of his men and machines. You can hand the pan back to SueChef."

"How did you mix him up in this? What's your scheme? I saw your video this morning. I've been getting calls and emails from so many people I lost count. Where have you been? Why didn't you tell me what was happening?" Her angry expression faded. She slumped back and slid the pan across the burners on the cooktop island. "Tell me what's going on."

Clay opened his hands and nodded gently. A good tactic occurred to him. "Where's Martin?"

"You care? What does he do every day at two? He's taking a nap." She closed her eyes and rubbed her forehead with her fingertips. "Your suv came home at midnight with the window smashed and you missing. I thought maybe the feds had arrested you. I called Nil and that's what he said—"

"He knew they'd arrested me. He told the feds I'd found out about the Free Samples Project."

She held her face without expression for a moment. "I thought he might. He seems that kind of man. You're going to get back at him?"

"Too late. He had a guilty conscience—believe it or not—and he helped me escape from the facility where I was held. But the feds caught up with us and he sacrificed himself so we could escape."

"He's dead." She leaned against the cooktop island and lost her gaze in the patternless terrazzo floor.

"He came clean before the end," Clay said. Jenny's head jerked up and her eyes widened. "He was worried about his position in America United when he informed on me, but later he decided our friendship was more valuable."

After a moment, she said, "I'm glad he had some conscience."

"The feds had ordered Roger's unit to hunt us after I escaped. He had harbored doubts for a while about whether Everton's regime deserved his loyalty. Seeing I was the target of the manhunt was the last straw. He helped Wally and I escape and joined us on the run."

"Wally?"

"You probably don't remember Osvaldo Guerra? He overlapped with us in college. I barely remembered him but he remembered me. He thought I would be the man to bring down Everton."

Jenny leaned away from him. "You?"

"I've grown as a leader." He cocked his head at an expression that fleeted across her face. "Any amount would be growth?"

"Why are you putting words in my mouth?"

Not another fight. He showed his palms. "It looked like what you were thinking. Sorry if I was wrong. And I know I had a long way to go but I'm getting there." He changed the subject. "We're going to New Washington. Roger, Wally, Roger's men, and I. Plus every concerned citizen who will join us. We'll stay there until Everton resigns—"

"Or attacks you. You think he won't send the entire army after you?"

Habitual anger, the product of neural pathways laid down in his brain over years of arguments, welled in him, but he closed the stopcock before the emotion reached his face. "He'll send soldiers, you're right. We've done a lot to psychologically neutralize the armed forces. But that's probably not enough. That's why we need your help."

Her eyes narrowed.

"If we can infiltrate sets of formix robots into the military bases in New Washington, we can disrupt their communications and monkey wrench their equipment. They wouldn't be able to move against us. Everton would have to resign."

"You think it's simple? Throw a couple of formix hives over a fence and five minutes later you're done? They'll be looking for it—"

"Everton's fallible too."

"Because he hasn't arrested you yet?" She scowled and shook her head, then turned away from him and leaned over the island. Her back was rigid. "Why did you have to come back?"

"We need your help."

She pivoted and glared at him. "*You* need my help."

"Your brother needs it too."

"What about what I need? Or what Martin needs? Have you thought about that?"

He could tell her a lie she would see through or disarm her with a truth. "No, not much. Tell me. What do you need? What does he need?"

"What does Martin need? His father. Do you have any idea how many nights he cried himself to sleep after your arrest? After you ignored him ever since the diagnosis? Can you make all that up to him?"

"I can try." He shuffled closer and spread his arms. If he could commit her to join him, he could fulfill his part of the deal, or renege, later.

She scowled at his arms and he tried to remember the last time she'd looked lovingly at him. "Don't think that's all."

Clay lifted his hand and pushed back his hair. "It would take a long time to close the gap between us. I know that." He inhaled slowly. "But if you don't help us then I know it could never close."

She released a breath. "Let me get Martin."

"I'll help."

Jenny looked at him with cold appraisal, then crisply nodded and touched his upper arm.

The safety gate at the top of the stairs swung open when it sensed an adult climbing toward it. Clay picked his way over the toys napping on the landing, plastic blocks with retracted spider legs and a white-furred Puca Sambuca sprawled on its back, and entered Martin's room. The boy woke as Clay lifted him off the bed. "Da?"

Clay forced up the corners of his mouth. "It's me."

"Da!"

"Hey, kidster, we're going to take a trip. Mom's getting some clothes for you. What toy do you want to take?"

Martin rubbed his eyes and then planted his face against Clay's shoulder. "No kno."

In a few minutes he would complain if he didn't have the right one. "You don't know?"

Jenny stood at the dresser wedging clothes into a backpack. "I'm bringing his counting robots and a set of flash cards."

"I'll pick something too." Clay carried Martin out to the landing. "See anything you like?" No, of course not. Clay knelt and picked up Puca Sambuca from the jumbled toys. It snored loudly but stayed asleep as Clay wedged it into the backpack Jenny held.

Martin came more awake when they walked through the garage to the waiting van. "Sea," he said, and pointed at Jenny's car.

She followed his gaze. "We need—"

"Forget the car seat. We're scoffing at bigger laws than that. Besides, when was the last time an autocar crashed?" Clay hunched forward and climbed into the van. Jenny followed and the door shut behind her.

"Ready to go?" Wally asked. The van started off and Jenny grabbed the edge of the nearest seat.

Clay reached his place and set Martin down beside him. "Do you remember Wally?" he said to Jenny, gesturing at him in the manual override seat.

She squinted. "You wore glasses, didn't you?"

Wally grinned at her, at Clay. "Ignored by men, remembered by women. I can live with that."

Roger took off his beret and slid away from the door. "Hi, sis. Have a sit."

Jenny sat next to her brother, her elbow on the top band of the seatback and her face in profile to Clay. She opened her mouth but said nothing, then shut it and gently shook her head. "I'm still trying to believe all this. You, Clay, and Wally," she said, then took in Hardin and the enlisted men, "and you gentlemen I don't know are going to bring down Everton?"

"There's more of us," Roger said.

"And other groups will join us," Wally said. "Treasures in Heaven and Greensmith."

"Who?" she asked. "Sounds like you need all the help you can get."

"How long does it take myfab or Youniverse to build a formix hive?" Wally asked.

Clay raised his voice. "Youniverse. I'm boycotting myfab. They collaborate with NCS and their network security is terrible."

Wally laughed. "Good points," he said, then turned to Jenny. "How much time do you need to program the hive after you pick it up?"

"Fabrication will take about six hours," she said. "Programming will be more but depends on what you need the hives to do."

"Way go?" Martin asked.

Clay frowned while deciphering the boy's words. "Where are we going?" Christ, how to explain it? "There's a bad man doing bad things and we're going to make him stop."

Martin dropped his gaze and pouted, lost somewhere in thought.

Clay blew out a breath and glanced at Jenny. Maybe she could tend the boy for a while. She turned her head slightly toward him and parted her lips, but a motion by Roger caught her attention. "Let's talk about what we need."

"Good idea," Wally said. "Why don't you two come up here—"

"I should sit in," Clay said.

"We've got it. We'll discuss it with you later."

Jenny stood. A wisp of hair hung down toward the narrowed eye she aimed at Clay. "His toys are here," she said. She patted the backpack sitting on the seat in front of him. "He'll enjoy the time with you."

Clay smiled weakly. After she walked forward, he reached over the seat and wrenched the pack next to him. Puca Sambuca was still asleep with its rabbit ears flopped over its face. Martin stared sullenly at the toy. "Want to wake up Puca?"

Martin shook his head.

"What about your flash cards? What can we do with those?"

"Pickas."

Did that mean pictures? Clay unzipped the backpack and reached past the puca doll. His fingers probed between cotton folds. Where were the flash cards? He found a hard plastic case near the bottom and tugged at it, spilling folded-up shorts and waking up the doll, only to find the case housed counting robots. Had they forgotten to pack the flash cards? No, there they were, encased in thick paperboard. He pulled them out and a T-shirt tumbled to the floor.

"No pickas."

"I thought you wanted to do pictures."

Martin shook his head and Clay seethed. All their talk of knocking over Everton and he couldn't even control his own son. Maybe there was something else on the flash cards. He held the paperboard case up to his eyes and started reading off the back. "Want to do numbers? Words?"

"No!"

"Then what do you want to do?"

"No!"

Clay leaned back and rubbed his temples. Maybe the boy would sit quietly for a while.

The van slowed and memories of arrest leaped into his fatigued mind. Clay whipped forward and stared in Wally's direction. "What's going on?"

One of the enlisted men behind him spoke. "Mr. Schieffer, we're picking up the crawlers."

He inhaled, leaned back, and half-turned his head. "I'd forgotten." He remembered what Nil would have said and turned further. He barely knew the two men but his freedom and his life might depend on them sometime down the road. "Thank you both for your work."

"It's our job."

The van stopped and the rear doors unlatched and swung open. They stood along the curb a few streets over from Clay's house. A storm drain horizontally slotted the curb. One of the enlisteds jumped to the street and whistled and the four crawlers emerged from the storm drain. "Stand down," he said to each in turn, then handed them up to his partner, who quickly wiped them down with a rusty towel and stacked them up behind the seat. After all the crawlers had been loaded, the other soldier climbed back in and pulled the doors until their processors realized he meant to shut them and their motors took over. The back of the van smelled damp from the storm drain and the crawlers' fuel cell exhalations. Martin stood on his seat, hands clutching the seat back, and his eyes wide.

"Want to watch?" one of the enlisteds asked. Martin nodded big. Despite a twinge in his knee, Clay shifted in his seat to better look himself.

"We're going to check them out before we put them to sleep," the soldier said. His hands gripped the front and back of a crawler's chassis and he raised it, rifle and paralyzer gun aimed at the floor. "Disarm." Two clicks came and clips sagged in their slots on the side of the crawler's turret. Clay reached for them and raised an eyebrow; the soldier nodded and Clay pulled them out and set them on the soldier's seat, near the window, far from Martin.

"Right tread, forward." The crawler complied; its wheels spun and its track rustled over them, grasping at air. The soldier rolled the crawler so Martin could see it edge-on. "How does that look?" he asked.

"Guh!" Martin said. He smiled and rocked up and down.

Could the NuGlands do something for him? Neurotransmitter mimics and antagonists could act only at synapses, of which Martin had too few, but there were more approaches they could try. Neuronal plasticity enhancers or perhaps even growth factors, if they could make his neurons grow more branches without inducing a neoplasm.

"Right tread, reverse," the soldier said, and Martin's eyes widened when the crawler did so.

The technology couldn't be on the market yet, or Jenny would have insisted it be tried; and no matter what might happen at New Washington, Clay could not hasten its arrival. But he watched the smile on Martin's face and wondered if perhaps he could tolerate his damaged boy until it did.

16

After the enlisteds finished the checkdown of their crawlers, Martin fell asleep, twitching with dreams. He woke when the adults extruded dinner from the MRE generators propped between the armrests and the windows. They flowed anonymously amid rush hour traffic heading north out of Dallas and ate their uncooked protein loaf discs and fibrous carb tubes. Even raw, the food tasted better than it had in the Hospital.

They picked up five hives, one each from various Youniverse stores in Oklahoma City's suburbs. Clay had probably seen photos of a hive but hadn't paid attention. Each hive was the size and shape of a lumpy football and skinned with a thick brown plastic. Closed zippers marked pockets or openings, and their slides lacked tabs… on the outside, at least. Gussets of pleated plastic ran roughly parallel to the zippers. Clay held up Martin and the boy poked his finger at the hive's skin. It bent around him until his finger hit something solid. He jabbed it a few times and Jenny pulled the hive away from him. "You don't want to hurt it."

Martin pouted but dropped his finger without protest.

Jenny sat in front of Clay and their son, next to Roger with the hive between them. She synched her wearable to the hive's controller and unfurled a smartpaper display, her new one, more colors and higher res that stayed more rigid when open and started working while the van drove to a sixth Youniverse and bought thin swatches of smart-camo, electric mesh, and adhesive. As the city's lights faded and a long Midwestern sunset stretched across the sky, Martin watched Jenny work until his eyelids drooped and he didn't fight when Clay laid him to sleep.

"Good news," Wally said.

Clay stepped past the sleeping boy and headed toward the front. "The Everton loyalty index fell again?"

"Not just that. The population is growing bolder." He waved a smartpaper at Clay. "A couple thousand people attended a yoga-in in San Francisco. A priest in New York called on Everton to resign. Federal agents came to arrest him but both other priests and a bunch of parishioners stood up for him and the feds backed down."

"When should we call on protestors to assemble outside New Washington? Tomorrow?" It didn't matter, did it? If the feds' morale was low enough, you could kick in the rotted wood at your leisure.

"New Washington will order a crackdown tonight that fed agents will enforce tomorrow. The crackdown will make the underground news and infuriate people." The newly strong parts of Clay's mind caught up and followed along. "We should make an announcement late tomorrow and get people to turn out the following day."

"Assuming you're right."

Wally was. The next day the van stopped at a rundown state park in the Oklahoma panhandle, and while Jenny and Roger worked on programming the formix hives, Clay and Wally watched low-res, bootleg video of feds bundling families, old women, and priests into black mariahs in New York and an America United mob swinging 2 x 4s in a fight in a parking lot of myfab store in suburban Atlanta. Even americaunitednewsservice.com mentioned the disturbances; it spun them as "an orchestrated campaign by anti-American factions," of course, but if its producers felt the need to say something, the protests had hit them hard.

Late in the afternoon, Clay prepared a second video, calling on all Americans alarmed by Everton's improper election and disturbed by the suppression of peaceful protests to assemble in Russell, Kansas, the next day.

Mid-morning found them on a U.S. highway entering Russell, Kansas, the town of more than a thousand original residents nearest to the USA Capital District. The original exit to the town from Interstate 70 had been joined by four more. Russell's population was now over twenty thousand and growing daily. Gupta Engineering signs marked the bare tamped dirt and the jutting concrete piers of the widening freeway and the new international airport. From the high point of an overpass, Clay saw fast food restaurants, upscale hotels, new shopping centers, and half-built subdivisions crawling across the plain toward USACD's southern gates but stopped a mile short, lapping at the edges of a fallow field.

His call had been heeded. Hundreds of people, men and women, old and young, clustered in the parking lots of the Holiday Inn and the Taj Mahal near the corner of the U.S. Highway and the Interstate business loop while men in sunglasses and dark suits watched from a distance. Word of Clay's arrival spread quickly, and Wally led them north toward New Washington.

The rising sun crowned the USACD's southernmost berms, ridges of packed dirt two hundred feet high, barely visible across the plain to the north of the interstate. Rumor had it more berms, impossible to see from the freeway, subdivided USACD. The official buildings were buried, half-buried, dispersed, all identical, twinned by dummies, overlain by camouflage netting.... Perhaps a dozen people had access to a complete map of USACD. Presumably none of them would league up with H-bomb terrorists. Contrails smeared the upper sky and gun emplacements glinted on the berms' redoubts.

They stopped at the side of the highway at a wheatfield owned by the highest-ranking America United gold member in the county. Three hundred yards to the north, a series of trestle bridges crossed a wide, shallow riverbed. On the far side, the highway vanished into the mouth of a tunnel through the southernmost berm of the capital district. Between the river and the tunnel mouth, the northbound lanes narrowed to one and chicaned to a guardhouse. Concentric fifteen-foot fences topped by uncoiled razor wire jutted on the far shore. More men in dark suits arrived at the guardhouse shortly after the protestors' arrival. Sunlight glinted on binocular lenses.

Clay looked at the gun emplacements atop the berms. Their barrels were still. "We're awfully alone."

"Not for long," Wally replied, but he tapped his foot faster than usual.

Again he was right. Lt. Treviño and the rest of his platoon arrived around noon and deployed its crawlers. The number of civilian protestors reached a thousand by early afternoon and among them came Lt. Wilson and most of his men and machines. Wider ranges of the wheatfield were trampled by car tires and human feet. Two American Bantu *ibuthos*, one from Denver, one from Kansas City, joined them. Sixty CFAers arrived soon after in a caravan of motorcycles and suvs; Clay sent them as far across the camp from the American Bantus as he could.

During the afternoon, Roger systematically lined up the cars along the highway and set up a front gate consisting of a web of ropes stretched tight across a rectangle formed from lumber. They also formed a command center of military hummvees, campers' tents, robot-dug trenches, and bags filled with soil and wheatstalks, and fitted Clay with subvocal microphones. They itched far less than Wally's formix had in the Hospital the night of his failed escape.

More civilians arrived, growing their numbers to three thousand by sunset. Members of Treasures in Heaven and Greensmith came, but a majority had no affiliation. Emma came with Roger's kids. All three, teary-eyed and shaking, plunged into his embrace. Delacroix, Kerensky, and Yamamoto arrived around four a.m., bleary-eyed from travel.

Most surprising to Clay were a handful of America United members who came to denounce Everton. Clay told Roger to keep an eye on them, but they did not appear to be *agents provocateurs*. They burned their AU membership cards and lapel pins in an impromptu ceremony captured on video and streamed live, their faces grim in the orange glow of the bonfire against the dark night.

Why surprise? He should have expected the NuGland hack to do this. After the bonfire, Clay sought them out and asked why they had come to protest. Their first answers were vague and selfless: "Everton stole the election." "We helped him, so we have to set things right."

Yet as they kept talking they betrayed themselves with subconscious revelations. They resented the golds and platinums; they fumed at being years down the Agerix queue. Clay almost pressed further, but the virtual Nil within his memory held him back. They'd said enough. The excuses were feeble, but if he didn't emphasize that they would not see through them. They clung to their reasons because of their feebleness, not despite it. They wanted to think they were in control of their own minds. Clay felt no sympathy for them.

Shortly after that, Jenny and Roger borrowed a pickup truck and wrestled the formix hives into the bed. They told Clay their plan. US-ACD covered parts of six counties, with all roads into the district torn up except for three: the one they parked along and two others, each about forty miles away to the northeast and northwest at Ft. Osborne and Ft. Stockton, respectively. On the north side of the district stood Steinmann Air Force Base, home of the anti-missile interceptor planes on patrol overhead and entrepôt for high-ranking visitors.

Jenny and Roger would take some enlisted men, ride around the perimeter of the district, and stop near each base to send out a hive. Each hive would take a couple of hours to enter each base. After one circuit, Jenny and Roger would ride another, checking the status of each hive and guiding it into position near the data trunks. Once there, it would lodge and send out formix to hack into the 3CI circuits and scavenge key parts from military hardware. After the second circuit, near dawn, they expected to be finished.

"A good plan," Clay said. He and Jenny stood awkwardly. There was risk; he didn't want to have to deal with Martin alone; but he also wanted her back in one piece. He reached for her, embraced her. He pulled away, hesitated, then kissed her cheek.

As the night wore on, Treviño's men and machines patrolled the perimeter and at the front gate a set of volunteers organized by Delacroix gave newly-arriving protestors an introduction to the camp, but Clay lay in the van and couldn't sleep, thinking about Jenny trying to coax her formix hives into place. What if something bad happened? They would radio in a mayday if they could, but as the sky lightened near dawn they hadn't returned yet. If the feds had jammed their communications and then captured them—

Using people might be easy in the abstract, but not if one were tied to them, by bonds of DNA and hormones, habits and memories. Clay mused and yawned as the sky lightened enough to show the contrails of the interceptors circling overhead, and another contrail descending on a straight line from the east into the capital district.

The ceedee caddy sat next to the foot of the mobile stairs on the taxiway at Steinmann AFB. The morning light glinted on the car's hood, its roof, and the sheet metal wall where the windshield should be, all painted as pale blue as the morning sky. General Johnson trudged down the mobile stairs, tired after a restless night and turning out of bed at oh-dark-thirty. The whine from the jet's turbines made him wince and the shutting of the caddy's doors came, for once, as a relief.

"Destination?" Thousands of copies of this model around the city, and all their voices sounded the same, like a housewife crewing a phone sex line while her children napped in the next room.

"White House."

The caddy remained unmoving for a time, accessing whatever server controlled travel permissions. "Right away, general."

It started moving and the sense of relief Johnson had felt quickly faded. He hated riding in these things. The caddy had no windows; soft beige trim, plastic and cloth, covered the inner surfaces of the doors. Video displays hung where the windshield and rear window should be but showed a visitor's guide to the city and the caddy system, useless to him after all his visits. He could use the display for personal use—NCS had cleared him for that—but he knew they would copy every output his wearable sent to it.

Some data was better left on one's wearable. Or in one's mind.

He'd heard the claim the cabin felt like a cocoon, but anyone saying that was an AU bootlicker convinced the President's shit smelled like rose petals; Johnson was convinced it was more like the inside of a rubber room at a mental hospital. The cabin's air did smell blandly sweet, like an air freshener output larded with citrus odorants, but he knew there were neuroactive drugs in it—hippocampal inhibitors, Doc Iammarelli had said. They made every trip in a ceedee caddy as hazy in memory as a half-doze and knocked people's direction senses off their gimbals. Johnson tried fighting the drugs, as always. *The car faced east on the tarmac. I got in and it executed a three-point reverse turn to head west, then turned south…* but in the diffuse artificial light inside the cabin, no cues of sunlight and shadow could help him counteract the swerving motion and disjointed pace of the caddy. South, east, west; he thought his way backward like someone lost in a cornfield maze before finally giving up.

Thirty years out of the Point and they treated him like a potential traitor. They wouldn't trust him to know where the White House was; they wouldn't trust him to think for himself. Thank god he had Iammarelli's morphine habit in his pocket. Johnson had built up favors with the division medical officer for years, waiting for the right moment to call them in. The order for loyalty drug brain implants had been that moment. Iammarelli had swallowed hard but checked the "implanted" box next to Johnson's name.

Could the AU bootlickers know Johnson had dodged their brain implants? Iammarelli would never squeal, but at some point scanners would get small and surreptitious enough that the doctor's brain could betray him. That point lay years away. By the time it came Johnson would be either retired or too high in the food chain to be touched.

Before then, the only tipoff could come from the implants themselves. They could receive distant signals, but could only transmit a few feet. Keep NCS agents away from his head and he'd be fine.

The caddy slewed and the engine noise echoed around it. *One mississippi, two mississippi….* Ten seconds lapsed before the echoes fell away. He'd passed through one of the berms. In quiet conversations on the golf course at Ft. Riley or over drinks with visiting senior generals at the officer's club, he'd heard the trip from Steinmann to the New White House passing through as few as three or as many as eight.

After passing through four berms and driving a winding road through an empty field, the sounds of concrete extruders and earth-moving equipment occasionally leaking through the closed doors, the caddy slowed and the engine echo indicated another tunnel. Outside the car, muffled voices called to one another and the echo had a smooth flutter to it, not the rough sound of unfinished concrete. He was in the *porte-cochére* running the width of the ground floor of the New White House. The caddy turned down a steep, sharply curving ramp and Johnson's stomach lurched.

The caddy stopped and popped its doors. Under banks of white incandescent bulbs, rows of ceedee caddies and stretch hummvees filled a parking garage. His vehicle had pulled up at a curb near a bank of escalators which led to a landing barely visible on the floor above. A young man with curly blond hair and weight room pecs under a bespoke tan suit waited for him. "General, follow me." Cockiness and naïve indifference from being twenty-five and working in the halls of power mingled on his face. *How platinum is his old man to land him this job?*

Up the escalators, then down a corridor thirty feet wide but with a badly proportioned ceiling—eight feet, yet it seemed lower. Johnson noticed taller people repeatedly ducking their heads as they hurried past. Phone conversations echoed in the corridor and improptu meetings took place along the walls near the recessed blast doors.

"Your meeting is in the situation room." The corridor widened into a cubicle farm on either side of the aisle. Johnson guessed he was under the New White House proper. Ventilation equipment hummed and smartpaper rustled on the desktops. The aide ignored the staffers at their stations and led Johnson to a pair of two-panel cherry doors lacquered to a fine sheen. Two NCS agents stood at either side, sunglasses dark. The doors opened and the aide gestured for Johnson to enter.

A conference table the same color and sheen as the doors stretched across the room. Smartpapers and the reflection of overhead lights glowed on its surface. The Secretary of Defense sat just to the right of center with the Joint Chiefs further to the right in their dress uniforms, gleaming buttons, and crisp piping. Their assistants stood behind them. To the left, NCS agent Ramirez sat next to another man in a dark suit, a beady-eyed, ruddy-faced, mustachioed white. Other civilians sat near them, cabinet secretaries, other senior bureaucrats, and others Johnson didn't recognize. The unknown man seated nearest to the center stood out, hair salted with gray at the temples, Italian suit and silk tie, and an arrogant gaze. Judging from their rapid glances at him, lazily terminated, they didn't recognize him either. The center seat was empty of the Presidential backside.

Johnson drifted to the right and sat across from the Chiefs. General Petrosian, Army Chief of Staff, eyed Johnson's smartcamo combat uniform and briefly frowned, but then one of his assistants spoke to him and any rebuke he planned to make was lost. Johnson spent the next moments gauging their pinched faces as they spoke with their assistants. As he had expected, all of them looked unhappy at having been summoned by the President. Despite Everton's excesses, he had never yet called on the military to suppress a peaceful and obviously civilian protest. The Chiefs wanted it to stay that way. Give them their sinecures and their cozy retirement packages on the boards of RTD contractors and they'd be happy.

As for Johnson.... Retired or untouchably high on the food chain? Was there really a question between the two?

The doors hummed open. This time, the rapid glances up stayed in place and the men at the table rose. Johnson pushed back from the table and also stood. Everton was shorter than he appeared on video; Johnson knew that and was not surprised. But Everton walked more slowly and his face had deeper lines and darker eyebags than Johnson had seen before. He'd always struck Johnson as a stuffed suit, telegenic and white enough to fool millions of people into thinking him leaderly; his tired expression made Johnson think the Schieffer situation had gotten the better of him. Four aides followed him two abreast around the far end of the table, where the standing bureaucrats nodded greetings and curtly said, "Mr. President." Everton perked up and greeted them by name, showed gleaming teeth, and slapped the Italian suit on the back and muttered a few words to him before he finally sat. Johnson was mildly impressed in spite of himself. *You're assuming he knows the depths of what's going on. He's probably just a grinning fool.*

Everton looked up and down the table. "I've seen the sitreps. Let's skip the rehashes and jump to the important question. What are we going to do about our unwanted visitors?"

Ramirez jumped in. "We should release the hounds. A military action with overwhelming force as soon as possible."

Everton nodded, rotated to his left. "General Pandolfini?"

The Air Force Chief, Joint Chiefs Chairman, sniffed in a breath. "We would submit two objections to the agent's proposal. First, there has been no Insurrection Act declaration—"

Everton raised his hand, then looked over his shoulder and spoke softly to one of his aides for a moment. He dropped his hand, turned back to the table. "We'll have one ready for my signature in ten minutes."

Pandolfini cleared his throat. "Our second objection goes beyond the Insurrection Act. The military's never been used to suppress a civilian protest—"

"These aren't civilians," Ramirez said. "These are enemy combatants. I was there when they attacked the NMHA facility in Missouri to break Schieffer out. I lost men to them. I know what they are."

Johnson looked away from Ramirez. The other NCS agent folded his arms and slunk back into his thoughts.

Everton watched him as well. "Assistant Director Haycock?"

The ruddy-faced NCS agent started and turned to his left. "Sir? What do I suggest? Military action is a card in our hand, but we've got a lot of lower intensity dirty tricks we haven't played. Some low-level AU members have done spontaneous disinformation via blogs and vlogs but NCS' black media unit hasn't been used. We can use aerosolized neuroactives for crowd control—"

"They already have countermeasures in place," Ramirez said. "It's in my field agents' latest report."

Everton nodded and turned to the well-dressed man immediately to his right. "Alex? What does AU's leadership have to say?"

The man smiled in business-deal charm and Johnson realized he was Alexander Fisher. "AU will stand behind the administration however you decide to deal with this crowd. If AU's organizational security auxiliaries could be of any assistance to you, we'll provide them."

"You've lost a few members," Everton said.

Damn, he's on. Maybe he needed to be pushed to the edge to figure out what he's capable of.

Fisher nodded. "A few bronzes. We presume they expected their dues to buy them the front of the line for agerix treatment. We're reviewing our psychological profiling and membership QC."

"Weren't they loyalty bonded?" Everton's tone was bland but there was a steely hint within it.

"We are certain one was. The others were due for it, if they did not yet go through the procedure. We're confirming and will have the report for your office this morning." Fisher was obedient but did not kowtow.

"I thought loyalty bonding provided a high certainty level."

Fisher blinked, put off-balance by Everton's grasp of the situation. "Relatively high, yes, Mr. President, but it only provides a statistical bias, not a guarantee for each individual. I believe that's a matter of common knowledge."

"Statistical bias? If we send the military there's no guarantee the soldiers and officers would remain loyal?" Everton looked disappointed, like a small child after Santa had forgotten to leave a Puca Sambuca under the Christmas tree. Petrosian and Pandolfini shared a cautiously hopeful glance.

Johnson cleared his throat and turned his gaze away from the Chiefs and toward Everton. "The fewer personnel you could commit, the less a concern with individual loyalties, Mr. President."

"I don't follow, General," Everton said. The Chiefs did, and turned cold looks on Johnson.

He ignored them. "I have three battalions of robots and teleoperated devices at Fort Riley. We could deploy within six hours."

"Never mind precedent," Gen. Petrosian said, glaring at Johnson but pitching his voice to carry to Everton. "Deploying robotic fighting vehicles to crush protestors will destroy sympathy for the government's cause. Remember Tank Guy at Tiananmen Square?"

The poor bastard, with white shirt and briefcase, photographed standing in front of a column of PLA tanks; his fate the subject of more urban legends than Elvis' or Michael Jordan's. Ramirez snorted. "Sympathy? The Communists ruled all of China for another twenty-five years after that."

"Sir," Johnson said to Petrosian, "I agree RFVs are a poor choice." He faced Everton again. "I would recommend the light robotics battalion. I know my men. Their loyalty has not wobbled."

"It hasn't?" Ramirez said. "What about Captain Sung?"

Johnson gave the NCS agent a flat stare. "You knew Captain Sung was Schieffer's brother-in-law. You deployed Captain Sung's company to arrest Schieffer. I would not have made that decision."

Ramirez' nostrils flared and he extended his fingers and pressed his hands onto the tabletop. Johnson turned back to the President, but a noise at the door made everyone look up. A muffled voice said in an odd accent, "It is important we speak to him."

"What's going on?" Everton asked, creases in his forehead. One of his aides muttered a reply. The President's frown deepened. "Mo wouldn't screw around. Let them in."

The doors swung open. The South Asian guy in the suit was obviously Mo—Mohammad? Monmahan?—and reminded Johnson of the premed and prelaw "friends" his college-age daughter was probably bunking with. He looked like he belonged in the White House, deferently smiling to Everton's face and backstabbing other bureaucrats.

The other belonged in a room filled with dry-erase boards and mathematics journals. He had a square face, curly hair, and a long, narrow nose. His shirt needed ironing—only the buttons kept the placket even close to flat—and his security tag dangled off-center, bearing the name G. Poisson. His accent was French and very nasal. "Mr. President, I am very glad you could see me."

Everton's smile didn't reach his eyes. "I'm afraid we haven't met, Mr?"

"Guillaume Poisson. There—"

Mo pressed his hand against Poisson's shoulder, and the other took the hint. "Mr. Poisson does sociological inflectology work for us in the Office of Special Operations. He earned his security clearance in large part through work with the late Dr. Boucher."

"I see."

"He's come to me with very important information. He has data—"

Everton nodded to cut Mo off. "Mr. Poisson? What do you have for us?"

Poisson nodded gravely. "Mr. President, in my work I measure the rise and fall of social forces and movements. You may consider it the epidemiology of ideas. I have observed various leading indicators of social unrest and I have come to a most unwelcome conclusion."

"Which is?" Everton's patience had thinned.

"Mr. Schieffer has reprogrammed the NuGlands of civilian government, military, and America United personnel."

Multiple people gasped, then the room fell silent for a moment. Everton turned a piercing frown on Poisson. "You're certain of this?"

Poisson raised his hands. "I have not cut open a man's brain and determined what his NuGlands have been synthesized to do, no. But I have observed the indicators of loyalty in many media, such as message boards, blogs, and internet traffic. Not only has disloyalty increased in recent weeks, Mr. President, but the peaks of increase of disloyalty have come in the places that should be most loyal. Within the government, within the military, and within America United. I can come up with only this explanation."

"I've seen his data," Mo said. "I concur with his conclusion."

Fisher broke the silence. "That's absurd. Schieffer couldn't do that."

"Didn't he build the things?" Haycock said.

Fisher looked down his nose at the NCS man. "The programmability is so secure that very few hackers could pierce it in only a few weeks. All the social network analysis we've done on Schieffer as part of due diligence shows he doesn't know any skillful hackers."

"Maybe your due diligence is wrong," Haycock said.

"Both of you," Everton said, "who the hell cares? Assume Poisson is right and fix it. Everyone, reprogram the implants for people in your organizations immediately."

Seated people spoke to their assistants and styluses scratched on smartpaper. "Sounds like your problem is taken care of," Gen. Pandolfini said to Everton.

"No no," said Poisson. "It is not so simple, General. It will take a few days to fix the security lapse, reprogram all the NuGlands, and then a few days more for the changes in the brain chemistries to be effected. Let us say it is a week. A week is a long time for the situation to remain as it is, Mr. President. From my observations, it is quite possible it would be too long."

"Thank you, Mr. Poisson." Everton stared past the man, his expression lost in thought. Even so, conversations around the room dropped to silence. Everton stared at nothing for more moments, but then his attention returned to the room and he nodded to himself, locking a decision into certainty. He shook his wrist and a wearable with an expensive watchface slipped past his cuff and into view. "I have 0814," he said. He lifted his gaze and turned it on Gen. Johnson. "I believe you said six hours, General?"

Johnson's heart thudded and from the corner of his eye he saw the disdain and fear lurking in the faces of the Joint Chiefs. By the end of the day he would be one of the most powerful men in the country. "Yes, Mr. President. Though I have a further request."

Everton raised his eyebrows, then nodded.

"It would greatly assist me if the guns on the south berm are assigned to my command." The Chiefs looked even less happy but said nothing.

"You'll have them," Everton said.

Long shadows crossed the trampled wheatfield when Jenny and Roger returned to the camp an hour after sunrise. The volunteer at the front gate radioed the command center with the news of their arrival, but it still took them fifteen minutes to press through recent arrivals and the furrows of thousands of cars to Clay, Wally, and Treviño in the command center. The three of them stood in the main tent. Its flaps were up in expectation of a warm day and lumps of bent stalks distended the plastic floor.

"How many people are out there?" Roger asked.

"Over ten thousand," Clay said. He turned to Jenny and relief flowed in him. "I'm glad you're back safe."

"Where's Martin?"

"With his aunt and cousins. How'd it go?"

She looked around and saw an unfolded chair. On the uneven ground, it wobbled under her but her face showed she was too tired to care. "We placed all four. They've spliced into the data lines and they're sabotaging vehicles."

"We've neutralized them and they don't even know." Clay smiled and the smile broke into a grin, toothy and awkward and he didn't care. "Great job. Both of you."

Roger did not mirror the emotion. He swept his beret off his head. "They're not totally ineffective yet, for one. For another, the longer the hives are in place, the more likely the federal forces will discover them."

"If we can make it a few more days without the hives being discovered, it shouldn't matter," Wally said. "The Everton loyalty index is still dropping."

"We may not have a few days." Roger exhaled heavily. "We came back through Russell. We saw an America United rally on the courthouse lawn. The crowd was about two thousand, twenty-five hundred."

"But we reprogrammed them," Clay said.

Wally shook his head briskly, but stopped when Clay turned to him. "We made them less loyal to Everton. It's a bias, not a certainty. You know that."

"We still outnumber them."

"Quality, not quantity," Roger said. "AU's a mob but its members are mostly armed and have some training at following orders. How many of our ten thousand have weapons?"

Wally bit his lip and frowned at a smartpaper. "About two thousand."

"A hunting trip or a few hours at the shooting range don't much make people into soldiers."

Clay frowned. "The numbers don't sound so bad."

"Us against the AU crowd? We would have a decent chance. But if they combine with heavy robots rolling out of USACD, or my former unit from Ft. Riley—or both—it would be difficult."

"We've shut down their heavy robots—"

From the chair, despite her fatigue, Jenny's tired voice carried through the tent. "Not yet, Clay. We don't want to flick the switch until we need it to defend ourselves."

He easily slipped into his new, authoritative voice. "We'll know when that's happening. What about Ft. Riley?"

Wally spoke. "I'll post to the forums and ask people to watch for military vehicles leaving Ft. Riley and heading our way. We should have a couple of hours notice, at least, if they come our way."

The tent suddenly felt warm. "More of our people are coming all the time," Clay said. He looked around the tent. Despite the firmness of his tone, the faces of the others were drawn. Roger cast a hooded glance in the direction of the south berm. Treviño looked like he had heartburn.

What would Nil do? "What am I missing, lieutenant?" His voice sounded charmless to his ears, but he hoped it would have its effect on Treviño.

The lieutenant blinked and straightened. "Morale is good," he said, "for now. But my men have reported some grumbling. The civilians can see the batteries emplaced on the berm. We also suspect there are AU spies among the civilians, spreading disinformation."

"You're saying we need to stiffen their spines."

"That's a good way of putting it, Mr. Schieffer."

"Wally?"

He rubbed his temples and yawned. "It's likely we'll have a correction in the zeal levels among the people on our side if we're in a state of siege for a while. Basic crowd dynamics."

"You don't have data on the people outside this tent?"

Wally blinked, slowly, heavily, and scratched patchy stubble on his chin. "Not enough." His voice sounded tired as well. Clay pressed together his lips and forced himself to look away. Wally had worked hard and wasn't superhuman. He'd earned the right to be tired.

Clay sat on the edge of an unfolded table that wavered under his weight. The formix hives had to remain secret from the mass of protestors if there were AU spies among* *them. He could make a vague speech, exhorting them to remain strong, but that might make the correction in zeal levels steeper than it needed to be. Then the answer came. "Do you know how many of our people are implanted with NuGlands?"

Wally frowned. "I can pull it up. Not many."

"Then we generate aerosolized neurotransmitter analogs and flood the area with them. Roger, Treviño, I assume you have enough spare nasal filters for us?"

Treviño frowned. "We do, but I don't follow you."

"We can stiffen our people's spines, lieutenant. Make the pacifists aggressive enough to beat up the AU thugs and the cowards laugh at the artillery on the berm."

Jenny looked at Clay with a querulous look. Roger straightened his shoulders and lifted his chin. "Is that why we're here?"

Roger's tone gave Clay pause. "What does that mean?"

"I thought we were here because Everton used your technology to turn people into puppets for his advantage. I must be wrong."

"Wrong?" Then Clay saw where Roger came from. "How can you think this is the same?" He inhaled and let the power of his reprogrammed NuGlands fill him. It tingled in his gestures, his facial expressions, his pitch and tone of voice. "Everton was using people for his own greed, you're right, but even if you could call what I'm talking about 'using people' it's for their sake. The only way they can survive this is by winning. All I'm talking about is making them better able to win."

Roger didn't back down. "You think I'm the only one who knows what he's risked to be here?"

The words forced Clay a half-step back. He glanced around the tent for support. Treviño stared at the floor. Jenny pursed her lips. He turned to Wally. "Tell me what you think."

Wally spoke softly. "You know why I saw you as the man to galvanize this rebellion, Clay?"

"I knew the technology."

"That's true. Better than anyone else. But I could have scraped by recruiting others who knew enough to make it possible. It was more than the technology. From what I knew of you in person, plus all the psych data I pulled up on you, I saw you were a rare man. A man who could lead others without wanting power over them."

Clay frowned. "I don't want power over anyone."

"The people who've chosen to join us see that too. What would happen if they come to feel they were deceived?"

"We're not talking about power. It's only things to help them—"

Roger spoke. "If it would help them, wouldn't they choose it themselves?"

Clay fell silent. The noises of the camp—thousands of conversations, the hum of vehicles—drifted into the tent. These people were not here because he had willed it, but because they had willed it. They had chosen to help him and that was as far into their brains as he could go. Nil would have gone further, but Nil wasn't here.

He stood straight and cleared his throat. "How else can we prepare them for what might come?"

The May sun climbed high over the wheatfield as the protestors fortified their camp. More vehicles added to the ends of the wall of parked cars along the roadside and curved it inward to ring the camp. More cars formed an inner, partial line along the roadside. Roger and Lt. Treviño circulated among the crowd and found some of the CFAers and American Bantus, along with a few ex-soldiers and marines, had started giving the armed civilians rudimentary training. Another military retiree, the cargo area of his station wagon jammed with plastics synthesizers and a miniature fab plant, was assembling and handing out gas masks. "If they try airborne crowd control agents," he said.

The flow of arrivals trickled to a stop. Posts on the protest's forums showed why, streaming video of AUers blocking the off-ramps at the Russell exit. Autocars slowed to a crawl and AUers shoved xenon flashlights against their tinted windows. A few people snuck in from distant exits and down straight flat gravel roads, but most formed a second camp of protestors on the south side of Russell, between the interstate and the razor-wire fence of the airport.

Other than the AU mob, however, the feds did not appear to stir. The formix hives fed data showing business-as-usual at the military bases in USACD, and the continual flow of protestors coming from Kansas City and points east reported no convoys rolling down the interstate from Ft. Riley.

After a quick lunch from an MRE generator, Clay put on his suit and tie and, with Jenny, toured the camp. Word spread. Despite the number of hits on his video streams very few people had seen him live. They turned his way and the hope on their faces pressed against him like waves on an incoming tide. Jenny gripped his hand and the skin crinkled around her eyes and he read her expression: he had to appear strong for the sake of the crowd. They saw, not him, but the role he played, and realizing that made it easier. He dispelled apprehension about the gun emplacements: "They haven't used them yet because they know they're in the wrong." When wild rumors came back to him—he was an NCS mole, the protest was designed to gather the opposition to Everton in one place to crush it, he said, "I'm sure Everton sent spies to spread rumors like that. They're welcome to burn their AU membership cards too."

He also found something that hammered home how wrong he had been in the tent. A trio of graduate students in chemical engineering at Missouri-Rolla eagerly showed off a jury-rigged collection of MuSynths and a tablet press. "Kumar designed drug combination to make people less fearful but more alert and Yi-Cheng and I synthed it and offer it to people," an acne-scarred, gangly young man named Sergei said with traces of a Russian accent. "Do you wish sample?"

Clay forced himself to smile. "I'd be honored. Are many people taking it?"

Sergei's expression showed the answer pained him. "Not many."

"Yet," Kumar said.

About two-thirty, shortly after leaving the graduate students, Clay encountered journalists. His nape was damp with sweat and, despite his reprogrammed NuGlands, his ability to be smooth with people felt as weak as his legs after a hard swim following an inactive week. He pushed through it. Not simply vloggers with video cameras and bandwidth, these were contract reporters for established news services, such as molecularfabricationtoday.com and Voice of Reason. "What are your goals?" the woman from VoR asked. Her tight bun and retro-styled eyeglasses made her look like a model posing as a librarian.

"Everyone elected in '20 and '22 with support from America United must resign."

"Won't that plunge the country into chaos?"

"The sudden, violent demise of a popular president, most of his cabinet, and almost all of Congress and the Supreme Court didn't do that on 6:19; why would peaceful resignations do it now? The Vice-President resigns; Everton nominates a replacement; Congress confirms the replacement; and then Everton and Congress resign."

The reporter from molecularfabricationtoday.com spoke. "And you should be that replacement?"

What would Nil do? "Me? Only if the American people think I should be." His earbud bonged lightly, and despite his poor pitch he recognized the tone for a call coming in from a member of the inner circle. "Pardon me," he said to the journalists, then turned and pressed the pickups for his subvocal microphone under his jaw. *Clay here.*

"It's Roger. Can you meet me at the command post?"

What's happening?

"We have bandits about five hundred meters east of the perimeter."

Bandits? AU? Military? Roger didn't respond. Clay strode toward the center of the camp, fighting off the urge to run. Nil would take his time and act like everything was under control.

An suv stood at the edge of the trench ringing the command center. Its doors were open and Roger stood on the running board with his elbows on the roof and a pair of binoculars at his face. "How many?" Clay asked. "Who?"

Roger shuffled his feet away from the center of the running board and held the binoculars away from his eyes. Clay climbed next to his brother-in-law and took the binoculars from him.

His gaze leaped twelve hundred yards across the wheatfield to a dirt road parallel to the highway. Two dozen tractor-trailers and about the same number of hummvees stood there. Their smartcamo shaded bottom-to-top from dirty beige to sky-blue. Men in smartcamo uniforms and black berets hurried between the vehicles. "Army?"

"My unit," Roger said.

His tone made Clay look away from the binoculars. Roger's expression looked professional and Clay saw no trace of any loyalty to the men and machines half a mile away. "They've deployed a platoon of crawlers across the front of their line. We're watching for further movement."

Clay returned his gaze through the binoculars to the Army personnel across the wheatfield. A soldier climbed onto a hummvee with a pack on his back and a crawler under his arm. "What sort of further movement?" he asked.

"What do you see?" Clay handed the binoculars over, then squinted across the field. The soldier was a tiny figure, his edges seeming to blur into the sky and the vehicle, but when he pulled something from inside his pack he saw its color, seemingly bobbing in air, even before Roger returned the binoculars to him. The soldier affixed a white flag to a length of stiff wire and mounted it on the crawler, then held it with its muzzles facing away from the protestors' camp and dropped it like a flat stone.

17

The white flag floated above the tops of the stalks like a low, tiny cloud as the crawler traveled toward them. "I'll take a guess they aren't surrendering," Clay said.

"Mueller wants to talk. It might even be Johnson."

"Talk? Or are they setting us up?"

Roger stepped off the running board and Clay followed. A smartpaper lay unfolded across the floor of the jeep's cabin and showed a map of the camp and the surroundings. A red dot moved toward the perimeter from the east, outnumbered by blue dots traveling with it. "If it turns hostile, our crawlers should neutralize it. If it's packed with explosives, ours will sniff that and stop it."

The crawler passed the smell test. Video feed through rows of wheat stalks, though blurred by speed and the interceding growth, showed the muzzles of both its paralyzer dartgun and its rifle pointed back at the Army formation. It stopped five yards from the perimeter and dropped an aluminum cigar tube to the soil. One of their crawlers scampered up, picked up the tube, and opened it. No explosives inside; the only content was a rolled-up piece of dumbpaper scrawled with ink:

Mr. Schieffer,
I'd like to pay you a visit to discuss matters.
Gen. Claudius Johnson, USA.

By the time one of Treviño's corporals brought Clay the message, a crowd had gathered outside the command center and Clay, Roger, Wally, and Jenny had retreated into the tent. "What does he want to discuss?" Clay asked.

"Maybe he'll offer us a chance to disperse before he opens fire," Jenny said. "Coming over I heard that rumor already going through the crowd." She squinted briefly. "Though he wouldn't need to meet with us to tell us that."

"Everton's loyalty index is still dropping," Wally said. His voice quivered but his tone was cheerful. "Insiders were going to start acting soon—"

"He wants to join us?" Clay asked. He turned to Roger.

"I don't know him well. He's too far above me in the chain of command. He seemed content with the status quo," Roger said, but then his face relaxed and his tone eased. "Before you hacked the NuG-lands."

Clay grinned. "Let's meet with him."

It took ten minutes to find a pen, but the delay helped them clarify what to say. Clay scratched out a reply to Johnson's message. Five minutes later the same corporal stuffed it in the cigar tube and tossed it at the silent crawler squatting outside the perimeter. It clacked over the tube and then sped eastward.

Forty-five minutes later, two figures emerged from the wheat field The first, black and round-faced, had large, intelligent eyes, and the only parts of his smartcamo uniform that didn't shimmer were two stars on each collar and the nametag *Johnson*. He pulled off his black beret with his left hand while his right hesitated near the pistol holstered at his hip before he moved to shake hands. "Mr. Schieffer?" he said. His voice was as buzzed and salted as his hair.

"General." Clay shook hands and glanced at the holstered pistol.

"I have no plans to draw it," Johnson said. "But we will defend ourselves, and Capt. Sung is familiar with vital signs telemetry."

To Clay's right, Roger nodded. He hadn't briefed Clay on the subject, but it was clear from context.

"We're here to talk," Clay said. "When we're done talking you can walk away." He turned to the other man, tall and thin with a long, narrow face. Clay opened his mouth to speak to the lieutenant colonel, but then felt a stab of *what would Nil do?* "Col. Mueller?"

His expression stayed cold. "Lieutenant colonel."

"Sorry," Clay said off-handedly. "Didn't mean to promote you."

Johnson peered at Clay, then dabbed at his sweaty forehead with the back of his left hand. "You said there'd be a place to sit?"

Clay nodded and gestured behind him. A long Lorelei sedan, gleaming black in the afternoon sun, idled outside the wall of vehicles. They walked toward it, surrounded by men from Treviño's platoon and armed ex-military protestors, and Johnson grunted. "Someone let you put their Rheinmädchen 880 in harm's way? You've built up a lot of popular support." Johnson and Mueller waited outside while Clay, Roger, and Wally went to the far side and climbed in. After, their door folded up and they joined them inside, in cold air thick with the aromas of leather and new car. Johnson relaxed for a moment and looked lazily across the cabin at them. "It's a shame that's all you have."

"All I have? There are ten thousand people out there."

"How many who know which end of rifle is up? Capt. Sung and Lt. Treviño are skillful tacticians, at least when it comes to ambushing an equally matched platoon, but we have—" Johnson pivoted his head to glance toward the waiting unit, "—at least two companies."

Next to Clay, Roger touched his throat. "We know that already," he said over their private channel.

"He might be bluffing," Wally said through his subvokes.

"They still outnumber us six to one—"

Clay raised his hand to break off their conversation, then realized how foolish the gesture must have looked to the officers across the cabin. Everyone looks foolish, Nil would have said, just fake confidence and plow ahead. "We have more military assets than meet the eye."

Johnson smirked. "White supremacists? Ex-soldiers with hunting rifles?"

It was easy to bluff when one had four formix hives in the hole. "At least."

Johnson's smirk faded. "What more do you have?"

Clay inclined his head toward Wally, but kept his gaze on the general from the corner of his eye. "It's slipping my mind," he said out loud, "but there's a poker phrase, isn't there?"

Wally mirrored his pose. "You have to pay to find out."

"You mean the hacking you did on the government and military brain implants?" Johnson asked. "That cat's out of the bag." To the general's right, Lt. Col. Mueller pursed his lips and frowned at his superior. "Everton, NCS, everyone knows about it."

Clay inhaled sharply, then realized it didn't matter if they knew. "Actually, no. I'm not referring to that. Assuming we even did that."

"Be coy, that's fine," Johnson said. "But if you think it made me and my men your puppets, you think wrong."

"Assuming we did that," Clay said, "I know how the technology works. Changing brain chemistry can only change the likelihood of target behaviors. The human brain isn't a blank slate. Nothing we can do can make people puppets."

"At least not yet," Johnson said. "But even if you could, I can't be one of them."

"It's natural to think you're immune—"

"It is when I don't have your implant, Mr. Schieffer."

Silence stuffed the sedan's cabin. Clay's heart pounded as he studied the general's face for signs he was bluffing. "That's not what our records indicate."

"Records can be falsified. Where were we? Yes, you claim to have some secret forces that could stop our two companies from crushing your protest. But there's a lot more arrayed against you than our battalion."

"The forces in USACD? We'll take our chances against them."

Johnson leaned forward and peered at Clay's face. "What have you got? Where is it?"

Clay sat straighter and stared back at the general. "You have to pay to find out."

Johnson slumped back, the seat squeaking underneath him. He lifted his fist to his mouth and brooded for long seconds. "It's time to cut to the chase," he said, but trailed off.

"Cut away."

"You have two choices. The first is your protest implodes when your people see the Army. You and your inner circle flee and maybe you get lucky and make it to Mexico before NCS catches you."

"What's the second?"

Johnson rubbed his forehead, then dropped his hand and stared across the cabin. "1 LRTD Battalion casts its lot with the protestors and helps them remove Everton from office. Afterward, a flag officer joins you on the… we can't call it a junta, we aren't a banana republic. The Transitional Governing Council."

Next to the general, Mueller looked aghast. "Sir," he said out loud, and then his hands fluttered to his throat.

Clay did the same, and listened for the baseline hum of noise on his private channel with Roger and Wally. *I assume "flag officer" means a general, Roger?*

"Exactly," came the reply through his earbud.

We thought he might join us—

"Join is not the same thing as become a coequal with," Wally said subvocally.

And 'Transitional Governing Council'? A junta by any other name. That won't work.

"Why wouldn't it?" Roger asked.

Clay's thoughts had wandered this route for several days, but only now did he frame them in words. *Because we have to paint ourselves as selflessly restoring the way things were before 6:19. We have to do it by the book. That's why the people inside the perimeter came here and that's the only way to make our effort to get Everton out of office look legitimate to two hundred million fence-sitters. The substance can differ, but we need to keep the forms the same. Hell, even Everton felt the need to follow the letter of the Insurrection Act.* Clay glanced across the cabin. The two officers faced each other, eyes glaring and muscles jumping around their throats. Johnson's offer to Clay had shocked Mueller, and from his expression Clay could see the lieutenant colonel had still not wrapped his mind around it. *But if we get him off that idea, should we take him up on his offer?*

"It means a fight with Everton," Wally said subvocally, but before his words trailed off he added, "but that's why Johnson came here in the first place."

"He wants a senior position," Roger added. "By law he can't

be SecDef, though we could force a change in that law through Congress.... but you're right, that's a bad idea."

The Presidency would be even worse; a hundred million apathetic people who could tolerate Everton's removal if it were spun as a restoration of the Constitution would see Johnson's ascension as a military takeover. *We could make him Army Chief of Staff or National Security Advisor, right?*

Roger nodded. Across the cabin the inaudible conversation broke up. Mueller breathed heavily and cast wary glances around the cabin. Johnson hadn't persuaded him, but rather appeared to have only talked him into confusion.

"That's an interesting possibility you mentioned," Clay said. "Despite the loyalty implants, I'm sure many members of the military resent the way Everton came to power and would join the effort to persuade him to resign."

Johnson nodded, his eyes lively. Mueller looked even more confused.

"And you made another good point. The United States isn't a banana republic."

A frown flexed Johnson's eyebrows. "I don't follow you."

"The American people don't know much about history or government, but one of the reasons they respect the armed forces as much as they do is the armed forces appear subordinate to civilian politics."

"They think of themselves as better than the people in those Latin countries," Wally added, "where the army comes out of its barracks to drive civilian governments from power and install a general as *Presidente.*"

Johnson brooded and Clay quickly filled the silence while hoping he talked slowly and calmly enough. "I said the armed forces appear subordinate to civilians. Behind the scenes they wield plenty of power, don't they? They get funding for their pet projects and new weapons systems, even now when our only enemies are Uighurstan guerrillas. The National Security Advisor and the Chairman of the Joint Chiefs can color the options when he briefs the President, especially if the President has no foreign policy experience. He can build up connections with private industry and retire to an easy seven-figure job." A sour emotion touched Clay but he kept it off his face. *This will be your life for the next few years*, he imagined Nil telling him.

Johnson cocked his head. "That's all true. But the President could do even more."

Clay stiffened and forced a dry swallow. Wally, though, jerked his head side-to-side and said, "Not if he's drowning in civil disobedience. Maybe even armed rebellion."

"Civil disobedience?"

Wally shook his head again. "I'm an inflectologist. If people see streaming video of tanks in the streets of New Washington and a man on horseback proclaiming himself President, they'll get off the couch. An attempted coup would strike at all the myths the people tell themselves about our country. Whites would be shown we're no better than Latin Americans, and Latinos would be reminded why they or their ancestors left Latin America in the first place. I've run the numbers. A man on horseback would have an ungovernable mess on his hands."

He hadn't run the numbers. The realization struck Clay so strongly he inhaled a strangled breath and hoped Johnson was not looking at him.

Johnson chuckled. "You overestimate people. As long as they get their videogames and vacations to Branson they won't care what's going on."

"We turned AU members into Everton haters," Wally said. "Want to bet no one could turn apathetic masses into a velvet revolution?"

No one spoke for a time till Johnson cleared his throat. "If you win through, you'll find General Petrosian, the Army Chief of Staff, and General Pandolfini, Joint Chiefs Chairman, are dyed-in-the-wool Evertonites."

Relief flooded Clay. "They wouldn't work for a president other than Everton?" he asked. "Even one who was duly nominated, confirmed, and appointed as his successor?"

"Not even. You'd have to ask both of them to resign and appoint a new Army Chief and Chairman. Of course, one man could hold both offices."

Clay nodded. "I have a candidate in mind."

A weak, but relieved, smile skewed Johnson's lips. "I think we understand each other."

"Sir!" shouted Roger, and into Clay's sudden confusion seeped the realization of the leathery, sliding sound of a pistol being drawn from a holster.

The red dot of Roger's laser sight spotted Mueller's chest. Mueller's nostrils flared and the fingertips of his right hand brushed his sidearm, still in its holster.

"Sir," Roger said, "put your hands on top of your head. No touching your subvokes on the way."

Mueller left his hands in place. He breathed so heavily his torso looked like a bellows. "You're all traitors. Every goddam one of you. Sung, I can understand you, blood's thicker than water, even though that's no excuse. But you?" he said to Clay. "And *you*?" His voice was a harsh whisper to Johnson. "Everton's our president and you're going to violate our oath to bring him down?"

"Everton's a murderer," Clay said. "He has to be brought down."

Roger nodded but the sighting dot held steady. "You know Ramirez murdered Monica Colbert. You saw him murder Nil Thomas. It was on Everton's orders to try covering up Everton's crimes in winning the election."

"Or did Everton know what was arrayed against him?" Mueller asked. He glared at Clay. "An enemy who would turn loyal officers into traitors and make up lies to soil the President's reputation?" Mueller glanced at the pistol as if trying to weigh it with his vision. He narrowed his eyes and slowly roved his gaze to Roger, to Clay, to Johnson. Mueller nodded to himself and his gaze swung to Clay and his right arm bent—

The gunshots roared through the cabin, the loudest sounds Clay had ever heard. The sighting dot remained in place over Mueller's chest, despite the shredding of his uniform and the piercing of his skin, the shattering of his sternum and ribs, the puncturing of his lungs and heart. Blood gushed from the cluster of wounds in Mueller's chest. His right hand crumpled away from his holstered sidearm and slid across the blood-slick leather seat. Mueller turned his head to Roger and opened his mouth, but all that came out was an ooze of blood and the choked gurgle of his last breath.

The only other sound over the ringing in Clay's ears were Roger's retches as he leaned over and vomited on the cabin's floor at the dead man's feet.

Clay stared at Mueller's blank eyes and slack face, not thinking, until he heard the squeak of clothed flesh against leather when Johnson slid away from the corpse. He shook his head at Mueller's body. "Why did you throw your life away," he muttered.

Roger sat up, but his face was pale. "He didn't want to believe he'd sided with the bad guys."

Johnson looked soberly at Roger. "It doesn't matter what he believed, captain. He made his choice and he followed it all the way to what he knew it would bring onto him. You made the right decision."

Roger wobbled and compressed his lips. "Thank you, sir."

Johnson nodded to him, then looked at Clay. "The next question is how do we get started?"

The camouflage pattern in Mueller's uniform still flickered, trying to match the pattern of his seeping blood. "I don't follow."

"You need to," Johnson said sharply. Clay pulled his gaze away from the dead man. "Ever since I found out what you'd done to the loyalty implants, I've been kicking myself for not having seen it earlier. The men are antsy and have little respect for Everton. But they aren't ready to rebel. Not yet."

"They need a spark," Wally said.

"I can start one. I can direct fire from the berm into your perimeter. To a spot you choose, to the meter, don't worry about that. The men don't know I've been given this, but when they see shells landing without provocation they'll flip. I don't need to be an inflectologist to see that." He grimaced at Mueller's corpse. "And maybe we can get something out this, too."

They parted the perimeter and the Lorelei rolled across the bent stalks of wheat, tires slipping across muddy ruts, to a stop twenty-five yards from the cluster of tents, lean-tos, and suvs that defined the command post. Roger had called ahead and Treviño's men and machines had cleared protestors from a fifty-yard radius around the command tents, allegedly a precondition for Johnson to be willing to enter the crowd. People thronged for a glimpse of Clay and the general on the fifteen-second walk to the tents. Johnson took off his beret, bowed his head, and walked a quarter-step behind Clay.

Inside the tent, Jenny hurried to him and had a concerned frown on her face. "What happened?"

"I'm fine," he said brusquely.

She glanced at Johnson and her mouth turned sour. "No, you're not." She glanced at the car. "What happened?"

No, she wasn't prying, she wanted what was best for him. He pressed his hands around hers. "Sorry. We'll talk later and I'll tell you everything. I mean that, sweet."

Johnson, Roger, and Wally stood around the smartpaper-strewn folding table. Johnson pulled his own from the chest pocket of his tunic and scrawled commands. Wally pressed his finger against his earbud. "Nearest hive reports fire orders coming from Ft. Everton to the artillery on the south berm," Wally said.

"Coordinates agree with the general's statement," Roger said. "The car."

Clay parted his hands from Jenny's. "Let it through." He looked at Johnson. The general's surprise was obvious. "You paid. You got to find out."

The first shell landed, exploded, tore metal. Clay expected it, but even then it sounded like the loudest thunderstorm he'd ever been in. He flinched despite himself. Jenny ducked. Protestors screamed, but a handful of voices—Treviño's men and former military personnel, Clay guessed—shouted authoritatively. Another shell landed around the command tents.

Clay knelt next to his wife. "I didn't have time to explain."

"Johnson flipped?" she shouted over the sound of another, distant explosion from south of the camp. From the tenor of shouts outside, the crowd's fear abated.

Johnson opened up his subvokes, but he spoke aloud for the benefit of the others. "Smith! Maldonado! Marsden! What are those fools in USACD doing?... I told them we'd settle it peacefully, we won't kill thousands of people even if we can!... I can't countenance this.

Yes, that's right.... What do I mean?... Yes. Hell yes.... I'm serious. What about you. Can you?..." More shells landed and Clay lost track of Johnson's side of the conversation for a moment. "So we're agreed? We're all in? I'll tell them. First, neutralize the artillery on the berm."

Jenny and Wally worked through their smartpapers and gave orders to the formix hives. They locked down robotic tanks and vehicles at all the bases and recalled the drone aircraft cover to Steinmann. Roger radioed Treviño and Wilson to tell them to prepare their robots to roll forward across the bridge.

Clay opened up a channel to all the protestors. Though his conscience needled him, he prepared to lie. *What would Nil do*, he thought with a bitter tinge.

"My fellow Americans, we have aspired to peacefully restore proper governance to our country. We have asked President Everton and other leaders affiliated with America United to admit their crimes and resign. But rather than speak to us in an effort to explain themselves," he said as a shell exploded twenty-five yards away, further mangling the ruins of the Lorelei sedan and Lt. Col. Mueller, "they have dealt us violence in the hopes of crushing our call for the peaceful restoration of justice. With this, President Everton has abdicated his last claim to leadership. We must bring him to justice. Don't worry! We are not alone! The armed forces have joined us!"

Clay and the others followed events across the smartpaper map. The blue dots of their robots hurried across the bridge, neutralizing the defenders there, and then fanned out across the berm. The emplaced guns controlled by Johnson fired a few more times, shells landing in the wheat fields between the protestor's camp and the America United mob lurking in the town, but then they fell silent and their red icons on the map turned warm gray and translucent as blue dots swarmed around them.

More blue icons, man-shapes in circles, popped up and then faded slowly from view. Clay raised an eyebrow at Roger. "People who aren't connected to the pervasive battlefield net. The *ibuthos*, retired soldiers, and people with rifles calling in sporadically." The wave of icons advanced over the outer berm into Ft. Everton. From the summit, blank areas deeper within USACD were seen and filled in—more berms, crossing the miles like the trails of giant moles, and between the berms large gray buildings that all looked identical.

Though the robotic tanks and fighting vehicles had been neutralized through the formix hives, and most of the personnel had hacked NuGlands, some of the defenders managed to form up around the mouth of the tunnel in the inner berm between Ft. Everton and New Washington proper. Reports came of gunfire and airborne crowd control agents, but too many of the protestors had gas masks for their advance to be disrupted, and Treviño and Wilson's crawlers soon knocked out enough defenders with muscle paralyzers for the morale of the effectives to reach a tipping point. Soon all of Ft. Everton had been cleared.

The mood in the command tent lifted, but Clay gazed at the map and he frowned. The cluster of blue dots and man-shaped icons was still advancing, but crumbling like a wave in the last few yards before a rocky shore; in the real world outside the tent, shadows grew longer as the sun climbed down the western sky. "We have to find Everton before he can slip away and make trouble. There's only one problem." Clay pointed in turn at each of the red icons indicating the large, identical government buildings. "Which of those is the New White House?"

In the situation room, under the constant white glow of the fluorescents, time ceased to exist until it surprised Haycock with cold coffee at his lips and the digits on a wearable's watchface. 6:17. Only three hours, or already three hours, since Johnson had turned into a traitor?

Why hadn't he sneaked a brainscanner into the morning meeting?

No help for it now. The dots popping in and fading out on the displays and the frantic conversations with men in the bases seemed like a videogame and it took an effort of will to make them real. Johnson's mutiny; military robots and armed individuals storming USACD; the soldiers and airmen in the bases immobile at best and treasonous at worst.

"Mutinous crawlers detected in four of fourteen zones of the city," Gen. Petrosian said.

Haycock checked the map on his personal display. The Joint Chiefs had high enough security clearance to know the general layout of the city, but even they were denied knowledge of where the New White House stood. Only Everton, Ramirez, and he had that level of clearance. Icons representing the mutinous crawlers were visible on the other side of the berm nearest the White House. Only two miles and a handful of fallow wheat fields separated them.

Everton stared at the map and his face stirred. The mutineer icons faded and their color leaked away to show the probabilities of where they might have reached since the confirmed observation. The front wall of the probability zone lapped at the base of the berm and slowly started climbing. "I can trust this?"

The Secretary of Defense cleared his throat. "It's the best data we have—"

"Or the best you're showing me? You told me I could trust your man Johnson and look what he's done!" Everton's eyes narrowed. "This was your plan all along."

The SecDef paled. "Sir?"

Pandolfini looked past him to Everton. "We did not recommend Johnson for this assignment, Mr. President."

"You're calling me a liar?" Everton lurched from his chair and planted one hand on the tabletop and waved his other fist at the Joint Chiefs Chairman. "I'll have your fucking head for this!"

Christ damn it! These were the only men who could preserve him and he was turning on them like a trapped animal gnawing its leg off. "Mr. President," Haycock said loudly enough to carry, "since, uh, events turned, we've ordered NCS HQ to rescreen all senior military personnel in the region. No anomalous calls between any of them and Johnson in the past month. He's a loose cannon, sir." Haycock pitched his voice higher and made his tone more subservient than usual.

Everton flared his nostrils a few times, then slumped into his seat. "Then they really are close," he said. "Where are our defenses?"

Petrosian began explaining the snarled communications with the bases with speculation Johnson had gotten to lower-ranking personnel. While the general talked, Ramirez leaned closer to Haycock's ear. "What the hell are you doing?" he whispered. "HQ hasn't rescreened anyone the past couple of hours."

"Ivar, if the SecDef and the Joint Chiefs are traitors, we're fucked. If they become traitors, we're fucked too. We can't do anything about it if they're already in league with Johnson, but why push them to his side if they're not there yet?"

"They need to know there's a price for failure." Ramirez' eyes narrowed and Haycock could tell he imagined how he would extract it from them. *Should've left him as a disgraced former agent working as a rent-a-cop.*

"Think! If POTUS fails, they're off the hook." On the map, the edge of the mutinous smear crested the last berm, but then it vanished. A single hostile-robot icon appeared at the peak of the berm.

Petrosian held up a hand and cocked his head, listening to someone through his earbuds while a frantic, appalled look reached his face. "Mr. President, the mutineers hacked into our wired C3I net. Ft. Osborne found a hive of formix robots and is clearing it. We're radioing the other bases to look for the same."

Everton blew out a breath. "We've beaten them."

"Sir, we can't make that assumption. It will still take several hours for the bases to return to full operations and deploy their men and equipment."

"Assuming their men can be trusted," Pandolfini added, "in light of Mr. Poisson's briefing earlier."

Petrosian nodded. "Depending on how close the mutineers are, we should relocate to another secure location closer to Osborne."

"There's no need for that," Everton said. His gaze was vacant. Haycock checked the icon on the map as it smeared down the slope of the berm a mile and a half away.

"Sir," Haycock said, "if I may, the general has a good point. There's no harm in abandoning the White House if need be. President Madison did so and we still won that war." With luck, POTUS even knew who Madison was.

Everton's gaze fell to the map. He listlessly nodded. "I concur. Let's move."

It was like a giant centipede had just woken up and nerve impulses were slowly transmitted to its myriad feet. Aides gathered smartpapers and telephoned orders to their underlings elsewhere in the building or the city. Haycock watched the hostile icon smearing toward them on the map and tapped his feet. Finally, the doors opened and they left the sitch room. NCS agents waiting outside clustered around them and hustled Everton and his advisors down the concourse to the parking garage. The cube farm had emptied out at the end of the shift, thank god, morale was low enough without employees being ordered to evacuate or seeing Everton run. Haycock sped up and fell into step with Petrosian, the Army Chief of Staff. He glanced around to see if anyone watched him and the general. "How's it look?" he muttered.

"We'll get him out of here."

"And then?"

Petrosian flicked a hollow-eyed gaze at Haycock, then sped his pace and started talking with Pandolfini and the other Chiefs. The group's footsteps and murmuring conversations echoed off the foamed concrete.

At the foot of the escalator, a motorcade of five stretch suvs waited. Haycock lurked close to the President, but the press of the crowd at the escalator's foot separated him from Everton. Only Ramirez, Fisher, the SecDef, the National Security Advisor, Petrosian, and Pandolfini and a handful of aides joined Everton in the fourth suv down the line. Haycock grunted and climbed into the third vehicle, cursing his luck at being cooped up with useless figures, like Navy Chief of Staff Morphy, Flanagan, the Secretary of State, and their underlings. Haycock sat near the front and checked the control panel—the vehicle was slaved to the line for now but could be detached to independent control with the right override. Morphy met his gaze and Haycock forced a weak smile.

"We're teats on a boar," Flanagan said.

Haycock caught his breath, nodded. "Along for the ride." The suv glided away from the escalator landing and he realized he should take the opportunity to talk to these men, however useless they might seem. "He'll need you when this is done."

Flanagan's mouth looked sour and he shook his head. "Admiral, how bad is it?"

Morphy weighed his words for a moment. "Ground combat is outside my area of expertise."

Flanagan laughed, an unexpectedly high sound for such a stout man. "That's the kind of frank advice the bossman's wanted from us for years. Glad to see things don't change even when the Russians are shelling the *Führerbunker*."

Haycock kept his face still and hoped his surprise didn't show. Everton had picked his cabinet for loyalty more than any other trait. Had Flanagan taken a NuGland? Had Schieffer hacked it?

The suv climbed up the ramp and followed the lead vehicles away from the New White House. The lawns fell away and long shadows stretched across the fallow wheat fields It felt like cheating in school, to be riding an autocar in New Washington and see the sun. "I might know how bad it is if I knew where we were," Morphy said.

Cultivate these men. "I've got clearance," Haycock said. He pulled out his smartpaper and unrolled it. Three rebel icons were converging on the New White House. He looked out the window towards the berm to the south, but couldn't see them.

"These are confirmed sightings?" Flanagan asked.

"Means there's others we might not see." Morphy looked at both of them and Haycock could see the wheels turning behind his face.

The rebel icons suddenly multiplied around the New White House. The battle between the rebels and the guards showed as flashes and clouds on the display. The icons for the guards turned gray and immobile. They'd been trained to fight scattered human enemies, not military robots with neural networks honed by recent use.

"POTUS better be glad he left when he did," Flanagan said, his tone flat.

"It's just a building." Morphy distended his lower lip with his tongue. "It doesn't mean Everton will fall."

"It's a propaganda coup for Schieffer. He can stand in the Oval Office and declare himself President now."

Haycock shook his head. "With all respect, Mr. Secretary, no. Schieffer's trying to play by the book. He has to capture Everton and force him to cede power."

Flanagan gave Haycock a withering look. "You think I haven't been paying attention? But it doesn't matter what Schieffer wants if he can't capture Everton. Then it becomes a civil war. Propaganda coups matter."

Haycock narrowed his eyes. NCS still counted for something and calling the service's assistant director an idiot was a bad career move. Either Flanagan had no fear of NCS or he thought its days were numbered. Looking at it that way gave Haycock a pause. But then the motorcade slowed and his appraisal of the other fell away from his mind. "What's this?"

Outside the front windows, the shadowed eastern slope of the berm west of the New White House loomed ahead. A monitor near the dashboard came to life and showed the face of one of the NCS agents riding in the point vehicle. Fair-skinned, with big brown sunglasses and thin lips, he looked agitated. "We have bandits interdicting the tunnel entrance to the next berm zone."

"Bandits?" Everton said over the common radio channel.

"Yes sir!" The display jerked, then resolved. The tunnel mouth was a black gash in the shadowed slope. Two pizza-box crawlers, fuel cells glowing in the infrared, stood at either side of the entrance, and the camera panned to show a half-dozen more scrambling along the berm to join the first two.

"Only eight? We can make it through."

Petrosian cleared his throat. "They're tougher than they look. Besides, there might be more out of sight behind the crest of the berm or in the tunnel. If the whole motorcade made it into the tunnel they could block us in."

Everton spoke with certainty. "Go around the tunnel and up the berm. These are suvs, aren't they?"

Top heavy, stretched out, and softened for luxury. Haycock envisioned them rolling down the berm and landing roof-down, wheels spinning. The emperor was nude—Haycock saw the realization in Morphy's lower lip and Flanagan's hooded eyes—but no one in the motorcade spoke for a moment.

Even without a lifeboat, it was time to jump. Haycock turned on his earbud microphone and said, "Mr. President, it's time for us to give this up."

"There's another way through the berm."

The other men in the cabin stared at him and Haycock licked his lips. "That's not what I mean. It's time to surrender."

Confused murmurs crossed the common channel. The display switched to show Everton's emotionless face. "You should repeat that, Haycock. I didn't hear you right."

"Mr. President, what's Schieffer going to do to you if you give him what he wants? He's painted himself into a corner; he can't lock you up as an enemy combatant. He'll let you retire quietly, but then what? He has good advisors but are they good enough to run the country? No. He'll stumble. The people will want you back. Then Flanagan can come out and say your resignation was coerced and illegitimate."

Flanagan stared sidelong at him. *Don't drag me into this*, Haycock read on his face.

Haycock stared back. *Don't insult me first.*

Everton raised his hand to cover the camera nearest him. More harsh whispers came over the radio, but the voices began cutting off abruptly. Haycock looked out the rear window at the tinted windshield of Everton's vehicle. Murky movements, impossible to gauge.

"The Assistant Director is right," Admiral Morphy said over the background whispers. "They've trapped us."

Ramirez' voice came on. "We can make it to a different exit from this berm zone," he said. His voice turned sharp. "Every loyal NCS agent will bend all his efforts to that goal."

"Even if you have to leave New Washington," said Fisher, "every AU member will rally to you."

On the monitor, Everton's hand sagged across the camera lens, and through his fingers Haycock saw slices of the President's face conferring with Ramirez. "Your suggestion is rejected, Haycock. We're going."

Haycock looked out the back window. The tailing suv jumped into reverse, backing up to an intersection to make a three-point turn, and Everton's followed. Haycock's did not move and he jerked his head to the front. The leading suv, full of NCS agents, moved into reverse and backed toward them while winding down its window—

"On the floor!" Haycock shouted. He crawled to the control panel. "Override! Off road, to the tunnel mouth, max speed, now!"

"Access denied," said the suv's flat female voice.

"Override!" He shouted the universal NCS override code, "Yankee Romeo four-seven-niner!" He glanced up. The suv full of agents had almost drawn broadside with them and the early-evening sun glinted on the mouths of pistols visible out the open windows.

Haycock's suv lurched forward as the first gunshots smacked the side and spalled the tempered glass. The suv sped off the road and the wheels slewed across the fallow field. *Please goddammit no mud no ruts.* More gunshots struck the rear window. The suv drove on and the gunfire from the road faded. Haycock bobbed his head up, then ducked again and recalled what he'd glimpsed: the NCS suv stopped on the road, a few agents on foot outside it at the edge of the field with their handguns drawn but their hands at their sides, heads half-turned to listen to orders over their radios. He took a second glance and saw the agents falling back to the suv. The other vehicles in Everton's caravan had traveled hundreds of yards down the road.

The suv returned to the road. The tunnel entrance loomed as a dark pit in the berm. The mutineers' robots ringed the entrance and aimed their paralyzer guns and rifles at them. "Slow down!" Haycock said. "Stop twenty yards from the entrance."

The suv's brakes whined and leaned everyone forward. Haycock looked around the cabin. Faces were pale and eyes wide, fear and anger mixed together. He'd almost gotten them killed. Bah, he hadn't; he'd even saved their worthless butts. So long as he could defuse anger at him he'd make it through.

"Work with me," he said, "and you'll be better off for switching sides. Weapons down, hands up. Suv, open the doors."

He stepped to the doors and sat crosslegged in front of them. He ignored the ache in his knees and the heaviness in his shoulders as he lifted his hands in front of him. The doors swung open. Two pizza boxes pointed their muzzles at him and a tennis ball tosser waited in readiness behind them.

18

As a red sunset streaked the western sky, Clay stood with Jenny, Roger, Wally, Johnson, and others in the command tent, watching blue icons fan across the map of New Washington, when Wilson cocked his head and pressed his hand to his ear. "Captain, General, Mr. Schieffer, I have a call coming in. My crawlers have captured an NCS official named Haycock and some other officials of Everton's government. Haycock and the others want to speak to you."

"Where are they?" Roger asked.

Wilson scratched an entry onto the smartpaper, and a red icon near an entrance to a crossberm tunnel glowed brightly.

Haycock? Clay didn't recall the name. One of Ramirez' goons? "What does he want?"

"He says it's important, but he will only discuss it with you on the line."

Roger looked at the map from a couple of angles, then glanced at Johnson. "We have things under control," Roger said. "Can't hurt to talk."

"Pop up a window," Clay said.

Harsh lights washed over three figures in a dark room. Haycock was a beefy man with beady eyes and a suit jacket gapping away from the back of his neck. Visible next to him were a man in a Navy uniform on one side and a face familiar from national media, Flanagan, the

Secretary of State. Though the other two probably outranked Haycock, their body language deferred to the NCS official. Clay glanced at the map and realized they were in the tunnel through the berm.

"Mr. Schieffer, I'm NCS Assistant Director Haycock, with Secretary of State Flanagan and Admiral Morphy, Navy Chief of Staff. I have some information you need."

"You do."

"I understand your tone of voice. Who is this guy and how can you trust what he's saying? Let me show you can trust me. The military in USACD have figured out how you tripped them up. Osborne's almost done overriding the damage your formix robots caused—"

"I don't know what you're talking about," Clay said. To the side, Jenny stepped closer to Roger and they scrawled notes on smartpapers.

"Believe me or not, but it's almost done." Haycock gave a beady smile. "Good operational security—you're not an amateur—but it's no secret. Everton knows what you've done and is on his way to Osborne right now. He'll be ready when that base unjams itself."

Jenny's eyes widened at something on her display and she hurriedly scrawled more commands. Haycock wasn't lying. If Everton reached a military base, could his force of personality overwhelm the hacked NuGlands of his palace guard?

Clay kept his voice calm. "Thanks for the intel. What's the information you really want to give us?"

"Where Everton is."

Conversations in the command tent ended with sibilant whispers. Clay nodded slightly, to show Haycock he'd heard him, but then looked away from the videophone window to the map of New Washington. Large unexplored stretches still filled the map and the red icons waiting in Ft. Osborne seemed numerous indeed. If Everton evaded them....

"What's your price?" Clay asked Haycock.

"Cutting to the chase. You'll do better than I thought." Haycock inhaled. "All three of us have a price."

Flanagan stirred. "The admiral and I want to keep our positions."

Clay focused on Haycock. "And?"

Haycock looked brazenly at the camera. "I want a promotion. Director of—well, you'll probably change the name. Whatever will replace NCS."

Clay glared at the window on the smartpaper. "We're going to talk about it. Cut the call. Leave them there." He sighed out a breath, then turned to Johnson and Roger. "Do we need them to catch Everton?"

"There's a lot of terrain for us to explore," Johnson said. "If he can reach Osborne—"

"He can escape to other military bases," Clay said. "Civil war."

"We're pushing the crawlers as hard as we can," Roger said. "We'll have to refuel them soon. We can do that on the fly, but it will slow us down."

Wally leaned forward, elbows on the table, and looked up at them. "Those are positions we'll need to fill. Flanagan will receive Everton's resignation and I can see a benefit to keeping him around afterward for continuity and legitimacy."

"He's an AU member."

"There's that."

"I don't know Morphy," Johnson said. "I have no reason to doubt his integrity."

"But Haycock," Clay said, and trailed off.

"You'll need NCS or a successor agency," Johnson said. "He has experience—"

"Someone like him threw me in a cell in South Dakota!"

"You're out now." Johnson flared his nostrils. "And capturing Everton before he can make trouble is better for all of us."

Clay's hands balled and he pounded his fists together. Normalcy was more important than revenge. He exhaled and shook his hands open. "Call them back," he told Wilson.

Their images returned to the smartpaper. Haycock was beady-eyed and insolence lurked behind his expression, but he kept his silence and waited for Clay to speak.

"Admiral, Secretary Flanagan, we accept your offer. As for you, Mr. Haycock, you'll get what you want but only if you help us. Pick a couple dozen people from among South Dakota, New Mexico, and New Washington to be prosecuted. We're also going to fire others—

you'll help us with a list."

"Why should I agree?"

"What would happen to you if Everton won a civil war?"

Haycock's face fell. "Look for a black suv heading north from the New White House to the berm tunnel. There were four in column last I saw."

Night fell by the time Clay and the others relocated their headquarters to the New White House. It was a long, low, windowless building, with proportions impossible to make out until their headlight beams washed over it. A hell of a place to call home. They pulled into the porte-cochere through the ground floor. The threat map was clear and Clay climbed out of his vehicle, into a darkness pierced by xenon lamps. Wilson's crawlers had cut the building's power on their way through, and a volunteer electrician went down to the basements to try bringing it back.

Signs of battle lay everywhere. The stink of spilled methanol rose from the cracked carapaces of destroyed crawlers. More robots dragged paralyzed government officials, NCS agents, and people left behind by Everton in his flight out of the building and laid them on the fallow wheat field Armed men from an *ibutho* watched the prisoners, but there was no point in resistance—Clay glanced at a few of the prisoners' faces and, despite the action of the skeletal muscle paralyzer, read their faces and saw they had concluded that. The forts had never shaken the formix hives, thanks to Haycock's warning and Jenny's brisk reprogramming, and the prisoners knew Everton had abandoned them. From across the wheat field carried conversations among the *ibutho* members, wondering about Everton's fate.

Among the prisoners was Vice-President Hu, abandoned by Everton in a basement of the New White House. They roused her first and she sat blinking on the rough grass, staring sullenly at the NCS agents and other government personnel lying paralyzed around her. Wally and a couple of volunteer guards took her aside. Clay didn't listen to what he told her, but he saw Wally hand her a sheet of paper. She signed it and slumped to a seat on the grass, looking as wrung out as a dishrag.

Spotlights recessed in the porte-cochere's ceiling snapped on. The electrician had done his job. Clay stretched his arms in front of him, elbows crackling, and looked up at the foamed concrete walls and ceiling and the steps leading up from the driveway to the New White House's formal entrance. Roger joined him on his left and Wally on his right. Jenny came closer, and Wally shuffled a half-step further to the right and opened his left shoulder to her and Clay. Nearby, Treviño, Wilson, Marsden, and other officers from 1 LRTD stood in a cluster and bent their heads over handheld displays. Johnson, grinning, spoke with Morphy. Flanagan stared at Clay and the people around him and looked like he needed an antacid. Delacroix chatted up the Secretary of State while Kerensky and Yamamoto hung back. Haycock drifted from cluster to cluster, speaking a few words, listening to a few more. He wore a pair of glasses that Wally had privately told Clay was a brainscanner swiped from somewhere. *Keep an eye on him*, Clay thought, and in his mind's ear he heard the echo of Nil's voice.

"The building is clear," Wilson said. "Our crawlers only. And more of ours are coming with company."

Headlights bobbed in the darkness a few hundred yards to the north. Military tow trucks from one of Johnson's units, their smartcamo black in the night, came closer, trailing black stretch suvs too long to be contained on their slanted beds. They pulled up under the porte-cochere and the smartcamo shimmered to match the gray concrete walls.

Some of Wilson's crawlers clacked to positions in front of the doors of the first towed suv. They lifted their rifles and paralyzer guns.

"He's inside," Wilson said.

"Take the vehicles to the basement," Clay said. No point passersby seeing the interrogations. The tow trucks rolled toward the ramp and Clay walked after. "I need to stretch my legs."

Everyone joined him on the descent. The basement held a vast parking garage. The crawlers surrounding the towed suvs were the only motion in the space. "Start pulling them out," Clay said. "One at a time."

The door locks chunked and the doors swung open. The front

door's motor grunted against the uphill slant. A couple of pizza boxes jumped into the cabin and the whine of their turret motors could be heard. Roger and Wilson reached into the slanted cabin and grabbed someone by the feet. They pulled him half-out and Treviño picked him up the armpits to carry him to the concrete underfoot, then bent over him and patted him down for weapons and items in his pockets. They stood and let the man become visible.

The smooth, sharp face made Clay's breath catch. Ramirez stared glassily at the ceiling. Clay's fists balled and he gritted his teeth. This man had come to kill him and now he lay helpless while half-glimpsed tortures danced in Clay's imagination.

Clay shut his eyes and inhaled while slowly counting to four. "Haycock, we talked about prosecutions. This man will be one of them."

Haycock nodded. "He was illegally working off the books for Fisher and America United. I'll testify to that."

Ramirez' gaze stirred and he tried to turn his head. Spit dabbed the corner of his mouth.

"Memory disrupt him, then keep him neutralized until we get him into a maximum security holding cell," Clay said to Roger. Crawlers extended grapples and dragged Ramirez to a ceedee caddy parked nearby while others held their weapons on him.

The next man pulled out of the suv wore a wrinkled Italian suit and his hair badly needed a comb. Clay had shaken Fisher's hand a few times during the final negotiations for the sale of TS to Titan, back when 6:19 was fresh in mind and America United seemed innocuous. Roger patted him down. "Rouse him," Clay said.

Fisher's eyes grew frantic as Treviño lowered the mouth cover and the antidote flowed. Even after Treviño pulled it away and the full play of emotions crossed his face he still looked frightened. He opened his mouth and his first words croaked out. "Don't kill me."

"We're not going to kill you," Clay said. "We aren't like that. We aren't like you."

"I've never killed anyone. You know that."

Clay sniffed out a breath. "Tell it to the judge."

Fisher pushed up on his elbows. A crawler moved to stop him but

Clay raised his hand. "Let him sit." Fisher lifted himself to a seat and took a couple of breaths.

"There's no need for a trial. I'm America United. You can use me."

Saving his own hide. Clay's mouth moued in disgust. "You made Everton who he is. Why would you turn on him?"

"We supported him at first, but look at what he's done to the country. Prison camps, throwing enemies into psychiatric hospitals—"

"So evil your conscience forced you to turn against him, what? Five minutes ago? Ten?"

"America United was trying to moderate him…" Fisher trailed off, his gaze on someone off to Clay's side and behind, and his expression hardened. Clay glanced in that direction and saw Haycock. "We can help you," Fisher said. "America United can support you."

"Why would we need it to?"

Fisher tried to smile confidently. "We have millions of members. Billions of dollars in annual dues. You can use the organization…. and if you don't, it can be used against you."

Johnson snorted. "You think you'll go free?"

"I think your civilian puppet here can't disappear me. It would dispel the illusion of restored justice he's trying to cast. You have to let me live."

Wally's high, fast laughter echoed through the parking garage. Even after he stopped laughing a smile forced the corners of his mouth wide. "America United is broken."

"You think your hack job took? I know my organization."

"So do we," Wally said. "AU's membership is going to collapse."

"And the organization's leaders will be prosecuted," Clay said. "How much money did you make buying up farmland out here before offering it to Everton as the site of New Washington?"

"Titan's stock price is going to collapse," Wally said. "I smell a hostile takeover."

"Disrupt his memory and get him out of here," Clay said to Wilson. Within moments crawlers dragged Fisher to the tunnel out.

Roger reached into the suv for another passenger, and as he pulled him out he hesitated and their backs straightened in surprise. Clay realized who it was in the moment before his face became visible. Roger and Wilson laid Everton on the pavement and patted him down while Jenny, Wally, and everyone else shuffled their feet and craned their necks to better see. Clay nodded and Wilson roused him.

Everton turned his head and coughed, then tried to sit up. He leaned unsteadily on his right hand. His brows were low and his gaze jumped nervously around the circle, returning to Haycock after first glimpsing him, before settling on Clay. "We can strike a deal."

"We can?"

"Don't give me that. Everyone has a price. What's yours? The Vice-Presidency? We can force Hu out easy enough. That's not it? Something else? Name it."

"You must resign."

Everton coughed again. "You're either just like me and trying to lie or you really think you're too good and pure for this. But if you were too good and pure, you wouldn't have gotten this far."

Clay pressed his lips together. "Either way, I'm here."

"But I'm still the President. How are you going to take that from me?"

Clay turned his head to Wally, who nodded and handed over a locked smartpaper that Clay pretended to read. "Vice-President Hu resigned. Secretary of State Flanagan has accepted her resignation letter to make it official. You'll appoint me to succeed her; we're rounding up a quorum of Senators who'll confirm the appointment. Then you'll resign. We'll broadcast your farewell address to the nation— time delayed, of course—and then you can ride off into the sunset, surrounded by a military honor guard, to fade into history."

"House arrest, you mean."

"No. You can travel and speak to whomever you wish. We will monitor who you talk to and what you say, but if you keep a low profile you'll have as much liberty as any other ex-President."

"What if I decline?"

Clay stared down at him. He'd hated the conclusion they'd reached on the drive from the camp, but Roger and Johnson had finally persuaded him. "You will be killed."

Everton stared back. "You are just like me."

"I'm not too good and pure. That doesn't mean I'm like you."

Everton stood up on wobbling legs and inhaled deeply. He was at least three inches shorter than Clay, but looked shorter with his slumped shoulders and shifty eyes. "You've got me. Where do I sign?"

Clay exhaled. It felt almost too easy, but that feeling seemed explicable: any ending would be an anticlimax after the past few days. He opened his mouth to speak when Haycock spoke subvocally through Clay's earbuds.

"Hold up! He thinks he's got you suckered."

Clay's heart slammed but he kept himself from turning his head to face Haycock. He stepped back and pivoted away from Everton, then touched his subvokes. *I'm pulling Wally in to listen. Can you tell how?*

"I can only see what's in front of me," Haycock said. "Behind his face Everton's gloating in expectation. Not just for going free, but he sees a way to avenge himself against you."

How?

"Can't tell."

What does he know that I don't?

Silence for a moment. "Shit. He knows what you did to the NuG-lands."

Wally said, "He's planning to release that information. Turn the public against you. If he times it well and takes advantage of a dip in your loyalty chart—"

We can't have that.

More silence, then Haycock muttered, "We have to kill him."

Clay imagined Everton glassy-eyed at their feet, lying in a pool of his drying blood. No, not here. Someplace isolated. One or two trusted men, they could take him into the Oval Office or the Residence and force sleeping pills down his throat or a noose around his neck. A few men to do the deed, several more to make sure the few didn't talk....

We won't do that.

"We have to," Haycock said. "You're afraid it will come out? I'll do it myself, no one will know—"

Three may keep a secret, if two are dead.

Haycock's only sound was harsh breathing that abruptly cut off when he dropped his hand. "Then what else?" Wally asked.

Haycock rejoined the conversation. "Keep hacking the NuGlands."

Clay shook his head. How much reprogramming of how many NuGlands would Wally have to do to nudge the country into what Clay would say was normal?

And how much could Clay authorize without ending up in a cage of his own conscience?

No. Thoughts churned half-formed in his mind when he opened his mouth, but by the time he finished saying the word those thoughts had crystallized. He dropped his hand and turned to face Everton. "I know your plan. After you resign, we'll let you tell the public what we did to their NuGlands. But first, we'll give them the keys to unlock themselves from anyone's cage."

19

Everton's face fell in genuine alarm, but Wally was the first to speak. "You're talking about making the NuGlands open source."

"Exactly."

Jenny frowned. "You'd tell people how to change their brain chemistry? Is that safe?"

"Safe?"

"What if people do strange things to themselves? Can we trust them to use it correctly?"

Her expression was so earnest Clay opened his mouth uselessly, fumbling in his mind for the right words. His head bobbed and he caught a glimpse of Everton in the corner of his eye. "Not very well, but who can we trust more? Not politicians," he said, and gestured at Everton. "Not security people like Ramirez, military brass like Pandolfini and Petrosian, business leaders like Fisher…." A recollection of the Hospital came to him. "…not even doctors can be trusted to use the NuGland for each person's benefit."

She didn't look convinced and shook her head. "But letting people change their own brain chemistry—"

"Is better than letting others change it behind their backs."

Johnson stepped closer and patted the pickups for the subvokes glued to his throat. "You're just saying this, right?" he said into Clay's earbuds.

Clay matched the gesture. *I don't follow your question.*

"You'll leave in a back door. Let us manipulate people's brains if we need to down the road." The general's expression looked guileless, as if his suggestion was proper and unremarkable. Nil would have said the same things with the same look on his face; but Nil was not here and would never be here.

No. We're letting the genie out of the bottle and won't try to put it back.

Johnson blinked and rocked his head back. "Mr. Schieffer—"

We might want to use a back door down the road, but it won't be on the table. I don't trust myself enough to know I'd never want to change how others think and feel, and I damn sure don't trust anyone else. Clay stared down the general until Johnson grunted, dropped his hand from his throat, and turned away.

"I'll start working up code," Wally said. "We'll need security modification, strip away any exploits, add an easy user interface and database system—"

Everton laughed. "You think that will work? You tell the people that I turned them into unquestioning zombies. How then did they turn apathetic or rebellious? It will become obvious that you turned them into zombies too."

"You underestimate the illusion of control," Wally said to Everton. "Everyone will think, 'he might have controlled everyone else but I chose to turn against him.'"

"He's right," Clay said amid a flow of memories of the Hospital and the day after his escape. "But we can't keep it secret forever. Better to come clean now than to let it blow open and do damage control. Right, Wally?"

Wally pressed his index finger to his lips and rocked his head from side to side. "You're probably right. Let me run the numbers to make sure." He pulled his personal display from his hip pocket and twirled his stylus in his fingers.

"Let me think what to say to the country," Clay said. "Everton manipulated them, we undid the manipulation, here's how you can tell if you were implanted, here's how to reprogram it, here's how to lock the program from outside interference… is that it?"

"That should do," Roger said. Jenny nodded.

Wally kept his gaze on his display. "Make sure you act like it was no big deal."

"Like talking to a three-year-old with a scraped knee?" Clay asked.

"I haven't talked to a three-year-old in a long time," Wally replied. "Aha! Definitely coming clean is better than trying to cover it up."

"Good," Clay said. "Anything further?"

Everton cleared his throat. "You win. Give me the paper nominating you as Vice-President and I'll sign it and my postdated resignation too. If you offer our Senators the same deal you'll get confirmed...."

Wally dug more paper from his jacket pocket and handed it to Everton. He sighed out a breath and shook his head as he scratched at the surface with an ink pen. He locked the displays with a gesture of finality and looked around the space.

"Haycock, Roger, find Everton a comfortable place," Clay said. "Preferably one with a display so he can watch what I have to say."

They led Everton away. The group around them broke up, Wally scurrying away with his display unfurled in his hands, Haycock and Flanagan murmuring under hooded eyes, Roger and Jenny ambling and talking in low voices. Delacroix and Yamamoto came up to Clay and shook his hand. "You're going to make this work," Delacroix said.

Clay grinned, shook his head. "We're going to make this work."

"We?"

"Someone has to be the Vice-President." Delacroix looked pleased and Clay turned to Yamamoto. "Phillip, are you looking to serve your country too?"

Yamamoto laughed. "Yeah. By going back to my lab and doing more research." His expression sobered slightly. "You're really going to make the NuGland code open source?"

"Absolutely."

"That's food for thought."

Clay nodded. "That's right, you're doing neuron/circuit interface work...." His mouth hung open and thoughts roiled. He craned his neck and sought out Jenny. She and Roger were a few steps away from the van they'd ridden from Houston. "Pardon me, guys." Perhaps it would look unpresidential, but no one would see; he jogged toward his wife.

"I want to thank you both," he said, while shaking Roger's hand and patting his shoulder. "Especially you, Jenny. The formix made all the difference."

She looked at him, her eyebrows slightly low and the corners of her eyes barely crinkled. "Everton had to go."

Roger looked from Clay to his sister and back. "I've been on my feet all day. I'll get in the van. Take your time, Emma called to say all three kids are asleep." He climbed into the van and the door swung shut.

Clay inhaled. "I met someone who might help Martin," he said, and then cringed. "Not that he needs it, he's a good kid and I hadn't seen that until recently—"

Her fingertips lightly brushed the fine hairs on the back of his left hand. "He needs it. It's okay to say that."

"Phillip Yamamoto. He works on neuron/circuit interfaces. He's looking at outsourcing brain functions to computers…. It might help Martin, but if it doesn't that's okay."

"I hope it will too," she said. Her hand closed around his and her face lit up with frustration that he could tell meant he didn't see something obvious to her. "Clay, it's fine. I saw you play with him. I know you love him."

"I love you, too." He blinked and hoped for better words to come, but none did, and he went on with the next ones to come to mind. "You put up with my resentment for years, and then, when NCS took me away, you could have put me behind you." He reached his right hand toward the side of her face but hesitated, half out of fear of clumsiness and half out of caution at the boundaries of her personal space. "But you stayed on my side and I can't thank you enough."

She shut her eyes and bent her head toward his right hand. He raised it and cradled her cheek. A tear leaked from her left eye and moistened his finger. He pulled her closer and wrapped his arms around her, her cheek warm against his chest and her heart beating between his arms and his torso.

After a time, she sniffled and pulled her head back, then stood on tiptoes and gave him a quick peck on the lips. "I'm with you," she said. "But right now you have a speech to give and a country to lead."

About the Author

Raymund Eich files patent applications, earned a Ph.D., won a national quiz bowl championship, writes science fiction and fantasy, and affirms Robert Heinlein's dictum that specialization is for insects. In a typical day, he may talk with biochemists, electrical engineers, patent attorneys, epileptologists, and rocket scientists. Hundreds of papers cite his graduate research on the reactions of nitric oxide with heme proteins.

Connect with the author at **www.raymundeich.com** or scan the QR code below.

Sign up for his mailing list to receive exclusive, pre-release content about his upcoming books. Your email address will never be shared and you can unsubscribe at any time. Go to **www.raymundeich.com/mailing-list** or scan the QR code below.

Other Books by the Author

Available wherever books are sold.

Learn more about these titles at our website, **www.cv2books.com**, or scan the QR code below.

Stone Chalmers

Earth barely survived the 21st Century. Biotechnological and nuclear terrorism, civil war, famine, and ethnic cleansing killed billions. Thousands fled on warpdrive ships to colonize planets around distant suns.

In the 22nd century, after the United Nations established control over Earth, it opened wormhole links to the distant colonies, to prevent a repeat of the previous century's chaos on a galactic scale.

Enter operative Stone Chalmers. Spy. Assassin. Instrument maintaining the UN's order on the settled galaxy.

Opposing him are hostile forces on colony worlds… and within the UN itself.

When Stone clashes with those forces, the UN—and every human world—will be transformed forever.

Learn more about the Stone Chalmers series at **www.cv2books.com/stone-chalmers**, or scan the QR code below.

The Progress of Mankind (#1)

To maintain order in the 22nd century, the UN relocates undesirables through artificial wormholes onto colony planets. Everyone benefits... except the planets' original colonists.

Now, the newly rediscovered colony of New Moravia learns the UN's plan and fights back.

The Greater Glory of God (#2)

Thousands fled the chaos of the 21st century on rogue warpdrive ships to settle colony planets. When Earth reunified in the 22nd, its fleets rediscovered the colonies and hunted down the warpdrive ships.

Every warpdrive ship but one.

To All High Emprise Consecrated (#3)

After unifying Earth, the UN has rediscovered the colony of Minerva. Prosperous and technologically advanced, Minerva quickly submits to UN supremacy.

Surprisingly quickly…

In Public Convocation Assembled (#4)

After unifying Earth, the UN controls all human colonies scattered through the galaxy by means of wormholes, warpdrive ships, and ruthless operatives. Operatives working to strengthen the UN.

Or destroy it.

The Confederated Worlds

The purpose of all other combat arms is to put the infantryman in sole possession of the battlefield.

A thousand years from now, while Earth sleeps in virtual reality, three polities—the Confederated Worlds, the Unity, and the Progressive Republic—strive to connect the scattered, terraformed worlds of humankind by artificial wormholes. When they meet, they clash, in a decades-long struggle of arms that will embroil every human world, in which dedication to duty liberates worlds—and oneself.

Learn more about the Confederated Worlds series at **www.cv2books.com/the-confederated-worlds**, or scan the QR code below.

Take the Shilling (Book 1)

The Confederated Worlds implanted in his brain the skills to make him a soldier. Tomas Neumann had to learn for himself how to survive interstellar war.

Operation Iago (Book 2)

The Confederated Worlds lost the war. Can Lt. Tomas Neumann win the peace against elusive, deceptive foes out to turn the Confederated Worlds against itself?

A Bodyguard of Lies (Book 3)

Assigned to the halls of power, only Capt. Tomas Neumann can save the Confederated Worlds from the ultimate treachery.

Novels

New California

After New California's founder committed suicide, two men vied to rule the colony.

Ashwin George, supported by the colony's elite and the Chinese company dominating half the settled galaxy.

Against him, Desmond Park, nanotechnology engineer, armed with the most formidable weapon of all.

A single idea.

Short Novels

The ALECS Quartet

He had a month to learn the planet's mysteries—and Juliette's.

His cover story: return to Elard to dismantle his sect's missionary work to the planet's natives.

His true mission: investigate decades-old mysteries of love and death.

His objective: return to Earth with his discovery.

If he can.

A Mighty Fortress

Theodore and his team from the Lutheran Interstellar Terraforming Society would transform a barren, rocky world into a refuge of faith and life.

Or die trying.

Collections

The First Voyages: The Complete Science Fiction Stories 1998-2012

From 21st century asteroid settlements to World War II Romania, from an Earth dominated by immortal aliens to Christ's empty tomb, a fresh, distinctive voice in science fiction will take you on journeys to the photosphere of the sun, the coding regions of DNA, and the complexities of the human psyche.

Stage Separations: The Complete Science Fiction Stories 2013-2018

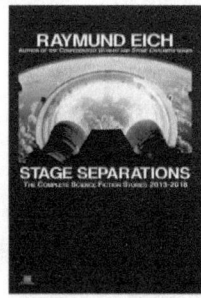

In these pages, you can...

...race against time to solve mysteries hidden in a planet's vast desert—and in a woman's heart ...learn the true story of a president's assassination ...journey 14,000 miles to a high-tech fountain of youth ...win or go "home"—to an Earth you've never seen

and explore six other worlds created by a distinctive voice in twenty-first century science fiction.